Dark Heart

By the same author

White Lies
Murder on Ward Four

DARK HEART

The Shocking Truth about Hidden Britain

NICK DAVIES

Chatto & Windus
LONDON

Published by Chatto & Windus 1997

4 6 8 10 9 7 5 3

First published in Great Britain in 1997 by
Chatto & Windus
Random House, 20 Vauxhall Bridge Road,
London SW1V 2SA

Random House Australia (Pty) Limited
20 Alfred Street, Milsons Point, Sydney,
New South Wales 2061, Australia

Random House New Zealand Limited
18 Poland Road, Glenfield,
Auckland 10, New Zealand

Random House South Africa (Pty) Limited
Endulini, 5A Jubilee Road, Parktown 2193, South Africa

Random House UK Limited Reg. No. 954009

A CIP catalogue record for this book
is available from the British Library

ISBN 0 701 16351 8

Printed and bound in Great Britain by
Mackays of Chatham

Contents

Prologue

In the winter of 1993, I researched several newspaper features which made me feel like an outsider in my own country. Each time it was the same. I would sit on a train watching the green and pleasant fields go by for a couple of hours, arrive in some city full of crowded pubs and shopping centres and, within an hour or so, with a little help from someone I knew in the city, I would be inside a crack house watching men and women sucking cocaine smoke out of the top of an empty Fanta can; or I would walk through the door of a council house and find a family who were living in some kind of throwback to nineteenth-century London; or I would befriend a prostitute who led me into a world of the most bizarre and cruel behaviour. Outwardly, all the landmarks of normality would remain clearly within sight. There would still be rows of red-brick terraced houses with televisions in the front rooms and cars waiting outside by the kerb; there would be crowds of people tracing the paths of their regular routines, buying and selling and building their futures – all the symptoms of an orderly community. But at some point, it was as if I crossed an invisible frontier and cut a path into a different country.

This is not a particularly original way to describe it, but it is the best I can find. This hidden country is a sprawling collection of battered old housing estates, of red-light areas and inner-city ghettos, of crack houses and shebeens and illegal gambling clubs and all the other refuges of our social exiles. To put it more broadly, it is the place where the poor gather. Unlike any other country, it has no borders nor even any name, it doesn't show up on maps or fly a flag, but the more I came to know it, the more

I came to see it as a country in its own right, nestling within the country of the affluent but utterly different in its way of life.

I set out to explore this place, pursuing rumours and news reports, being passed from one contact to another, looking for patterns and themes, trying to record everything I saw like some Victorian explorer penetrating a distant jungle. But this journey of discovery did not really begin until I met the children of the Forest, a group of children in Nottingham who were behaving in a way that was so shocking that I could not come to terms with it without going back into their childhoods to find out what it was that had shaped their disfigured lives. They had all grown up separately in different parts of the country, but all of them had a common source in the old council housing estates which are scattered through every community in Britain. Almost at random, I chose a housing estate in Leeds and I spent weeks there working my way deeper and deeper into its daily life, discovering more and more about what was happening to those who lived there and finally realising that what I was looking at was simply poverty and the damage which it inflicted on those who lived with it. From that moment, the journey had a shape. I set out to map this damage in all its different forms – physical, emotional, social and finally, I realised, spiritual.

The single point about this country that was hardest to believe was that even though just about everyone in Britain has seen at least some of the signs of its existence, just about no one knows anything about the detail of its daily life. It is riddled in among the familiar sights of commonplace existence, and yet for almost all of its neighbours, it is an unseen world.

In its way, despite all its chaos and confusion, the undiscovered country enjoys the most sophisticated network of communication. Everybody talks, exchanging fears and warnings, deals and promises, threats and propositions. Perhaps it is because they are thrust away from the mainstream country that they are forced into such an intense familiarity with each other. They are linked by family, clannish networks of reliability and loyalty; by their geographical patch; by an endless history of past events, which has forged friendships and feuds; a whole scatterwork of demarcations. Every incident is the mother of a brood of rumours running wildly at her heels. This whispering might well remain inaudible to the rest of the world – even to the police, who work so hard to hear it – but inside this country, there is always the sound of people talking.

This book is built out of the stories of hundreds of people who live in this other country and most of these stories are set between 1994 and 1996. I went to all kinds of lengths to corroborate what I was told, but I could not have started if these people had not talked to me in the first place. In some cases, I was steered towards them by professionals such as social workers or police. In the case of some of the prostitutes, I persuaded them to talk by paying them the £20 they would have earned from a customer if I had not taken them away from their work. A few of them hoped to gain something else by talking to me. (I know that a group of street thieves and burglars helped me in the hope that they could use me to hurt the police.) But in the overwhelming majority of cases, these are the stories of people who agreed to talk to me because they wanted someone somewhere to know what was happening. I want to acknowledge their help and, also, their bravery.

In itself this is an odd thing. Quite often, I admit, I was frightened of them when I first approached them – physically frightened that they might hurt me. It never happened. On the contrary, I often discovered that they were frightened of me. It worried them that I might expose them to the law or to their neighbours or to people who had reason to attack them. The prostitute was frightened to talk about her pimp; the crackhead was frightened to talk about his dealer; the old man was frightened to talk about his mugger. With the exception of a few people who were doing things so horrible that I set out deliberately to try to expose them, I willingly agreed to disguise the identities of people who were worried that this book might hurt them. In a few cases, this meant that I needed not simply to give them a false name but also to omit their location. Where I have concealed the true identity of any character, I have printed their name in italics on the first occasion that it appears.

However, for the most part, the names as well as the stories in this book are real. A small amount of the raw material has appeared previously in newspapers, particularly in the *Guardian*, and I am grateful to the editor, Alan Rusbridger; the features editor, Roger Alton; and the editor of *Guardian Weekend*, Deborah

Orr, for supporting me, often for allowing me to disappear into the darkness when neither they nor I had very much idea of what I might bring back. There is no other newspaper in Britain that would take that kind of risk for stories like these.

Apart from my own research, I have also relied on various academics and other specialists and I acknowledge, in particular, the considerable help which I have received from the personal advice and/or the published work of: Carey Oppenheim, formerly of the Child Poverty Action Group and now at South Bank University, London; the Joseph Rowntree Foundation; Richard G. Wilkinson at the Trafford Centre for Medical Research at the University of Sussex; John Jacobs at the University of Sussex; Major Ray Oakley and Captain Bill Cochran of the Salvation Army; and Gerry Smale at the National Institute for Social Work.

Most of all I acknowledge the help and the inspiration and courage of the children of the Forest. You'll see why.

Part I

The Children in the Forest

This volume ... is curious as supplying information concerning a large body of persons of whom the public had less knowledge than of the most distant tribes of the earth ... and as adducing facts so extraordinary that the traveller in the undiscovered country of the poor must, until his stories are corroborated by after investigators, be content to lie under the imputation of telling such tales as travellers are generally supposed to delight in.

Henry Mayhew,
London Labour and the London Poor, 1851

I

The daylight was fading. Some of the cars were already using their headlamps as they prowled northwards from the centre of Nottingham, skirting the edge of the patch of green which was all that remained now of the ancient forest which had once engulfed the area. It was the night before the annual fair was due to open and all across the Forest recreation ground, there were pools of yellow light spilling out of the caravans and the crooked rows of stalls. The whole place was alive with activity: men in oil-stained dungarees spannering the joints of the fairground rides; more men dabbling with streams of black cables that trickled across the grass; women lugging armfuls of fluffy turquoise toys from car boots to stalls, or standing over washing-up bowls scraping the skins off great piles of potatoes. There were locals, too: kids yelling while they weaved their bikes through the gaps between the caravans; some early customers taking a peek at tomorrow's fun; a few stray commuters walking home from work.

No one paid much attention to the two small boys standing in a doorway in the middle of the fairground. They were not very old – no more than twelve or thirteen at the most – and, at first sight, they were simply two silhouettes, hovering in the light that welled out of the open door behind them, with their hoods pulled up over their heads and their fists crammed into their pockets, occasionally slapping their elbows against their sides to beat out the autumn damp, engaged in nothing in particular. Yet there was something about them that commanded attention, a restlessness in the way that they glanced into the faces drifting by, something faintly furtive about the way that every so often, one of them would dodge inside the door for a few moments and then dart back out again to report on developments. His mate would nod, and the two of them would stand there again, silently surveying the scene, like two bouncers watching a dance floor. They knew what everyone was up to, but it wasn't for them to go and join in.

Then one of them spoke out. It was the smaller of the two, the one with the curly blond hair. He had seen a man walking by close to their doorway and now he cocked his chin and lobbed a single word into the gap between them.

'Business?'

Not a question. An invitation. The man walked on by and the two boys stood silent again, and in the light that shone behind them, the truth began to be clear. They caught another man's eye, tossed out another invitation, watched a woman on a hot-dog stand pummel an onion into submission, lit cigarettes, stepped back to let a man go through their doorway, darted back inside just to be sure, and then stood some more, watching and waiting, like hitch-hikers on the highway, with all the patience of necessity. There was little doubt now about what was happening. This doorway in which they were standing was the entrance to a public toilet. This business in which they were engaged was the sale of themselves.

How old were they? They looked horribly young. Who were they? Where had they come from? Why were they doing this? And who were their customers? If they were standing here so deliberately, offering to sell, they must have good reason to believe that there were other people out here who were willing to buy. And why here in particular? Was it simply that people were gathering here for the fair and they knew that they could rely on any group of adults to contain some customer in its midst? Or was this a regular meeting place where normally those who were involved in this business could enjoy the anonymity of the night undisturbed by a whole fairground full of witnesses? And were these two boys the only sellers? Or could there be other children concealed out here as well, selling the same thing to these unseen customers? And where were the police?

Half an hour later, they sat in the McDonald's in St Peter's Gate in the middle of Nottingham like two boys on a family outing, grabbing at the comics that lay around on the table, blowing bubbles into their milkshakes, chewing on fistfuls of cheeseburger as they competed to explain.

Jamie was the smaller of the two, the one with the curly blond hair, and in the bright white light of the restaurant, you could see that he had a face like an angel – big blue eyes with long lashes, soft pink skin and a cheeky smile that almost never left him – and you could see, too, that he was not yet thirteen. He was certainly younger. He turned out to be just past his eleventh birthday.

He was trying to explain who he was. He had been born in Nottingham and he recited his address and his phone number and the full names of his parents as though he were filling in a form, but his story came out in unconnected fragments of half-remembered scenes. 'My mother is kind of cute, but she's a bit fat. She used to take buses but now she doesn't do that any more, she just walks . . . I've got nine brothers and sisters, eight or nine, I think. I've got eight brothers and I've got two sisters . . . I have been on holiday about three times: Blackpool, Weymouth, I think I've been to Weymouth, there was sand and caravans and food and sea . . . My dad's a mechanic, he used to be a mechanic, I don't know, I had three dads . . . I can remember having cereal, Weetabix. I can remember playing with a truck.'

There was nothing so unusual here – just a boy with a tendency to babble – but slowly, out of the fog of disjointed recollection, the outline of a shape began to appear. 'My first dad, I don't see him any more. The second one, I don't really remember his name. It was the third one, that's the one that got rid of me and my brother and my sister, got me put in care. I think he planned it . . . I can remember I was sitting at this woman's house, Thelma, and I swore and she hit me with a slipper and I fell down on the step and I felt something dripping, and I said "Thelma, I'm bleeding" and then they felt sorry for me. And it was them that'd hit me with the slipper! . . . I didn't like me mam and I didn't like me dad either . . . My dad used to beat me mam up. I saw me mam being beaten up and me brother being beaten up. That's all. When I was about five, he left . . . I just mostly swear by accident. My mam says, "Right, that's it." Fairy

Liquid down my mouth. Vinegar down my mouth. Soap, salt, pepper, everything down my mouth . . .'

He was animated as he spoke, eyes bright, hands conjuring shapes in the air to illustrate his point, sometimes giggling, occasionally throwing back his head and laughing like a donkey before plunging on, with never a hint of pain or sadness. 'Don't know why I got put in care. That's personal and private and confidential. Nothing. I stole some biscuits. Me bedroom door didn't have no handle. I used to get up in the middle of the night . . . At school, I used to get beat up, get my head pushed down the toilet, get kicked up the whatsit. Everything happened to me . . . I don't remember Christmas, don't remember Christmas presents, I had a truck . . . I stole me mam's jewellery and I sold it at school. I ran off from school. I kept on running off, stealing. Sometimes I didn't go to school . . . Me door didn't have no handle. One time I had this knife and I stuck it in the door really hard, really hard, and I went downstairs and I stole some biscuits. I had to break down half the door . . . Me mam says I raped my sister, but I didn't. I was found in the room but I was just asleep, me brother was in there too. She says "Right, that's it" . . . She kept on smacking me and that. She did it with a belt, slipper and that . . . Once, in the front room I was sitting watching TV and I shouted at me mam "Yikes" and this mouse ran out and into the kitchen . . . I got sent to a home because I went with my sister, she were seven, and I touched her up. Me brother an' all. Me mam came in and told me to get out. That was the time she put me in the children's home. She just couldn't put up with me. I were nine then . . . I did phone her up but she said she didn't know me. She doesn't want anything to do with me. She doesn't let me phone her up, she doesn't let me see her . . .'

Even though the shape of his story was becoming clearer, he himself seemed barely able to see it. All the time that he was talking, he was fidgeting in his seat and fiddling with everything around him, tearing little strips off the pages of the *Beano*, jiggling the straw in and out of his milkshake, occasionally reaching out to cuff his friend, *Luke*, who was sitting chewing on a hamburger, still in his anorak, with the hood pulled tight around his pudgy, pink face. Luke was a couple of years older than Jamie, quieter, more solemn, and even when Jamie paused and put his straw to his lips like a blowpipe and blew a sticky white arc of strawberry milkshake into his face, Luke just grinned quietly and palmed it away.

They had met in the children's home. Luke started to explain that he had been born in Mansfield and he had two brothers and a sister, all of them in care, but Jamie was off again. 'This first home, right, I got bullied there, kicking and thumping and strangling and robbing . . .' Luke nodded and said that was right, Jamie had got picked on because he was the youngest, and Jamie powered on with his story. 'And I got sexually abused by a lad called *Liam*. He were fifteen and he got me and he said, "Come in here, Jamie, I've got something for you." So I went in and he locked the door and barricaded it and the staff were banging on the door and he were doing everything to me. He was naked and he was doing it up me arse. I was shouting, "Get him off me!" And the staff broke the window. After that, he was doing it to me all the time and I used to let him. One day, he got me really pissed off so I said to one of the staff, "Can I speak to you for a minute?" I told him all about what Liam did to me and that stuff. So he got moved. And I got moved an' all . . .'

Luke was still quiet, turning out his pockets in search of a cigarette, while Jamie was beating the air with the stump of his cheeseburger like a politician with an order paper as he approached the object of his speech.

'There was these two bigger lads, *Wayne* and *Anthony*, and they got me in the shower and Wayne said, "Get some money for us or we'll blow your knees off." So I had to get a load of money, but that's not how I got started. That was *Michael Jones* who put me on the game. He was fifteen. He was in the home with me. He took me downtown and he asked me if I would get some money for him. I said, "How?" He said, "Go to that man and ask him if he wants business and he will say what he wants you to do."

'So I said that to the man and he took me round the corner, and the man said, "What do you do?" I said, "I don't know." And I shouted at Michael, "What do I do? He wants to know what I do." He shouted back, "He'll 'T' ya, tell him you'll 'T' him." That means toss. "T" for toss. Only I didn't know that then. He took me round the corner and I said, "How do you toss?" and he said "Do this." I did it and he give me £50. He looked like a rich man. I gave £25 to Michael and I spent mine on sweets. That's when I was ten . . . I been with loads of men. I do tossing for ten or twenty. I don't do sucking. I let them screw me in between the legs. I can't make money any other way. There's bus fares, fags, sweets, toys, drugs . . . I get frightened sometimes. The punters try and do things to me that I don't want, putting their dick up my arse, telling me to suck them off . . . I don't like it when they're telling me to do it, forcing me. That's it really.'

He slumped back in his chair, scratched the curls on his head for a moment and blew out a lungful of air. The table in front of him was strewn with aggravated litter, bits of paper and hamburger and milkshake container, all of them ripped to shreds as he had talked. He bubbled his lower lip and stared at them as though he were staring back at his own life and, while he was silent, Luke spoke again.

He began to describe a boyhood which was apparently more or less stable and happy, in a council house in Mansfield with his mother and father, and his two brothers and a sister, himself addicted to Notts County footballers and pictures of high-performance cars, proud owner of a goldfish called Alf. His memory was sharper and better organised than Jamie's and he recalled quite vividly the Christmas when the teachers at primary school had given them all presents which they had opened on the bus going home even though they were supposed to have kept them until Christmas Day, and he had a clear picture of a day trip to Skegness with his family when he was a toddler, when they had all swum in the sea and then suddenly realised that they were late for the bus home and his mum had run round the corner to the bus station so fast that she had tipped over his buggy and spilled him onto the pavement. There had been problems – his father had been arrested and sent to prison for robbery – but then he had been released and the family had stayed together.

It had all changed when his dad died. He seemed to think that everyone had read about it in the paper. His father had fallen from a window though it wasn't too clear whether this was an accident or a suicide. Luke had been six at the time, and it had exposed some hidden weakness in his family, his mother had been unable to make ends meet and had started to find it hard to cope with the four children. She had got stress, he said, and he remembered how he and his older brother had tried to help one day when things had got on top of her. They had gone to a friend's house and borrowed a pound – it was a rich friend, he explained – and they had bought her a packet of cigarettes to make her feel better. It hadn't worked, at least not for long, and by the time he was seven, someone had called in the social workers and all four children had been taken away.

Calm as ever, he described how he had been separated from his brothers and sister, going first to foster parents (*Auntie Linda* and *Uncle John*) and then, quite soon, to another set of foster parents (*Auntie Doreen* and *Uncle Alan*) and then to a children's home. He said he didn't mind. And just as calmly, with his solemn little face still tightly framed by the hood of his anorak, he began to describe events that had nothing to do with childhood.

He had first had sex at the age of nine, he said, when he was in care, with a couple of girls who were both more or less the same age as him. *Karen* was the very first. He recalled the event with a profound indifference. 'She gave me a blow job. I licked her out, licked her tits and I shoved it up her vagina.'

He sniffed and rubbed his nose with a podgy hand. At about the same time, he said, in the children's home, he had started smoking hash. 'You get a big Rizla,' he said, unfolding an imaginary cigarette paper on the table in front of him, 'and you put your tobacco all along it like this and then you get your draw like this and you put it in and then you smoke it and you get mashed.' Jamie giggled through his nose and nodded in agreement and Luke explained – casually, as though it were so obvious that it was barely worth the effort – how he had started selling himself.

'I was in this home. I went to this one where I hadn't been before and I heard them talking about being rent boys – give a man a blow job and then you get paid for it. So I thought, Well, I ain't got much money for fags and things, so I went down there with them. The first one I did was called Terry. I spent the night with him, at his house. I done loads. I was all right with it but I got molested. I was walking down the canal, it was about two in the morning, and this punter followed me and he jumped out at me and he started touching me up. He didn't pay me. And he was pulling at my trousers and he tore the button off and he was trying to get them off me. He was trying to kiss me. He was trying to shove his dick up me.'

For the first time all evening, Luke looked alive, and he got up and stood by the side of the table to finish his story. 'So he was like this – behind me – and I elbowed him one in the stomach and got round so I could kick him in the balls and then I just ran, but my trousers were all down round my knees like this.'

And he waddled across the restaurant waving his backside and jerking an imaginary pair of trousers up round his thighs. Jamie cackled with delight at the performance while a few of the families who were out for a Thursday night burger looked round and could not quite make sense of it.

There was something about the two of them that was not quite real. They described lives that had become one long sequence of misery and pain and yet they did so with all the appearance of indifference or even, occasionally, of enjoyment. Maybe they were lying and it was all a fantasy, designed to earn a free cheeseburger. Maybe it was some kind of joke. But the certain fact was that they had been there, in that doorway in the dark, touting for business, and now they insisted that everything that they said was true, that that doorway was a regular marketplace for their trade and, more than that, they declared airily that there were loads and loads of other kids doing the same thing in various different places around the city. The cops knew about it, they said, and the social workers, too. There was boys and girls. Same age as them. Loads of kids. What was more, they said, they could prove it.

Outside the streets were slick with rain. Jamie and Luke skirted around the taxi rank in the Old Market Square where the drivers sat flicking their fag ends in the dark, passed within sight of the end of the queue outside the Odeon cinema and crossed the road in front of Yates' Wine Lodge, whose walls were already bulging with booze and music. They were heading back up towards the fair in the Forest recreation ground, and as the bus pulled up, they tried to dive in among the passengers who came flooding out of it, only to be spotted by the driver who hauled them back and made them pay their fare. Ten minutes later, they were back in the Forest, back on the edge of their own world.

Once again, there was this confusing sensation of entering the unreal. Any stranger on the street could look around and see motorists pouring down Gregory Boulevard, a clutch of people hugging their arms at a bus stop, a newsagent's with a metal grille over its window, the fair slowly growing in the background. Jamie and Luke stood on the same streets and saw a different country, populated by others like themselves.

This woman, for example, down at the bottom of Balmoral Road, just around the corner from the recreation ground. She was tall and elegant with long blond hair on which the rain sparkled slightly in the streetlights. She was waiting for her husband to park the car, or she was on her way to the pub to meet a girlfriend, or she was taking her dog for a walk. No, she wasn't. She was *Lisa*, she was fourteen, and Jamie and Luke knew all about her.

She had been walking this beat for three years now, ever since she was eleven years old. And with the same matter-of-fact detachment that coloured the pictures painted by the two boys, she attempted to sum up her experience. She said she'd never been that good at maths, but when she thought about it, she reckoned that she had been earning about £800 a week for all of those three years, and if she was charging, say, £20 to £40 for each punter, depending on what he wanted to do and where he wanted to do it, then she must have been doing about twenty-five punters a week, so that, even if you took into account that some of her punters were regulars, that meant that by now, having reached the age of fourteen and a half, she must have sold herself to something like three thousand different men. Could be more. She wasn't sure.

She was tall for her age, even taller on her shiny black high-heeled shoes, and she was wearing the clothes of an adult on a Saturday night out, a tight, white skirt which barely covered her backside and a white blouse hanging open to reveal the flesh of her chest. But when she spoke, she did so with the voice of a child.

Although her memory was cluttered with the debris of her time on this pavement, she still remembered a life she had had before. She had been happy then, an only child, who had had a mother and a father and who went to school and ran around in the playground and who hardly ever thought at all of what she would do when she grew up and who certainly never dreamed for a moment that she would end up here. Looking back now, she could see how the danger had always been crawling towards her – never enough money in the house, her mum and dad arguing all the time, getting worse and worse, sometimes coming to blows, finally splitting up and breaking the news that they were sorry about this but it was all too much and neither of them could keep her any more and she would be much better off with someone else to look after her. So her mum and her dad had gone their own separate ways, and Lisa had gone into care.

She had been aged ten then, but she had soon grown up. The other children in the children's home had started practising their boot work on her, kicking her out of bed in the morning, robbing her food at breakfast, hassling her on the way to school, jogging her pen in class, threatening her with burning cigarettes in the playground, pummelling her on the way home and kicking her back into bed at the end of the day. There was no special reason for them to pick on her, just that she was small and weak. She ran off. The social workers brought her back. She ran off again – London, Scotland, Manchester, Birmingham. They kept bringing her back and after a while, she stopped running and just hid. She'd spend the day skulking about in the middle of Nottingham, watching the pigeons on the Council House steps, and it was when she was doing this one day, about a year after she was first taken into care, that she met this woman. The woman was on her way to pick up her dole and she started talking to Lisa and she said, 'You've got the figure to go on the game.'

'What's the game?' Lisa asked.

The woman said, 'You know, sell your body like.'

Lisa didn't know, but the woman soon explained that she could get £400 a week, in fact maybe more because most of the punters wanted younger girls, so being only eleven, with her looks and her figure, she'd get maybe £700 or £800 a week. Lisa shrugged. The woman said she'd help her. She took her hand like a mother takes her daughter's and they went to the shops together and bought this very short miniskirt and a very low-cut T-shirt and then they went up to the Forest.

Lisa didn't know what she thought. She'd more or less given up thinking. But the woman said it would be OK, and Lisa liked the woman and she liked the idea of stabbing the social workers in the guts, so she thought she'd give it a try.

Well, why not? she thought. I've got nowt else to do.

The first time she went with a man, it made her feel sick, but the second time was easy and so she moved in with the woman and helped her pay the bills. Every so often the social workers would come and take her back to the children's home and give her a lecture and some leaflets about diseases, and she'd just turn around and walk right out again. They couldn't stop her. She didn't want anything more to do with that world – mothers and fathers and social services and being a little girl. That was all somewhere else now, somewhere far away.

Jamie and Luke pressed on through dark city streets. All the while their eyes pierced the tangle of ordinary life in search of signs of their own world. The two boys had been born in this other country and they knew their little patch of it like rats know a barn. They knew all its secret byways and hiding places. Other people might walk through the centre of Nottingham and see shops and restaurants and multistorey car parks. Jamie and Luke walked through the same streets and saw a window that they could get through at night if they were short of somewhere to sleep; an alley where they could hide to get away from the social workers; a newsvendor whose security screen didn't fit so they could steal a copy of the *Beano*; a cinema queue where they could beg some sweets. Other people might see pavements littered with shoppers and office workers. Jamie and Luke saw a steady stream of lucrative possibilities – an old man with food sticking out of his shopping bag, a woman sitting on a bench and ignoring her handbag, open scaffolding outside a building, a bike with no chain, a door with no lock, a man with a smile and a pocketful of fivers. Jamie, in particular, could spot a cop car in the distance with the speed of an instinct, as quick as another child could shout 'Snap' in a game of cards.

Right here, for example, not far from the Forest recreation ground, the two boys had stopped on a street corner, at the junction of Gedling Grove and Burns Street. It looked entirely unremarkable, just another patch of pavement. But no, they said. This was a special place. This was Girls' Corner, which – as everyone in their world knew – was the number-one meeting place for all the working girls in the Forest. There was another place for boys, they said, down in the city centre, in Victoria bus station – on the bench there, right outside the men's toilet. That was no ordinary bench, they said. That was the Renters' Bench, the prime shop window for the display of boys who were renting out their bodies. They went there often.

With Jamie and Luke as guides, it was like walking through a gallery of ghostly images which would materialise suddenly and then fade away. Some of the streets were empty. Some carried only groups of drinkers on their way to a pub. Then around some corner, they would point to a girl child standing as if on show on the pavement – in the shadows at the end of Hardy Street, outside the grocer's shop on Bentinck Street, alongside the car park by the Vernon Arms, all wrapped up in fishnet and leather, her teeth chattering in the autumn cold, raising her eyes to the passing strangers, sometimes ducking through a driver's door and disappearing into the dark, all of them just as obvious as two boys standing in a doorway in the middle of a fairground full of people, and just as invisible.

Here they found *Bernadette* with blond curly hair, who said she was twelve, but looked much younger; here was *Tricia* who was ten at the most, maybe only nine; here was little *Nina* with the black pudding-bowl hair and the coarse, lumpy features, who fiddled with her fingers (speckled with self-inflicted tattoos) and said that things had been OK until her dad got killed in a car crash and even then it was OK with her stepfather, he was her closest mate as a matter of fact, like when she was eleven and she needed a bra, it was him she went to for advice, not her mam, and then when she was twelve and they were alone together one night and he had had a bit to drink, he had tied her to her bed and raped her. She'd cried and complained. She'd complained to everyone. Her mam never believed her, but the police arrested him and there was a trial and she went and told them what had happened, but they said she was lying, and he got off, and her mam wouldn't have her in the house no more.

Here, too, was *Shelly* with the soft, wide mouth and the smoky blue eyes and the tangle of nearly blond hair, who left Jamie and Luke to lurk on the pavement while she came to a pub and solemnly pushed the loose ash of a cigarette into little circles on the table and nursed a glass of brandy and told very quietly how she had arrived in this place.

She was twelve years old when it started. Shelly had never really worked out exactly what had happened. She had been in care, she said, because her parents drank too much and her mum kept cutting herself up. She talked about a home life of chaos, getting herself out of bed in the morning, getting her own breakfast if she could find any food, taking herself off to school, returning on one particular fearsome afternoon to find her mother ketchupped in blood where she had taken a razor blade to her own breasts. Shelly had called the ambulance and then the police had arrived and the social workers, and she had been taken away.

She knew that some of the other girls in the children's home had been working on the street, and she supposed that one of them must have told this woman, *Wanda*, that she would be good at getting punters. Anyway, one day, during the lunch break from school, Shelly had gone down to a chip shop near the Forest, and a taxi had pulled up beside her, and inside it there was this Wanda and two black girls. They had pulled Shelly in and taken her to some flats in Radford. She had still been in her school uniform but they had made her change and taken her to see this old man, who was disgusting, really dirty and smelly, and Shelly had been made to give him a hand job. She'd never had sex before, though she'd had some boys play around with her a bit, and it had made her feel sick. Then Wanda had taken her back to this flat in Radford – Wanda lived there with her dad, but he was an old alcoholic and he was never there – and she had kept on slapping her and then the next night she had taken her to this other punter and she'd made her have full sex with him.

After that, Wanda had put her on the streets near the Forest and stayed with her to make sure she didn't try and get away. She even used to come with her in the car with the punters so she could get the money and keep an eye on her. Once when Shelly argued, Wanda had cut her arm. Another time, after she had been working for a couple of weeks, Wanda had told her to go to meet a punter in this house and Shelly had tried to pretend that she didn't know which house it was, so she had walked straight past the door, and Wanda had caught up with her and given her face a good slapping right there on the pavement.

In the end, it had all come out. Wanda had been driving her through town one day on the way to do some business and the police had stopped them – someone must have told them what was happening – and Shelly told the police everything, so Wanda was arrested.

By that time, Shelly didn't care that much any more. Her dad had left home and her mum took her back out of care and told her everything was going to be all right, but it wasn't. Life at home was still wall-to-wall chaos, no work, no money, no routines, no future. By now, her mother was selling herself through an escort agency, and Shelly started going back on the street on her own. She didn't exactly like it, but she liked the money. And what else was there?

She finished her brandy and lit another cigarette and looked up with her eyebrows raised in a hopeless kind of way. She was silent. Her story was over. It sounded like something from another era – from Dickens or *Fanny Hill* or the Marquis de Sade. The whole idea of this ruthless woman procuring a child off the street raised again that feeling of unreality, of doubt. Had this really happened? Or was Shelly just swimming in fantasy, just looking for attention?

The more the children talked, the more difficult it became to doubt them, as the separate threads of their different stories overlapped and twisted together in unbreakable strands. The same kind of childhoods, the same kind of life in the children's homes (and almost without exception, these children turned out to be living in children's homes), the same kind of experiences out on the street. Shelly's story of her life at the hands of Wanda was echoed and enlarged by stories told by other girls around the Forest of another, even more ruthless procurer.

Fat Natalie, they called her. Her real name turned out to be Natalie Meadows. She was nineteen, from Canada, and she'd moved to Nottingham, where she used to spend her days hanging around the Victoria bus station looking for children to put on the game. And she found them. She was running all kinds of children – boys and girls – until she pushed it a bit too far.

She had this one particular client, a car salesman called John House who was obsessed with whipping young girls. Fat Natalie said that that was no problem, there were loads of girls who'd let him whip them, and she went and found him a couple. One of them was Nina – who had described how she had been raped by her stepfather – and the other was a girl called *Terry*. John House had driven Fat Natalie and the two girls to the bank so that he could get out the money to pay them. By that time, Nina said, she was getting scared because she knew what this guy wanted, so she bottled out, but Terry stayed in the car.

John House paid Natalie for her work and gave Terry £120 for what she was going to have to go through and then he set off, driving calmly through the traffic, with the fourteen-year-old girl beside him. He drove out of Nottingham, way out into the countryside near Ilkeston and found a quiet lane where he stopped the car and told Terry to strip naked. Then he tied her face-forwards to a fence post and used his thick leather belt across her back and buttocks while she sagged and howled. When he had had enough, he drove her back into Nottingham and left her to go back to work on the pavement.

That would have been the end of it, but John House had enjoyed it so much that a few months later, he went back for more. Terry wasn't going to go through that again, but Fat Natalie knew another girl. She was just what he was looking for. She was called *Emma*, she was fifteen and she was desperate. She had run away from home, she was obsessed with crack cocaine, she was in a total mess – she reckoned she'd been raped four times, some black boys had broken into the place where she was staying to try and steal her money and someone else had tried to strangle her while she was asleep. All she wanted to do was to get out of her head. Emma would do just about anything. And Fat Natalie knew it.

Emma knew what John House had done to Terry – Terry had told her all about it – but she let Natalie make the same deal again. And John House had his fun again, just the same way. He even used the same fence post. But this time it all went wrong. Emma's mother knew she was working on the streets to buy herself crack cocaine and since she knew she couldn't stop her – she'd tried, and it was just no good – she had made up her mind to protect her. Often at night, Emma would be standing up on Gedling Grove not far from the Forest with her pale pimply face and her little skirt up round her thighs, waiting for punters, while her mum sat on the wall nearby and watched her and talked to her and, when the punters came and took her away, she wrote down their car numbers and looked at her wristwatch and waited for her to return.

Fat Natalie knew all about Emma's mother so that when she sold her to John House for the afternoon, she made sure she got Emma on her own. But after it was over, when Emma limped back to her room, when her mother made her tell her what had happened and made her show her the crazy red lash marks all over her back, her mother insisted that no matter what she thought of the police, no matter what Fat Natalie would threaten to do, the two of them were going to the Vice Squad. So Fat Natalie got put away, and so did John House. And Emma covered up her bruises and went back out on the pavement. There was no doubt that the story was true. Some of the details might have slipped and slid in the telling, but the hard facts were certainly true. One of the girls had newspaper cuttings to prove it.

As the stories unfolded, each overlapping more or less with the others, it became clear that the world where these children lived was a peculiarly dangerous place. Unseen threats came suddenly out of the darkness, sliding out of the night, striking with an intensity of pain and fear. The children spoke not only of female procurers but of men, too, who attempted to run their lives. Some of them spoke about a particular man, whose name was Lucky Golding.

Nina said that it was Fat Natalie who had originally put her on the game when she was fourteen, but it was Lucky Golding who had taken her over. She had gone to his house one day to pick up an umbrella for her sister *Kerry*. Kerry was on the game as well but it was months before Nina realised that Kerry must have set her up with Lucky, must have sent her round there to pick up this umbrella on purpose because Lucky wanted to get her working for him. He had been really nice to her, treated her really well, made her feel special, and so she had stayed with him and loved him, she said, loved him to the bone. They had spent their first two months together, just the two of them, listening to music, smoking weed, lying in bed, talking about going away to Tenerife together. She had never felt so safe and so warm, and she was happy to work for him. She was proud to. She loved him. And what better way was there for her to show her love for him than to earn him money? So she had worked for him on the pavement and been proud to give him her earnings. Then one night, he beat her all around the room. She wasn't that worried. Beatings were a way of life for her, she said, and it only made her all the more anxious to please him, so she worked harder to pull in more money – to pull in more money than any other little bitch that was working for him, so he'd care for her the most. But he still knocked her all around the room. She never knew from one moment to the next whether he was going to hug her or hit her. It got to the point where she didn't dare look at him, in case he went off on one of his rages. She'd sit in the pub with him and his friends and she wouldn't say a word, for fear she'd say something wrong and get caned for it when they got home. All she wanted was to please him.

Then the police got on to him. He had been running these two other girls, *Michelle*, who was thirteen, and *Stacey*, who was fifteen. They were in the same children's home and they had started going out at night together to work. It was Nina who had first seen them and told Lucky that he should get them to work for him. He'd started hanging around outside the children's home in his gold Datsun 2000X. One evening, he had seen them come out and he had followed them down to Radford Boulevard where he had stopped them and offered them a lift. As soon as they were in the car, he had told them, 'You gonna work for me.'

They said they weren't and they tried to get out, but the doors were locked, and he told them straight that if they didn't work for him right now – and he meant right now, this evening, no messin' around – he would have their bones broken. So they agreed. That night, they worked a couple of punters, while he drove around the block in the gold Datsun, keeping an eye on them until they were finished. Then he took all of their money and drove them back to the children's home.

Michelle and Stacey didn't like it, so they told a social worker, who called the police, who went and arrested Lucky for pimping. When Nina found out what had happened, she went wild. By now she was pregnant with Lucky's child, and these two little bitches had taken her man. They were going to stand up in court and give evidence against him. She went out looking for them, found them in a pub and she grabbed a pool cue and started beating the blood out of them right there in front of everyone.

She was charged with assault and interfering with witnesses, but she was proud of what she'd done for her man. Lucky didn't seem to get the message. He was out on bail and just as crazy as ever. One night, Nina told him she'd had enough, she wasn't going to work for him any more, he could go and earn his own money. It was a mistake. He drove over her in his car, broke both her arms and fractured her skull. She was in hospital for six weeks. Then he said he was sorry so she went back with him. A few months later, Lucky Golding was sent to jail for eighteen months. Nina waited for him loyally with her baby son and her desperate love.

Almost without exception, there was a pattern to the way the children talked about the pimps: they all said that they knew pimps but most of them insisted that they had never been pimped themselves. Lucky was one of the few who had a name. The others simply drifted shapelessly in and out of stories. Like the two men who had kidnapped Leona.

She was a tall, slim girl the colour of milky coffee, aged fifteen and addicted to crack cocaine. She described, as casually as though she were describing her breakfast, how she and her friend had been snatched off the street by two black men who had driven them to Birmingham and forced them to go to work. These men had simply driven up beside them in the Forest, grabbed them, thrown them into the back of the car, told them to shut up unless they wanted to be hurt, and then dumped them on the pavement in Balsall Heath in Birmingham and watched while they earned for them. These men had no names and no faces, they were simply shadows.

Or there were the pimps who had kidnapped a Spanish girl in Brighton because her boyfriend had failed to pay money he owed them. They had raped her and put her to work to pay off the debt and kept her locked up at night in a house near the Forest, from which she had escaped eventually only because two older working girls had taken pity on her and broken into the house to release her.

The pimps were not the only danger. There was danger from disease, particularly among the youngest of the children who insisted on believing that it was safe to work without condoms. Lisa, at fourteen, admitted she had been riddled with gonorrhoea.

There was danger from the older prostitutes. Up by the cemetery on Forest Road West, Della started to rant through clenched teeth about these little sluts who didn't use condoms and did punters for a tenner a time. She had run one of them off herself, she said with pride, some little thirteen-year-old. She'd cracked her head against the cemetery railings and told her if she came back again, she'd scratch her face off.

There was danger, too, from the police who from time to time would mount purges around the Forest, arresting anyone they saw, pressuring them to move away, sometimes as far as Leicester or Derby, but never for long.

These children seemed hardly to notice the dangers. They breathed them. Down in the Victoria bus station, where Fat

Natalie used to look for children, Jamie and Luke found a boy
called *Slim*, who liked to sit on the bench just outside the men's
toilets. He said he was there almost every evening, hunched over
his elbows with the ends of his sleeves pulled up over his hands,
shivering in the cold, sniffing with almost every breath he took
and occasionally yawning like a horse.

Slim was older than Jamie and Luke – fifteen, at least – but he
was playing the same game, and he had been since he was thirteen. He more or less lived in that bus station. It was a huge
place, like an aircraft hangar, full of fumes and the roaring of
engines, drenched in harsh white light which poured down on
the queues of people reading the *Evening Post* and nursing their
shopping, so that all their faces looked tired and pale. On the
wall behind Slim's head, there was a sign which declared: 'This
bus station is privately owned. Skateboarding, roller skating and
cycling are strictly prohibited. By order Chief Executive.' On the
concrete pillars that supported the roof, there were more signs
which said you mustn't feed the pigeons. But no one stopped
Slim. No one could.

If trade was slow, if there were too many other boys competing
on the bench beside him, Slim would wander away and limp
along the side of the bus station towards the shopping centre. (It
turned out that he always limped – he dragged his left foot – and
although he said it was because he'd just been in a car crash the
week before, the truth was that it was a habit, like a barrister
feeling his braces or a model swinging her hips; he limped because
it suited him. It felt right.) He'd wander along flapping the loose
ends of his sleeves, with his blue jeans swimming round his rib-
thin waist, and he'd stop and stare into the shop windows, sniffing
to himself, gazing at the goods, gloating at the prospect of having
them to handle, longing out loud for a new Sony Walkman if only
he could find a bloody punter: £10 for a hand job, £20 for a
suck, £30 for both. That was it. That was all there was.

He always had his eye open for the law and the social workers
and for that little gang of black boys who liked to come down
here and beat up the rent boys and take their money. No one
ever seemed to stop them. There was a rank full of taxi drivers
outside and they had seen it happen, seen Slim or one of the
others splayed on the floor with their money being kicked out of

them, but they never did anything. They said it was the kids' fault if they wanted to hang about these places all hours of the day and night. Slim didn't care.

The social workers at the children's home and the cops all knew what he did and they'd threatened to lock him up in a secure unit if he didn't stop. He didn't give a fuck if they did lock him up. They'd have to let him out sooner or later and then he'd just carry on. They couldn't keep him locked up for ever. They told him he'd get diseases. He wasn't afraid. He told them he wasn't afraid of nowt. They said he'd get hurt, someone would have a go at him. He knew a lad who'd had a razor taken to his scrotum by some weirdo and another who'd been raped in front of a video camera. So he carried a little knife in his pocket. Slim said he wasn't afraid of no one. He didn't give a fuck, just so long as he had his punters.

And yet it became clear that the greatest danger of all was from these very punters. Some of them made Jamie and Luke cackle with contempt – weirdos who did mad things with cream cakes or wanted the girls to do cartwheels in the nude. Others were not so funny.

Lisa had had a bad one. She'd been standing out on the pavement one night, around half past eleven, and she was thinking about going off home – she'd already earned £220 and the pubs were closing so there were a lot of freaks about – and this man had picked her up and said he wanted to go back to the flat which she rented for her business. So she had taken him there, and she'd just got undressed and laid down on the bed when he turned round and put a knife to her throat. He had kept her there for nine hours, mucking about with her, pleasing himself. He had used the knife on her, on her thighs, teasing her and tormenting her and occasionally splitting the skin to show her he meant business, and then he had broken off a chair leg and started shoving that into her. She had thought he'd never stop, but eventually he had given up and got dressed and driven away in his car, leaving her there all on her own. She'd never forget it. It was just before her thirteenth birthday.

Nina too had been attacked by a punter. This was a couple of years earlier, when she was fourteen. She'd been in the car with him, he'd paid for a full strip, she was all naked and ready to do business, and he'd pulled out a hammer. She'd escaped but only by throwing herself out of the car and running down the street without her clothes on.

Sara, a young Asian girl who worked the beat at the top of Arthur Street and who had the most beautiful features, had been around for five or six years. She'd worked down in London in a flat which had been robbed at gunpoint one night by some guy who realised that the working girls in there would have rolls of cash. In Ipswich, she and a mate had taken punters in two different cars to a car park near Portman Road, and Sara's punter had taken a wrench to her head. All he wanted was her money, and once he had got his hands on it, he had let her go, but she didn't know that while it was happening. All she could think about was her friend who had been murdered in Leicester: the guy had taken her back to his house, where he had had the knife laid out on the stairs waiting for her. He had stabbed her forty-seven times. He was an ordinary, everyday kind of guy, Sara said. He just didn't like prostitutes.

Now there was no room for doubt. Jamie and Luke belonged to a small tribe of children who worked out here in the shadows around the Forest, confronting a host of dangers, but never flinching from their task. It was illegal but just about nobody stopped it.

There were these two different worlds, each of them appearing alien to the other, and yet the two of them existed in a state of intimate entanglement. These children slipped between the two worlds like Peter Pan. There was Jamie in a fairground with his friend – and there he was again, in a toilet cubicle with his customer. There was a man in a neat, new car with his jacket hanging on a hook behind the driver's seat, a family man, a respectable man, an ordinary man – and there he was again, beckoning Jamie to the passenger door, buckling him into his safety belt like a father buckles in his son, and then heading south through the city centre and out over the wide new bridge, over the railway yard and the broken Victorian warehouses with the heaps of sodden mattresses and twisted rust outside, past the rigid tower blocks like fists in the sky; out onto Daleside Road, lined with discount stores and empty industrial units and the Magpie pub where the businessmen in nylon shirts sit eating chicken in the basket; all the way out to the nearest edge of the city where the little blue sign with a picture of an adult leading a child by the hand marks the entrance to Colwick Park. Lots of people drive out here. They go to the greyhound stadium or to the racecourse; they stay the night at the Colwick Hall Hotel or they stop by the picnic area or the trout lake. But the man drives Jamie past them all, over the tufted grass to the parking place on the banks of the river Trent, where Jamie can watch the wind scuffing the face of the big, brown river while the middle-aged man in the family car hunches over the little boy's hand, pumping like a dog on a bitch. And then he returns, back to his world.

It was late now. The rain had faded, Jamie and Luke had done their work. Together they travelled back to the centre of the city and sat by the statues of the lions outside the Council House and watched a couple of stray pigeons prodding their beaks into the cracks in the paving stones. They still chattered on, about their mothers and how they might write to them, about some woman who was a cleaner in the children's home who they liked because she gave them cigarettes, about a convertible Mercedes that Luke wanted to have, about an underground house where Jamie was going to live when he was bigger. They both agreed that they would never have children and they wondered out loud whether they might be punters when they grew up. They thought maybe they would.

Slowly and carefully, as they talked, Jamie started leaning forwards in the direction of a fat, black pigeon that had come hobbling towards them, cautiously spidering his two hands across the paving until he was close enough to lunge and grab it. He held the bird softly between his hands, looking into its anxious black eyes, stroking the back of its neck with his forefinger, cooing gently. Then he leaned forwards and lowered the bird's head towards the paving so that he could wipe the end of its beak in a mess of its own shit. Kindness. Cruelty. What was the difference?

They talked a little more and then it was time to go. Jamie threw the pigeon in the air and watched it flutter back to the ground. Luke got up and shoved two pudgy hands in the pockets of his anorak. He sighed.

'You know what they say?' he asked and nodded quietly to himself. 'Life's a bitch.'

Then they were gone, side by side, padding off into the darkness, two small boys in the middle of an English city in the 1990s.

3

Why is it happening? Everyone who knows about the streets agrees that there have always been prostitutes and there have always been a few children who would run away from home and turn to selling themselves to stay alive. But it soon became clear that everyone who knows about this agrees that something new is happening – the sheer scale of it, as if there were some invisible conveyor belt tipping an endless supply of children out onto the streets. Why suddenly are there so many of them behaving in this way? It can't be coincidence. It has to mean something – something rather important. But what?

The Nottingham detective was a decent, honest man. He knew Jamie well, he said, and he thought he knew Luke and he knew a lot of the other juveniles up around the Forest as well. It was true, he said. They were prostituting themselves. There had always been a few children up there, but suddenly, a couple of years ago, the number of underage girls had leaped up, more than doubled, without any obvious explanation.

It was the older prostitutes who'd noticed it first and started complaining about it, telling the police that it was disgusting and they should do something about it (even though the real reason they were complaining, he knew very well, was that the young girls were stealing their business). That didn't mean the number was doubling every year, and they had done their best to get those girls off the street, but there was no denying it: for some unknown reason, there were a lot more juvenile girls out there now than there used to be – not hundreds, but certainly dozens. The youngest one he had dealt with himself was twelve, though he had heard the older prostitutes talking about girls a lot younger than that.

And for some reason, it had been the same with the juvenile males. The city had never had male prostitutes on the streets, though it had had its share of cottaging in the public toilets, but suddenly in the last twelve months, there were young boys – and he meant 'young' – hanging around these toilets selling themselves, taking their punters out to Colwick Park or wherever. He himself had dealt with eleven-year-old boys – Jamie's age. It was hard to explain and just as hard to deal with. The truth was that there wasn't very much that they could do about it at all.

Part of the problem was the law, he said. As long as they were over ten years old, the girls could be arrested for soliciting and the boys for importuning, but then what were the police supposed to do? If the children were being maintained by the local authority – and almost all of them were – they could send them back to the children's homes, but they walked straight out again. In addition, they could caution them. At least that meant that they were in the system, that their details were recorded and the police could try and keep an eye on their movements, but it didn't stop them working. They could fine them but it didn't seem right to punish them and, anyway, fining prostitutes of any age, he had learned over the years, was completely counterproductive. It only forced them to work harder to earn the money to pay the fines. There was one older woman who had been fined thirty-nine times in the last year, and it hadn't made the slightest bit of difference. She paid her fines the way other people might pay taxes (which meant that she paid them late if she paid them at all). It was the punters who ought to be punished, he said, but where they were concerned, the law was even more impotent.

The police could see these men cruising the area looking for a juvenile for prostitution and they wanted to arrest them and charge them with unlawful sexual intercourse, which was what they really were engaged in, but in reality all that the police could do was to charge them with kerb-crawling, which was a minor offence, and failed to recognise whether the target of the kerb-crawling was an adult or a child. These children were not interested in giving evidence against their own customers so the only way that the police could charge them with having sex with children was if they actually caught them physically in the act. It was unlikely that that was going to happen by chance and it was improper if it happened by design – if the police deliberately watched and waited until the man was having full sexual intercourse with a juvenile.

Apart from the weakness of the law, the police didn't have the manpower to deal with the problem. The Anti-Vice Squad in Nottingham consisted of an inspector and half a dozen officers, and they were supposed to investigate paedophile rings, the production and distribution of obscene publications, and the activities of professional pimps; street prostitution had to take its place in the queue. As long as the prostitutes were not causing a public nuisance, the inevitable fact was that it could not always be the highest of priorities. It was a losing battle, the detective confessed, because the cause of the problem – whatever it was – lay beyond their reach.

The executive from the Social Services Department was also a decent, honest man. He knew Jamie and Luke and Lisa and Stella and Nina and just about all of them – because just about all of these children were living in his children's homes. At least, they were absconding from them. Pimps sometimes hovered around his homes like gulls around a garbage tip. One of them had even telephoned a Social Services office, posing as a social worker from outside the county, using all kinds of technical jargon to make himself sound credible, trying to find out what had happened to a particularly vulnerable young girl who had been moved out of a city-centre home at short notice.

The executive from Social Services shook his head. Yes, he knew these children, he knew their histories and he was afraid, he said, that he knew their futures, too. He didn't like it at all but the sad fact was that there wasn't very much that his department could do about the situation.

It was partly a problem of law. The social workers in the children's home had no right to physically stop the children walking out of the door unless there was an 'immediate risk of injury'. And the social workers knew what would happen if they tried to stop them. There would be lawyers on the line in no time: just the other day, one of the children had attacked a care worker and there had been a struggle, at the end of which the child had phoned his parents, his parents had phoned the law and the social worker had ended up being interviewed in a police station.

They were more or less powerless, he said. Not far from the Forest there was a children's home which was run by a kind man who was more experienced than most in his position and who had watched in sadness every evening as a group of young girls, aged twelve, thirteen and fifteen, slapped masks of make-up across their faces and slipped their adolescent limbs into the uniforms of their trade and sauntered off to the streets. He was determined that somehow or other, he would stop them. He knew he couldn't lock them in, he had tried to talk to them and watched them walk away, he had seen the police arrest them and fail to make any difference. One day, he decided to try a new and simple tactic: he confiscated their working clothes, all the stockings and garters and skimpy strips of black leather, and he hid them away in the attic and locked the door. It worked. For a very short time. Then he ran into problems.

He wanted to destroy the clothes but he couldn't do that unless he had the permission of the children's parents. However, when he contacted them, they were not too sure. Even when he spelled it out to them, that their adolescent daughters were using these clothes to sell themselves to strangers on the pavements of the city, they were still not sure whether they would allow him to burn them. And in the meantime, the girls hit back.

The first that the man in the children's home knew of this was when one of the boys who lived there shinned up a drainpipe on the outside of the building and busted his way into the attic, from where he retrieved the black bin bags full of working gear and returned to the ground floor. Why had he done this? The answer lay in the bout of oral sex with which he was greeted by the grateful girls when he succeeded. The social workers had tried to intervene to stop it happening, but it had been made very clear to them that they were in danger of having their heads kicked in, so they had backed off and the girls had got dressed and gone out on the game again.

The senior social worker said it wasn't just the law that made them impotent. They lacked staff. Their staff lacked training.

Everyone did their best, but no one pretended that they were doing enough.

The real difficulty was that the roots of the problem grew terribly deep: 'In our experience over the last few years, the nature of the young people we are dealing with in care has changed. We have tremendous problems of management with them. What we find is that our community homes contain a combination of the most damaged, deprived, depraved and delinquent children and they are incredibly difficult to work with. And our problem is that we are the ambulance at the bottom of the cliff. We pick up these young people when a lot of this damage has been done to them. This problem has become far worse in recent years.'

Here is the real clue. These aren't child prostitutes in the classic Victorian sense, pushed out on to the street by sheer want of food and shelter, selling their bodies simply because they have no other means of survival. Children like that might be rescued with care or driven away by the threat of punishment. This is quite different. For a start, these children are surrounded by offers of help. They are being virtually ambushed by policemen, social workers, church workers, voluntary workers, all begging to rescue them, to give them homes and food and clothing and education. In truth, these street children are unusually rich in material terms, pulling in hundreds of pounds a week in untaxed cash, paying for their own homes, dressing in slinky gear, carousing in nightclubs, spraying away cash on cocktails and crack cocaine.

But if they aren't pushed on to the streets to fend off destitution, why are they there? Is it the pimps and the procurers? Are the children there because they are being forced to be there, working out of fear? It is clear that this is sometimes so, but it is not the real story. Shelly was forced on to the street by Wanda and her slapping, but when Wanda was arrested, Shelly returned to the pavement of her own free will. It was the same with Nina. When Lucky Golding finally stopped caning her and she was free to do what she wanted, she went straight out into the Forest and stood at the top of Balmoral Road of her own free will. But why do they choose to do this? It is something to do with the children themselves, these 'damaged, deprived, depraved and delinquent children'.

Just look at Emma, propped up on the pavement with her

mother in the shadows. She stands there for hours, absolutely quiet and still, waiting for her next event. There is something almost serene about the way she stands there. She is a frail creature, small and thin, with a sickly air, the kind of child that would be no good at games. She is not pretty either. She has no figure to speak of, and although her face must once have been pleasant enough in a pale kind of way, it is now hacked up with spots and sores. She is in the wrong place, doing the wrong thing, yet she stands there at the end of Gedling Grove like a rock in a storm, absolutely determined to carry on. Ordinary life sweeps past her – not just the cars on the road and the people on the pavement, but all the everyday feelings of ordinary people. In her position, they might feel pain or shame or loneliness or distress, they might run away in fear or scream in rage or simply go mad from the pain of it all. But not Emma. She is homeless, she is a crack addict, she is a child prostitute, she has been raped, robbed, strangled and whipped, and yet she makes no protest. Something inside her is different.

It is the same with the others. When Lisa talked about how her parents had given her up and walked away, she rubbed her nose and sniffed and said she didn't really think about it, it was up to them. Jamie sat in a McDonald's, jabbering about violence and rape, and then he laughed until he choked on his cheeseburger. When Shelly said she just didn't think about her mum no more – with her booze-soaked life and her blood-soaked shirt – there was a bit of bravado in there but, more than that, she meant it. She really didn't think about it, she really didn't feel anything about it, or about anything else either. They are all the same, all these children, they never show a thing – because they have learned never to feel a thing. If someone lands them with a bruise, they just hide it or cover it with make-up. If someone lands them with any other kind of pain, they just shrug it away. They are totally split off from ordinary people, sharing with each other their own peculiar hollowness, all of them different together.

In one sense, this is simply a matter of survival. They are very tough people. The girls said that if there was a punter who hurt one of them or ripped them off by grabbing their money after he'd had business, they'd go straight off and get some of the black boys onto them. They could usually find the punters easily enough. Most of them were local men, and the girls knew the cars, and when the black boys found them, they'd beat the blood out of them. Very simple. Sometimes, the children just plain ripped off the punters. A girl would arrange for the punter to drive to a particular spot, or else she'd take him back to a flat, where she'd have a couple of men waiting with baseball bats. Once the punter had his trousers down round his ankles, the men would jump out and start battering him and take everything he had – cash, cards, watch, rings, everything. And they'd just haul him out and leave him bleeding on the street while the children went off to enjoy the proceeds. If he was hurt, that was his problem. That was life.

In this hollow state, the children can tolerate almost anything. More than that, they can actively incite the kind of experiences that would otherwise have broken their hearts, like meat crying out for the knife. And so it is that, despite all of the dangers, their lives are not frightening for them – not the sex, not the loneliness, not the violence or the law or the diseases or the drugs. In their own minds, there is a logic to everything they are doing. Something has happened to these children.

Something has not merely thickened these children's skins but distorted their whole view of life. These are children who think that they are adults, who think pleasure is the same as pain, who think sex in the back of a family car is the same as affection, who think that money is the root of all life and that power is the only point, who can be roped, raped, beaten, buggered and abused and still come back for more because for them, in some mysterious fashion which they themselves most certainly cannot explain, this is the logical way to lead their lives. And their lives are logical. They need money and so they get it. They want power and so they have it. They chase excitement and here they grab it. They want to advertise their utter disregard for everyone who has ever claimed to care for them – drunken mothers, treacherous stepfathers, transparent care workers – and this way is perfect. And somewhere in there, despite all that has happened, they want somebody to want them. And these punters do. In a way.

Everything these children have learned in life has taught them to do this. For them, this is not an aberration. It is the natural outcome of childhood. This is the real meaning of those two small boys standing in a yellow-lit doorway in the fairground evening. They are like little symbols of ruined childhood, guards on the doors of darkness.

But what is it that has happened to them? What experience is it that has so scrambled the personalities of these children? Was it the children's homes? Almost without exception, they have spent years in homes, where they have been forced to eat some bitter fruit. It was painful enough for them to be wrenched away from their families in the first place, but in the care of the state they have been wrenched and wrenched again as they have been passed from one foster family to another, from one residential home to another, learning along the way that whatever else happens they must never start caring for the people around them. But that miserable experience – made even more miserable for many by beatings and molestations at the hands of other children – is only a fragment of the whole picture.

They have been subjected to another experience, far more powerful and far more widespread, an experience that damaged them almost beyond repair, long before they reached the care of the local authority, long before they reached the ambulance at the bottom of the cliff. They grew up in a world of chaos and violence, which comes seeping through the detail of all of their stories of home – slappings, leatherings, rows late at night, knives, bottles, broken windows, shattered homes, evictions from houses, exclusions from schools, people going into hospital, people going into prison, people going into care.

Where is this world of chaos and violence? Why is it suddenly pumping out these deeply damaged children? Is it that this world is a new creation? Or is it an old world which has subtly changed? Somewhere in these childhoods is the beginning of an answer.

Part II

Inside the Secret Society

> In their memories, there dimly floated a story of
> a land which grew darker and darker as one trav-
> elled towards the end of the earth and drew nearer
> to the place . . . Ah! then the ancients must have
> referred to this, where the light is so ghastly and
> the woods are endless and are so still and solemn
> and grey; to this oppressive loneliness, amid so
> much life, which is so chilling to the poor dis-
> tressed heart; and the horror grew darker in their
> fancies.
>
> Henry Stanley, *Darkest Africa*, 1890

4

Outsiders know very well that this hidden Britain exists. Everyone has seen the beggars on the street or read about the muggers and the joy-riders who come creeping out at night. Anyone who travels with their eyes open can find out very quickly that there are children like those in the Forest selling themselves on the pavements outside Kings Cross Station in London, and within sight of Anglia Television headquarters in Norwich, and in Spencer Place in Leeds, Melbourne Road in Leicester, Chorlton Street in Manchester, Portman Road in Ipswich and in Sheffield and Bristol and Birmingham and Huddersfield – in almost every city in the United Kingdom, where it has become a simple matter for an ordinary man on his way home from the office to stop and buy a child to have sex with. Yet, for all that outsiders may see, most of them know nothing about the reality of this other country.

Although the most obvious signs of its existence are on the streets of the cities, where the walking wounded of the battle for life work and beg and sleep, its most important embodiment is in the hundreds of battered council housing estates where its people were born and where most of them spend their whole lives. These estates are the heartland of the undiscovered country and they are the places where the children of the Forest were born.

Leeds is the second largest metropolitan area in Great Britain, one of the busiest hives of financial and legal activity outside of London; it has the West Yorkshire Playhouse and the Headingley Cricket Ground and the Leeds International Film Festival; it has a city centre full of Victorian pride, all funked up with pedestrian precincts and riverside chic; it boasts that it has more parkland and open space per square mile than any other city in the country; and, most important, in the 1990s, it has been the scene of an economic boom that has generated 20,000 new jobs and more than £700 million of new investment, and a cacophony of claims for the credit, most of which centre on the partnership between ambitious northern entrepreneurs and the self-consciously moderate socialists of Leeds City Council. Yet it also has its share of problems. It suffers from crime and unemployment. In the spring of 1995, nearly 30,000 men and women were out of work, 7.5 per cent of its workforce. Leeds reasonably could claim to contain just about all of ordinary life in Britain at the end of the millennium.

Just to the northwest of the city centre, near the University of Leeds and the General Infirmary, there is an area called Hyde Park and Burley. It is neither famously rich nor notoriously poor, neither overwhelmingly white nor particularly black, a place that appears to offer a cross-section of city life. It has its middle classes, not only in the chunky detached houses along Cardigan Road but more obviously in the swarms of students who descend on the place each term; it has elderly people, single mothers, black families, Asian families and, most of all, young people whose lives have been shaped here.

Outwardly it was an unremarkable place. There was the long, straight stretch of Hyde Park Road running down from the crossroads at its northern end, where Patisserie Valerie advertised oven-warm croissants, and the shop next door offered handmade shoes, and the window of Trader Dick's was full of stripped-pine beds and kitchen dressers. The road ran southwards past the rows of tall Victorian villas standing stiff-backed like old soldiers on parade on its western edge, past the swings and the tennis courts on Woodhouse Moor on its eastern flank, down the hill, through the council housing estate towards the junction with Burley Lodge Road, which ran along most of the southern edge of the area and which housed the Burley Lodge Centre with its orgy of meetings and outings to which all local people were invited. Over to the west of Hyde Park Road, behind the Victorian villas, the old back-to-back terraces huddled together in tight-knit families, all sharing the same name. There were the Harolds (Avenue, Walk, Road, View, Mount, Square, Street, Grove, Place and Terrace), the Autumns, the Brudenells and the Kelsalls, each of them a cluster of streets so tight that they were like little villages on their own, all teeming with life. And, finally, there was the council estate itself, most of it over to the east of Hyde Park Road, where some of the old back-to-backs had been swept away by bulldozers to be replaced by the neat 1970s flats and maisonettes of Hyde Park Close and St John's Close. The estate was serviced by three churches and a health centre and a little row of shops with a post office along Woodsley Road on the eastern edge. This was Hyde Park and Burley.

Something was wrong here. The narrow back-to-back houses to the west of Hyde Park Road, for example, looked now just as they would have done a hundred years ago – slightly scruffy, quietly colourful, busy with men and women going through their daily routines – but there was one odd little difference. Almost all the ground-floor windows were scarred with thick iron grilles. A lot of the doors were, too. Like leaded lights and Viennese blinds in the posh new houses on the nouveau-Barratt estates, grilles appeared to be almost compulsory extras for every home here.

Who would pay for an iron grille? Presumably someone with something to fear and, most likely, the object of this fear was crime. Even so, an iron grille was an expensive fixture. So it wasn't going to be bought by the victim of a single crime, not unless the crime was a real horror, it wouldn't be worth the expense; and certainly not by the mere neighbour of a victim of crime. Each of these grilles must mark the exasperated victim of a series of crimes. But could that be right? Why would these houses attract criminals in such numbers? They showed no signs of great wealth. (Indeed, the grilles were the most expensive possessions on show.) Just around the corner, on Clarendon Road, which ran along the western edge of the area, there were fine, large houses full of electronic swag, but here in these dense streets, these were humble, ordinary houses. Who would steal so obsessively from places like these?

Down the bottom of the hill, Burley Lodge Road cut past the

bottom of Hyde Park Road. It was a quiet street; most of the access roads had been blocked by the council to keep out passing traffic, to encourage its residents to enjoy the street. But something was wrong here too. It was not only the iron grilles, although they were here again in great numbers. From the Antiques and Collectibles shop at its western end, whose face was masked by a dense steel grid, past the burglar alarm which screamed like a demented cat near the junction with Autumn Grove, the line of houses with their barricaded front doors made the whole road look like Coronation Street in Harlem.

But there was something else. The shops were dead. The one that used to stand at number 121 was boarded up and converted to a house; another at 119 was boarded up and empty, with Class War posters about Nazi scum plastered across its face. Here were three façades in a row, Leeds Chamber of Commerce, Training Services, Arts Programme, all abandoned. And again, at the junction with Autumn Place, there were more shops deserted behind their screen of wooden boards. Jan's Salon – closed. Di Clementi's general store – closed. The printer's shop – closed. There were a few shops still open, over to the east on Woodsley Road, but most of them seemed to have fallen victim to some kind of invisible plague.

And then there was the writing on the walls. The abandoned shops offered a canvas for the graffiti artists, although not for love hearts pierced by arrows, but for a hand that wrote a more essential message: 'Kiss it, bitch.' And over and over again: 'Fuck the police . . . Fuck the law.' On the crumbling red brick walls in nearby streets, there was more: 'Don't it make you feel you've got nothing to lose? . . . Save the Earth – kill yourself . . . One World Under One Boot . . . Class War . . . PC Blakelock. Chop. Chop. Chop.'

Around the corner, in the new council estate, Hyde Park Close curled around its small car park in a tight horseshoe, which was lined around the outer edge with flats and maisonettes, broken occasionally by narrow alleyways leading off to other modern houses set further back from the road, to the old people's home at Benson Court and to St John's Close further east. It was a red-brick maze. Here, the clues began to multiply. Numerous hands had signed their names in white paint, like dogs squirting on their turf: Luke, Clint, Duane, Dean, Sharelle, Khalim, Tyrone, Nicola.

Several of the houses were closed to the world by wooden boards nailed tight against the doors and windows. One of them was sealed with thick metal sheets. Empty (although one of them seemed to have music leaking out of it). Every little corner in the street had captured its trophies: battered milk cartons, ripped-up rags, empty crisp packets, Coke cans bent double and tossed aside, a disembowelled computer lying helpless on its back, puddles of broken glass, a suitcase all sodden and twisted in the grass with its cardboard lining on show. There were bars over the windows, boards over the broken glass in a front door, a deep sea of brambles in one of the gardens. A vicious little dog, like some monstrous beetle, raced snapping down the street. There was no sign of anyone, though the walls were still eloquent. Some of the words were printed on neat little metal plaques: 'No Motor Vehicles In This Area . . . No Ball Games. By Order . . . No Tipping. By Order.' The rest were written by hand: 'I don't want nobody but Alistair. Alistair is sexy. Written by Debbie . . . J loves nobody in perticler . . . Charlie smells . . . Nina is a tart . . . Fuck the law, smoke the draw . . . Fuck the law . . . Class War.'

A police car prowled quietly around the corner from Hyde Park Road and slowed to a halt in the car park in the middle of the close. Silence. Two thickset policemen in uniform stepped cautiously out of each side of the car and made to walk along the pavement. Their feet had barely touched the kerb when a fistful of brick soared out of nowhere and hurtled through the air towards them. They ducked. The brick exploded in fragments on the road behind them. Somewhere behind the houses, there was the sound of footsteps running.

_____

5

Jean Ashford had a story to tell. She wasn't too sure quite where it began, though the ending was clear enough, nasty enough. It was all about her, but it was also all about Hyde Park – or any other place like it, any place that was attacked without warning.

In a way she supposed that it started one evening a year or so ago, when she found herself walking past the pub that used to stand on Hyde Park Road, almost exactly opposite Hyde Park Close. The Newlands, they called it, though Jean Ashford had never heard any good reason for the name. 'Badlands' would have been more like it. She never did feel comfortable walking by there. Well, no one did really. If she hadn't been in such a hurry to get to her daughter's house that evening, she would have made a detour round the place, but it was the quickest route and, to tell the truth, she really didn't take kindly to being bossed about, and she didn't see why she shouldn't walk down any pavement she chose.

This particular evening, it was about six o'clock and it was autumn, so it was getting a bit grey but she could still see quite well, well enough to see the two lads on the other side of the road up in front of her. She recognised them straight away: Jimmy Clarke and Dean Boyle. Jimmy was small with thick mousy hair which tumbled down across his forehead. He looked quite boyish and innocent in a way – and he was only sixteen or seventeen – but she had seen what he could do before. The other one, Dean Boyle, looked the way he acted. He always reminded Jean of a rat; he was a skinny, mean-faced little lad with his hair cropped so short that it looked like a shadow on his skull.

Jean dropped her eyes and hurried her step. Her daughter's house was just around the corner. She would just ignore them. Only twenty yards and she'd be past them.

'Foogin' grass.'

It was Dean's voice. Her heart started to thump. She'd just ignore them. Only another ten yards.

'Hey! I'm talkin' to you. Hey!'

She was almost level with them now, eyes down, head down, hands clasped together in front of her, walking as fast as she could without losing her dignity. They were crossing the road. She could see them out of the corner of her eye. Keep walking. Too late. He was on her. It was Dean. He had one hand on her throat, gripping. She flinched. He twisted her round and pushed her hard against the wall of the pub so that the back of her head thumped against the brickwork. He had both hands on her throat now and he was shoving her backwards.

'I'm gonna get ya. I'm gonna burn ya foogin' house down. D'ya hear?' Her neck was hurting. And the back of her head, too. She was afraid she couldn't breathe.

'I'm gonna foogin' murder you. I'm gonna come round your house when you're asleep and I'm gonna foogin' murder you.'

She could see his little black eyes right up in front of her face. He was almost shaking with hatred. She wanted to shout for help, but his hand was too tight around her throat. She wanted to fight him, but she didn't have the strength.

'Ya foogin' grass.'

She looked for help. The street was empty, except for Jimmy Clarke, standing right behind him, sneering. Dean was swearing at her now, not saying anything that meant anything, just swear words, horrible words, and he was still gripping her throat.

There was a shout from across the road, a man's voice, telling someone to clear off out of it. It was Mr Mangan. She knew Mr Mangan. He lived right there opposite the pub and he had dogs, two great big Alsatians. He was opening his gate, and the dogs were with him, he was letting them out into the road. Dean and Jimmy turned and vanished.

Mr Mangan came across and asked if she needed help. She thanked him and said she was sure she'd be all right, and she caught her breath and put herself back together again and hurried on around the corner towards her daughter's house.

Mr Mangan thought they had been trying to mug her, but Jean knew what it was really about. She knew the whole story, and that had all started a lot earlier. In a way, it had started years and years ago, in the spring of 1972, when Jean Ashford had first moved into Hyde Park with her three young children.

Jean was happy to be there. She had been born in Leeds, a couple of miles away, in Beeston, in an old terraced house that backed onto Cross Flatts Park. Then she had got married and drifted away for several years, but when her marriage had broken down, she had wanted to come home, to be close to her parents, and she had been lucky to get this brand-new house in St John's Close.

It seemed a very fine place. The council had bulldozed all the tattered old housing to make way for this new estate and the houses were lovely. Hers had three bedrooms and a big kitchen with a dining area. There was St John's Close and then right next to it, a bit closer to Hyde Park Road, there was Hyde Park Close. The two streets were connected with little footpaths. In fact, the whole place was a bit of a maze until you got used to it.

She wasn't saying it was perfect – the garden was just a patch of mud, and it was hard work bringing up the three children on her own without very much in the way of money – but it was all right. Pretty soon, the other houses in Hyde Park Close and St John's Close were filled with their first tenants, and some of them became very good friends and neighbours. There were the Garbutts next door – they had young children too; and Julie, the Irishwoman, with her three youngsters; and the Baileys, who had two small boys; and Mrs Miller, who was a very nice woman most of the time except when the kids played around her door and she'd suddenly turn into the dragon woman and shout at them all to clear off. There were Doreen and Tina who lived together as man and wife. There was Clarence Jones, who was a West Indian chap, a very cheerful, happy man; Sam the man, with his wife and three girls; a couple of young students who had got married and settled down together, though it didn't look as if they were going to last very long the way they carried on; the Bennetts (she was German, he was English); the Mathews (she was Scottish, he was Indian); Ron and Phyllis; Fred and Pauline. It was a good street, a good mix, and since they were all new at the same time, everyone soon got to know everyone else. Although they had the occasional difference of opinion, they generally got along pretty well. The children ran in and out of the houses, playing on the grass or going up to the swings on Woodhouse Moor. It was all right.

These were busy days. Jean had the children to look after, and although the two bigger ones were old enough to walk over to Westfield Primary School and Emma spent part of the day at nursery school, Jean still had her old mother to look after all day – she was too ill to live by herself. And at the same time as she was running the house, Jean was trying to do four jobs to bring in extra cash. With her mother to keep an eye on the children, she was working most nights as a nurse at the maternity hospital next to the General Infirmary in the city centre; on her nights off, she was a cashier at the Lyceum bingo hall; on weekend mornings, she went to cook breakfast at the bail hostel on Hyde Park Road; and one day a week, while the children were at school, she was the cashier at the Odeon cinema. It was hard work, but she had always been a bit of a fighter, and she was not going to give up.

The whole place was busy. Jean would see the men going off to work in the morning, to the old foundries and factories which still stood along Kirkstall Road to the south of the estate. She had married again and her new husband, Jack, went off each day to work in the bottling plant at Associated Dairies. It was dull work but it brought in the money. A lot of the women went off, too, to the General Infirmary or to the university. Those that didn't work were soon out in the streets, heading for the shops. There was a Co-op down on Burley Lodge Road, Clayton's bakery, Hemmingways the grocers, Mrs Oddie's china shop, a sweet shop on the corner, a fruit shop, two barbers, Mr Sidebottom the fishmonger, several butchers and two confectioners. Jean liked it. Hyde Park was like a self-contained town. It had its own football teams, its own churches and clubs. She hardly ever had to go into Leeds.

The change came slowly, almost invisibly, like waves wearing down a cliff. Years passed before she had to admit that something was wrong. The children had grown up, Jack had fallen into ill health and given up work, Jean was into her mid-fifties and a grandmother. It must have been around 1989 or 1990 that she first noticed it: a little raft of places that she had come to rely on as part of everyday life in Hyde Park suddenly seemed to sink out of sight.

The community centre up at Belle Vue was one of the first to go. There were all sorts of activities up there, play schemes and meetings, and the local youngsters used to go there to play pool and listen to music. Suddenly, there was talk of trouble. Parents were saying that they didn't want their children going up there any more, that there was drug-taking and vandalism. Some of them said it had something to do with the black boys who went there – and it was true that more black families had moved into the area – but Jean didn't really know the ins and outs of it. It didn't sound like Hyde Park at all. Her own boy, Mathew, who was in his early twenties now, wasn't interested in the place. Anyway, the upshot was that the white children stopped going up there, and pretty soon afterwards, for some reason, the whole place closed.

Then there were the churches – three of them suddenly went. There was the United Reform Church on Woodsley Road, which used to have a lot of activities for local people. Without warning, it shut up shop, and they sold the building to the Muslims, who used it as a mosque. There was the Catholic church, Sacred Heart, which closed down for good. Apparently, there just weren't enough people going to the place. That one was sold to the Muslims as well and it became the Grand Mosque for the whole of Leeds. And then there was Hyde Park Methodist Church, on the corner of Woodsley Road and Belle Vue, which closed down as well, though eventually they rebuilt it on a new site near the back of St John's Close. It was strange, really, as if people around here weren't interested in the church any more, or even as if the church weren't interested in the people. It felt as though her familiar world was starting to crumble at the edges. It worried her, but there was something else that worried her even more – the people.

There was violence on the streets, not riots or anything, but people being mugged or stabbed or bashed or simply chased away from whatever business they were about. The small children wouldn't go up to Woodhouse Moor any longer, they said they were scared. Some of them wouldn't go outside at all. The old people wouldn't go out at night. Jean couldn't understand what had happened. She would see these little gangs of youngsters hanging around the car park on Hyde Park Close, smoking and spitting and doing nothing, just looking for trouble. Jean knew most of them, the McGibbons and the Hooks and the Clarkes and the Boltons, half of them seemed to be related to each other somehow, like some kind of clan. She couldn't help feeling there was something really wrong with them. They were only kids, some of them only ten years old, but they'd look at you and stare right through you as if you were nothing to them, just meat. When they weren't leaning on the wall in the car park, they were across the road in the Newlands, finding the trouble they were looking for. She couldn't make it out. There was one thing she did know. There were drugs in Hyde Park. She'd seen the dealers herself, selling the stuff on the pavement outside the Newlands pub, and she'd heard that there were big dealers who came down from Chapeltown to sell there. One night, her granddaughter Amy, who was twelve, went to stay the night with another little girl who lived in St John's Close – just a perfectly ordinary night with a friend – and she came back talking about the mother there using drugs in front of the children.

The people on the estate weren't the same any more. A lot of Jean's old friends had gone. Some of them had died, like Clarence, the coloured chap, and Mrs Bennett, the German woman. Some of the families had broken up: the student couple had given up; Sam the man had split up from his wife, though Doreen and Tina had stayed together. But a lot of them had taken advantage of the new laws and bought their houses off the council and then they'd waited three years, like the law said, and sold them to cash in. There weren't that many people who could afford to buy these houses – not ordinary people, not with interest rates the way they were – and so most of them had been bought by professional landlords, people who lived miles away in Dewsbury and Bradford who didn't know anything about Hyde Park and probably didn't care much either.

The landlords split these little houses into even smaller flats and rented them out on short lets to anyone who would take them, so the estate, which was once one big gang of friends, was now filling up with strangers who came and went before you had a chance to get to know them. And because they were only staying for a while, they had no reason to care about the area, and Jean was afraid it showed in the way that they treated the place. Selling council houses and giving people choice was all very well – Jean had voted for it herself – but it hadn't done any favours at all to a place like Hyde Park.

She looked around her now and she could hardly believe some of the things she saw people getting up to. She'd be sitting at home, minding her own business, and she'd suddenly hear a rush of footsteps and one of the little gangs of youngsters that hung around in the Newlands would come racing down the steps at the end of St John's Close, carrying armfuls of record players or radios or computers. They had obviously stolen them, and they used this maze of footpaths around the estate to escape. She'd be asleep at night and be woken by the sound of kids joy-riding stolen cars around the area with the engines roaring and the tyres screaming. Sometimes she'd wake up in the morning and find a car burned out in the car park – the kids had used it and then just set it alight for fun.

The young people didn't seem to care at all. There was this one young girl, Beverley Clarke, who had three small children. She lived in a flat right next to Jean, and Jean could see her through her window and so sometimes she could see quite plainly when the young lads took all this stolen stuff into her house where she would store it for them. She was the most foul-mouthed girl. In the end, the police got on to her, and she was taken to court for receiving stolen goods. But it didn't stop her.

Just across the road, there was this young man – Chad, he called himself – who was selling drugs from his front door. Jean could see him clearly. Well, he made no attempt to hide it; there was a halogen light outside his home at night so it was lit up like Blackpool, and Jean could see all these strangers coming up and knocking at the door and handing him money while he handed them little packets.

There was a girl called Sheralee, she must have been fifteen or sixteen, a nice little girl whom Jean had known for quite a few years; she knew her mother too. Jean watched in horror as this child slowly slid downhill.

Jean used to see her sometimes sitting all alone on the bench on Woodsley Road, on the eastern side of the estate, just sitting there, slumped back, staring in front of her, with a polythene bag screwed up in her hand. Jean didn't know what to make of it at first, but she soon found out. There was a friend of hers who had been clearing out her son's satchel and found traces of solvent in there. She was a bit more clued up than Jean and she had known very well what it meant. There and then, she had gone straight up to the boy's school and burst into the assembly, where all the children were gathered, and she'd told the lot of them what she had found and what she thought about it. Maybe it was because he finally understood the danger or maybe it was just that he couldn't stand the embarrassment of his mother acting like that, but the boy had never touched the glue again. Sheralee was different. Apparently she was sniffing glue and also those little canisters of lighter fuel. God only knew who sold lighter fuel to a fifteen-year-old girl each day. But it turned out that a lot of the kids around there were doing it.

It hurt Jean's heart to see Sheralee like that. No one seemed to be able to do anything to help her and, one day, Jean heard that Sheralee's mother had come in and found her daughter lying on the floor in her sitting room, dead.

There was something else, too, a kind of desperation about people. It was as if life was just too hard to live. A few doors down from Jean, there was a couple called *Eric* and *Nada* who had moved in some years ago. They were very intelligent people, they'd been at university, but they had mental problems and, years earlier, both of them had been in Highroyds Hospital. Now they lived all day in their little flat with the curtains drawn across the windows, more or less hiding from the world. Eric was a computer programmer, he had a whole cupboard full of books about computers, but he was terribly nervous and shy, his hands shook uncontrollably almost all the time, he couldn't work and he spent his days sleeping in bed. Nada was a manic depressive, she often couldn't sleep at all, and she'd have terrible mood swings from one day, when she'd be so blacked out that she could hardly move, to another day, when she'd be so pumped up with adrenalin that you thought she might explode. She'd talk gobble-degook and go on about Helen of Troy and tell people that they had blue lights shining around their heads. The two of them were stranded in the darkness in this flat of theirs with a couple of guinea pigs running around on the floor. Once a month a community nurse came to visit them, but that was all. Apart from that, they sheltered behind their curtains on their own.

There was another, older couple, called *Fred* and *Edna* whom Jean used to visit. They were alcoholics. They had nothing but their state pension to survive on, and every week they spent almost all of it on cans of beer. They had nothing. No food. When they got too hungry to bear it, they used to go around to the church and beg a bit of bread off the caretaker there. Jean and her friend, Anne, who had moved into St John's Close a few years after her, used to go around collecting food for them from friendly neighbours. They had no gas or electricity either. The fuel companies had put them on token meters so they would only get fuel if they paid for it in advance. But they owed money from previous bills, so that even if they went to the post office and spent £10 on a token, they would find that their meter had been set so that it deducted a portion of the £10 to go towards paying off the old debt. They often had no lights at all and, in winter, it was freezing in their flat. It was terribly dirty, too. And there seemed to be no one to help them.

Edna was well into her seventies, a tall, emaciated woman. From time to time – especially on pension day when she'd had too many cans – she would fall over in the flat. Because she knew Jean had worked as a nurse, she would pull herself up and come hobbling over to ask to be patched up. Sometimes, she came across with a teapot to ask Jean if she could mash her a cup of tea. Sometimes she asked for underclothes. Once she came over because someone was coming to visit them and they didn't have a tea towel. They had nothing.

All of this was new. There had never been anything like this in Hyde Park when Jean first moved in. No one used to be frightened to go out for a walk. Children didn't sit on benches and die. You didn't get mentally ill people left all alone to fend for themselves or old women coming out of their flats to beg a pair of knickers from you. Jean couldn't understand what had happened.

Years ago, before it all changed, there had been a very industrious Asian man called Abba who had lived in St John's Close, and he had taken great trouble to plant strawberries and blackberries and all kinds of other fruit in his garden, at number 31. Then he had bought his house and sold it to an absentee landlord, and others had moved in. The new people had not been bothered to look after his fruit plants and very soon they had started to grow out of control; now the whole garden was just one big briar patch, and anyone who felt like it used it as a dumping ground for old carpets and cardboard boxes. That one garden summed it all up really. From a place of plenty to a rubbish dump in less than twenty years.

Jean Ashford got sadder and sadder at the sight of it all and she wasn't quite sure how it happened, but at some point she made a decision. She decided to fight back – for her children, or for her grandchildren, or for Jack, who was suffering from presenile dementia and was more and more upset about the things around him, or just because she had always been inclined to stand up for herself and she couldn't bear to see things getting any worse.

Her fight eventually became a war between two worlds: between one that believed in living in peace and harmony in a community to which everyone belonged, and another which believed in nothing. Like many other wars, it began quietly.

6

Jean Ashford tried to recruit reinforcements for her fight by writing a questionnaire, asking everyone in the area for new ideas to help the place. It took her a week to cover the whole patch and then only a few people replied. They had some useful thoughts: somewhere for the children to play safely; somewhere to get reliable legal advice; somewhere for black people to go that wasn't up in Chapeltown where there was too much street violence. But when Jean circulated the results, it all went dead. Even her Methodist church in Oxford Place in the city centre sat on it for several months and then decided that she couldn't use their premises. No one else said anything. That was the end of the first clash of the war.

It was disheartening, but she didn't give up. She couldn't. The estate was getting worse and worse. There was an epidemic of burglary now. It was as if some kind of crime circus was being staged there. There were these gangs of kids who seemed to spend all day hanging around, just staring and watching, and then they'd disappear and the next thing you knew someone had been burgled or someone had had their car stolen. Jean and her friend Anne used to be on the phone to each other half a dozen times a day: 'Have you seen what they're doing now? Have a look. Quick.'

The police seemed to be powerless. Sometimes, when they tried to drive into the estate, these kids would attack the patrol cars, throw stones at them or even surround them and start rocking them and then melt away into the muddle of footpaths. There was one day when Anne's husband, Paul, looked out of the window and saw a group of these kids spray-painting all over somebody's car, so he picked up his video camera and filmed them doing it. After a while, they broke into the car and tried to drive it away. He filmed the lot and he took it to the police and to the council housing office. Nothing happened. These kids were running riot.

The first time they tried to get into Jean's house, she and Jack were sitting there reading newspapers in the front room when they heard this tremendous kicking at the back door. It was these lads trying to get in. Jean jumped up, ran to the door and let the dog out on them. She saw three or four of them running off towards Hyde Park Close, flicking V-signs and swearing over their shoulders. They were just kids, kids she knew – they were her neighbours.

They soon came back for another try and this time they found the house empty and they took several hundred pounds' worth of things. It was bad. Even worse: the insurance, which they had paid for twenty-one years, had run out. She had known it was due for renewal but, with Jack being out of work with his dementia, they were so short of money that she couldn't pay it until the end of the week. The 'grace period' had run out that Monday morning; the burglary had been on Monday afternoon.

It was only a couple of weeks before the youngsters were back again, and this time they took everything that was worth anything: the microwave, the old knitting machine, the TV and the video, her son's computer, all her little collection of jewellery, a silver christening bracelet that had been worn by a baby daughter who had died. All gone, just because she had dared to leave their house unattended. It was the same all down St John's Close and Hyde Park Close.

Fred and Edna were safe, sitting in their filthy flat with their tins of beer. They never left the place and, besides, they had nothing to steal. But Eric and Nada were not so lucky. From time to time, they ventured out from their heavily curtained flat, and several times they returned to find that their absence had been noted and the place had been raided.

These kids were operating in broad daylight, they seemed to have no fear at all of being caught. There were two or three burglaries every day.

They got to know that one particular house in the close was left unattended quite often and they broke into it ten times; they used it as a kind of alternative home, just went in and helped themselves to anything they wanted. The house next door to Jean belonged to a woman who lived in Cheshire and she let it out to students, most of whom were completely unable to deal with life on the estate. It was burgled over and over again. And that was how Jean got sucked into the trouble.

One night, just as she was about to go to bed, Jean Ashford looked out of her window and saw a little gang of lads coming from Hyde Park Close and instantly she thought to herself that something bad was about to happen. The next thing she knew, there was a loud banging outside; she looked out of the window again and saw the same little gang trying to kick in the door of the neighbouring house. She rang Anne and by the time she got down into her back garden, Anne's husband was already there, shouting at the lads to clear off. She saw them going off down St John's Close – not running, not worried at all that they had just been caught attempting to burgle a home, but strolling together down the road with their hands in their pockets. One of them was waving a V-sign over his head. Another turned round to yell some abuse – and that was a mistake. She saw his face clearly in the streetlight, and she knew it. It was Jimmy Clarke, the brother of Beverley Clarke, whom Jean used to see through her window storing stolen goods for the lads.

Jean had had enough. No one had been arrested for any of the raids on her house or anyone else's, including poor Eric and Nada's (though Eric was distantly related to the chief constable), and so she called the police and told them what had happened, and when they asked her if she had recognised any of the boys, she told them that she had. They came to her house and she made a statement and she named Jimmy Clarke. The police arrested him. She agreed to give evidence. That was how the trouble started.

For a few days, it was nothing worse than glares and threats from the gangs of kids and them all hissing 'grass' when she walked by. Then came that evening when she was walking past the Newlands, and Jimmy Clarke and Dean Boyle grabbed her. She was a 55-year-old woman, she was alone and defenceless, she'd done nothing worse than try to use the law to defend her neighbour against crime, and yet here were these young men grabbing her by the throat and shoving her up against the wall, the better to frighten and threaten her. It was only the beginning.

She went back to the police and made another statement, describing the attack outside the Newlands. The police charged Dean Boyle with assault and gave Jean a leaflet about witness protection. It meant very little to her. She couldn't go out of her house now without walking a gauntlet of threats. And it wasn't just Jimmy and Dean, it was Jimmy's family, including his mother, and their friends, too. Shouting, swearing, spitting.

People Jean had never set eyes on pointed at her and called her a grass – adults as well as children. She would look out of her window and see half a dozen of these kids sitting on the grass bank outside, just watching her, staring her down, trying to intimidate her. She felt like some kind of sport to them.

When the day came for her to go to court, the police sent two men to escort her from the main street in Leeds city centre, Headrow, into the magistrates' court on Oxford Row. She sat on the bench outside the courtroom and immediately found Jimmy Clarke and his mother sitting right opposite her, muttering abuse at her. She turned her head and tried to ignore them, and then the usher came and gave her a copy of her statement, but it really wasn't very easy to read it when the person it was all about was sitting there sneering at her. The case went ahead. She gave her evidence, and Jimmy Clarke was convicted. He got a conditional discharge and a £50 fine with something like ten weeks to pay. Jean told herself it might have been worth it to see justice done, but it wasn't worth it for the punishment he got and, in the meantime, the insurance on her house had shot up from £68 to £169 – she was paying twice the fine that Jimmy Clarke was.

Her friend Anne had come to court to support her, and the two of them walked out into the street together with a policeman on either side. They got to the Headrow, the policemen said goodbye and thanked them for their help and, about five seconds later, Jimmy Clarke came striding along the pavement, with his mother and some other people beside him.

The two women glanced at them. Jimmy shouted. Then the mother shouted. Then the whole lot were shouting at them, f-ing and blinding at them, giving them thumbs-down signs and yelling,

'You're dead!' Jean and Anne turned quickly and crossed the road to the pub and phoned for a taxi. Jean went home feeling physically ill.

Now it was like living in a permanent blizzard of threats and abuse. Everywhere she went, people followed her and jeered. If she wanted to visit her daughter Susan around the corner, she had to wait until there was no one lurking on the grass outside her house, sneak out in the opposite direction down the back of the houses into Woodsley Road, and go off on a great detour to avoid Hyde Park Close and the Newlands.

Jimmy Clarke's mother used to see her in the street and literally cross the road to spit at her. Sometimes, she'd hit her target. Jean would take Jack out to visit the hospital, but these kids all knew about his dementia so they came and laughed at him.

There were so many of them. They kept telling her they were going to burn her out of her house. She had heard of people starting fires by shoving burning rags through people's letter boxes, so she filled a bucket with water and stationed it permanently behind the front door, where it might catch anything that they tried to push through. She kept her key permanently in the lock on her side of the front door in case they needed to escape in a hurry. She'd get up in the middle of the night and pad around the house making sure that the windows were closed and the doors were locked, peeking out through the curtains to be sure there was no one closing in on them.

There were times when she just got fed up with living like an outlaw in her own home and she threw caution to the winds and went straight out and walked through them. One day, she needed to go shopping and she couldn't wait until the coast was clear, so she put her chin in the air and set off with her basket. She was all right for a few minutes but when she went into the chemist's on Woodsley Road to pick up a prescription, she realised Beverley Clarke was right behind her in the queue, standing right up against her, whispering 'grass, fuckin' grass' at the back of her head. Jean stood quietly, doing her best to ignore her. The next thing she knew Beverley was grinding her fist into her shoulder blade, screwing her knuckles up against the bone, doing her very best to hurt her. Jean stood her ground, picked up her prescription and went home on legs that felt like jelly.

It all made her scared. But it also made her angry. They were pushing her into a corner. Either she ran or she stayed to fight. And she didn't really know what it was about her – you might call it pride, or maybe it was just her natural stubbornness – but whatever it was, she knew she wasn't going to run anywhere just to please people like this. She decided to fight on.

7

Jean contacted the police, and they told her that the trouble was that they were short of real evidence of the crimes that these people committed. They had thought about putting in an observation vehicle to record what was going on but they knew that if they put it anywhere near Hyde Park Close or the Newlands, where all the action was, it would be spotted within hours and burned out. So Jean agreed that they could use her spare room to watch what was going on. She knew there'd be hell to pay if anyone found out, but the police made sure that they slipped in and out at night, coming down the back of the houses from Woodsley Road. She watched them set up their camera and she brought them cups of tea and prayed that she was doing the right thing.

She tried once more to recruit reinforcements. Once more, she failed. She talked to a couple of the local councillors, Brian Dale and Gerry Harper, and they advised her to start a proper tenants' group, because this wasn't just about crime, this was about the whole area falling apart. She wrote a little leaflet and sent it all around St John's Close and Hyde Park Close, inviting all the residents and also the police and the churches and the city council to a meeting in the old people's home, Benson Court, on Hyde Park Road, just near the end of Hyde Park Close. Only six residents turned up. They did their best to set up the tenants' group, and the council people said they would clear up the litter and try to repair some of the houses. They agreed to keep meeting, but people wouldn't come. They gave all sorts of different excuses about being too busy or it being a waste of time because nothing would change, and a few of them even complained that she was giving the area a bad name, but Jean knew the real problem: they were afraid. Jean could see what they meant: these kids didn't just burgle to get money, they would break into people's houses to teach them a lesson, almost as if they were disciplining people to run things their way.

Using her spare room, the police got some results. They arrested Chad in the house opposite and found loads of stolen goods in there and they busted another of the lads for stealing and burning cars. But nothing had really changed.

There were syringes in the gardens now. Her own daughter had found one, with traces of blood in the perspex barrel. It was horrible. There was no end to the burglaries. There was a young teacher who had bought one of the houses on the estate who had been burgled over and over again, because the kids knew she was out at work during the day. It got so bad that she decided to sell to try and escape, but she couldn't. No one wanted to live on St John's Close any more, not now, and, anyway, her house wasn't worth nearly as much as she had paid for it. Prices all over the country had dropped, but they had dropped even further in a place like Hyde Park Close, so that even if she did sell, she'd have no chance of paying off the mortgage that she'd taken out to buy it. She was trapped. She went to the police and tried to get some of these kids arrested and, pretty soon, she was being yelled at and spat at, the same as Jean, and they were still burgling her house whenever it suited them and, in the end, she just gave up. She abandoned her own house, just went off to live with friends or relatives and left her home to its fate. It was all too much.

Jean spoke to the police again, and one of the superintendents, Colin Haigh, arranged a big meeting at Millgarth police station in the middle of town. This time, seventeen residents turned up and talked and agreed to try to help themselves. Haigh organised a confidential hot line for them so that they could phone straight through to report crime without being identified as informants. Jean felt that they were really beginning to move now. Mind you, the hot line didn't work too well.

Even if people did get arrested, as far as Jean could see, they just walked out on bail or supervision orders. The police had charged Dean Boyle with assaulting her, but the Crown Prosecution Service had let him plead guilty to disorderly conduct, so he'd got away with a supervision order to keep him away from her. And people complained that often all they got on the hot line was an answer machine. Jean's friend Anne had seen a gang of kids one night ambushing some man in a dark corner of the estate. He looked like an Asian, and they were all at him, swiping him with an iron bar, chucking stones at him, kicking him in the legs and back. She'd got straight on the phone to the police while it was still going on, and they'd been very calm.

'Tell us exactly what you can see,' they'd said.

'Just get down here,' she'd told them. 'Just get down here now!'

But by the time they'd got there, it was all over; the boys had run away, and their victim had limped off to get help on his own.

All the same, people were finally admitting there was a problem and finally they were looking for solutions. The chief superintendent at Millgarth, Steve Smith, set up a summit meeting and invited two local MPs, councillors, council officials, all the different community groups as well as the residents to come to the police station to pool their ideas. They talked about getting new streetlights and blocking off some of the exits from the estate to make life more difficult for the thieves. They talked about finding good new tenants and organising a football team, and Jean said she would start a credit union.

On the estate, Jean was fighting harder than ever. The kids were still burgling with never a care in the world, and they were so sure of themselves that they had slipped into a steady routine, which gave Jean a chance to strike back.

One of the kids would ride around on a bike to find an empty house and to make sure there was no one around. Then he'd whistle loudly, and a few second later, you'd hear the crash as his mates smashed their way in. Or, at night, you could always tell when they were about to break in somewhere because they'd smash the nearest streetlight. Jean and Anne and some others on St John's Close replied by setting up a kind of mobile ambush. They'd all keep an eye out and as soon as they saw any warning sign, they'd get on the phone to each other and try and get as many people as they could to converge on the house to frighten them off. It worked once or twice.

Jean and Anne started working as a duo. If Jean had to go out shopping, Anne would go with her and go into the shops ahead of her to make sure there was no one hostile in there. At night, the two of them started to go out together on patrol, with Anne's little terrier, Angus, trotting along in front of them, as if he could protect them from anything. If they saw any of their neighbours, they'd clutch each other's hands for comfort.

'Keep going,' they'd mutter. 'Don't stop now.'

If they saw any trouble starting, they'd go and warn people, try to raise the alarm. Anne was embarrassed one night, on one of these patrols, to see her own son's car racing by at breakneck speed. She said she'd wait till he got home and give him a dressing-down, but when she got home, she found he had been there all evening. It was just another joy-rider who'd taken a fancy to his car.

A few of the other neighbours finally started to show some spirit. There was a lady in her fifties who lived alone, who had watched the stolen goods going through the estate, in and out of certain houses. One afternoon, she had a couple of tots of brandy, armed herself with a can of white paint and a brush, and went out onto Hyde Park Road, where she found a wall and painted a clear and straightforward piece of information for all comers: 'Bent Goods This Way. Second on the Left.'

Even better, Jean heard rumours that, behind the scenes, the police were up to something special. The first thing that happened was that the brewery which owned the Newlands suddenly decided to get rid of the landlord, whose own sons had been arrested for drugs. Everyone reckoned that it was the police who had got rid of him, that they must have put a bit of pressure on the brewery, maybe threatened to oppose the licence when it came up for renewal if they didn't make some changes. Now, they changed the name of the pub and started calling it the Jolly Brewer and they put in a new manager, a man named Bernard Sherry who was described in the local newspaper as being 'a former hairdresser to the stars' on *Coronation Street*. Jean had heard that the police were working with him in some way. She didn't know exactly what was happening, but she could see that at last they had a chance of winning.

She knew there was still a long way to go. There was this dark side to the estate now – not so much the crime as this feeling of sadness about the place, a sadness which Jean had never seen before and which seemed to have captured so many people.

She saw it sometimes in the post office on Woodsley Road. An old man or woman would come in, looking tired and dejected, and they'd queue up and collect their pension and straight away she'd see them handing back their money for some tiny chance to escape from their lives, by buying a scratch card for the lottery. Often, she'd see them buying five at a time, handing over more and more of their precious pensions. Most often, of course, they would lose. Or they'd win and hand the money straight back again to get more cards, a bigger chance to escape. And then she'd see them shuffle away, across the street, still captured, but poorer.

She saw it on the bench in Woodsley Road, the one where she used to see Sheralee, before she died. Someone else sat there now, a middle-aged Jamaican woman called Eve. She would sit there all alone, usually wearing nothing more than her nightie; sometimes she was crying, sometimes she was eating a take-away meal. She'd sit there, sighing, soaking up the rain, watching her life go by.

She could see the sadness in the young mothers pushing their children out of their front doors to look after themselves on the streets and she could see it in the physical state of the place, in the broken windows unrepaired, the litter uncollected, the bitter messages sprayed across the walls. They had started letting young people move into the sheltered housing in Benson Court and there was a young mother in there now who used to change her baby's nappy and often just chuck the old one out of the window. It was as if she hated the place.

The house in St John's Close whose garden had been overgrown with briars had been left empty by its private landlord, and the kids had started going in there to muck around. Nobody had stopped them and the next thing you knew, one of them had set fire to it and burned it to a wreck. One of the private landlords had rented out another house for a few months to some Malaysian students. One night, they had cooked up a meal which, for some reason, they had decided they didn't want, so they'd hurled it out of their door up on a garage roof, where it had started to rot. Eventually there was this lump of decayed mess up there, seething with maggots which occasionally dropped in clusters into Anne's garden.

It was as if other people could smell this sadness. And there were those who liked the smell, who were drawn to it like rats on a refuse dump. There were these finance companies, for example, who used to send round neatly dressed salesmen with glossy brochures, offering all kinds of special, attractive deals, but Jean knew that all they were really after was debt. They wanted to get people into debt so they could lend them money and charge them ridiculous rates of interest. They'd never get away with it on posh estates but here people were desperate for anything that looked like a bargain.

There was an old lady who lived upstairs from Eric and Nada's flat who had been persuaded to borrow some money, and Jean used to see the man from the loan company striding over to her place at seven in the morning, to make sure he nailed her before she left the house. Edna and Fred, who had no more than two empty beer cans to rub together, were up to their eyes in debt to companies like this.

And if people didn't pay, they'd put in the bailiffs and seize goods out of their houses. The end result was no different from what the gangs of kids did to people.

8

The fight went on. The crime still flashed through the estate like flames on oil. One day, it was one of the Hooks using a stolen car as a battering ram to destroy a garage door. The next day, it was a woman who lived with one of the McGibbons, coming round the estate with carrier bags full of shoplifted clothes, selling them on the doorstep and taking orders for her next trip.

'Does your little boy want a tracksuit?'

There were a lot of rumours, too, that some of these kids now had guns. There was a robbery at a baker's in the city where two men had pulled guns, and the police seemed to think that they were Hyde Park kids. And there had been a nasty incident where two men had been kept prisoner in their own home while three armed robbers ransacked the place: the robbers turned out to come from Hyde Park and they were aged eighteen, fourteen and thirteen.

On the advice of the police, Jean set up a crime prevention evening and symbolically chose the reformed pub, the Jolly Brewer, as the venue. It turned out to be a mistake. People told Jean they wanted to come but they'd be scared to go to the pub. She told them there'd be safety in numbers, but when she turned up at the Jolly Brewer on the evening of the meeting, she had to pick her way through groups of youths hanging around outside with hoods pulled over their heads. An inspector from Millgarth came with another officer, but there were only five other residents and Jean ended up apologising for inviting them in the first place. Although they did stay for about an hour, they didn't agree to do very much and, when they left, the two police officers had to escort them home. Jean said it only went to show how right they were to fight. The new people at the pub agreed. Bernard, the new manager, seemed determined to turn things round. Already, he had banned the worst of the kids from using the pub and now he installed bright new floodlights in the car park to keep the drug dealers away at night.

The kids hit back, smashing the pub's windows and smashing them again as soon as they were repaired. The pub put up boards and padlocks; the kids removed them and smashed the glass again. Bernard Sherry didn't seem to worry. There were a lot of rumours about him on the estate, mostly that he was an ex-policeman and even that he was allowing the police to use the pub to spy on the kids who were still dealing drugs in the street outside.

The kids themselves were looking sullen and angry, strutting round the car park, flicking stones at passing cars, occasionally walking round to Jean's house to lob a lump of concrete at her gable or just to stare. Jean stayed well away from them. Then one night someone went into the pub and told Bernard Sherry he was needed outside. When he got there, two young men told him he was a grass and attacked him with baseball bats. They broke his wrist and several of his ribs and put him into hospital.

A few days later, Jean noticed a little pile of charred rags and burned matches just outside her back door.

By now, the police had gathered enough intelligence to act and, at six o'clock one morning, they pounced on the estate, banging on doors, rounding up sixteen of the kids. They took them to Millgarth police station and charged them with a total of seventy offences – burglary, car theft, robbery, possession of drugs, intent to supply drugs. Then they came back to the estate looking for six more who had slipped through their net.

A couple of nights later, not long before midnight, the opposition hit back and, this time, they went all out for victory.

Jean was just settling down in the spare room to do some paperwork before she went to bed, when she heard a lot of shouting and banging. She went to the window and saw people running, people with big sticks and dustbin lids in their hands. They seemed to be coming from every corner of the estate, heading westwards toward Hyde Park Road. She went to her telephone and called her councillor, Gerry Harper.

'There's something going off,' she told him. 'I think there's going to be a riot.'

At that moment, there was a bang and a burst of flames, and Jean realised a car had exploded somewhere in the street. She heard alarm bells. There was more banging and crashing from the garages and from the north, towards Woodhouse Moor, and then a much bigger bang. Now, she could see flames reaching up towards the night sky from somewhere over in the car park. Something dreadful was happening out there.

She heard a new sound, a steady thumping, like a jungle drum, and she realised it was the sound of sticks being beaten rhythmically against the road. There was another bang – a deep, soft whoof of a sound – and a balloon of orange light burst into the night. That was bigger. That was the pub. They were burning the Jolly Brewer.

The sounds of battle rumbled through the night – shouts and muffled bangs, flames crackling, sirens, footsteps running. When Jean finally ventured out the next morning, the streets of Hyde Park were littered with the burned-out wrecks of cars. There were police on every pavement, and journalists and gawpers were wandering from house to house. And on Hyde Park Road, just opposite Hyde Park Close, there were fire engines still spraying water over the blackened remains of the Jolly Brewer. It was burned to a ruin.

That morning, the chief constable, Keith Hellawell, reviewed the damage and warned that gangs were tearing the city apart. He blamed illegal drugs – 50 per cent of robberies and burglaries, he said, were committed by young people trying to find money for drugs. 'We have lost a generation who are now in their teens and are being left to their own devices. We can expect 30 per cent of today's youngsters will be involved in drugs by the age of thirteen and 50 per cent by the age of sixteen.'

That afternoon, by coincidence, bulldozers tore down the old Belle Vue building which had once given young people in Hyde Park somewhere to go.

That night, the opposition struck again, even though there were police all up and down Hyde Park Road. Just before midnight,

Jean looked out of her window and saw people gathered outside her house, looking towards her. There were about thirty of them, most of them young men, most of them with their hoods pulled over their heads. Some of them were shouting the usual abuse and, as she watched, they started battering at the steps at the end of St John's Close, tearing up lumps of paving stone and running back to sling them at her home. They started yelling that they were going to burn down her house. She ran to the phone, called the police, called her local councillor and watched again, standing well back from the window, as the youths prowled outside until the sound of approaching sirens scattered them into the darkness.

Now she was frightened, far more frightened than she had ever been in the past. That night, the police put a van at the end of her road. On the streets the next day, every face seemed to be snarling at her. She tried to ignore them, but their voices still pierced through to her. So many threats – to break her legs, to burn her home, to kill her. There were notes through her letter box. And, once again, she found burned rags by her back door. Her daughter Susan found that someone had spray-painted 'Kill the grasses' on some boards outside her home. Susan tried to continue as normal but when she left her house to go shopping with her baby son, Sam, in his buggy, she found herself surrounded. Someone grabbed the handles of the buggy and before she knew it, she had lost Sam. While she pleaded, they took him out of her reach and started pushing him backwards and forwards across the street, taunting her with their strength, and then running off to leave her with her fear.

The police had taken away the van from the end of Jean's road and told her to call them if she had the slightest worry. Three days after the burning of the pub, the streets seemed quieter. She was looking after another of her grandchildren, Joshua, who was two, and she arranged to meet his mother, Emma, at the bottom of Woodsley Road to give him back. She strapped the little boy into his buggy and walked quickly down St John's Close, looking directly in front of her, somehow hoping that if she saw no one, no one would see her. As she turned the corner into Woodsley Road, she discovered her mistake.

Two big lads came at her. These weren't boys, these were grown men in their twenties. One of them in particular was thickset and strong. They were swearing, hissing through clenched teeth. She tried to walk by them, pushing Joshua in front of her. One of them grabbed her from behind, spun her round to face him and punched her in the ribs. She tried to double up, but he was already punching her again. She had one hand across her midriff, trying to protect herself, but she had to keep the other on the buggy, clutching it for fear that if she let go, Joshua would roll off down the hill into the traffic. Now they were both punching her, shouting – no, louder than that, they were screaming at her. And kicking too, thrashing their heavy black boots into her shins. Vaguely, in the background, in another world, she was aware of other people walking down Woodsley Road with their shopping bags, not stopping, not doing anything to save her. Then it was over. The two men turned and disappeared into the estate. Jean stood, doubled up, one hand still on the handle of Joshua's buggy, all alone in the street full of strangers.

She couldn't go home, not like this. Jack would be too upset. There was no sign of her daughter down the road. She had to go somewhere. She turned and pushed the buggy into the butcher's shop. She knew them there. As she came through the door, she vaguely heard a woman who was already in there say something to her and, more clearly, she heard the butcher tell the woman to be quiet and she opened her mouth to tell what had happened and finally, she started to cry.

The police said she had to go. As soon as she had found her daughter and got home, still pouring tears, she had gone upstairs, where Jack wouldn't hear, and telephoned the police. At first, they said that they would give a quick-response alarm so that she could push a button and have the police straight round to her doorstep within minutes, but then they considered the threats and the burned rags by her back door and now this latest attack and they told her that in truth there was no way that they could guarantee her safety here any more. She would have to go.

That afternoon, the police arranged for the council to show her another house in another part of Leeds. They did the same for her daughter Susan, who, they feared, would no longer be safe living in Hyde Park. That night, plain-clothes police guarded her home.

In the papers, the home secretary, Michael Howard, was visiting the ruin of the Jolly Brewer and promising that the perpetrators would be brought to justice. But everyone knew there was no chance of that. No one was going to give evidence against them. Not any more. They'd won.

They were children, but not the kind of children who had once lived here, not the kind of children who played games and enjoyed life and looked forward to growing up. These children were wild and hard and impervious to pain – theirs or anyone else's. Something inside them was different. And they had won.

Jean had lost. She had lived there for twenty-three years. Now, she had only twenty-four hours to move out. When the furniture van came to take them away, it had to be protected by a police escort.

9

Now they were notorious. They were in the *Yorkshire Evening Post*, they were on the early evening *Calendar* programme on YTV, they were in the national newspapers. It was the chief constable himself who was having to explain things to the press. It was the home secretary personally who was promising they would be caught. They were not just the kids who hung around in Hyde Park Close. They were the Hyde Park Gang, the ones who had burned down the Jolly Brewer, the ones who had taken on the law – and won.

The simple facts that began to emerge about them were enough to guarantee their notoriety, even without their assault on the Jolly Brewer. Police sources made it clear that they had watched from various secret places and that they had seen a fearful exhibition: children as young as nine smoking cannabis on the pavement outside the Newlands pub; children of similar age helping to break into houses in order to steal their contents and 'bricking' police cars that strayed too close to them; adolescents from Hyde Park Close using heroin; others using ketamine, which was designed to sedate horses; joy-riders who were apparently so obsessed with driving other people's cars that several of them were stealing two or three a day. Some of them were stealing local cars in order to cruise around the city looking for high-performance alternatives, some stole cars which they then donated to their friends as 'community cars' to be used by whoever needed one, and one was so addicted that he admitted that, single-handed, he had personally stolen more than six hundred cars, most of which had ended up stripped of their fixtures and burned to a wreck.

It turned out that there was a street in the north of Hyde Park which had been picked on by the national tabloids a year or so earlier and named as the most burgled street in Britain. Now, local people said that the tabloids were wrong. There was another of their streets that had suffered even more. And they knew who was responsible. Pick any street round here, they said, it's the same kids who've robbed them, the same notorious kids.

Now, when people asked what had gone wrong with Hyde Park, they thought they had their answer. It was that gang. They were terrorising the place. That was why old people were afraid to leave their homes, why so many shopkeepers had fled the area, why the whole place had become so run down and ruined. They were the ones who had torn the heart out of this community, that gang, and they were still out there somewhere, out on the streets of the city, lurking in the dark corners of the car parks, padding around the back alleys looking for a weakened door, with their baseball bats and their petrol bombs.

Hyde Park Close was an intimidating place. Approaching from the east, from St John's Close, it was noticeably rougher than the rest of the area – more litter, more graffiti, more broken windows, more boarded-up houses, and an entire three-piece suite, two heavy armchairs and a sofa, sitting burned out and blackened in a puddle of ash in the car park. There was no sign of anyone. There was only that pricklish sensation that someone certainly was watching and a fear that at any moment, they would sling a welcoming lump of brick through the air. Only at the far end, where Hyde Park Close opened onto Hyde Park Road, was there any obvious sign of life.

There were two of them there. They looked about sixteen, both of them skinny, both of them wearing torn trainers, dusty jeans and baggy T-shirts, the uniform of city boys. They were sitting on the pavement, with their backs to a red-brick wall and their legs splayed out flat along the pavement in front of them, dangling their hands in their laps. Neither of them spoke to the other. Both of them were oddly still. In fact, the only thing about them that moved was their eyes, which prowled slowly across the breadth of Hyde Park Road, apparently watching for something.

They must be the ones. Along with their mates, they must be

the ones who had signed the walls and smashed the windows and broken down the doors, the ones who had battered Jean Ashford and burned the Jolly Brewer to the ground, the ones who lobbed bricks at policemen, the kids who ran riot in Hyde Park. This was their patch. It was as if they were guarding its gateway.

Minutes passed. From down the hill to their left came a shriek like a witch in flames, and a car swung into the bottom of Hyde Park Road and roared up the hill towards them, shiny and black and very, very fast. As it came level with them, it screamed again and juddered to a halt so suddenly that its rear end bucked off the ground and landed alongside the driver with the front of the car twisted round to point directly towards the two figures on the pavement. Clouds of white smoke churned up around its wheels. A lad with a Spanish look about him grinned out of the driver's seat and suddenly swung the car again so that it pointed back up the hill, its engine panting.

The two on the pavement eyed him, still not moving. Then one of them spoke.

'Thought you was gonna get a Bim.' A BMW.

The Spanish boy's eyes were as bright as his smile. 'Couldn't find one,' he called.

The engine started to yell again. He flashed a grin of madness through the window of the driver's door. 'I'll go find one now.'

Roaring and squealing, the car leaped off up Hyde Park Road, leaving behind a bitter smell and a long, black streak in the road. The two lads on the pavement shrugged and went back to their silence.

They were the ones. They had that same matter-of-fact indifference that Jamie and Luke had relied on. They sat there and life passed them by, except that every so often they got up and declared war on it, burning and burgling and spreading distress. Most of the time, they just sat inside their armour of indifference. But why would they be like that? After all, this was not one of the notoriously bad parts of the city. It wasn't like Gipton or Seacroft or Halton Moor, the estates that were ravaged by social problems. This was Hyde Park, in the shadow of the university, the place that Jean Ashford had been so pleased to move to.

For a while, they refused to talk. They just shook their heads and stared at the pavement or looked away and wanted nothing to do with nothing. Then one of them said something about students.

'They're the foogin' problem round here,' he muttered. 'Students! I feel like ripping all their hearts out.'

Close up, he was even thinner than he had looked in the distance. He was not very tall, probably not much more than five foot, he had coal-black hair so short it was like a shadow on his skull, and the skin drawn tight across the bones of his face was scattered with pimples and sores.

'Foogin' students,' he went on, shaking his head in disgust. 'They throw all their rubbish out in the streets. It's not healthy. Place is full of students. They're going through the streets in big groups, twenty or thirty of them, going through the streets together. They're taking the place over. It's all right for them. Students can get good jobs. Students can get good money. You see 'em coming down here with their parents in their cars. I foogin' hate 'em.'

He paused and sniffed and turned away and, for a moment, it looked as though he would say no more. Then he went on.

'You know what I'd like to give 'em?' He smiled grimly and spoke slowly and deliberately. 'A foogin' Colombian necktie. The next bloody student I see, I'd like to cut his throat from ear to ear, rip his foogin' tongue out and leave it hanging down the front of his shirt. Then d'ya know what I'd do? I'd lie down on the floor and I'd bloody laugh. I'd laugh till I cried. Yeah. Foogin' Colombian necktie.'

He smiled. His face looked better. He was animated now – now that he had shared this confidence – and he started to talk quite freely.

He said he'd lived in and around Hyde Park since he was born and he'd probably be here for the rest of his life. He'd gone to the City of Leeds School, over the other side of Woodhouse Moor. He hadn't gone to school every day, he confessed, and he had passed no exams. He had never worked. He had never done anything. He shrugged and said he had nothing to do now. That was what really got to him, he said.

'Every foogin' day is the same round here. I can't think of one thing to do all day. There's no point going to town – you need money. I wake up in the morning, and I don't think about it, I just do the same thing. You're used to doing it, every day, every week. You can live in Blackpool and there's a beach an' all. There's no beach here. There's no arcades. Students have arcades.

'I wake up in the morning. Sometimes I sleep in, I sleep till the afternoon. I come out. I call for my mates. I just hang around, wait for something to happen. That's the only thing there is to do in this whole area. Just hang around, hang around, just be there on the street, looking trampy, then go home. Every day is the foogin' same.'

'And smoke draw.' The other one spoke for the first time. He had a younger, fleshier face, which was lightly decorated with pubescent fur around his throat and chin and upper lip. 'You get charged out your head and then you just chill out.'

'But there's still nothing to foogin' do. Is there? "Shall we go to your place?" Nah – been there. "Shall we go to my place?" Nah – been there. Nothing.'

The lad with the furry face sniffed and rubbed the palm of his right hand deep into one of his eyes. 'The only thing we do is, we smoke draw.' Slowly, he wriggled his back against the wall behind him and screwed up his face as though he were in pain. 'You get up in the morning and you take £10, and you go and get some draw, you have a spliff, you get out your head, and you just chill out, just pass time. That's what you do.'

His mate snorted. 'There is not one thing to do round here. No point going to town. It's like three pounds to get in to Stoggy's, six to get into Bedrooms – it's a dance hall, got a chill-out room – then you gotta spend money on beer and stuff. There used to be a youth club, up Belle Vue, but that's closed. TV's all shite. There is not one thing to do. Every foogin' day is the same.'

Now, at least, one thing made sense – their stillness as they sat on the pavement. They didn't move, because they had no reason to move. They meant what they said. Literally, they had nothing to do. But even if all they did was just to smoke and sit on the pavement, they'd still need money, wouldn't they? Where would they get the money to buy their draw?

It was the very skinny one who answered. 'I don't sign on. I can't, not allowed to. There's no benefits for sixteen-year-olds. Anyway, I don't want to sign on. Don't want to crawl to a bunch of people for foogin' £30 a week. I want a job. Don't matter what it is. A packing job, mechanic, don't matter what it is, long as it brings in money. See?' He started to stab the air with his right index finger. 'I want to have a job, earn some money, save it up, get a girl, have a kid. Look at me. Will you look at me? I live like a tramp. I live like a foogin' animal. Don't I?'

While he was talking, he had started to crouch forward from the wall, but now he sank back again so that he and his mate looked once more like two shadows on the pavement. What about their parents? Did they work? Did they give them money?

'They got no money. Why they gonna give me money? No foogin' way.'

The furry one leaned forward and spoke thoughtfully. 'My dad works but I don't really know what he does. I don't really live with him.' He rubbed his face. 'I think he used to work at Myer's once. I think he still works somewhere. I dunno. I don't see him. My mum don't really work. She's done some cleaning, some cleaning jobs.' He shook his head and laughed suddenly as though he'd just thought of some ridiculous joke. 'She got no money. No money at all.'

But when they were younger, did they think they'd get work? What had they wanted to be when they grew up?

'Fireman,' said the furry one with a shrug. 'I wanted to be a fireman. But I can't do it. I've got no exams. I do want to go to college, but you have to pass a test. Don't ya? I'd do anything, me. I'd just go anywhere, to stop being bored.'

And his mate? His skinny mate sighed and took a plunge. 'What I want to do, what I would like to do . . .' He was looking upwards with his eyes half shut. ' . . . is to go up in an airplane and parachute down, come down from the clouds. I want to float. I want to foogin' fly. Down from the clouds. I've always wanted to do that.'

For a moment he was alive, his face flushed with excitement at the memory of his dream, no matter how far away from his real world it might be, but then in the next moment, his energy had passed and he was slumped back inside himself again. There they sat: the boy who wanted to be a fireman and ended up an arsonist; the boy who wanted to fly free and ended up . . . well, like this.

And they still hadn't answered the question. What did they do for money?

'I foogin' rob students, don't I?' He almost shouted the words, as if he was showing an idiot to his own front door. 'Whaddya think I do? Look. Listen. The only way to get them out is rob them. If they don't like it, they can fuck off. They trash the area and then leave it. They are loving it, not being with their parents, changing their image, all that. So every night, they get foogin' robbed.'

He was burning with anger now. 'There's a pizza shop for students. If you've got a student card, you get a reduction. There's banks'll lend 'em money, coz they're students. There's rooms they can rent, coz they're students. Why should they get privileges like that? Normal people don't. They're building all student accommodation in this area. But people who were born in this area can't get a house. It's just coz they've got money. Isn't it? And we've got fuck all.'

While he was raging, four or five others had strolled out of Hyde Park Close, evidently aware that something was going on, and they had gathered in a group, staring down at the two on the pavement. They were listening, checking, starting to nod, trying to butt in, starting to talk now, muttering their agreement, returning to the one great reality of daily life. There was nothing to do and nowhere to do it. So what did they do with their time? The answer came in a chorus.

'Twocking'. Taking cars without the owners' consent. It was easy, they said. City workers left their cars in Hyde Park on the way to their offices, so they were just sitting there, waiting for twocking. Break a window. Stick a screwdriver in the ignition. Burn it up.

One of the newcomers was wearing a battered baseball cap with a dirty kangaroo on the front and every time he opened his mouth to say something, he twisted the peak from his forehead round to the back of his neck, as if this somehow turned on his speaker. Then he'd finish his speech and twist it back again. He wanted to talk about burgling. He switched on his hat and explained, 'All the kids round here do burglary. Well, most kids. And they drive without a licence and insurance and all that.'

'I wouldn't tax my car.' It was a very big lad, like a giant in jeans, older than the others. 'There's no point anyway. One o' youse lot would only twock it.'

'Well, twock it back then,' said the lad with the revolving hat. 'Anyway, what I'm saying is, we don't pay no fines, we don't have a TV licence – '

The giant interrupted, 'No point in having a TV licence. Don't make the picture no better.'

A few of them laughed and the lad with the hat swivelled his peak right the way around his head to indicate that he was coming to his main point. 'It's war against the law. Innit? That's what it is. Innit? War against the law.'

He switched off his hat and others took up the theme: 'I was on bail for eighteen months and they come and took the door off five times . . . Police round here, they take the piss . . . Three Sundays on the trot, they come into our place, never found nothing, never charged me wi' nothing . . . They done me for drugs, right. Some draw and some Es. But they were me girl-friend's. They weren't mine, right. But she's a junkie, real junkie. And this copper, he tells her she'll be all right, he won't arrest her, if she makes this statement on me. So she does. And she's still fucking scared shitless of him, right, so she lets him do it with her, she lets him screw her. Right. Are you tellin' me that's allowed? . . . They'll strip-search you up against the wall. It's illegal, that . . . There's a cop who buys stolen gear off us . . . They come in, they shout abuse, it's like they want to get a reaction so they can arrest you . . . It's not law and order. It's out of order . . . They do you for Section Five, disorderly conduct. Nothing happens, just a fucking waste of your time . . . They picked me up once, didn't charge me with nothing, kicked me out at one in the morning. No way of getting home. And it were cold, it were winter. They don't give a fuck . . . They batter people, I seen 'em do it . . . They're in uniform, they think they're terminators . . . There's a kiddie goes to special school, T-Bone he's called, he's backward, and they picked him up and this copper put his fingers right up this kid's arse . . . They say we're lowlife. They're foogin' lowlife.'

They started to vie with each other with stories of their first assaults on the law. One reckoned he had set fire to a doctor's surgery in Chapeltown when he was seven; another said he'd put bricks on a railway line to try and kill people when he was five. Someone had robbed an ice-cream factory in Burley with his brother when they were five and six years old, and they had spent the whole night eating their way through a great big box of chocolate flakes until some Asian lads had grassed on them and the police had come to pick them up.

There was an older lad, tall and thin with curly blond hair – he looked a little like the England cricketer Michael Atherton – who spoke for the first time and, although his manner was quiet and almost bashful, the others stayed silent while he said his piece. 'We're not animals. Our houses are pleasant and tidy. I've got a family, three kids and another on the way. I'm not skint, I can afford to raise them, because I have my ways of bringing in cash. Then I see families walking together and I look at them and I think they must have a job, and I would love to be just like them – go to work in the morning, have the weekend off, live a straight life. All I want to be is a family man. All I want is to support my family legally.

'I've had loads of jobs. When I first left school, I installed Skysat dishes. I was on two hundred and fifty a week. Then they found out I had a criminal record, so they kicked me out. I've done scaffolding, but I kept taking days off to go to court. It's like you can't get away from it. It's like I've got chewing gum stuck to me back, always keeps pulling me back. I don't want my son to do what I do. My dad has always said to me, "If you don't work, you've got to thieve." You've got to have some income, you've got to. Money talks. You know that yourself. Without money, where are you? You're living in a cardboard box, you're pissing up a wall. Breaking the law, it's a way of life.'

The lad with the hat switched on again. 'War against the law,' he announced. 'That's what it is.'

Michael Atherton said that people didn't understand that they hardly ever got caught – 99 per cent of them got away with 99 per cent of what they did. 'Look at the crime rate round here. Look at the number they catch. They think they're wired. I've done fifteen months for burglary. That's all I've ever done. If they do get us for something, it's only one thing. Most of what we do, they never get on to.'

A car pulled up alongside them. A thickset lad with red hair and a black T-shirt leaned out and said Hello to no one in particular.

The giant in jeans stepped over and peered into his car. 'How come you've got keys in your car?'

'It's my bloody car.'

'I never seen ya with keys before.'

'Couldn't find me screwdriver, could I?'

The lad with the furry face spoke up from the pavement. It was easy, he said. Burglary was really, really easy. You just mooched around, saw a house that looked empty, rang the door-bell and if anyone came to the door you asked some directions – how to get to Woodsley Road or something – but if no one came, you started kicking. Kick 'n' run. That's all it was. You got the door open, ran in, grabbed whatever you wanted, ran out again. And it was exciting, too. 'You get hypervibes,' he said. 'Specially if you're out your head, fucking great hypervibes.'

Michael Atherton didn't like all that. 'We don't just rob anyone. You don't just kick down any door. People think that because we're thieves, we're evil or something. I burgled a house two weeks ago and there were a woman, she started screaming. We'd put the stuff in the car in front of her house and she pulled up in her car just as we were leaving. She were screaming, coz she knew we'd taken her stuff. I felt gutted. We all felt gutted. When we drove away, everybody went quiet. I felt like saying, "Very sorry, lady, please don't cry." I felt really sick, I felt like dropping the stuff off at her house.

'You never rob a house that's got toys on the floor. There's things you don't do. Like there's a fella round here who's just robbed three girls, and he used a knife. It's in the paper. We know who's done that and we're not pleased with him, to tell you the truth. If somebody robbed an old lady, they'd get chinned. We'd do it. And that person who robbed those girls is going to get beaten upside and down. He has done something stupid and he's going to pay for it.'

The others nodded and agreed that they had rules, and some-body mentioned *Cecilia* and they all started vying with each other again, chipping in with details of the story of Cecilia, the heroin addict, who'd do anything for money, who'd suck ya cock for a bag of brown powder – 'she opens her legs like a pair of scissors' – because her boyfriend is inside and she's got all these kids to look after, she's only about twenty-five and she's got three or four kids, and she was grassing. She was grassing everybody she knew. And the law must think everyone is stupid or something, because they were driving her around in a cop car, and she had got stolen stuff in her house but she never got arrested, she was seen getting out of a police car at two in the morning, and people were accused of stealing the stuff that she had got in her house and there's nowt worse than a grass. So her house got smashed, inside and out. Foogin' smashed. And that was the end of Cecilia round here. She had to go and live in a hostel.

Even though it was not clear that they necessarily always obeyed these rules of theirs, it was clear that they thought they did. This was a war against the law and they were all bound by its rules. But how serious was this war? Did they have guns? If they were going to fight a war against the law, did they need guns? Michael Atherton nodded grimly. 'They see us as thieves, that's all. They are going to get fucking shot. If I need a gun, I know where to find it. Most of us do.'

Had they taken them out on the night of the riot? 'We didn't need to,' he said, and he smiled.

Then they talked about the great victory, the burning of the Jolly Brewer. The young lad with the furry face started, sadly recalling the joys of the old pub. 'We owned the Newlands. It were ours. It's our area, this. It were very dark there, it had all ripped seats and no decorations. It were like an old saloon and you could go in there and do what you wanted. You could smoke a joint. Everybody were on a good vibe. You could relax. There were a pool table and a jukebox. There was some bands some-times. Karaoke. It were ours.'

The lad with the hat switched on. 'We went in there and we weren't doing no one no harm. It were better than lying on the street.'

'And they banned us from the place,' the boy with the fur continued.

Then they all pitched in: 'Nobody wanted that place to get burned down. It only happened because of the law . . . The new landlord were a grass and he let the law put cameras in there. They were filming us . . . This is our area. They thought they were so clever, running around at night. We saw 'em the first night they went in . . . They brought this van with sliding doors.

We saw 'em. They shouldn't have involved other people . . . It had to happen.'

And together they described how they had reclaimed their pub by destroying it. They had planned it. It wasn't obvious who were the leaders but it was clear that they had sat down and planned the assault on the pub. It had started earlier in the evening when a couple of police cars had come onto their patch. They knew that there were houses the police had raided a few days earlier where they hadn't found the people in, so everyone knew they were looking to make more arrests. So they had stoned the police cars and beaten them out of the area. But they had known that it wouldn't be long before they were back with reinforcements, so they had moved in quick.

They had spread the word to get everyone there and then they had broken into all the cars that were parked around the pub and shifted them into the middle of the road as barricades, to keep out the police and the fire brigade. Once they had got the whole area sealed off, they had set fire to some of the cars and then they had broken into the empty pub. It was closed – the landlord was still in hospital from when he'd got beaten up – and they had grabbed anything they wanted, bottles of booze, bags of crisps. They had even dragged the fruit machines out into the street so that they could spill out the coins from inside them.

When they had taken all they wanted, a couple of them had climbed onto the lowest roof, at the side of the pub, broken a couple of windows and set fire to the curtains. From the road, they had lobbed in a couple of petrol bombs. It had gone up fast. Within minutes, they reckoned, there were flames all across the top floor. Then they had set fire to the rest of the cars in the road, and Hyde Park had belonged to them. One of them had phoned the *Yorkshire Evening Post* to tell them what was happening. Another had grabbed a video camera to record the happy occasion.

And Jean Ashford? 'She were grassing,' said the skinny lad, from the pavement. 'There's nowt worse than a grass. She were putting all this police harassment on us. She should keep her nobby little nose out. If she didn't like the area, she should have moved out.'

It was chaotic and it was violent and the rules that they wanted to keep were punctured with holes, but there was a kind of logic to it all. They had no money, no excitement, no status, no skills – except what twocking and burgling gave them. If they weren't breaking the law, they could only sit inundated with inactivity, almost physically paralysed by their own boredom. This war against the law gave them an income and it gave them a purpose. It gave them heroes and villains and something to excel at. And once they were committed to waging this war, there were certain necessities that flowed from it. They had to stop the enemy spying on them and so they had commandeered road blocks and organised an assault and successfully taken out the enemy's forward position. And then they had dealt with their traitors.

But not all of it was logical. They knew that themselves. There was a kind of chaos around them that had crept inside them, as if they had been force-fed on some sort of bitter bile which eventually started to seep through them, poisoning their everyday life. It was there when the skinny lad at the beginning talked about students. He wasn't just talking about students, he was talking about everybody – everybody who had everything that they didn't have, the people who had qualifications and jobs and cars and houses and families and futures. The students were just the nearest and most blatant example of the world that went on without them (like the mighty advertising hoarding that stood over the top of Hyde Park Road with a huge picture of a £10 note and a bank's offer of cheap loans, but only for students, not for the rest of them).

They all had their own dreams, most of them very mundane. They wanted to go to college, to get a job or simply to have something to do all day. In real life, as they readily described, there were only two things to do – thieving and twocking. They wanted much more. Their lives refused to let them have it, so they became frustrated and hopeless and bitterly angry. And they fought their war against the law with a furious rage.

The lad with the black T-shirt stirred up the engine of his car, twisted round behind him and popped open the back door. Several of the others, including the one with the furry face, climbed into the back. Where were they going? No real need to ask – off to work, off to the front line. The others started to drift away, back into Hyde Park Close.

The skinny lad was still spread out on the pavement, lifeless, but suddenly he leaned forward and started to speak with a passionate intensity, as if he were warning the world: 'Things are going to start getting rough round here. Students are going to start getting killed.' He stabbed his index finger into the air. 'Everybody has started to get so mad with these students. They'll get their houses smashed in. They'll get their schools smashed in.'

He was now hissing through his teeth. 'I'll smash foogin' students. I've done it before. The next one I see, I'll kick his foogin' teeth in. I'll pull his foogin' eyes out. I'll bite his foogin' ears off.'

He threw himself back against the wall, as if he were deflated by his own aggression. He shook his head and sighed very deeply. 'Look at me,' he said, after a moment, holding his palms out to each side. 'I'm sixteen and I feel like foogin' killing somebody.'

He covered his face with his right hand, dropped his chin onto his chest and mumbled, in a voice that was heavy with the sound of defeat, 'This area's fucked up.'

10

It was not the way that it had seemed. Here, still, was this ordinary patch of this apparently successful city. Here, still, was the sweeping green space on Woodhouse Moor, the row of little shops at the top of Hyde Park Road, the Victorian villas and the neat, new estate and the community centre. Every morning, the people delivering post and newspapers ambled through their familiar rituals as the commuters parked their highly polished cars along the kerbs and marched off into the city with the *Daily Mail* under their arms. Every night, the lights went out and Hyde Park slept in peace. And yet it wasn't like that.

The darkness had descended on this place. Walking around it now was like looking at a sheet of water which reflected its surroundings and, by doing so, disguised its own contents. Tucked away behind the signs of normal city life, there was a community suffering from some kind of collective nervous breakdown.

To an outsider, to the reporters kicking through the ashes of the burning pub, to the home secretary looking for a name to blame, it was easy to explain that all the horrors of Hyde Park were the work of these devil children. But it was clear now that they were not themselves the cause of whatever disaster had overtaken this place. They aggravated it, they provided some of its most painful and obvious symptoms, they inflicted real despair on their victims, and yet when you listened to them talk, when you listened to their lives – bored, listless and stoned, clinging for comfort to their Colombian neckties – it was as plain as the pain on their faces that they were not the origin of the problem. They were part of the result of whatever had happened, victims just as much as Jean Ashford and the others of whatever had happened to Hyde Park.

And what had happened?

The answer – like so much else in Hyde Park – turned out to be hidden, scattered across the whole neighbourhood behind the countless doors of endless houses: the people of Hyde Park held the clues to the disaster that had overcome them. Like fragments of shrapnel embedded in flesh, their stories were the vivid clues to some past explosion which had swept across their lives. Taken on its own, each story amounted to nothing more than an isolated individual incident – painful, crazy, touching incidents. But taken together, they began to form a pattern, all of them pointing to one common source.

It took weeks to uncover these stories, weeks of knocking on doors and trespassing into intimacy, of promising not to reveal names or mention addresses. Even then, some never told their stories. Some told stories only of those they knew, but never their own, and, for sure, there were other stories behind other doors that would have told as much. But, in the end, they told enough, enough to see quite clearly how the darkness had come to Hyde Park.

She was well into her sixties, very small, probably only four foot seven, and severely disabled. Her name was Sarah. When she wasn't in hospital, she lived alone and used the phone to stay in touch with the rest of the world, until she received a bill for £400, which she could not pay. British Telecom cut her off.

She had relied on her phone, not just to stay in touch with people but also to contact the doctor when she needed help in an emergency with her illness. Now she was frightened. She offered to pay off the debt by taking £2 a week from her pension. At that rate, it was going to take her more than three years. BT insisted that as long as she owed them any money at all, they would not give her back her phone. She tried to get a crisis loan from Social Security, but she had already borrowed a little money to replace her cooker and they wouldn't lend her any more. She had no choice but to cash in the death policy into which she had paid over the years to cover the expense of her funeral. It yielded only £150. She was still facing two years without a phone.

The Social Services heard of her problem and, together with the community centre on Cardigan Road, they agreed that they would pay her future phone rental and her future bills, but they weren't allowed to pay off her debt. It was against their rules. British Telecom said that as long as there was debt, she could have no phone, no matter who agreed to pick up the bill.

The next thing that Sarah knew was that she was being sued for the money. BT had sold her debt to a debt-collecting agency, who had added an extra £40 to cover their fee and hired a lawyer to take her to court. To rescue the old lady from sinking deeper, the community centre agreed to bend their rules and to pay off her debt. But when they applied to have her phone reconnected, BT told them they wanted a further £300 as a bond, because she had a history of debt with them. She was trapped.

Without her phone, she spoke to no one and she lost her medical lifeline. Her doctor said she was clinically depressed. She stopped going out, she saw no one. She started to talk about ending it all. But there was nothing that could be done for her. She had fallen over the edge.

There was a meeting of a girls' group at the Anglican church in Hyde Park. A ten-year-old black girl arrived late and in tears. She said she had been stopped in the street by some policemen who had pushed her up against a wall and called her a little nigger.

Her only good day was Monday. She had two children, aged two and five. She lived with them on income support of £94.15 a week. She was often tired, almost always depressed. But on Monday, she picked up her benefit and, for once, she could live a little – buy food, buy tokens for the electricity, buy soap and toothpaste, sometimes even buy a drink. By Tuesday, she was usually short of money again. By Wednesday, she was usually broke. And soon after that, she'd start to run out of food. She always bought plenty of potatoes, so by the end of the week, the kids were on chips for breakfast, chips for dinner. By Sunday, bloody Sunday, she'd often have nothing, not even potatoes. Starve on Sunday. But Monday was a good day. At least, it always had been.

On this particular Monday, she was feeling low. There was no special reason for it, she'd just had enough, so when she picked up her benefit, she bought enough food for the day, and then she went and bought herself a four-pack of lager and she started drinking. When she'd finished that lot, she went out and she got some more. That night, she hit the pub. On Tuesday morning, she was still drunk, she'd got no money to buy food for the rest of the week, she didn't know what to do, so she took what she had got down to the off-licence and spent it all on lager. On Wednesday morning, she was in trouble. The kids were yelling. There was no food to be had anywhere. There were no tokens for the light and the heat. She had no money, none at all.

She tried the Social, asked for a loan, told them she was starving, that her kids were starving, too, but they said she'd have to wait for Monday. She managed to beg some food for the kids off a friend of hers. Then she borrowed £5 off her and bought some more lager and while she was drinking that, she came up with a plan.

That night she went to a flat which belonged to a woman she knew. She took a box of matches with her, she found a newspaper, she screwed it up, shoved it in the letter box and lit it. The flaming paper fell into the flat. But it was all right. She might have been a bit drunk but she was sure it was all right. The woman who lived here hated the flat, she'd been asking to be rehoused for ages, but they wouldn't listen to her, so she reckoned she was doing her a favour by burning the poxy place. She'd made sure there was no one in the house, so no one would get hurt. And now she'd go straight off and call the fire brigade, and they'd come and put it out. The thing was that she had to do it. She had to do something. Something to tell people what was going on. She had to get somebody to help her.

She failed.

The fire brigade came and put out the fire. It had burned some carpet and scorched a wall – not enough to get her mate rehoused. The police came and they charged her with arson. When she got to court, she tried to explain why she had done this thing. Her lawyer tried to explain that no one was hurt and very little damage was done and it was all a cry for help. The court said that that was all very well, but the fire could have spread next door. They told her she would have to go to prison for thirty months – two and a half years. When they led her away, she knew very little of where she was going but she did know that if she ever got out, nothing at all would have changed. She'd still have only one good day in a week.

An old lady was burgled. She lost a lot of her most precious belongings and she had no insurance. She had lived in the same house in Hyde Park ever since she had arrived from Jamaica in the late 1950s and she had never been worried before. But now she was hearing of so many others who were suffering the same way, that she decided that she must get her belongings insured. She was told it would cost her £200.

She could not afford it. She had nothing but her pension to live off and almost no savings, but she had to have it. She was determined to be safe.

She made a decision. That week, she spent half her weekly pension of £58.85 on a stock of rice and peas and on the following Monday, instead of going to collect her pension, she simply stayed in her house. The next day, she did the same. And the day after. For days, merging into weeks, she sat there. She went nowhere that might cost her a penny. She did nothing that might run up a bill. Simply, she waited and, once a day, she went to her kitchen and boiled herself one bowl of rice and one cup of peas and put them together on a plate for a meal.

For four weeks, she lived like that, frozen in penury, all normal life suspended until finally, on the Monday morning of the fifth week, she pulled on her coat and went to the post office and collected her pension for all four weeks and gave it all, along with her savings, to the insurance company. Then she felt safe.

There was a stabbing in Stoggy's Bar on Kirkstall Lane. Two men had an argument, one of them pulled a knife and stabbed the other to death. The police had no trouble catching the man who had done the stabbing: the whole thing was caught on tape by the security cameras in the bar. So they closed the case and more or less forgot about it, until a few weeks later, when they discovered that copies of the tape were being sold around the city for home entertainment.

A stranger drove down Burley Lodge Road and parked his car

outside the Chapel of Rest. He wanted to go in there to say farewell to his mother, who had just died. But a group of lads saw his car and told him that if he left it there, they would set fire to it. Maybe they wanted him to pay them to protect it. But he was a stranger and he didn't understand, so he climbed back into his car and drove away, leaving his mother to lie there alone.

The Church of England vicar in Hyde Park took a new job in York, and his curate went with him. The church could not afford to replace them immediately and so, for fifteen months, the church and its hall stood empty. The hall had been used as a meeting place and as a youth club: there was a pool table and a vaulting horse and some tables and chairs.

During the months when the hall was empty, the young people who had been using it broke in and started to destroy the place. They smashed all the fixtures, ripped out the plumbing and the wiring and destroyed the pool table and the vaulting horse. By the time the new vicar arrived, the inside of the hall was a ruin.

One of the first things that the new vicar did was to organise a survey of opinion among young people, to ask them what they thought of the area. Overwhelmingly, they complained that there were not enough facilities for them.

This woman wanted to be an artist. She had a home and a husband and two small sons and, when she had time, she imagined she would paint and be happy. Several years ago, her husband lost his job. He was unable to find a new one and although she started working to bring in some money, her husband became frustrated and angry. He started to take out his moods on her and on the two boys and, eventually, she walked out, taking their two sons with her.

She moved to Hyde Park and, because she was caring for the two boys, she was able to find a house through the council. However, living alone, she had no one to look after her children while she went out to work and she could not afford to pay anyone, so she had been forced to give up her job. Having lost both her marriage and her work, she started to sink into a deep sadness. The deeper she sank, the less she did with her life and so she sank deeper. Soon, she lost the energy even to get up in the morning. She stopped going out, apart from a few essential trips to the shops. She refused to answer the door. She simply lay in her bed or sat in her front room, while life slipped away around her.

Her two sons, who were by now aged nine and ten, were able to get themselves out of bed in the morning and make their own way to school. Sometimes, by the time they came home in the afternoon, they would find her awake, sitting in her chair. Other times, they would come home and fend for themselves, make sandwiches for tea, turn on the television, wander the streets, while their mother lay quietly, with no reason to rise.

One Tuesday a year or so ago, some workmen from the City Council spent the morning in Burley Lodge Road, planting flowers in big concrete pots so that the area would look a bit brighter and more cheerful. By Wednesday morning, all the flowers had been pulled up and thrown away.

Just about everyone in Hyde Park knew Ruth. She was a long, tall, black woman with an air of sexual arrogance that stopped streets when she came walking by. She used to strut down Burley Lodge Road with her shirt slashed open to the navel, her backside wrapped in a bright, tight strip of leather, her long legs naked from thigh to ankle, all poised on heels like steeples. She looked as though she wanted to be some kind of plaything for men, but she was not as she appeared.

She had moved to Leeds from the Midlands with no money and no friends or family and she had survived on her wits. She was very sharp and whenever she wanted anything, she twisted men around her finger, wheedling and arguing until she got what she wanted. But that wasn't the point. The real point was that she was a man.

Sometimes, when Ruth was frustrated, he would drop his female mask and instead of using his wits, he would use extreme threats and physical violence to get his way. Soon after he arrived in Hyde Park, he strode into the housing office near the Methodist Church and saw on the noticeboard that an old man was offering to exchange his council house for another in a different area. At the time, Ruth was living in a small and unpleasant flat just off the northern edge of Hyde Park, in an area called Little London, and he decided that he liked the sound of the old man's house. Unfortunately for the old man, he had written his address on the card on the noticeboard. Ruth marched round to see him, hammered on the door and informed the old man that the two of them were swapping homes and explained that if he did not get out immediately, he would pull his head off. The old man went.

But, most of the time, Ruth wore his femininity with extravagant pride, waiting only for the day when he could change his sex forever, surgically. He was serious about this, and he had talked to the doctors about having an operation. They had sent him a gender counsellor who had done his best to understand Ruth, although Ruth had greeted him in the street on his first visit by yelling abuse at him because he was a stranger.

Ruth told everyone that the doctors had agreed to go ahead with the operation. He claimed they had given him a date and it was all set. It was the biggest thing in his life. Then something went wrong. No one knew the entire truth. All they knew was that suddenly he exploded. Apparently, for some reason, the doctors had changed their minds. Ruth had argued with them in his usual way, informing the professor that if he didn't perform the operation, he would disembowel him and eat his intestines, but it had made no difference. Ruth was trapped as a man.

Rapidly, he retaliated, abandoning all pretence at femininity and disappearing deep into his masculine self. So it was that one day soon afterwards, Ruth swaggered down Burley Lodge Road with his head shaved to the scalp apart from a clump of hair at the back which he had twisted into a pigtail. He was wearing a tattered denim jacket, biker's jeans which were soiled with filth, metal bands clamped around his biceps, and he had a gold ring through one nostril. From now on, Ruth was a man. From now on, he became seriously violent.

Faced with any kind of human obstacle, he would grab anything that came to hand as a weapon – knife, hammer, screwdriver, lump of wood – and throw himself at the opposition with an uninhibited lust to inflict damage. He was always in fights. Usually, he won – he was fit and strong and his violence was so sudden and so complete that its victims had no chance to defend themselves. Soon he was at war with almost everyone around him. Children chucked stones at him and ran for cover. Occasionally, the victims of his violence would try to take revenge and come after him mob-handed with their friends or family to ambush him in the street, but he always fought back with his fists and his feet and his endless supply of aggression.

He walked into the community centre on Burley Lodge Road, started a row with the chairman of the management committee and dragged him downstairs with a knife in his hand. A few weeks later, he was in someone's office in Hyde Park, arguing about something, when he noticed a skinhead walking by in the street, decided he was a racist, grabbed the nearest weapon he could find, which happened to be a length of four-by-two wood, jumped through an open window and launched himself at him, battering him around the head and shoulders with his makeshift club.

It was soon after that that he took a Stanley blade to a man in the street. The man was just walking to his pick-up truck when Ruth intercepted him and started abusing him about his manhood, suggesting that he had bigger genitals than the man did, telling him he must be jealous. When the man turned to walk away, Ruth snatched a Stanley blade out of the back pocket of his trousers and ripped his back and then, as the man spun round towards him, he slashed the blade across his face.

For those who watched Ruth's raging journey, the strangest point was not so much his madness as the almost complete failure of anyone to do anything about him. He was obviously ill, but no one came to help him. He was obviously very dangerous, but no one came to stop him. It appeared that the different authorities had neither the resources nor the motive to get involved. In truth, they had tried. At one point, a dozen workers from different agencies had met to discuss him and had concluded finally that the best that they could do was to ask a social worker to go round and make a psychological assessment. The social worker did try, but he didn't get very far. The community centre persuaded its chairman to go to the police to complain about Ruth dragging him down the stairs, but Ruth was released with a caution. He failed to pay any rent on the old man's house. Housing officials told him he had to pay; he told them he would pull out their intestines. Eventually, they evicted him, using a flat-bed truck to carry away his possessions. Ruth perched on top of his pile of belongings like a raja on an elephant as the truck prowled down the road. Then he spotted a flat he liked and forced his way in there, threatening the residents with cannibal bloodshed if they resisted. Still no one helped him.

Eventually, he was charged with assault for his attack with a Stanley blade on the man in the street. While he was waiting for the case to come to court, he lived in the new flat which he had commandeered and continued to try to play his supermanly role. On the stairs of the block of flats one day, he saw a nineteen-year-old girl who was trying to visit some friends. Ruth grabbed her and started dragging her into his flat. A neighbour heard screams and came out. Ruth banged the young woman's head hard against the wall and swore at her, telling her never to cross him again.

'This is a domestic dispute,' he shouted at the neighbour. 'Get back in your flat.'

The young woman took advantage of the lull to scramble down the stairs. A few weeks later, Ruth went to court and was jailed for two years for the Stanley-blade assault. Hyde Park was left to wonder how much more quickly he would have been dealt with if he had lived in a wealthier part of the city, where the limbs of the state had not withered away, and to count the days until he came back to them.

She couldn't get out of her chair. She was old and disabled and she suffered from some kind of dementia, so she sat in her chair in her front room, occasionally wetting herself. The council said they'd send help, so she arranged for the front door to be left open for them, and while she was waiting, someone came in and stole the rest of her house – not just her belongings, but her furniture, too, and the pictures off the wall; they even stole the carpet. All that remained was her front room with the bitter, damp chair.

Two policemen in a tow truck arrived in a side street on a hill in the western part of Hyde Park to retrieve a stolen car which had been dumped there. While they were out of the truck, inspecting the stolen car, some children crept up and released the handbrake in an attempt to send the tow truck rolling down the hill. The two policemen had to leave the area and then return with half a dozen officers to cover their backs while they did this simple job.

John was a skilled man, a carpenter and cabinet-maker, and he had the tools to prove it – hammers of different weights, chisels of different breadths, screwdrivers of different sizes, wood saws, jigsaws, fret saws, hacksaws, keyhole saws. But he was unemployed.

By the time he was thirty-four, he had been made redundant five times. The problem was that employers were interested in taking on a skilled man like him only on a short-term contract. That way, they could pay him a probationary wage which was far below the going rate; they need give him nothing towards his pension; they could show him the door if he made any kind of complaint; and at the end of the contract, they could make him redundant and take the next man from the queue.

When he was a single man, this didn't worry him too much. He simply took his box of tools and went out and found himself bits and bobs of work from friends and neighbours. But now he had a wife and two small children to support (and his friends and neighbours had very little money nowadays) so he signed on for state benefit.

He and his family found it hard to get by on the money they were given, but when he tried to do a little carpentry work on the side to make ends meet, as he always had done before, he was warned very sternly that if he was caught doing that, he would lose benefit. There was still no work for him. He went on a couple of training courses and improved his skill, but at the end of them, he was still trapped. No work, not enough money, no chance of doing anything about it. So slowly, over a period of time, to cover the costs of keeping his family, he sold each and every one of his tools.

Mr Lovett was a man with power. He was a small man with a shiny suit, a bald head and a neat moustache and he was employed by Leeds City Council as the housing manager for the Burley area, which included Hyde Park.

Mr Lovett had the power to grant wishes. He could take a

young couple who were stranded in the back room of their parents' house, desperate to move into their own home so that they could start a family, and he could spirit them out of the endless waiting list and move them into a house with their own front door. He could send in the workmen so that the lone mother with young children need no longer put them to bed in damp rooms, so that roofs need no longer leak, doors need no longer hang off their hinges, windows need no longer let in the winter cold. He could provide heating or a new bathroom or a new kitchen. He could authorise transfers for old people trapped in homes with staircases so steep that they could reach their beds only by crawling slowly upstairs on their hands and knees, or for families whose children were sleeping two to a bed for want of space. But Mr Lovett wanted something in return.

He wanted something for himself, something personal that would satisfy him, something that the women of Hyde Park could give him, particularly the young, single women. And he insisted that they did. They didn't want to give it to him. They had husbands or boyfriends, they had lives of their own, they weren't interested in this man, but some of them found that they had no choice, because they had nothing, and Mr Lovett had power.

Eventually, some of the social workers caught on to what was happening. There was a house where they suspected that the children were being abused by paedophiles and so they were keeping an eye out for any adult male who visited. They heard about Mr Lovett, who was certainly no paedophile but could not explain why his job required him to visit the woman of the house so often. They noticed several other young mothers who had been the targets of Mr Lovett's attention, who had suddenly found themselves well housed. Then, as luck would have it, he was transferred to another area of Leeds, Holbeck. The fuss died down.

Holbeck is a working-class area where families are desperate for homes. There, Mr Lovett exercised the same powers as he had in Hyde Park and with the same private conditions. Eventually, in 1996, he asked the wrong woman. She went to the council and complained; he denied it; the council looked at the evidence. In November 1996, they sacked Mr Lovett. He appealed. His sacking was upheld. He left.

There are women in Hyde Park who will never forget him.

Marina knew she recognised the boy. She might be old and she might be infirm, but she still had her wits about her and she was sure she knew that face.

She knew most people round here. She had lived here all her life, since the days when they used to have one outside lavatory to share between houses (they used to keep candles burning in there in winter to stop the pipes freezing) and it didn't take her more than a moment to realise that this was the boy who had mugged her.

It had happened a few weeks earlier. She had been walking to her flat about ten o'clock one Saturday night and she had noticed this young white lad hanging around outside the Chinese take-away. He had crossed the road towards her and there had been something about the way he walked that had made her hurry up along the path to the communal door. But before she had had a chance to get inside, he had been on her, grabbing her handbag out of her hand and skidding away through the car park at the back of her building. Well, she had known straight away that he would have to come past the front of the building to get away, so she had walked back that way and, sure enough, a couple of seconds later, he had come walking by with his jacket turned inside out and with no sign of her handbag.

'Where's my bag?' she had demanded. 'What've you done with it?'

He had denied all knowledge and walked on. As it was, he had missed her purse which had been tucked away in her pocket, and when a student found her handbag under a car in the car park, it turned out the young lad had rifled through it and found nothing to steal. The police had shown her some mugshots, but she hadn't found him anywhere in their book of pictures.

Now, here he was a few weeks later, sitting outside the Skyrack pub on Headingley Road with a drink in his hand. What was she going to do? She knew very quickly.

Marina believed in ordinary people. She never held with Con-servatives and she always said that if the Labour Party had looked after those at the bottom as well as the Conservatives looked after their friends at the top, they would never have lost power. She could not understand why she was paying £249.12 a year in water rates while some millionaire businessman in the *Daily Mail* was complaining because he was paying £175. It had made no sense to her when she'd gone to the chemist's on Cardigan Road a few years ago and she'd seen a man walk out of a Porsche and claim free medicine for his child, and yet there she was working all day and Saturday mornings, too, in a baker's shop, taking home just under £100 for her work, and when she wanted a prescription, she had to pay for it.

So she thought it was all wrong, a terrible sadness, that working people would steal from each other. She had a friend, a woman who was even older than her, who had been more or less ambushed coming out of the post office with her pension money at half past nine in the morning. Two lads had thumped her and taken her money. She had another friend who'd been walking by a school just as the children were coming out and she'd been distracted by all the noise and commotion and the next thing she knew, someone had come up behind her and pulled her bag off her shoulder. But Marina was determined not to be afraid of her own people. Every day, she went out of her flat on her own, to the public library, to read the daily paper because she couldn't afford one of her own, and most days, she went shopping or to visit her daughter and she suffered no ill.

Now, she wanted this young lad to know that she knew who he was and that she wasn't one bit frightened of him. As long as he knew that, he wouldn't try hanging around her flat to have another go. She knew he was just a lad who had wanted his beer money on a Saturday night and he'd seen her and thought she was a little old bod who'd give him no trouble. In a way she felt sorry for him. He would have seen other people who had money, going off to discos and wearing fancy clothes, but there was no point telling him to go off and get a job and earn his own money. There were no jobs. She'd seen others like him – there was a group of them, even younger, begging money at a bus stop just a few days earlier – and she knew he was more sad than bad.

So, one way or another, when she saw her mugger sitting there outside the pub, Marina decided very quickly what to do about it. She caught his eye and she nodded at him.

'Hello,' she said, quite polite and friendly.

He looked up and she could see he knew her face.

'Hullo, love,' he said. And he seemed to mean it.

There was an old man who had suffered all his life from an addiction to alcohol and who eventually ended up losing his home and living in a hostel for single men. After a while, the Social Services Department found him a little flat in Benson Court, the sheltered housing at the end of Hyde Park Close, and they moved him in there and left him to get on with his life.

Four months later they discovered how he was living. He had nothing in his room. He had no stove or oven or any means of cooking anything, not even a saucepan. He had no fridge nor anywhere else to store his food. He had no bed, not even a mattress on the floor. He had no bedclothes, not one blanket. He had nothing. He didn't even have curtains to hide behind, so the young kids from Hyde Park Close could peer in his window and watch the way he lived, like a creature in a cage.

For four months, the old man lived like this, signing on every couple of weeks, buying food which slowly went rotten in the corner, seeing no one, going nowhere, too full of remorse to dare to complain. He thought it was better than being on the streets.

When a social worker finally visited him and found him alone with the smell of rancid meat and rotten milk in the air, he tried to persuade his own department to find the funds to supply this man with furniture and some means of storing and cooking his food. But there were no funds. The social worker knew something had to be done and so he tried to organise a crisis loan from the Social Security, but they wouldn't give him one. It appeared that they had already spent their allotted funds for the year. In the end, the social worker took money out of his own pocket to buy a cooker for the old man. There was nothing else for him.

A family who ran one of the shops near the bottom of Hyde Park Road one day decided to clear out their garage, which was one of a row behind their house. They were glad that no one had broken into it, but as they set about their work, they were sad to discover that in the shadows behind the garage, the ground crackled beneath their feet as they stepped across a carpet of used syringes.

Standing against the bar in the Royal Park pub, to the west of Hyde Park Road, he drinks his Skol straight out of the bottle and watches the fruit machine and he describes a loser's life.

He had a bad upbringing, he says. There were six kids, three boys and three girls, and when they were all pretty young, his mum left. They ran a bit wild, they all got into trouble with the law – boys and girls alike. Most of them ended up in care and all of them ended up in jail. He was fourteen when he was first locked up by the law, he was eighteen when the full care order on him finally lapsed and, by that time, he had left school with nothing, not even an ambition.

He is only a few feet away from the fruit machine but, even though he watches it and checks out every punter pushing its buttons, he never makes a move to play it himself.

He says he had work, a few years ago. He was a presser in a clothes factory, he had to iron the insides of jackets. He was on piece rates, paid by the number of jackets he pressed, and the money was bad. Then the whole place closed down. He got another job, working in a peanut factory, picking out the bad nuts as they went by on a conveyor belt, but he lost that job and now he hasn't worked for years.

He has a girlfriend and they have two little kids and they do live together, although they tell Social Security that they don't because that way, he gets about £70 a fortnight and she gets about £90 a fortnight. If they told the truth, they'd only get about £120 a fortnight, so they'd be that much worse off. He tips Skol down his throat, his eyes flicking across to the fruit machine. He would work, he says. He wants to work but all he's been offered is Restart courses. He's been on four of five of them, learning how to write a job application and what to say at an interview, but he's never had to write a job application or go to an interview and the only reason he goes on the courses is that the Social tell him he's got to, or else he'll lose his benefit. But he's never learned a real skill.

He's not proud of his life, he says. He's twenty-five now, and still in trouble with the law. They've done three search warrants on his place in the last couple of weeks, they turned the whole place over, they were going all through the kids' clothes, looking for stolen credit cards, and they found nothing except an ornamental sword which they reckoned had been used in a big brawl in a pub where a fella got killed. He told them they must be kidding.

He used to do a lot of burglaries, but he doesn't do them so much now, though it's true he'll help people get rid of stuff they've got. He used to drive without tax and insurance, but he's legal now. If his eyes were drills, he would have bored a hole straight through the back of the student who's now standing in front of the fruit machine, blocking his view.

He says he's worried for his kids. There's nothing to do round here – all he ever does himself is sit at home or come down here, to the Royal Park. He can see his kids growing up just the same. If he had his time again, he'd do it all different, he'd do his exams, he'd get a decent job, get out of this place, but it's too late now. This is it. This is what he's got. This is what his kids have got to look forward to.

Suddenly, he moves – Skol on the bar, darting forward, elbowing through the people – and he starts to play on the fruit machine. His hands move as quick as a concert pianist's, flying over the buttons, holding and nudging and spinning, and he is intent, totally absorbed, suddenly alive with the prospect of winning – and he does. The machine clicks three times, coughs and starts to churn out tokens, dozens and dozens of them spewing out of its belly into the metal bowl beneath. He's not surprised in the slightest. He knew it was getting ready to pay out. He was watching for his moment, he knew he could win. At least in here, he can win.

May has three children. She doesn't know why she has three children. It was just the only thing there was to do when she was younger – get pregnant. She doesn't have that much to do with them. She drinks. Every day, she drinks.

All May's children are girls. The oldest is eighteen now and when she was about thirteen, she refused to go to school, she said there was no point, and no one could make her change her mind. Now she, too, has three children, all of them aged under four. She doesn't know why. She doesn't have a partner – he's in prison. She doesn't have a home – she was evicted from a council house because she wouldn't pay the rent – so she lives with May and, most days, she goes out and leaves the children behind.

May's second daughter is fifteen. She stopped going to school a couple of years ago, and she spends her days in front of the telly. She's expecting a baby but she doesn't know why. The baby's father doesn't want to know.

May's youngest daughter is twelve. She hasn't been to school for a year, she says there's no point. She spends a lot of her time wandering the streets around Hyde Park with her baby niece in her arms. She says she wants a family of her own.

When Pat was in the army, in 1945, she used to say, 'The wogs will take over. You see if they don't.' And they did. She has lived on Burley Lodge Road for thirty-seven years and it used to be all right, but now there's too many bloody Pakis. She goes to the doctor and there's more of them there than there are white people. Pakis should have their own doctor. They've taken over the whole area. There's nothing for white people. And they don't speak the language.

Pat remembers when there was a riot round here, must be nearly thirty years ago. 'The Burley riots.' That was bloody Pakis started that. There was this fella, Kenny, who came out of a café there used to be down the bottom of the hill, and the Pakis stabbed him, stabbed him to death. Pat remembers there were thousands of white people came from all over, chanting about the Pakis and marching through the area. She didn't watch telly for a fortnight, she just stood on the doorstep and watched the trouble. Kenny's father went out and told them all to go home, but they didn't listen to him, they went and burned out a Paki off-licence, they did a load of their shops. She heard that the Pakis had had a go at Kenny because some white fella had stabbed one of theirs, but she didn't know much about that. They taught them a lesson in the Burley riots. But there's still too many of them.

In the old days, she used to belong to a ladies' social club, the Burley Blue Belles they were called. She still has her badge. There was Pauline and Jessie and Madge and Margaret and they all used to get together every Thursday and listen to the gramophone and have a chat, but then they said they couldn't do it any more if it was just for white people. They couldn't use the room in the community centre, unless they let the others join in. So they stopped it.

Now, as far as Pat can see, the whole world's gone mad. It's like this beer allowance they give to the alcoholics. Had you not heard? They give them £29 a week just to buy beer, because they're alcoholics. They get that on top of their ordinary benefit. That's what Pat's heard anyway. It's madness, if you ask her.

Everything belongs to the Pakis now. All the shops belong to them. That Newlands pub that got burned down, that was a Paki pub. She tries to be friendly to them but she wants to know where they were when she was fighting for her country. They were out in the jungle, weren't they? Cannibals. That's what people used to call them. She tries to be friendly. She's got a good friend called Jim and he's a Jamaican. Pat doesn't like Jamaicans. But Jim's all right. Pat likes him. Jim can't stand Pakis either.

Carla gets tired. She is a big woman with purple stains around her eyes and hair that lies exhausted on her shoulders. But she has a way of getting by. She goes round the corner to her mate *Angie*'s house and gets something to keep her going.

'Speed's like a cup of tea round here,' she says.

There was a woman in Hyde Park who got into trouble with loan sharks. Everyone said she was a bad lot. Week after week, she would spend all her income support down in the bookie's on Woodsley Road and, week after week, she would go off to borrow more. In the end, she owed these loan companies a fortune, more than a thousand pounds, and their men were on her doorstep, threatening her and making all kinds of demands. Everyone said she was a bad lot until they found out why she'd gone down to the bookie's in the first place. It turned out that she had five kids and she thought that the best way to show them that she loved them was to buy them toys, the best toys she could find. Often, she won at the bookie's and at Christmas, she had bought all the children mountain bikes; she had been trying to get them a computer when the loans got on top of her.

The loan sharks sorted it out. The men on her doorstep went into her house and took away all the mountain bikes and all the special toys she had bought and her telly, too. Then they were even.

Chantaille had three babies. All of them had different fathers. None of the fathers wanted to know.

Each time she got pregnant, Chantaille got worried. She had no job and she couldn't afford to buy all the stuff – buggy, cot, clothes. She had nowhere to live. She put her name down with the council and the housing association, but they both had long waiting lists and, in the end, the best that they ever offered her was something out in Moortown, right up on the edge of town, with the ring road roaring by and with no one she knew in sight.

She knew she was better off than the Asian girls who got pregnant without being married. Some of their families were so strict that they had to have abortions, and they had to do it all on their own without anyone knowing or they'd be shamed, maybe even beaten. At least Chantaille had the choice.

But in the end, it was always the same. Chantaille put each of her babies up for adoption, one after another, more or less as soon as they were born. She hoped they'd go to someone who was better off than her.

Simone was only nine the first time she tried it. All the girls in the Girls' Gang did it – Beverley and Jane and Sheralee and the others. So she did it, too.

She went round a shop that all the girls used and she bought a can of lighter fuel. Then she went off round the back, crouched down, took off the lid, laid the end of the nozzle between her front teeth, bit hard and pushed. The gas sprayed into her mouth and down her throat and up the back of her nostrils. It smelled like puke, it made her want to puke, it chilled her skin and made her want to fall over, and then it poured into her brain, and she didn't know whether she was awake or asleep, alive or in a dream, like being caught in a shower of dreams. Then it wore off and she did it again.

That was what the Girls' Gang did. They bought lighter fuel from this shopkeeper and they got out of their heads sniffing gas. Sometimes they bought glue instead and got out of their heads on that. That was their life, although, in truth, the deal wasn't quite that simple. The shopkeeper wanted something out of it, too. That was why he sold them the lighter fuel in the first place. He'd give them other things, too. He'd take them to the pictures, or buy them food if they hadn't eaten. He'd give them sweets and cigarettes to do what he wanted. Sometimes, he'd give them cash. He was a rich man, he always had handfuls of banknotes in his pocket. There was one girl he gave £150 in cash. She was only thirteen and she really didn't want to go with him, but when she saw that much money, she changed her mind and she gave him what he wanted.

But Simone never went with the shopkeeper. She hated him. He was always on at her to let him kiss her, let him touch her, let him take her for a ride in the stinking car that he used to take all the girls for a ride in. He offered her money if she'd let him do it to her. She always said no. Simone had other things to do.

She lived with her mum and dad and her six brothers and sisters in a small house on Hyde Park Road, but she wasn't interested in a little girl's life. She had three elder brothers and she spent all her time following them around, trying to catch their attention, and when they started hanging around on street corners with other lads, Simone did too. And before anyone could stop her, she was drifting into trouble. When she left home in the morning to go up to school on Bedford Fields, she hardly ever made it as far as the school. She couldn't be bothered. She had a better time with her mates in the Girls' Gang. They did a lot of thieving, mostly shoplifting. The first time Simone got arrested and cautioned, it was for nicking a chocolate bar out of a sweet shop. But they did pensioners, too. They were easy, especially if you were only nine years old like Simone when she started. You knocked on their doors and smiled nicely and got friendly with them and then, once you were inside their houses, you just stole things off them. Cash was best, but anything was all right. The Girls' Gang didn't do burgling and twocking, like the boys did. But, if they had no money, there were always men who'd buy something off them.

There was one old man who lived near the Newlands, who used to pay Simone just to stand near him while he looked at a porn magazine and played with himself. She didn't want to do it, but she had no money and she couldn't get any, and it wasn't so bad just standing there watching him. She was eight when that started. He died in the end of a heart attack while he was fooling around in front of one of the girls. At about the same time, her friend Esther told her about this fellow down on Burley Road who liked taking pictures of little girls in their underthings. He had all this photographic equipment down there. Simone started going there and posing. Some of her friends started doing the same. There were six or seven of them going round there to earn their money by the time the police heard about it. One of the coppers told her dad, and he was a big, strong man and he went round and broke the place up.

When she was eleven, Simone was taken into care. They had heard about the photographs and they said she was out of control and, from that time, she was in and out of care for six years. Some of the other Girls' Gang were in care, too. While Simone was in the children's home, she started doing a lot more robbing and other bits of law-breaking – criminal damage, assault, robbery, grievous bodily harm, assault with intent to rob. She was always in and out of court. She wasn't worried. She looked such an innocent with her big brown eyes and her long, fine, black hair, like a Spanish dancer, that the magistrates kept letting her off lightly. There was one time when she got done for fraud. She'd been punting out stolen cheques and she'd got away with all of them except the last one, when she'd been caught doing it on a security camera so she couldn't really deny it. All the same, she did deny it, but they found her guilty and hit her with a big fine. But she was in care, she couldn't pay it, her parents couldn't pay it, so Social Services paid it for her.

When Simone was about eleven, around 1991, she hooked up with Sheralee. She was three years younger than Sheralee but they got along all the same, like sisters. Sheralee was a bit of a tomboy, always joking and fooling around, a big Bros fan, but the main thing that the two of them had in common was sniffing gas. The other girls did it too, but it was Simone and Sheralee who did it the most. They'd go to the shop and buy two or three tubes of lighter fuel at a time. The shopkeeper knew what they wanted it for – they hardly ever bought any cigarettes and, if they did, they bought matches to light them. They weren't going to waste good gas on lighting cigarettes. Sometimes, if he was feeling generous, or if he fancied his chances with them, he'd help them out by taking the lids off for them, in case their child-hands were too small to do the job. Then Sheralee died.

Simone wasn't with her when it happened. They'd been sniffing stuff together all day, as usual, and Sheralee had ended up going back to her mum's house on her own late at night, with a couple of tubes of gas. No one was quite sure what happened, but they thought she'd been in her bedroom and done too much of it. It could freeze your lungs, Simone had heard. Sheralee had tried to get out of her room, she'd made it downstairs and into the living room, and then she'd collapsed. Her mum had found her, but by the time the ambulance had arrived, she was dead and gone. She was sixteen years old.

Everyone was very shocked by Sheralee's death. Her mum had idolised her and she had never wanted to believe that Sheralee was doing anything so bad. It drove her right into herself when she died like that. Some of the Girls' Gang were so frightened that they stopped sniffing gas, but Simone didn't stop. She carried on just the same, filling her head with gas and glue, robbing people, battering people, in and out of care, in and out of court.

The shopkeeper didn't stop either. By the time that Simone finally left care for good, when she was seventeen, he was plugged into half a dozen of her friends. They were all pretty girls and they were all short of cash and they were all messed up on drugs and gas. One of them was fifteen; she was in care, though she already had a baby of her own, and she was having to go round and sell herself at the shop to get cash. There was another, called Lindsey, who was living with foster parents. She was fourteen or fifteen and she was doing the same thing, until her foster mother found out and told everyone. Then some men went round and battered the shopkeeper and his shop. He was a bit more careful after that.

There were two particular girls from Armley who had started selling themselves for the shopkeeper's cash a few years earlier, Chantaille and Maxine. They were nineteen now, both of them, and they were still making the same deal with him so they could get cash for food and drugs and things. One day, Maxine was in Hyde Park, looking for some guy who was going to sell her some drugs, and she came across one of Simone's little sisters, Jade, who was out riding a brand-new mountain bike that her mum had bought her. Maxine asked her if she could borrow the bike. Jade agreed. Maxine went off and didn't come back.

Jade was really upset. That bike had been her greatest pride and it wasn't insured – you couldn't get bikes insured around Hyde Park. When Simone heard what had happened, she knew who Maxine was and she went straight round to the shopkeeper's and told him she wanted her address. The shopkeeper tried to make out that he didn't know who Maxine was.

'Course you do,' Simone shouted. 'You're fuckin' shagging her.'

She threatened to tell his wife what he got up to. She threatened to call the police and tell them, too. She got the address.

That evening, one of Simone's brothers went round there with a mate, but they got jumped by a bunch of the Armley lads, who gave them a beating. The two of them went back again and they waited until they saw one of the ones who'd given them the beating on his own. They weren't sure if he'd got the bike, but they got hold of him and battered him just the same. They never did get the bike back. They guessed Maxine had sold it for drugs. Jade just had to get by without it.

Simone shuffled from one place to another. For a while, she had a council flat of her own, but everyone else used it as a dumping ground: lads used to turn up and sleep there or leave stolen stuff there or stash gear. A couple of times, she got her dad to come round and clear everyone out. But in the end, they totally trashed the place, and Simone just walked away. She moved to Bradford, but that didn't work out. She got a place in Chapeltown, but these black lads accused her of stealing a bike that went missing from the front hall, and they beat her up, so she left. She spent a bit of time in a hostel called Hollies, then she moved in with a girl called Sarah in Harold Road, in Hyde Park. But this Asian guy wanted Sarah to do a robbery with him and Sarah didn't want to do it, so the Asian guy smashed their window and stole their stuff, and Simone moved on. She moved in with a lad called Dave, who had a flat on Cardigan Road, but there was a fight round there and some of the windows got broken, so they all got evicted. She ended up in another hostel, St Michael's, but she didn't like it there, it was too strict. So she moved on, to another hostel, while she waited for another place to come up.

As often as she could, she was still sniffing gas. When she talked to you, you could smell it on her breath, a sweet, sticky, sick smell. And that was her life. All the other girls she knew were the same. She was nineteen now and there were younger girls following her, the way she used to follow Sheralee. There was Heidi, who'd been raped by a friend of her mum's, who'd just given up sniffing gas because she was pregnant by some Asian guy. He was married and he didn't want anything to do with the baby, but Heidi said she wanted it all the same, she was going to love it and be good to it and not do any more gas. She was fifteen. There was Donna, who was being blackmailed by her own boyfriend. He had beaten her and she threatened to go to the police, but he said that if she did, he'd tell the cops and the social workers that she smoked draw and sniffed gas, so then they'd take her kid off her. So she didn't go to the police. She didn't even go out, because he ordered her not to. She wasn't even allowed to talk to anyone on the phone, or he said he'd bray her and get her kid taken off her. She was sixteen. And there was Sandra, a thin little white girl who used to sniff gas. She ended up selling herself on the pavement up in Spencer Place, in Chapeltown, and then some guy took her off to Bradford and locked her in a room. He used to go in and beat her and sell her to punters, and he wouldn't feed her. In the end, she died. That was the first Simone knew about what had happened to her. Simone and Heidi went to her funeral. She was only fifteen. That was her life.

Soon afterwards, Heidi had her baby. It turned out it had nothing to do with the Asian guy. The baby was black; Heidi thought she knew who the father was, but he didn't want to know. Heidi did her best with the baby, but after a few months she gave it up to be adopted.

Simone stumbled onwards, on her own sweet way. Recently, she was down in the middle of town and she heard this girl had been talking about her, so she battered her, used her fists and her boots on her, made a right mess of her. She was taken to court and they gave her community service, 180 hours, and £160 fine. They said she could pay it at £6 a fortnight. She paid the first week, then she couldn't be bothered with it. She didn't do the community service either. So they stuck her inside for two months. She was scared at first but once she got to the prison, New Hall in Wakefield, she found several of her mates were in there, so it was OK. She says she doesn't care. That's life, in the Girls' Gang.

She goes out once a week, to pick up her pension and do her shopping and to go to the library. That's all. She's got an old mongrel dog called Tom, but she won't take him for walks, not any more, not on your life. She wouldn't dare. She has a friend who got mugged a year or two back, outside the Newlands pub. He was eighty-six and had a pacemaker. They knocked him down on a Saturday afternoon and kicked him in the face and took his money. So now he doesn't go out either. The house next door to her got kicked in. It's happened all up and down Burley Lodge Road, she says. She stays in now, she takes Tommy and ties him up outside the front door and she watches television. That's what she does. She watches the soaps and the quiz shows and she keeps the door locked. And apart from the one day when she goes to the library, that's all she does.

There were not many who were literally starving. People often talked about running out of food in the last few days before their giro came from Social Security, but most of them managed to make do by borrowing off friends or family. But there were a few who had no one to turn to, who would reach a point where simply they had no food and they were condemned to be hungry until the next giro appeared. They were the ones who really suffered, and they were the ones who tended to turn up on the doorstep of the Methodist church at the back of Hyde Park Close.

Some of them knocked on the caretaker's door. There was one young woman, probably in her mid-twenties, who lived in a house in Autumn Avenue which, in the eyes of anyone passing by, appeared to be derelict. It was dirty and overgrown, some of the windows were cracked and broken, guttering hung down like broken branches in a tree, there were gaps in the roof through which the darkness of the attic leaked out, there was never any light in the windows. But this young woman lived there with her brother and, from time to time, when they had nothing, she would turn up at the door by the side of the church, with a weak smile and a simple request.

'Will you give me money?' she would say.

'We can't,' the caretaker used to say, honestly enough.

'Will you give me food?' she'd say.

And the look on her face meant no one could doubt that she needed it, so the caretaker would give her something to go away with. The young woman didn't come every week, but there were others. Five or six times a week, someone would knock on that door – a young boy on drugs looking for 50 pence, an adult needing £5 for an electricity token, an old man so hungry he could barely move until the caretaker gave him baked beans and lemonade.

Others found their way to the home of the Methodist minister, Gary Hall, a young and thoughtful man who worked part time as the chaplain to the prisoners in Armley Jail. Several times a week, he would answer the door of his terraced house in Hyde Park and find one of his parishioners standing there, begging for food.

He knew these people. He knew they were living to the last penny. He knew there were others who managed better to survive on what they had, but he knew equally well that there were a lot of families in his parish who really were very hard up, who were struggling to find some of the basic necessities of life. He knew because he saw them in their homes – short of food because they had run out of money, living without fuel because they had run out of tokens, the children small and wiry and skinny because habitually they ate too little. He knew because in wintertime, when their electricity tokens ran out and the cold got to them, he was called upon to bury them and supervised far more funerals than during the warmer months. He knew they suffered not only a lack of material things but also a deep lack of opportunity to do anything about it. There were many people here who would never escape and who knew that to be the fact of their lives; they felt a deep despair which occasionally erupted in aggression and crime. He knew that because they had broken into his own home along with everyone else's. He was not going to pretend: he found it very annoying to have his possessions stolen. But when he spoke to them, it was terribly clear that they really had no idea of the people they were hurting. They came from a sort of shadow world where it was normal to survive by burgling and shoplifting and twocking. And by begging.

The ones who turned up at his door were the most serious casualties from a war that had swept across most of this community. Some of those who came to him were children. They had fallen foul of an adult at home and found themselves pushed out on the street until things calmed down and they could creep back inside. Some of them were the parents of young children and it filled him with horror to think that life in this prosperous society could possibly have sunk to the point where mothers and fathers had to go begging at a priest's door to find food for their children's bellies. So he gave them what they wanted and sent them on their way with a prayer for their safety and a surge of frustration for those who liked to pretend that there was no such thing as poverty in Britain in the 1990s.

II

Ｉt is, indeed, as if some powerful explosion has swept through Hyde Park, laying waste everything in its path, and all the fragments that have been left behind form one clear, over-whelming pattern. This community has collapsed and, surely, Gary Hall is right about why it has done so. There is poverty in Hyde Park.

There is something a little uncomfortable about this con-clusion. In the immediate past, there have been well-documented occasions when some of the most prominent people in Britain have declared unequivocally that absolute poverty has been ban-ished from the country. The former secretary of state for Social Security, John Moore; the Duke of Edinburgh; the two Conserva-tive prime ministers Margaret Thatcher and John Major; numerous journalists and academics; all of them have declared forcefully that there is no such thing as absolute poverty in Britain, that it is a problem of the past. Yet the detail of what has been happening behind some of the closed doors of Hyde Park seems to demand this description.

There are some people in Hyde Park who, for at least some of the time, lack at least one of the four essentials of life: food, fuel, shelter and clothing. Surely they have to be described as 'poor'. Yet, the truth is that these people amount to a small minority whose circumstances often have become intolerable only because they have failed to organise their affairs in the most efficient way. Can the Duke of Edinburgh and the others then argue that this is their own fault and certainly not evidence of a real social problem?

That, too, seems wrong for a couple of reasons. First, beyond the small minority who lack even the basic necessities of life, it turns out that there are numerous people in this community who live in real need and who avoid disaster only by living in the social equivalent of an iron lung, surviving only because they allow themselves to be encased in rigid self-discipline – to control themselves and their instincts, to measure every penny and plan every action, so that they never give in to temptation by spending the evening in a pub or giving their children new toys or buying new clothes or going out to the cinema. If they control every detail of their lives and strap themselves down within strict limits, then they can cling to the four essentials of life. But these lives of quiet desperation are always on the edge of disaster. One mistake, one weakness or one extra problem: that is all it takes to plunge them into trouble. An unexpected bill, a crime, a physical sickness, a mental illness, a violent partner, an aggressive neighbour, an accident at home, a bereavement or an addiction. Some stumble over the edge accidentally, like the old lady with her phone bill. Some deliberately jump, like the ones who drink knowing that they are blowing an entire week's money in a single night but preferring six days of trouble to a lifetime without laughter. Common sense demands that the circumstances of these people should be described as 'poverty'. So why can't the Duke of Edinburgh and the others see it?

Apart from the fact that they have never entered the lives of these people, the larger obstacle is the very idea of 'absolute poverty'. These people use the term to indicate the state of complete material deprivation in which people once lived on the streets of Victorian England and in which they continue to live on the streets of Calcutta or in the deserts of Ethiopia, conditions in which men and women have none of the essentials of life. On this definition, there is no poverty in Britain. But is that a fair way to think of poverty? What would happen, for example, if they took a similar approach to the idea of prosperity? Following the same line of argument, they would have to say that since absolute prosperity involves a state of complete material fulfilment, it can be found only in the palaces of Saudi Arabia or in the heights of Hollywood, where men and women live in conditions in which they lack absolutely nothing. On that definition, they would be compelled to say that despite all that has been claimed on behalf of the British economy in the 1980s and 1990s, there is, in fact, no prosperity in Britain. The idea of poverty is being stretched by these people to a point where it loses its meaning. If the idea is allowed to return to its original shape, to describe a state of material hardship, it is clear that Gary Hall is right. There is poverty in Hyde Park.

Under its strain, the lives of many individuals in Hyde Park have collapsed. With some, like the woman who set fire to a flat to call for help, the link between the collapse and the poverty is direct and immediate. With others, like Jean Ashford, the link is indirect. Jean herself, though often short of income, always managed to get by, always had the necessities of life. It was the crime that grew out of the poverty around her, like nettles in a dungheap, that ruined her life in Hyde Park.

In the same way, the lives of whole families have been destroyed, leaving the daughters to produce children for want of anything else to do, or the mother to lie in bed all day in a coma of sadness.

Of course, it is complicated. There are some people, including many families, who suffer from poverty yet manage to survive without collapsing. A few individuals not only survive but also manage to prosper and to escape. Others are forced to stay but nevertheless manage to hold their lives together. They have that much more inner strength, moral or physical or spiritual, than their neighbours. They have luck. They have relatives with savings who will bail them out of a bad time. But most are unable to defend themselves, perhaps because they are weakened by one problem too many, perhaps because they are simply unlucky, and so poverty's assault finds out some weakness in their armour and penetrates their lives with all its destructive force.

Some of the Hyde Park social workers whose job it was to pick up the pieces after this explosion had swept through the area, said that it was like watching a flu epidemic: some people went down, others remained steady, and often it was impossible to say why some escaped and others didn't.

The ways in which poverty has wounded this community are infinitely subtle. It has bruised the minds and bodies of those who live with it, spoiling their health, undermining their self-respect, spreading hopelessness and sadness, loneliness and anxiety, provoking frustration and anger and crime and alcoholism and drug abuse, corroding all the fibre of daily life to the point where a place like Hyde Park almost ceases to exist as a community and becomes instead a collection of strangers, living with or without each other's support, in surroundings for which many of them can feel nothing but estrangement. Some of them have tried to fight back. They organised a Unity Day, they teamed up with students to clean up the streets, they organised basketball and football and dance classes and outings to the country, but, for all their hope and all their effort, they are, for the most part, like Jean Ashford, unable to rebuild a community that has collapsed.

And why did all this happen? It is obvious that Hyde Park has not always suffered in this way. At some point during the twenty years of Jean Ashford's life in the area, it tumbled into decline. Something pushed it over the edge. Beneath all the complexity of the effects of poverty, there lies one simple point of origin – the detonation which released this explosion of scattered damage.

In the spring of 1995, a couple of months before the children of Hyde Park set fire to their streets, a team of public servants from Leeds City Council decided to make a study of the area. This was a coincidence. They had been working their way systematically around the city, picking one patch after another, gathering every available fact and figure, interviewing thousands of residents, looking to see what help was needed in each area.

In Hyde Park, very quickly, they uncovered a striking, though familiar, pattern. Looking at the workforce of the area, they found that a quarter of those who were available for work (25.6 per cent of them) had no work at all: they were either unemployed or temporarily attached to a government scheme. Among young people who were available for work, the figure was even higher: nearly a third (29.1 per cent) of those aged between sixteen and twenty-four who were able to work had no job. The largest single source of earnings in the area turned out to be not manual labour or office work, not private business or the public sector, but income support: just over a third of the families in Hyde Park (34.4 per cent) were signing on for this bottom-line benefit paid to those who had no work and no other source of funds. Coupling together the unemployed among the workforce with those who had retired or who were unable to work through disability or long-term illness, the team from the City Council found that a sweeping 58.5 per cent of this community had no work. And this was not the way it had been in the past.

For years, the terraced back-to-backs and modern homes, where Jean Ashford had once been so proud to live, had housed men and women who rose in the morning and trooped off to earn a living in the old iron foundries and textile factories along Kirkstall Road and Cardigan Road. Life in Hyde Park had had a rhythm and a reason.

But during the 1980s this community had been shaken to its foundations by a series of massive quakes as the underlying structure of work shifted and splintered: new electronic technology, which cut away some jobs for ever; the deregulation of finance and markets, which allowed British-based companies to use cheap labour in the developing world; the stripping away of union power and labour laws, which allowed employers to shed workers in order to improve their productivity. George Brays, the engineering firm which had employed several generations of men and women from Hyde Park and Burley, cut its workforce from hundreds to dozens. The British Screw Company on Kirkstall Road, the forge, the brewery, all the old textile plants and engineering firms were either cut or closed for ever. It was as if someone had drilled a hole in the underside of Hyde Park and drained away its jobs. This was the beginning, the key ingredient in the chemistry of despair which now overwhelmed the place.

The material hardship which then settled over the community was equally clear. As the team from the City Council moved into Hyde Park, systematically interviewing nearly six hundred local people and gathering fragments of numerical fact from every conceivable file and database, they could see the results of what had happened.

In families where the breadwinner was out of work, nearly half of them (46.2 per cent) reported that they had trouble affording clothes, and more than a quarter of them (26.9 per cent) said that they had trouble even paying for food. As a result, there were some people who sometimes went without. Among lone parents, the position was even worse: nearly half (42.4 per cent) reported that they had trouble paying for clothing, more than a quarter of them (27.3 per cent) said that they had difficulty affording food, and a fifth of them (21.2 per cent) said that they could not afford toys for their children. And so, sometimes, they went without any or all of these things.

A fifth of all of those who were interviewed – 20.1 per cent of the whole community – said that they had serious difficulty paying for fuel and water. Again, as a result of this, some of them sometimes had no heat and/or no light and/or no water.

When it came to luxuries – even simple luxuries of the kind which were taken for granted by many in the developed world – the picture that was uncovered by the City Council team was just the same. Nearly two thirds of the people who lived in Hyde Park (64.4 per cent) had no car. The council team asked 597 people in the area whether, in the last three years, they had been away anywhere for a holiday lasting longer than a single weekend. Just about a third of them admitted that they hadn't.

This material hardship, in turn, spawned a collection of personal problems. Some of them were obvious. The team from the City Council asked how the residents of Hyde Park felt about money. Nearly half of the people they questioned (42 per cent of them) – not just the workless workers – said that they felt financially insecure. Lone parents said they felt even worse: 82 per cent of them were worried about money.

Some of the problems were more profound. As the team from Leeds City Council trawled through Hyde Park, looking for clues to its nature, they asked those who lived there how they felt – not how they felt about any particular thing, but how they felt inside themselves as each day unfolded. Once again, a pattern quickly became clear.

Nearly a third of the people they spoke to (29.8 per cent) reported that they were seriously depressed. They said that they had trouble sleeping, that they suffered from stress. Doctors in the area reported that often they dealt with people who were suffering not from some definable physical illness but from loneliness or fear or from sheer despair at the circumstances of their lives. The council team found that a fifth of those with children (21.6 per cent) said quite simply that they never relaxed. Among the single parents, even more (30.3 per cent) said the same thing. This community was riddled with worry.

The price of a family – emotional as much as financial – often proved to be too high. Nearly a third of the children in Hyde Park (29.5 per cent of them) lived in homes where one of the parents was missing. When the team from the City Council went to visit the nearest Social Services offices, at Buckingham House, just outside Hyde Park, they found that a disproportionate number of the children who were registered 'at risk' or taken into care from their region of the city, came from the poverty of Hyde Park.

The social workers told of children who hadn't been to school for two years, children whose teeth were rotten brown, children as young as four who wandered alone through the streets, children who were left alone and ended up banging on a neighbour's door for attention, children who were smacked and beaten as a matter of routine. 'It's neglect,' they said, 'but it's all to do with poverty.'

They told, too, of a more insidious threat, from 'Section One offenders' – paedophiles – who targeted single mothers living on breadline benefit. They offered money to a woman who had none, they offered affection to a woman who had none, they offered to help with the children, to take them for walks, to baby-sit them – anything to take the strain out of the woman's life. The woman found it hard to decline. But soon she would find that her new lover was not so interested in her. Sometimes his sudden indifference might remain a mystery to the woman. On other occasions, it might become painfully clear that the real object of his physical affection had always been her children and, on those occasions, the social workers had discovered mothers struggling to persuade themselves that it was all right to allow this man to stay, that for the sake of the money he brought and the support that he offered, they might deny the reality before them. The real problem for these mothers was that whatever they did – whether they kicked out the man and his money, or let him stay in his corrupt way – the children would suffer. It was a choice of pain.

In this fertile soil, where material poverty and emotional distress were so potently mixed, the crime rate had started to surge upwards. Parents who were interviewed by the City Council team said that their two greatest fears for their children were that they would have no jobs to go to and that they would become involved in crime. But, in its own right, crime had become an additional problem for those who lived there. More than a third of the people of Hyde Park reported that they had been the victims of crime within the previous twelve months. More than half of them said that they were scared to go out on the streets of Hyde Park at night. Some of them were scared, too, of the streets of the city centre at night, but even more of them were frightened to be in their own homes, knowing that there was only a flimsy wall between them and their neighbours' children.

It wasn't just individuals or individual families who had collapsed under the strain of their circumstances. All across Hyde Park, institutions too had staggered under the burden and occasionally they too had fallen apart. That was what had driven away the shopkeepers from their places along Burley Lodge Road, now standing deserted and concealed by boards – not the wild violence of the local children, but the commercial impossibility of surviving in an area where people had no money in their pockets. Big companies had a name for it. They called it 'redlining': they would look at a map of a city and identify the areas of high unemployment and low income and then they would draw a red line around them and ensure that they would invest nothing inside them, for they were useless to them.

The centre of Leeds, only a mile or so away, could boast of its success in attracting £700 million of new investment from private companies, but precious little of it was finding its way into Hyde Park. There were no new banks here, no new supermarkets, no fancy new restaurants, only the vacuum where so many of the old enterprises had folded and gone. Worse than that, employers in other parts of the city seemed to turn away workers who came from a red-line area. To them, a post code in Leeds 6 seemed to be worse than a bad reference.

And slowly but undeniably, this same process of withdrawal had also afflicted the public institutions around them. The welfare state which had once, briefly, protected the needy was withering away.

The social workers and police – the two groups who dealt most directly with the effects of poverty – were themselves suffering from institutional poverty. Social workers confessed to the team from Leeds City Council that they were too busy to offer anything more than 'minimal support work' to their clients. They were effectively unable to engage in the kind of preventive work that had once been their proudest and most productive activity, and were reduced now to mere 'first aid', racing from one crisis to another without being able to attack the cause.

The police, from Millgarth division, had once used a team of fourteen community constables to patrol their area, including Hyde Park, on foot. But during the year before the children burned down the Jolly Brewer, this system collapsed. The patrolling constables were uncovering so much crime that they were drowning in work. The division pulled them back and renamed them 'beat managers'. This had two advantages: it stopped them uncovering so much crime, which made the crime figures look slightly better; and it allowed them to form teams to target particular kinds of crime in the hope of making arrests. They dressed in plain clothes and took bicycles to mount mobile ambushes on joy-riders who tried to steal the cars that the commuters left behind them every morning. They lay in wait outside the old grammar school on the eastern edge of Hyde Park, where wealthy parents paid thousands of pounds to educate their children privately and where the children had discovered that a school cap was as good as a banner marked 'Mug me'. They got some results but the truth was that, caught between the plague of crime in Hyde Park and the shortage of officers, the police were fighting a losing battle.

One of the beat constables, Glen Brady, wanted to start a basketball team to keep the kids off the street. But the police had no spare cash to set it up. A few months before the Jolly Brewer burned, the inspector at Millgarth discovered that he had £10,000 unspent in his annual budget, so he decided to invest it in extra overtime for uniformed officers in Hyde Park. Within weeks, by sheer bad luck, Hyde Park saw its first two murders in four years – both of them incidents of domestic violence – and he was caught with no money to pay for the CID inquiries. He ended up borrowing £12,000 from the contingency fund and learning that the power of the state was not what it was.

The problems of the police were multiplied by the problems of the National Health Service which, in the name of community care, had slashed its funding of the mentally ill and pushed out of its hospitals men and women who found life in the outside world almost intolerably difficult. A tiny number of them went berserk and committed terrible crimes which caught the head-lines, but the mass of them settled into a life of daily difficulty, sometimes sinking into despair, like the old alcoholic alone in his flat with his rancid bacon, sometimes stumbling into a war with those around them – like Ruth, striding through the streets with his fists and his sexual confusion, or the former patient who played his drums all night, or the woman in one of the old back-to-backs who was reduced to terror by the sounds of phantom attackers on her stairs. They bounced like bagatelles from the social workers to the police cells and back to their homes, bereft of rescue, devoid of hope.

The schools, too, were struggling. The City Council team were told that children who were coming into Hyde Park primary schools were already at a disadvantage: they had 'delayed lan-guage development, restricted experiences, limited vocabulary and limited social skills'. And it was these troubled children who were most likely to be turned away from the local schools. Head teachers knew that in the new 'free market' in education, these disruptive children would produce poor exam results which would drag the school down in the league tables, with the result that some parents would avoid the school, thus cutting their pupil numbers – and, therefore, their budget. For the sake of the school's bank balance, head teachers had to consider excluding the very children who most needed education. An overwhelming majority of these excluded children came from poor homes. Many of them ended up in special schools in the area, where staff reported that 80 per cent of their pupils came from families who were living on income support.

Trapped in their homes, often without books of any kind, sometimes without anyone who was able even to read, distracted by chaos and stress, children soon lost their way in school. The City Council team found that all twelve of the primary schools that took children from the area were turning in exam results which were below the national average. At Royal Park, one of the two primary schools based within Hyde Park, only 28 per cent of the infants could read at the expected standard, and only 22 per cent could spell. Among the older children at Royal Park, the results were even worse: only 18 per cent reached the expected standard of English and science and only 9 per cent met the standard for maths. It was not that the schools were bad – just that life in Hyde Park could be very bad for its children.

Among the adults in the area, there was a significant layer who had left school by the time they were fifteen (22.4 per cent of them) and about the same number reported that they had no qualifications at all. And yet, repeatedly, the people of Hyde Park told the City Council team that they wanted to improve themselves. Among the workless, 86.5 per cent said that they wanted to go back to school or college. Lone parents had the same message: 69.7 per cent of them wanted more education. But few of them obtained it. They had no one to look after their children, they lacked the essential qualifications, some of them could not read or write, many of them could not afford it or could not find college places. So, they were stuck. The welfare state that might once have helped them was no longer able to do so.

It had retreated like an exhausted mother, too tired to offer her children anything but indifference.

The library in Cardigan Road had been forced to cut its hours, and the librarians could see the results. Where once they had been lending eight or nine hundred books a week, they were now lending only six hundred. Now they were having to cut the stock of books as well. It wasn't just the cuts, the librarians said, it was the whole social mess. Schoolchildren used to come to the library in groups, but now the schools could not afford the escorts, so that had stopped. People were afraid to leave their homes in case they were burgled, they were afraid to be out on the streets in case they were mugged. So, things like visiting a library became too threatening for some. When they had tried to plant some trees opposite the library to brighten up the street, people had complained that glue sniffers and muggers would hide behind them, and so none was planted.

The housing department was also enfeebled. More than half the houses in the area turned out to be unfit for human habitation, according to the guidelines of the central government. When the City Council team interviewed residents of Hyde Park, just under half of them complained that they had nowhere adequate to wash their clothes. More than half of the council tenants said the repair service was poor.

Old people were living in houses where they had spent most of their lives. The houses were now slowly decaying and often they had staircases that were far too steep for them to negotiate. They couldn't move out. There were just about no council flats for old people in the area and none being built. They couldn't afford to rent anywhere else. Some of them couldn't bear to move, abandoning their memories and moving into a strange place. The ones who couldn't get up their staircases ended up camping in their own front rooms, with a kitchen on the side and a commode next to the stove. Others fought running battles with the damp. There was one elderly man in the Autumns who had installed six damp courses in his dilapidated home and still not succeeded in drying the walls.

The City Council team interviewed Hyde Park people who were disabled or trapped by illness and found that only 22.5 per cent had been able to adapt their homes to their disabilities. Some of the housing stock had become a black joke.

'We live in back-to-backs. There's only one wall between us so we're very close. If they do burgle you, at least you know your stuff hasn't gone far.'

A whole layer of support and supervision had disappeared. Where once there had been bus conductors and lavatory attendants and park-keepers and petrol-pump attendants, now there were few, if any. With their departure, the community had lost a degree of security and care which had not been replaced.

Even the churches, the final fall-back of the poor, were staggering under the burden, imposing their own version of 'redlining'. The Catholics and the Presbyterians had seen their churches closed and sold away. The Anglicans had seen theirs closed for fifteen months while the diocese looked for the money to fund a new vicar. The Methodists now had a new church hall, which stood at the back of Hyde Park Close, but Gary Hall, who was its minister, confessed that they were so short of money that 'we're running an emergency service, that's all'.

Gaps had opened up in the fabric of daily life. To fill them, the team from the City Council reported that Hyde Park needed more play schemes, an organised baby-sitting service, more full-time nurseries, more school clubs, more after-school clubs, more weekend clubs, local services for drug addicts, more social workers, training for parents, more outreach workers for young people, more playing fields, more youth clubs, more home-care help, more and cheaper public transport, more doctors, a health-centre service on Saturdays, more homes, more repairs to homes, more security in homes, more cooking facilities, more laundry facilities, more damp-proofing and heating, roofs without leaks, doors without draughts, more police, more streetlights, more college places, more college funding, more courses in office skills and English language, more traffic control and road-safety measures, a clean-up campaign, more special-needs teachers, more cashpoints, a local supermarket, more street cleaning, more library books, a community centre, a council gardener, a nice pub with a garden, more money and, above all else, more jobs. In other words, the fabric of this once vibrant area is now riddled with holes. Weakened by the loss of its jobs the community has collapsed under the weight of its poverty.

12

What has happened to Hyde Park is an almost perfect recipe for the destruction of a community. You close down the factories and the other employers so that for a great many men and women there is not only no work, there is also no prospect of work, ever. You sell its houses to absentee landlords who have no interest in their upkeep or their tenants. You bring in groups of people from other cultures who don't speak the language or understand the ways, and you make no attempt to smooth their passage. Just at that moment, just when these men and women are starting to plunge into anxiety, you start stripping away the old safety nets which had previously promised to break their fall. You cut their dole, you peg their pensions and their child benefit, you cut back their housing benefit and stop building public housing, you close their youth clubs and you do your best to suffocate their libraries and colleges. To add further chaos, you release the mentally ill into their midst and do just about nothing to care for them, and cut back the budgets of all those who might be able to help, particularly the social workers and the police.

If you can do all this, you can start to generate a combination of emotions which are essential to the effective destruction of any community – sadness, bitterness, hopelessness, despair. Some people will continue to fight, to struggle to survive. But many people will surrender, particularly young people who have been born into this and who have had no experience of a better world to lend them resolve. And soon, this community will start to destroy itself, as those among it who have abandoned hope turn their anger and indifference on their surroundings. This means that they will destroy not only the physical fabric of the place – by smearing it and smashing it and burning it down – but also the subtle, fragile webs that bind its people together.

The children in the Hyde Park gang reek of all this, with their boredom, their savage indifference to their surroundings, their seething hatred for the middle-class students who have more than they do. But they are only the most visible among all those who have lost their faith. Once people went to the library and stopped to talk outside. Now they are too scared. Once, the old people stood around outside the post office after they collected their pensions, exchanging friendship. Now they are too scared and they collect their pensions by taxi. (It is like paying tax, really, to pay out a slice of their pension to a taxi driver before they can put it in their pocket.) Once, people went to work and they came home, not only with money in their pocket, but with some stimulation inside them, however small, with some interest or even excitement, some self-respect, some status. At work, they had found friends and enemies and fools and heroes, jokes, stories, gossip, a life. Now they sit at home or lie on the pavement.

They don't necessarily speak of themselves as being poor. That is too frightening or too shaming. Inside themselves, they feel like ordinary people, like people who have homes with light and heat and food and clothing – and, for most of the time, it may be just about true. They may have no car and no holiday, they may have give-away furniture and hand-out clothes, their homes may have broken windows and battered doors, they may very well look to other people as though they are poor, but inside themselves, they feel like everyone else. Even so, there are some days, the days when the giro runs out, when they have to behave as though they are paupers, as though they have nothing, not even pride, and they have to take themselves out to plead and wheedle, to act like the paupers they have seen, to barter their pain for comfort.

When the work drained away from Hyde Park, it took with it not only the material wealth of the area but also its emotional health. There are numerous families here who protect and love their children, but some of them have capitulated to the stress to the point where, rather like rats in an overcrowded cage in some grotesque laboratory experiment, they start to attack each other and even their children in perverse and brutal ways.

In the mid-1990s, Leeds City Council became so alarmed at the number of children who were being seen by their social workers for physical or emotional or sexual abuse that they set up a working party to consider its roots. Its chairman, Bernard Atha, a Labour councillor, was precise and honest in explaining their conclusion:

> There is a very strong correlation between poverty and child abuse. The bulk of child-protection work can be clearly seen as being almost identical in geographical areas with high unemployment, low per capita income, poor housing and other aspects of social deprivation ... Affluence is no guarantee that abuse will not occur. In fact, abuse in the more affluent families may be much more difficult to identify and investigate. However, poverty and deprivation appears to guarantee increased levels of child abuse of all kinds. Abuse abounds where family stress exists.

The children who run amok in Hyde Park are the same children who are exposed to this risk of abuse. The clearer the picture becomes, the more it looks like a nightmare. If this is the deepest damage, there is yet another kind of damage that spreads wider.

Life is hard if there is no money, and even harder if there is no hope, and so some of these families now live like refugees. Real life has been torn away from them. They have no future, no possibility of planning one. They have lost their connection to this place: it does nothing for them, and they do nothing for it. Even those who have work are troubled: they can see what has happened to their neighbours, their children can see what the future holds, they have no right or reason to feel secure, to trust life round here. They have lost touch with each other.

An overwhelming majority of the residents of Hyde Park (79.5 per cent of them) told the City Council team that they played no role in any part of the community or any group in it. They had no hope for its future: two thirds of them felt the area was changing for the worse. They hardly even knew their neighbours. Half the people who spoke to the council team said that they had lived in their homes for less than two years. The old stability of the council estates had been broken by the new market in 'right-to-buy' houses. For many of those who want neighbours as friends and supporters, there is only frustration. For those who turn to crime, it is much easier to steal from neighbours who are strangers.

And they are trapped – like the old lady locking herself into her house with her rice and peas, like Simone with her addiction to her own destruction. There is no point to life, no point to families, no point to neighbours, no point to going to school. Life is traipsing in the rain to the Netto supermarket where everything is cut-price and traipsing home, hoping nobody notices your shameful Netto bags. Life is queuing for giros, propping up a wall on the corner of a street, sleeping till the afternoon and watching telly till dawn. Life is nothing. It is being pregnant for no reason, being jobless with no hope. It means nothing. It has fallen apart.

And it is there – in the hollow inside them, in their indifference to everyone, including themselves, in their total acceptance of pain, in their contempt for the law and for all the rest of their surroundings, in their 'damaged, deprived, depraved and delinquent' way of being – it is there that the children of Hyde Park and the children of the Forest in Nottingham show their common origin, in these thousands of battered council estates which together form the heartland of the undiscovered country of the poor.

Part III

Damage

Talk about Dante's Hell, and all the horrors and cruelties of the torture-chamber of the lost! The man who walks with open eyes and with bleeding heart through the shambles of our civilisation needs no such fantastic images of the poet to teach him horror. Often and often, when I have seen the young and the poor and the helpless go down before my eyes into the morass, trampled underfoot by beasts of prey in human shape that haunt these regions, it seemed as if God were no longer in His world but that in His stead reigned a fiend, merciless as Hell, ruthless as the grave.

William Booth, *In Darkest England*, 1890

13

For most of her life, Natalie Pearman was a walking portrait of an ordinary girl. She lived with her four brothers and sisters and her cat called Lucy in a neat little council house on the edge of a peaceful village in Norfolk. She liked ballet and horses and watching *Neighbours* after tea, she was good at drawing and painting and she had the idea that when she grew up, she would like to go into the Air Force so that she could be independent and travel around the world.

Her family was indistinguishable from any other in their street: the father, Chris, going off to work each day as an engineer in a plant-hire firm; the mother, Lin, who had given up her career as a nurse to manage the home; the children clambering on to the bus that took them down the road to school; all of them running through the routines of an ordinary existence. Then it changed – at least, Natalie did. It was as if she had decided to take a knife to that ordinary portrait of herself and hack it to shreds and start all over again. She was fourteen when it happened and, when she re-emerged, everything had changed: her clothes, her hair, her likes and passions, her friends, even her name. Natalie Pearman had vanished. And nobody really knew why.

In place of the skinny little schoolgirl with the mousy brown hair, there now stood a willowy blonde who called herself Maria, who drank and smoked and played around with dope. She no longer lived in the little council house or had anything very much to do with her family at all. All they knew was what they heard from the police when she was picked up from time to time – for breaking and entering, for stealing a car, and then for soliciting on the streets of Norwich. The truth was that Maria was a whore.

The last time she came home, her mother barely recognised her. Lin hadn't seen her for more than a year and it was like having a stranger in the house. When Lin made her a cup of tea, she had to ask her whether she took milk and sugar. She could barely understand the things that Natalie talked about – pimps and punters and the guys in the Vice Squad. And when Lin looked at her daughter, she saw what she could only describe as a fog of evil hanging around her.

All this might have remained a private mystery if there had not been a terrible sequel to the story. A few days after that final visit home, Natalie died. In the small hours of a dark November morning, somebody used her for sex and then choked the life out of her and dumped her body in a lay-by outside Norwich. She was sixteen. Her murder turned the riddle of her life into a public puzzle. In many ways, it seemed to be a classic story of self-destructive youth, corrupted by drugs and ruined by reckless self-indulgence, the kind of case that has adults shaking their heads in despair. But then again, it wasn't quite that simple.

The key to the mystery lay in the very ordinariness of Natalie's childhood. Police and social workers and neighbours, too, took a long, hard look at her past, but they found only the everyday tensions of family life: Natalie used to fight with her brother, Jon, who was two years older than her and inclined to push her about, like older brothers always do; and she sometimes resented Chris, because she knew he was not her real father. She and Jon had been fathered by Lin's first husband, an oil worker named Rod Earp. But the marriage had collapsed when Natalie was only one, and Chris had played the part of her father since she was eight. They were things that might have upset her sometimes, but no worse. There was something else which was equally common but which appears to have upset her more. The Pearmans were poor.

It wasn't that the family were starving; they were nowhere near the kind of desperation that envelops the destitute. But they were trapped at the bottom of the financial cliff, with Chris working full time and bringing home only £120 at the end of the week, and Lin juggling her child benefit to fill in the gaps. They had enough to get by, but no more. They had no car, so if they wanted to go anywhere they had to travel by bus, and since there were only four of those a day, they tended to stay in the village. They had no holidays abroad or any extravagance at all. Life was strictly limited. And when Natalie was twelve, it got a little worse.

Lin had fallen pregnant with her youngest child and began to have a very difficult time. She needed 24-hour care and the only person who could provide it was Chris. He asked his employers if they would let him take time off to look after her and then come back when the baby was born, but they wouldn't have it, so he was forced to give up his job. When the baby was born and Lin had recovered, he went out to look for more work. There was the canning factory in North Walsham, the gas terminal at Bacton, a couple of pig farms, but no one was hiring. Once, he was offered shifts at a place near Cromer, but he had no way of getting there. Another time, he signed up with a friend who was starting his own business, but there was no money in it and it all went sour. Now, this family's life had changed. Now, they were struggling.

Natalie hated being poor. It was not that she was ashamed of it, it was the practical fact that she could not enjoy the things she wanted, even simple things. There were times when she came home from school asking if she could go on a day trip with the other children and she had to be told that they couldn't afford it. Some of her friends went to Brownies, but Natalie didn't; there was no money for the uniform. She had to give up her ballet lessons.

And then there was Mundesley, the kind of village that looks right in the rain. It is a tiny place, with a population of 1,500, perched on the clifftops overlooking the muddy brown sea about half an hour's drive north of Norwich. There are a couple of caravan parks, which fill up with trippers in the summer months and then sit soaking up the drizzle for the rest of the year. There's the Haig Club with its star cabaret night featuring compère and vocalist Phil St John; a pub or two; a scattering of guest houses pleading for business ('All rooms en suite'); and the Coronation Hall, built of red brick and pebble dash, with four concrete tubs of ageing flowers collecting dust outside, and a poster that says 'Come to Sunny Mundesley'. Natalie spent most of her life here and never found much to do. There was the little amusement arcade with the sign over the door telling local children to stay away unless they could demonstrate to the satisfaction of the management that they were on holiday. No cinema, no youth club. There was the beach, bristling with rules: no dogs on the beach, no parties on the beach, no barbecues on the beach unless they take place in the designated area with the written permission of North Norfolk District Council. The nearest town was a six-pound taxi-ride away. Natalie stayed at home. She'd sit in her room and draw. Sometimes, on a Saturday morning, she'd go to a jumble sale with Lin. And for a long time, that was enough.

When Natalie started to change, she did so with dazzling speed. The beginning was simple: a few months after her fourteenth birthday, she got herself a weekend job at a little take-away hamburger bar next to the amusement arcade and earned herself pocket money for videos and clothes and, while she was working down there, she saw something that caught her eye – a group of village children having fun. To an outsider's eye, there was nothing to it, just a bunch of boys and girls on a sheltered bench, chewing gum and sharing cigarettes. But they had their little secrets, which Natalie soon discovered.

One of them was dope. There was an older boy who had a room of his own in the village, who used to buy little lumps of hash in Great Yarmouth, and then they'd all sit around on their bench, spitting at the grass and giggling while they tried to get stoned. Then there was sex, lots of groping and screwing down on the beach. Natalie started to sit around with them on the sheltered bench and then to join in. Some of the adults from the village saw what she was doing but they had no worries about it. Village kids had always done it. What else was there to do when you were penniless in Mundesley?

Back in their neat little council house, Chris and Lin saw within weeks that something new was happening but when they asked her, she shrugged them off. They told her to behave herself and wrote off to the RAF for glossy brochures about life in the Air Force, but Natalie wasn't that interested any more. Lin wasn't too sure what to make of it, until one of Natalie's friends came to see her and told she was afraid that Natalie was on drugs. Now, Lin had always believed in what she calls 'tough love': you lay down the rules and you offer your children love, but on your own terms. The door is always open but the child has to come to you. Lin told Natalie in no uncertain terms that there was no place in this family for anybody on drugs. But years of squabbling with her big brother had taught Natalie to stand up for herself. She said she wasn't on drugs – not the way her mother thought – and anyway, she was having fun at last. Then she got pregnant.

Natalie was ecstatic. It was the best thing ever. The father was seventeen, three years older than her, a local boy with his own motorbike (and a more or less permanent plaster on the leg he kept breaking). She was in love. They'd have their own house together and both of them would go out to work so they could afford to buy furniture and, while she was at work, Lin would look after the baby. It was going to be great. But Lin said no: there was no way she was going to look after Natalie's baby. If she wanted to have the baby, that was up to her, but she would have to take responsibility for it herself or give it up for adoption. And that was final. Natalie turned to her boyfriend for help, but he took fright and told her he didn't really want to get involved. She said she'd bring up the baby with her friend Julie. When she was ten weeks pregnant, she miscarried, and so the dream was over.

Natalie started to stay out late at night. Chris used to go out at midnight, fishing in the dark corners of Mundesley until he found her and brought her back for a good ticking-off. Lin was going through a rough time herself. She had just miscarried and was feeling bad, her eldest son had joined the army and been posted to the Falklands, and Chris's mother was dying very slowly from cancer. She told Natalie they really didn't have time to deal with her silliness. Natalie started drifting further afield, to North Walsham and Great Yarmouth, so that Chris couldn't find her when he went out looking, and, without a car, he and Lin ended up calling the police to find her. They decided to get tough. One night when two boys brought her home full of cider, Lin took off her slipper and beat her from one end of the house to the other. They started locking her indoors, but Natalie fought to get out, smashed a window once, tried to squeeze herself through the cat flap another time and nearly succeeded. By now, the family was at war with itself. The tighter they pulled at Natalie, the further she ran away. The more they shouted, the less she heard. When the police brought in a social worker to try to help, Natalie gritted her teeth and announced that she wanted to be taken into care.

She found a new boyfriend, Simon, a young farm worker, five years older than her, with a ring in his ear and an old Cavalier and two best mates called Dean and Delbert. They hung around together, smoked a little dope, got stopped by the police, got away with it, broke into an empty house and legged it when the police came, got caught, got cautioned, carried on having a laugh, while Chris and Lin sent out the police to bring her back.

The social workers talked to Natalie, who was full of anger at her family – at her real father who was lost in the past and at her stepfather who was too tough on her. She threw up a whisper of a clue that she had once been physically abused by a friend of the family. She said she couldn't care less: if people didn't like her, then she didn't like them. When she was out, Lin read her diary, scattered with hints of dope and sex, and then she told Natalie in no uncertain terms that she did not like what she had read. Once when she came home late, Chris hit her and she wore the bruise like a medal the next time she saw Simon. Then one night, she didn't come back at all and the police couldn't find her until the next morning when they spotted her wandering alone along a beach. They picked her up and called Lin and asked what she wanted them to do, and Lin said she didn't want Natalie home, she wanted her taken into care. The police agreed. And so Natalie was out of her family – less than six months after she first went to work at the hamburger bar and joined the other kids hanging around on the sheltered bench.

Now the war became a stand-off. Lin stuck to her tough love: if Natalie wanted to come back, that was fine, but Natalie would have to make the first move. Natalie told her friends that she couldn't care less about being in care. She hated Chris and she was better off without them. In the children's home near Cromer, she was caught sniffing petrol.

That week, Chris's mother finally died of her cancer and when the news reached Natalie at the children's home, she said she wanted to go to the funeral. Chris wrote to the social workers to say that his family did not want her there; she had caused too much upset. The social workers felt Natalie ought to be there, so they ignored Chris's letter and took her along to the funeral, where Natalie sat alone at the back of the church while Chris and Lin and their friends and relations pretended they had not seen her. Back at school, Natalie sniffed lighter fuel and was suspended for a week. Chris's family decided that she should no longer call herself Pearman; she should use her real father's name if she was going to be so bad.

Natalie spent just over a year in care, most of it with foster parents, calm for months at a time, running around with Simon and the lads at weekends, occasionally pitched into sudden panics if things went unexpectedly wrong. Once, Simon wondered out loud if they should stop seeing each other so much, and Natalie went back to her foster home and said she'd swallowed fifty contraceptive pills. Simon raced over, but she was fine, though she fell into a long sulk, snarling at others in the home until her foster mother said she should leave. Natalie didn't wait to be pushed; she ran and, from a phone box outside a pub, she called her family. Chris went and fetched her and returned her to the social services. Back in the children's home, she warned the social workers that she was full of heroin. They had her blood tested and found she was clean. She settled back into the stalemate. Her family did not visit her; Lin thought it would teach her a lesson. They were supposed to go for family therapy, but Lin couldn't afford anyone to look after the baby and, anyway, she had no transport, so the sessions fizzled out. At Christmas, Chris delivered some presents to the home, without seeing her. Natalie was alone.

She reached her sixteenth birthday, struggled free of social services, walked out of school and headed for Norwich. She had no job, she was too young to sign on, and for a while she lived in the YWCA, but she still had her mates – Simon and the lads and a whole network of other young people who had fallen out of the bottom of village life and drifted into the nearest big town. They showed her how to survive. For a girl, it was easy. Within weeks, she was working on the pavement. 'Maria' was born.

She used to stand outside a pub called the Ferry Boat in the middle of the network of streets which have been used by prostitutes for years and are collectively known in Norwich as the Block. Fifteen pounds for a hand job, £20 for a blow job, £30 straight sex. At first, she worked only part time, selling just enough of herself to pay for her rent and food, but after a few months she became more confident and started to work routinely.

Now, in a twisted way, she began to find what she wanted. She wasn't poor any more. She was pulling in £500 a week and then blowing it in great gushes of extravagance – videos, clothes and anything else she wanted. She talked about buying a flash new car and a mobile phone. She used to get together with one of the girls who worked round the corner from her, Louise, and the two of them would go out and raid nightclubs together and get completely paralytic and then stumble into a taxi in a heapful of laughter. She was having fun. It wasn't the kind of fun she had dreamed of as a child and often it was only the synthetic excitement of something she'd stuffed up her nostril, but it was more fun than she'd ever had when she was penniless in Mundesley.

Maria was not so much a new self-portrait as a caricature, a grotesque parody of the life that Natalie craved, but everyone who was with her at the time agrees on one thing, that she was happy. She wasn't the mad-eyed junkie whore of legend at all. In fact, she wasn't a junkie of any kind. All her friends say the same thing: that she smoked some dope and, when she was working on the Block, she played around with heroin and cocaine, but she was never very interested, certainly not addicted. She wasn't trapped and dragged down by sinister forces. She chose to do what she did, because when she looked at her life she saw she was trapped and when she looked at her future, it was even worse – getting pregnant, getting married, getting a house and stewing slowly in front of a television for forty years. What else was there?

When she went back to see Lin on that last visit, just before she died, she wasn't interested in going home. She went back to collect her birth certificate because she wanted to get a passport and go off to France or Spain. 'There's nothing here for me any more,' she said. And she glided round the house with her dyed blond hair and her skin-tight trousers with her nails polished and her eyes painted up, and she was saying she'd won the war with her past. Her visit wasn't an offer of peace, it was a victory roll.

The next night, she was back on the Block. Just before midnight, a taxi driver picked her up and used her for half an hour. At about one in the morning, a man paid her £30 to come back to his house where his baby daughter was asleep upstairs. Then, just after half past three, a lorry driver, who was working his way through a narrow road to the northwest of the city, spotted a bundle of clothes in a lay-by. He stopped to look and, in the lights of his lorry, he found Natalie Pearman, stripped from the waist down, scarlet bruises round her neck. The police set up the biggest inquiry in the history of Norfolk, but the killer eluded them. They collected her property and found she had acquired almost nothing: a few tacky dresses, some make-up and a little box in which she had kept the medals she had once won for ballet – just the possessions of an ordinary girl.

14

What happened to Natalie Pearman was unique and yet some of the pressures that bore down on her are familiar. The jobless parents, the desperate boredom, the sense of pointlessness, the final dive to self-destruction all hark back to the experiences of the children of the Forest and Hyde Park. This, in itself, must have some importance. If places as far apart and as different as Nottingham and Leeds and Mundesley all show similar signs of breakdown, this hints loudly at the scale of the poverty which has created this undiscovered country. It must be huge.

Like the idea of poverty itself, the scale of the hardship turns out to be a subject which has been stretched and pulled from different sides like a toy in the grip of squabbling children. And yet, despite all the different approaches of different people who have attempted to measure it, with striking regularity they have come to the same conclusion. On the best estimate, by the late 1990s, the number of men, women and children in the country of the poor in Great Britain amounts to nearly 14 million – just about a quarter of the population. It sounds like a wild exaggeration and yet the best minds with the best information have all arrived at this figure even though they have travelled along different routes.

Some said they could measure poverty by tracking the number of people who relied on the most basic state benefit. Its name has changed – from National Assistance through Supplementary Benefit and Income Support to Jobseekers Allowance – but its significance has remained the same. This is breadline benefit, the bottom line below which the poor cannot be allowed to sink.

Westminster civil servants have been the key group that has used this measure to count the poor. By 1992, the official records showed that there were 13.7 million men, women and children in the United Kingdom who were living on or below this poverty line.

Others, who used different routes to try to chart the size of the undiscovered country, came to the same conclusion. The European Union, for example, use a different measure. They work out the average income for the entire population of the country and then suggest that if anyone is living on less than half of this average, it is reasonable to say they are poor. In the case of the UK, the European Union's records show that by 1993, there were 13.7 million men, women and children in Britain who were living on or below this poverty line.

Despite the clarity of this evidence, there have always been some who want to claim that these are not real poverty lines: if anyone's income were too low, they say, they would be allowed to claim benefit and, if they claimed benefit, they could not be poor. The state would be looking after their needs, they say. Margaret Thatcher told the House of Commons in December 1983: 'People who are living in need are fully and properly provided for.' However, this is not correct.

On two occasions in the early 1990s, a special unit at the University of York produced detailed figures for a 'modest but adequate budget', then they compared these figures with the spending power of those who lived on the two poverty lines. In both cases, they found that these people were unable to afford to pay for the reasonable basics of life. A couple with two children would need, they calculated, £351.21 each week to pay for their needs, including housing. But income support was giving them only £115.15 – 38 per cent of the money they needed. If the same couple were living on half of the average national income, they would receive a little more, £166 a week – still only 55 per cent of the money they needed for a modest but adequate budget.

When the Church of England produced its *Faith in the City* report in the late 1980s, highlighting 'grave and fundamental injustice' among the inner-city poor, the government denounced the report as 'Marxist theology'. One of the most senior civil servants from the Department of Social Security told a House of

Commons committee: 'The word "poor" is one the government actually disputes.' The last Conservative secretary of state for Social Security, Peter Lilley, refused to heed the UN Social Summit's call for a national strategy to fight poverty on the grounds that, in Britain, it was unnecessary.

In 1990, two academics set out to find the truth once and for all, by approaching the issue from a completely new direction. Joanna Mack and Stuart Lansley secured the backing of the Rowntree Trust and London Weekend Television to set up a sweeping survey of people all over Britain whom they asked for a definition of poverty. What possessions were essential to life in twentieth-century Britain? The answers to this mass survey produced a list of twenty-three items – things like an indoor toilet, heating in winter, a damp-free home, a bath, a bed, and three meals a day. In the eyes of the British people, these were the essentials of modern life. Then the two academics went out and conducted more research to find out how many people were living without these essentials.

They discovered that roughly 10 million men, women and children in Britain did not have adequate housing – their homes were unheated or damp. About 7 million people could not afford essential clothing, such as a warm coat in winter. Around 5 million were not properly fed by today's standards: for example, they could not afford two meals a day. They found that 2.5 million children were forced to go without their own essentials, such as three meals a day or toys or out-of-school activities.

Looking back at all they had found, Mack and Lansley concluded that anyone who was living without three of these twenty-three essentials could reasonably be described as poor. Using this new poverty line, they arrived at exactly the same conclusion as the Westminster officials and the European Union. When they completed their research in 1990 (before the recession of the early 1990s had its effect), the two accepted poverty lines showed that there were some 11 million men, women and children in the UK who could reasonably be said to be living in poverty. In that year, Mack and Lansley, using their own original approach, arrived at the same conclusion. Over the following years, the recession had lifted the figure higher – to 13.7 million people. Almost exactly one quarter of the population.

It is huge. It is arguable that the true figure is even higher than this. None of these studies takes account of the numberless mass who disappeared off official records to avoid the poll tax, or those who are homeless, in hostels or hospitals or prisons. On the other hand, it is arguable that since the end of the recession of the early 1990s, the figure would have fallen. The bedrock reality is unchanged. By any available measure, by the mid-1990s, there were some 13.7 million people within the boundaries of the UK who were suffering genuine material hardship. The country of the poor has a population four times the size of Ireland or New Zealand, a population bigger than the whole of Sweden and Norway put together.

It is huge. Yet for all everyday purposes, it is hidden. The obvious signs of poverty – the homeless person or the beggar – are there for all to see, but the scale is not. And the reason for this lies in the experience of the other three quarters of the population. Since 1979, they have become more prosperous.

The very rich have done the best. By 1993/4, the wealthiest 5.5 million people in Britain (the richest 10 per cent) were each enjoying a bonus of £650 income for every £1,000 they had been receiving in 1979. In other words, as a result of the changes in salaries and taxes and benefits, they were 65 per cent better off. This has nothing to do with inflation. The figures have been adjusted to take account of changes in prices. The very rich simply have become much richer.

It is true, too, of the mass of other people. By 1993/4, the population of Britain as a whole saw an increase in their income of 40 per cent since 1979. Again this is a real increase, nothing to do with inflation. This is simply the result of changes in salaries and taxes and benefits. In the mid-1990s, if you picked four people at random in the middle of Oxford Street in the West End of London, you could reasonably have expected to find that three of them were better off than they had been in 1979. On average, they would have been able to buy 40 per cent more goods than they could have done in 1979. It was only the poorest quarter – the 13.7 million – who were left behind.

The Treasury's own figures show that by 1993/4, the 5.5 million people in Britain who had the least money (the poorest 10 per cent) were something like £11 a week worse off than they had been in 1979. This took account of all their spending, including housing, and, again, this had nothing do with inflation. In 1979, they had been able to buy £78 worth of goods each week. By 1993/4, their disposable income – a combination of wages and taxes and benefits – had fallen so that they could afford to buy only £67 worth of goods at the same prices. They were 14 per cent poorer. For every £1,000 which had come their way in 1979, they now had only £860.

At that point, there were another 5.5 million people who were slightly better off than these very poor, but who had also missed out on the new wealth. Within that group, some of them – a lot of pensioners, for example – had simply stuck where they were, while others were clearly worse off. Among the 11 million poorest people in Britain (the poorest 20 per cent), couples with children were worse off by about £9 a week. Single people without children had lost even more. By 1993/4, the changes in Britain during that time were costing each of these people something like £1,352 a year – £26 a week which they were paying, like a kind of levy, a compulsory payment for a project which was destroying them, rather like the custom of Saddam Hussein's executioners who would kill a man and then send his widow a bill for the bullet.

This is how the scale of the undiscovered country remains so hidden – because three quarters of the population look around them and see nothing but prosperity. There is a veil over the experience of the other quarter. When the then prime minister, Margaret Thatcher, told the House of Commons in May 1988, 'Everyone in the nation has benefited from increased prosperity – everyone', she was drawing this veil deliberately across the truth, but for most people there is nothing cynical about it. For the most part, they simply do not see it.

Who are these 13.7 million people? Once again researchers have collected a mass of raw material. There are all kinds of different poor people in this country. There are literally millions of children. In 1993, the executive director of Unicef, the UN Children's Fund, warned that Britain's children were the poorest in Europe. By 1993/4, a third of the boys and girls in Britain, 4.2 million of them, belonged to families who lived below the two accepted poverty lines.

There are adolescents. On an average day during 1996, there were 161,600 young people, aged seventeen or under, who were out of work. The Unemployment Unit in London estimates that the overwhelming majority of them, 140,400, had no income because they were no longer allowed to sign on for benefit. There were some 450,000 other young people, aged under twenty-five, who were also out of work and living on benefits that had been reduced for their age group. By 1996, a survey by ten housing charities found that 250,000 young people were homeless – either sleeping rough or living in squats or sleeping on the floors of friends or, occasionally, in local-authority hostels.

There are old people. In December 1995, Age Concern found that more than a third of pensioners found it hard to manage on their income and a further 50 per cent only just managed to get by; more than two thirds of them never took holidays; a third of them had trouble paying for heat in winter. There are disabled people, single people who live lives of stunning isolation, young mothers with their children, people like Ruth who have been patients in mental hospitals but who are now trying to live on their own. But for all their differences, over and over again, they share one common burden. They have no work.

In 1993/4, among the 13.7 million in poverty, there were 10 million who lived in households where there was no wage earner. The number of households like this had soared upwards, from one in twelve in 1979 to one in five by the mid-1990s. It is the kind of statistic that is hard to absorb but it indicates the dramatic scale of poverty in Britain. There are some households like this that manage to climb above the poverty line, usually because of their savings. But, on the best figures available, seven out of every ten households without work end up living in poverty. This includes not only the families of those who are officially listed as unemployed. By 1993, the government had changed the way that it measured the unemployed thirty different times. Each time, they had shuffled more people away from the official figures, until some 2 million jobless workers had been airbrushed out of the picture. This 10 million includes the families of all those who were 'hidden unemployed' as well as the families of pensioners, the mentally ill, the physically disabled, single mothers, all of whom live without work, most of whom live in poverty.

The other 3.7 million have work but they have been swept into poverty by a tide of low pay. The number of 'working poor' trebled between 1979 and the mid-1990s. The main reason is simple: the government abolished the wages councils and withdrew the regulations which had once built a financial floor beneath which no worker was allowed to sink. Beyond this, the government stripped power from the trade-union movement, which had previously used its strength to lift wage levels. By August 1995, 78 per cent of the jobs that had once been protected by the wages councils were offering pay that was below the level that a family with two children would receive on income support. In other words, the employers were paying below the poverty line.

During this time, there was an explosion of part-time jobs and jobs on temporary contracts. Most of these were taken by women. Most of them paid low wages.

The clearest sign of poverty, quite simply, is shortage of money. Families cannot pay for a cot for their new baby, for a bed for their growing child, for shoes to replace those which wear out, for gas and electricity. While three quarters of the population save for holidays, the other quarter save for bus fares. The signs of this are clear enough. In 1981, for example, official figures showed that 1.3 million households were in debt. But eight years later, in 1989, the number of families who had paid out money which they did not have had soared upwards to 2.8 million. In the same way, whereas in 1980, only 3,480 homes had been repossessed, in 1991, the figure had spiralled by more than 2,000 per cent. In that year, 75,540 homes were taken back from owners who could no longer afford them. As the property market has recovered, this figure has dropped back somewhat.

But there is much more to poverty than merely running out of money. That is simply the beginning. The point that emerges from the Forest and Hyde Park is that poverty inflicts real damage on those who live with it, even on those who manage to organise their affairs most efficiently and who escape the worst of the material hardship. Poverty is not neutral, not just a passive background against which people act out their lives. It is aggressive, destructive. If it is fair to speak of the poor living in another country, then it is right to see this country not as some kind of liberal democracy in which the citizens are free to develop as they choose, but as a totalitarian state which is profoundly oppressive to its subjects. Part of this oppression is emotional.

15

There is a small boy in the playground, probably about eight years old, and he is crying while his young mother stands and looks away.

In a flat voice, she says, 'Shut your mouth.'

He cries on.

'Shut your mouth!'

He cries on. She turns and leans into his face. 'Shut your mouth or I'll slap you.'

He shuts his mouth and starts to cry through his nose instead, and his mother looks away again.

The school doors have just opened for the day, and the children are arriving from every corner of the estate: out of the tower blocks with the spray-paint on the walls; past the empty houses with their windows all 'tinned up' against the thieves; down the road where the young woman was murdered; round the corner where the old Alsatian dog shouts; and into the playground. Just about nobody arrives by car. Outside the doors, it is chaos. A boy shows off the ear-stud he has been given for his birthday. A girl falls off the school wall and takes a cuff across the shoulder from her mother. Somewhere, a car alarm starts screaming. A mother in a dirty tracksuit shouts 'Stop it off now!' at the baby in her buggy. The boy loses his ear-stud and starts to scream. Two small boys and a girl scavenge among the rubbish that the wind has collected. Then the parents start to drift away, the school doors close, and something rather strange begins to happen.

This primary school survives in a state of siege. It sits in the centre of an estate that has been ravaged by hardship. It happens to be in a city in the north of England, but it might as well stand in any of the 'sink estates' which now cling to the ring roads of towns and cities across the country. The poverty invades the school. You can see it in the fabric of the building, which has bars on its windows and a spiked fence around its grounds: even so, joy-riders career around the playing fields at night and intruders routinely rob the place at weekends, leaving behind them a trail of broken windows, graffiti and syringes. It touches the physical wellbeing of the children, who sleep in damp houses and turn up wheezing; who wake up to find no food in the house and come to school crying with hunger – in such numbers that seven months ago, the school started laying on an emergency breakfast service for its pupils. But most of all, it touches their personalities as they grow up in families that have collapsed under the weight of their hardship.

And yet, the school fights back. Within five minutes of the doors closing, some two hundred children are sitting cross-legged in lines on the floor of the main hall, and the teacher says, 'Good morning, everybody'. They chime back, 'Good morning, everybody', and she starts to tell them a story. They go all quiet and serious as she explains that this is a story about a girl who could not see and could not hear, and her name was Helen Keller. She tells them how this girl grew up angry and tried to damage everything and everyone around her, kicking and fighting and scratching.

'We sometimes say to you that your behaviour is bad, but no one here behaves as badly as Helen. Because she was frustrated. She used to have the most incredible paddies.'

Looking at the children now, you can see only the tiniest hints of their lives outside. A couple of them are heaving with fatigue. Others have shabby clothes and broken shoes and there is something oddly adult about some of them: the eleven-year-old girl with her tight black miniskirt and her T-shirt that says she's '100% babe'; the little boys with men's faces. But for the most part, as they sit here now with their thumbs in their mouths, listening to their story, their poverty is invisible and they seem immune to trouble.

Still, they understand how Helen Keller felt. There is a six-year-old boy here who is quite bright but who cannot handle anything going wrong and suddenly throws terrible tantrums in class and says he wants to kill himself. As far as the teachers can tell, the problem is that his mother is working as a prostitute and parks him with friends while she goes out on the street or, worse, brings men home while he is in the house. There is another boy, slightly older, who mutilates himself, digging into his arms with any tool he can find, acting out some unnamed horror at home. Sometimes the clues to the damage are obvious, like the children who have been acting out hardcore pornography in the playground, copying videos they have seen at home; or the eight-year-old who decided to settle some score with another pupil by bringing a six-inch knife to school. Sometimes, the clues are harder to see: the boy who was suddenly sullen because, in the background, his elder brother had been jailed for five years; the strange excitement between unrelated children after the holidays when, it turned out, they were involved in some kind of sexual abuse between their two families. On another occasion, there was an outbreak of friction in the playground between an eleven-year-old boy and some other children and, when the teachers investigated, they discovered that the boy's father had fallen out with another family in his street and persuaded his son to set fire to their house by stuffing a flaming rag through their letter box. The next day, the boy was at school, along with the children whose house he had burned, who knew very well that he was responsible.

There are times when the teachers can help. There is a girl in the hall now who is swollen with fat, something that happened over the last year without any explanation until the school discovered that her mother could not afford to pay for any fuel at home and was reduced to feeding her daughter on nothing but chips from the fish shop on the estate. And there are times when help seems futile. Last week a mother came in to tell a teacher about her attempt at suicide. The teacher found an excuse to send her three children out of the room, so that they would not have to hear the story. But then the teacher realised that that was pointless. The children had been there, like ringside spectators, when their mother had tried to kill herself. They had already seen it all and heard it all and taken it all in.

But right now, the children are not thinking of their problems. The teacher is telling them how a governess broke into Helen

Keller's world of darkness by offering her kindness, how she persuaded the girl to stop throwing tantrums and to start to learn, and when the teacher asks how anyone could teach a blind child how to read, dozens of them shoot their hands in the air, using their spare hand to push their elbow even higher in hopes of being noticed.

There are children here who will survive, perhaps because their families have managed to resist the stresses of life on the estate, perhaps because the school itself will offer them a way out. There are pupils from this school who have gone on to succeed. One is a policeman, another is a teacher, some have gone on to college after secondary school. But those are exceptions. The most famous graduate of this primary school is a boy who was tortured by his family life and became a notorious child-thief with dozens of arrests to his name before he even reached his twelfth birthday.

The school has seen new shoots broken off, like the little girl who was a natural gymnast but couldn't come and practise after school any more because she had to take over the care of her younger siblings; or the difficult boy who wanted to be a Cub Scout and was offered the chance by the school, who arranged to pay for his uniform and to recruit the Cub leader as an assistant at the school. It looked like a turning point in the boy's life, but then his father said he couldn't take him to Cubs, even one evening a week, because it did not fit in with his timetable. The teachers sometimes ask the children what they want to be when they grow up, and invariably they hear the same answer: 'Nothing.'

These children have no dreams. The nearest they have to role models are junk heroes from pulp fiction. In the nursery school the other day, they kitted out a four-year-old girl in a nurse's uniform and when they asked her what she was dressed as, she had no idea. She looked at her cape and took a guess. 'Batman?' The school is trying to teach them not only how to be adults but also how to be children. When they first arrive, many of them cannot play, simply because they have no toys at home and they have never been near adults who had the energy or interest to play with them.

The teacher has reached the end of her story now and told

them all how Helen learned to read and write and to escape from the troubles which had beset her.

'There is nobody here who has the problems that Helen had, yet how many times do we hear children saying, "I can't do it, it's too hard"? But there is nothing that you can't do.'

And when they wrinkle up their eyes and put their pudgy hands together and pray for the courage to keep on trying, they mean every word of it.

These seeds of hope are allowed to grow for about six hours and then the school has to uproot them and send the children home – home where a two-year-old sister fell out of an upstairs window the other week because no one was looking after her, where one of their fathers is suspected of murdering the young woman who died on the estate earlier this year, where many of them are left to fend for themselves while their parents deal with their own struggles.

It is not that the parents fail to love their children. When the school puts on a play at Christmas, the parents pack the hall and cheer with pride, but they have themselves grown up in chaos and despair. Many of them have no books for their children; and if the school tries to solve the problem by sending books home, they find some parents angry and confused because they never had books themselves and never learned to read.

At the end of the day, as the children start to trail away, kicking and fighting and scratching again, their head teacher sometimes remembers the time the Archbishop of Canterbury visited the school and watched all the children singing. Afterwards, he asked her about the children's eyes – why was it that the youngest ones had a sparkle when they sang, while the ten- and eleven-year-olds looked so dull and lifeless? And so she told him the truth.

'These children have no hope,' she said. 'They live in a state of despair.'

16

Joey had just been arrested yet again for yet another burglary. His solicitor had come to see him in the police station. Sitting down opposite him in the interview room with all the graffiti on the wall, he sighed and asked him straight, 'Joey, why do you do it?'

And Joey looked straight back and told him, 'Fook, I dunno. I gotta buy fags, drink. There's drugs and things. I gotta girl. It's money. You know . . .'

Joey shrugged, like any man with a weight on his mind. Joey was then eleven years old.

Soon afterwards, he became famous when he was locked away in a secure unit in the northeast of England where he was three years younger than any other inmate, so young that his incarceration required the personal authority of the secretary of state for health. As he was led away from court, he flashed one defiant finger at the press and then disappeared in a dust cloud of publicity. He was 'the Artful Dodger', 'Britain's most notorious young crook', 'Crime Baby', 'the Houdini Kid'. He made all the papers. So, too, did the eleven-year-old brother and sister in Reading, whose attempted arrest caused a riot at a wedding party; the six 'Little Caesars' from Northumbria who were blamed for 550 offences; the thirteen-year-old armed robber from Cheshire; the fourteen-year-old multiple rapist from south London. Soon their cases were being used as ammunition in a sustained assault which saw the home secretary, the Police Federation, the *Daily Express* and various chief constables campaigning to lock up more children, as though Joey's kind of problem was the kind that could be locked away.

Joey grew up in a maze of red-brick council houses which appear from the distance, even now, to be models of working-class contentment. Closer, they are dishevelled: tattered scraps of litter in the grass, gutters hanging loose, mongrels humping on the pavement, 'Fuck You' sprayed on a wall. Behind the doors, they are a glimpse into a Victorian ghetto: bare boards, bare bulbs, damp walls, carpets sticky with dirt, the rich stink of dogs, women with fags and saggy faces, and children everywhere – barefoot, sticky-nosed, hand-me-down packs of them. It reeks of poverty.

Joey grew up here with his father, *Gerry*, a Southern Irish labourer who has not worked regularly for many years; and his mother, *Maureen*, also Irish and barely literate, who was only eighteen when she married Gerry, fifteen years her senior. The neighbours remember Joey playing with his go-cart in the street, running around with his two smaller brothers, banging on the door to scrounge a fag for Gerry. He was crazy about football, though no one ever took him to a game. They say he was a nice kid. The neighbours remember him skiving off school, too, and thieving, but they don't remember it well. Almost everybody's kids skive off school, and a lot of them go thieving. Round the corner from Joey's house now, there is a family where all three sons are awaiting trial, though one of them, called Andy, who is fourteen, is on the run. On the same street, David, aged ten, has been arrested for burglary. Another boy has been caught putting sugar in petrol tanks, just for the hell of it; his father recently finished a sentence for manslaughter and he has been hanging around the family home, even though there is a court order which forbids him to go near the place. Kids steal. Adults steal, too. Sometimes they pocket the stuff that their kids steal for them. The pub round the corner from Joey's home was known for years as the Burglar's Arms, until the police closed it down.

Gerry says he's not too sure when Joey first broke the law. He thinks he stole some crisps for his dinner when he was four. But he might have been three. In Gerry's family, there has often been trouble with the law: petty thieving, handling, the occasional fight, a succession of brothers and uncles behind bars. His family are more like a clan, an endless network of cousins and uncles and old folk, who all stick together and live in each other's houses, looking after each other's children, taking part in each other's schemes. Gerry says that his boy stole because he wanted things and he couldn't pay for them. Everybody did it. Joey was just a little brighter than the others, a little braver.

There is something else, although Gerry does not mention it. Maureen had a boyfriend and when Joey was eight, she ran away from Gerry and the dingy council house and went to live with him in a van, taking Joey and his two small brothers with her. All through that summer they roamed from town to town, the five of them cramped into their travelling home. They had no fixed address and so they had trouble signing on. They were so short of money that they were beginning to starve, but the boyfriend came up with a solution. He told Joey to go out and thieve for them. By this time, Joey was well used to thieving. Like most of his friends, he had been pinching whatever he thought he could get away with and, like most of them, he had been arrested by the police. The first time was just after his seventh birthday, but the police could only tick him off and release him: he was still three years short of the legal age of criminal responsibility. Since then, he had been arrested a dozen times and released in the same way. Maureen's boyfriend said it would be easy. Joey would steal, and so they would eat. It wouldn't even matter if he was caught. The police would have to release him. But Joey didn't want to thieve for Maureen's boyfriend and he told him so. The boyfriend thumped him. So far as anyone knows, the boyfriend thumped him a lot to persuade him to steal and, eventually, Maureen decided it had to stop. So it was that early one August morning, Joey and his two brothers, then aged five and six, were found wandering alone around their old council housing estate. There was no sign of Maureen or her boyfriend. The three boys had been abandoned.

Gerry took them back and, a month later, without explanation, Maureen returned home. Social workers came to help, put the three boys on the Child Protection Register, went to court and got a three-year supervision order which gave them the power to run the family's erratic affairs. But it was too late. Joey was now thieving with a vengeance. He was being arrested routinely, sometimes three times in a week, almost always for burglary. The child who had once been happy with a go-cart and a football was now devoted to taking on the police and the courts. He didn't want fun. He wanted action. He didn't behave like a little boy, he behaved like a pro, paying his way in life by clambering through other people's windows. Everything around him, on the estate and in his family, had conspired to do this to him, to confuse him and abuse him, to shred his infant personality. Joey's childhood had been stolen from him.

And yet, in a way, it was still only a game. He would steal hundreds of pounds in cash and give it away – to his family, to his friends, to people he hoped would be his friends. When the police arrested him, they had to lift him up on a desk to search him. He was always honest with them, admitted everything he had done and then he walked straight out and did it again. He abandoned school. By the time he was ten, thieving was the only game he knew; he had thirty-five arrests behind him, and the social workers decided he had to be locked up. They had tried taking him into care, but he had simply walked out of the homes where they put him and so he was sent for the first time to the secure unit.

He liked it there. It wasn't like a prison; there were no peaked caps or truncheons. It was more like a school with extra keys. Tucked away in there, far away from the mean crescents of the housing estate, he was a child again. He played with Lego. He ran around in a football strip. He practised joined-up writing. He woke up feeling ill in the night and cried on the principal's shoulder. He behaved so well that the Social Services Department no longer had any legal excuse to hold him there and, after three months, they were forced to put him back in a residential home. Within days, he had walked out and started burgling his way through life again, buying a television, a hi-fi and a computer for his bedroom at home. The police kept arresting him, but they had no legal power to hold him. Joey was now bored by appearing in court. He'd sit beneath the beak, swinging his legs off the edge of the chair and muttering to his lawyer, 'Fook, do we have to go through all this?' Once, when his impatience got the better of him, he escaped from a police station by squeezing his tiny frame through the feeding slit in the cell door, wriggling through the iron bars at the end of the corridor and disappearing into the night. Another time he escaped from the police in Rotherham by slipping his tiny hands through the cuffs. He was just too small for the law.

In and out of the secure unit, in and out of residential homes, in and out of cells, he was now running rings around the law. He was burgling houses and pubs in broad daylight, often in handfuls. In one typical afternoon, he burgled three pubs in two hours, escaping with £805 of cash and valuables. The only thing that ever put him off was dogs. Sometimes, he worked with other kids. One of them was his cousin, also aged eleven. He took to stealing cars and, with two other boys, he crashed one right outside the home of the director of Social Services. Every so often, the police would catch him; he would confess; they would take him to court, where a magistrate would look at him solemnly and send him back to a residential home; then he would abscond and start burgling again. Twice he absconded after less than an hour in the home. Once, he absconded before he even got there – simply listened to the magistrate's speech, turned on his heel, ducked out of the court, down the steps and off into the streets. But it was no longer a game.

Sometimes, as he ran from the children's home, the social workers could see adults waiting for him in a car. They drove him off and used him. They stuck him through fan lights and toilet windows. They took him into pubs and let him sneak upstairs while they drank. He did whatever they said. In the living quarters above one pub, he came across a dog that he said was as big as a donkey, but he steeled himself and crept over it to do his job. The adults let him take the risks and then they kept the money. They drove him all over the country: to Skegness and Boston in Lincolnshire; to Poole in Dorset; to York and Wakefield and Rotherham and Selby. Once, the police found him in Pontefract. He admitted burgling five places that afternoon, but he had none of the jewellery and cash left on him. The adults who had used him had taken it and driven away, abandoning him again.

Now, he no longer ran home to his mum and dad. He stayed in the red-light area, among the hookers and the pimps and the hooded young black guys selling wraps of crack cocaine on the corner of the street. Here, he sold his stolen gear – he once sold £4,000 worth of jewellery for £50 to a man on the pavement outside a pub – and he bought himself safe haven. He paid £500 in cash for a sofa for the night. He could afford it. He was taken in by a prostitute. She had peroxide blond hair and she was eighteen, though she made herself look much younger because the men in the cars preferred her that way. Once, when Joey was arrested, when he had just turned eleven, he admitted with his usual frankness that he had just stolen £1,000 from a pub, and when the detectives asked him what had happened to the money, he told them that he had spent it all already – £500 on drugs and £500 on a blow job from the prostitute he lived with. The detectives looked at Joey. He had always been small. Even now at the age of eleven, he was barely four foot tall. He was obviously not sexually mature. They guessed he must be making it up about the prostitute. But with Joey, you never could tell. It looked as though he might be telling the truth about the drugs. He was pale, thin, he had black rings under his eyes. A couple of weeks later, an eleven-year-old boy who matched Joey's description was admitted to hospital suffering from a heroin over-dose. He recovered and ran away before the social workers could get to him.

Joey went back to the secure unit. It was his third visit and this time, the staff saw that he no longer relaxed and became a child again. He wasn't interested in Lego or anything that smacked of childhood. All he wanted to do was to play the part of the pro-fessional thief. He boasted to the older boys about his many burglaries. They ignored him, so he sneered at them because they had been given longer sentences for stealing far less than he had got away with. He wrote letters to his old partners in crime, some of them children. 'Come and get me over the wall,' he told one of them. 'Then we can screw some more pubs.' He wrote about sex he'd like to have with men and women and about various people he thought should be bumped off. He left the letters lying around where the staff could read them, as if he were punishing them for their care. The English teacher tried to get him to write a story. She showed him a picture of a crowd at a football match and asked him to imagine what happened next. He told her that he would pick money out of everybody's pocket and then run away with his mum so that they could spend all the money together.

She showed him a picture of a rock concert, and he came out with exactly the same story.

The outside world kept creeping in. After his first visit from his mother, Maureen, the staff discovered that Joey had acquired a lighter and some cigarettes. When she next visited, the staff took her aside and asked her about it. She said it must have been her seven-year-old son who was to blame. She was sure he was smoking, and he had probably passed something to Joey. During this second visit, the staff watched discreetly and they saw Maureen pass a lighter and more cigarettes to her seven-year-old son and send him off to the toilets with Joey. When the visit ended, staff found that the two young brothers had pinched several things from them and stuffed them into their pockets. Maureen appeared unconcerned.

There was no cure for Joey's disease. The social workers could keep him locked up, but they knew that however hard they tried, this was bound to be bad for him. It would break the bonds with his family, stigmatise him, float him in a pool of older criminals. Anyway, the whole idea of jailing an eleven-year-old smelled barbaric. Alternatively, they could let him go – back to the streets of the city. But they knew better than to believe that that would offer him any chance at all. By nature, they knew, Joey was anxious to please. In the secure unit, he always conformed and obeyed the rules, just as outside, on the dog-turd council estate, he had conformed with everything around him, and been ruined by it.

17

He says you always know the houses where the big drug dealers live. It's easy. Look here. Look at this place now. See the main waste pipe, the one that runs down the side of the house from the first-floor toilet down into the drains. Look down at the bottom. It's missing – the last three or four feet have been cut off at the knee.

'That's the police. They go in through the front door. The dealers run upstairs and flush their stash down the toilet. The police get nothing. So now, they put someone round the side with a bloody great axe and when the front door comes off its hinges, the waste pipe loses its legs. They stick a bucket underneath and catch everything the dealers flush away.'

When a senior social worker looks at the streets of his inner-city manor, like this one in the north of England, he sees a world of trouble. Even more than a policeman, he knows its secrets – all its intimate vendettas and hidden pains and its tactics for survival. In this area, it means that as he drives slowly from street to littered street, he observes the signs of a savage wildness.

Here, now, for example, is the burnt-out shell of a council house with scorch marks still visible around the outside of the ground-floor windows and a couple of blackened beams still angling up into the sky like fingers from a grave. 'Someone's face didn't fit. In fact, it was a whole family whose faces didn't fit. And round here, they don't put up with you for long if they don't like the look of you. They'll put your windows through a couple of times to warn you, and then they'll really do you. They'll do one of these "total burglaries" where you come back to your house and find they've taken everything, even the plumbing. Or they'll burn you out.

'They do it to sex offenders, people like that. And grasses. There was a fire on some wasteland. Some kids started it, they were burning down some builder's shed because they didn't like what he was building, and they had a scanner, they heard the fire brigade being called and they found out who had called them. So they went round and called them grasses and burned them out to teach them a lesson. They'll do it to anyone they don't like. Black families can't survive in here.'

Here, now, is the off-licence where the owner has been attacked so often that he walks around with a knife in his hand. Here, a little further, is the zebra crossing where the Samaritan Boy likes to do his turn. He's about twelve years old and he specialises in falling down, crying a bit and pretending that he's in pain. As soon as a car stops and a driver gets out to help him, he's up and into the front of the car, grabbing whatever he can see – a jacket, a handbag, a bunch of cassette tapes if there's nothing else – and running into the block of flats across the road, where he disappears like a bat in a barn.

The senior social worker knows about victims. Here, for example, is a house with a brightly painted wooden handrail attached to its outer wall, alongside the path that leads to the front door. 'That's a terrible mistake to do that. It's like a neon light flashing outside the house, telling people that the person who lives there is elderly or disabled – so they get robbed. If these kids see anyone vulnerable, they go and rob them. A wheelchair ramp's just as bad.'

He knows, too, about the heroin, which used to belong only in the back streets of the red-light areas but has now established itself in every residential street on his patch. It is the mothers who like it best, he says, the young mothers. They don't want crack cocaine, with a rush in the brain that lasts no more than a couple of minutes; they want soft, warm, gentle heroin to take them in its arms and lull them to sleep. He knows a lot of young mothers who have started using it and a few who use their children to run and get it for them.

'There are a lot of kids round here who know all about drugs. You go to a house and knock on the door and the kids come and check you out through the letter box – not like a normal kid that's just being curious and having a laugh. They look through the letter box to see if you're a source of danger and then they go back and tell Mum. Then, if you're OK, she'll come and open the door. These kids know all the different names for different drugs – what they look like, how much they cost, where to buy them. They're bound to. They're growing up with this stuff all around them. You'll see them out on the streets on their own, as young as four or five years old, just roaming around, looking for trouble. If you come down here at night, they're still there, sniffing glue, setting fire to empty houses, just roaming around.

'We've got a few kids who have more or less left the parental home altogether and they're looking after themselves. Maybe not very well. There's a couple of fourteen-year-olds we're trying to find who've been reported just wandering around the place, stoned on something, and looking like skeletons because they're not getting enough food. God knows where they sleep. But there are houses where they know they'll be OK, where the adults have gone off and left the place or where there's some adult who, for some reason or another, doesn't mind the place being used by all comers. Some of these kids have been on the streets so long that being cared for would be totally alien to them.'

Most of all, the social worker knows about the abuse of children. Here, round the corner, in this street, with its tinned-up windows and its graffiti walls and the Rottweiler chained in the muddy front garden on the corner, he starts to point more or less randomly to the houses as he drives past. 'There's a family there – lots of physical abuse. Next door, same thing – physical and emotional abuse. Next door, physical and sexual abuse – very bad sexual abuse, parents were abused as children, take it for granted that they should abuse their own children. All of the children are currently with foster parents. Next door, empty. The house after that, there is a known Section One offender, we're looking at him, we're as sure as we can be that he's abusing the kids in there. Same problem all down the street. In this one street, I would say that we have dealt with child abuse of some sort or other in something like 70 per cent of the houses. And that's bad. But it's not the worst. It's not like that in every street, but it's not that unusual. Not any more. And when you talk about this kind of abuse, you're almost always also talking about neglect – at some level or another, often pretty serious.

'I mean, you can argue that we know more about abuse now than we used to, that it's more likely to be noticed and reported and recognised. And that's true. But the sheer scale of it now – physical, emotional, sexual abuse of children. It's terrifying.

'And we've been very cautious about making the link between the issues of abuse and poverty. I mean, you have to acknowledge that there is abuse in middle-class homes. But the reality is that there is a correlation between these very deprived homes where the structure of the family has collapsed and all routine has gone and all the barriers have gone – between all that and the abuse of children. There are families here who do a great job with their kids. Considering their circumstances, they should get a medal. But if we tell the truth – and we've been reluctant to – the truth is that if you want to find child abuse, you should come to a poor area in the inner city. We're talking about parents who are at the ends of their tethers – they take out their feelings on their children, and it is deeply damaging.'

He pushes on round another corner, past a garden piled with sodden mattresses, up another hill. An old man shuffles along the pavement, painfully slow, with a supermarket carrier bag hanging from the claw of his right hand. He stops to breathe and, from a garden path at his elbow, a middle-aged woman in a mac emerges, stops beside him, puts one hand gently on his shoulder blade, takes his carrier bag in her hand, slips her arm through his and helps him up the hill. There is human life. But it struggles to survive.

Here now is the home of a young woman who has escaped. She has got into Oxford University and she is soaring away into her future. But she has a younger brother, fourteen years old, who is already frantically delinquent, using a knife to rob elderly women on their way back from the post office. Brother and sister both suffered from the same surroundings. The difference appears to be that by the time the boy was born, their father had developed schizophrenia. As a result, he lost his work and, under the combined pressure of poverty and his illness, the family collapsed. The girl was already strong enough to survive. The boy was not.

In the next street is the home of a boy with a skill. 'He can act.

163

He can really do it. It's some God-given talent he has. He has had some decent roles in three or four big Shakespeare productions. So, you know, he ought to be a success. He has an interest and an ability. But he has no self-value because he is black and because his father happens to be a right bastard. In fact, the father has now left home, and there's this lad, who's nearly fifteen, and a lot of elder sisters. But the damage is done. He is screwed up. And the trouble is that, like most of the other lads round here, he has started committing some serious criminal offences. He's done some serious muggings. And right now, he is missing rehearsals because he has been remanded in custody. It's a classic story. He would get out if he could. But he can't.'

The senior social worker has watched families and children succumb to crime and confusion, seen the children taken into care, the adults into custody. And he has watched it get much worse. 'Twenty or thirty years ago, people were having children and they were leaving school and there was a good chance of them finding work and earning a living of some kind. Now, they know that they're not going to get a job, they know that from an early stage. One result is a lot of them just stop going to school. There are plenty of kids round here who have not been to school since they were ten or eleven. Why would they bother going to school? It's better for them to get out there and get involved in some crime. The other result is that families start falling apart. Twenty or thirty years ago, families tended to stick together because the youngsters could contribute something financially. Now the reverse is actually happening, at least with some of our clients. They feel that they are not part of the family because they are not contributing something towards it, so they don't belong to it, they feel guilty and unwanted and very often it's true. They're not wanted, because the adults can't afford to keep them. So the family breaks up.'

He halts the car outside a nondescript semidetached house with grimy white pebble dash on the upper half of its façade. 'Look at this,' he says. 'Look at that drainpipe. Down the side of the house, the main one. Look at it.'

The bottom ten feet of the pipe are encased in a welded iron cage. Axe-proof.

18

When *Tina Sampson* was three years old, her father walked out of their house in Bradford and all through the rest of her childhood, she never saw him again.

When she was four, her mother, who was still very young, met another man who moved in and became her stepfather. Her mother gave up her job in the matchstick factory where she had been working and began to have more children. By the time Tina Sampson was seven, her mother had given birth to four more daughters. Throughout these last four years, Tina's stepfather had been beating her. He said she was a cheeky little bitch and she needed to be taught a lesson. Sometimes her mother tried to defend her. Her stepfather would be pulling on one arm, trying to get hold of her to teach her a lesson, and her mother would be pulling on the other. Her stepfather usually won and gave her a good battering. Just before her eighth birthday, the social workers came and took her away.

For her first three years in care, Tina saw nothing of her mother. She noticed that other children had visitors, but, for reasons she could only guess at, she had none. Her four young half-sisters did not get taken into care. She knew they were still at home, with her mother. Instead of her own family, Tina now had foster parents, but they kept changing. She was bewildered. She would arrive in the home of one foster family, get used to the layout of the house and the way things worked and maybe start to get to know the mother and father, and then the social workers would say that there were other children who had to come here and she would be moved on to a new family. It meant she kept moving school, so each time it happened she'd lose her friends and she'd lose her way with her learning, too, so she started to get a bit backward. By the time she was ten, after three years in care, she had been through six different sets of foster parents.

When she was ten, Tina was placed finally with a foster family who were allowed to keep her. She began to settle down. It was very nice where they lived, not nearly so rough as the estate where she had started, and she had her own room and clean clothes. It was so nice that Tina was afraid she was becoming a bit snobby. While she was with this foster family, her mother started to visit her. She only came once or twice and Tina didn't find it very easy to talk to her, but she did her best.

When she was thirteen, the social workers told her that her mother was willing to have her back. They told her that she must choose: she could stay with the foster family where she had settled for the last three years; or she could return to her mother, who was now living on an estate in Leeds. She chose her mother.

'Wrong choice.'

Tina Sampson sits now in an empty room. There is no carpet on the floor, there are no curtains at the window, no wallpaper on the wall, no lampshade over the bare bulb burning above her head, no furniture apart from the broken old armchair on whose edge she is perched. She flicks the end of a cigarette and watches the ash float down to the dusty boards below as she looks back across her life.

'Going back to me mam were the wrong choice. On the day I got home, she laid on this big party, she invited all the neighbours, spent all her week's money on food. In the middle of it, she came up to me and she tried to put her arm around me and I wouldn't have it. I told her to leave me alone. It were like there was this wall between us.

'When I came back here, I just got scruffy. I went downhill. I suppose it's my fault for mixing with the wrong people. When I came back, I weren't close to me mam. We used to have arguments and I'd go right up against her. I'd say, "All right, hit me if you're gonna hit me."'

She trusted no one, neither adult nor child. Something had happened to her inside. She didn't care for herself. Why should she, when no one cared for her? She cared for nothing. She thought about dying, she thought about it a lot. She took an overdose of paracetamol, but the doctors pumped her stomach and brought her back to life. She did it twice more, only this time she did it just so she didn't have to go to school and, if no one had found her and she'd died, she didn't care. She started cutting herself, splitting the skin on the insides of her arms with a kitchen knife or a razor blade or a jag of broken glass or anything at all that would open her up so that she could see the pain coming out.

Now, in her bare-boarded room, she rolls back her left sleeve and twists the underside of her forearm into the light of the naked bulb that hangs down from the ceiling. There must be fifty scars there and she points them out, the ones that dug right down into the thin blue vein until the ambulance came, the ones that were only looking for attention.

When she was sixteen, like her mother before her, she gave birth to her first child, a son. 'Everything changed for me when I had kids. I had something to do. You know? It weren't just me on me own any more. I don't know if I loved the boy's father. It was half and half really. With me never having had a father when I was a kid, I were more into my boyfriends being one for me. He was twenty-three, this one, quite a bit older than me. But he never wanted to stay. He was always off behind the sheds with me mates, shagging. So that was that, really.'

Tina still had her baby, but, just like her own mother before her, she had been left on her own to look after it. It went badly. She couldn't cope. She loved the baby but he made her tired and angry and she couldn't seem to get things organised. She wanted a bit of a routine, but she was always running out of things and there were people in and out of the house, distracting her. The house was a mess, the whole estate was a mess. There was a gang of kids who broke in and used her house for glue-sniffing when she was out. There were drug dealers on the street corners. There were fights and feuds. One of the houses in the street got burned down. She couldn't sleep sometimes for the noise of people getting on each other's nerves.

In the end, it all got too much so she decided to ask her mother to look after the baby for her. He was still her baby, still her son, but she wasn't going to look after him every day. She'd visit him.

When Tina was seventeen, she gave birth to her second child, another son. This boy had a different father. But the same thing happened: he left, and Tina couldn't cope. Her mother took over this son as well. Over the next three years, Tina had three more children, all of them boys, all of them with different men. All the men said they would stay, but all of them left. With each child, Tina tried to be a mother, but the muddle inside her and the chaos around her always conspired against her and eventually, each time, she turned to her mother for help and handed over her boys. She guessed it wasn't the life she had dreamed of, the happy family life, but the one thing she was certain of was that it was better than letting them go into care, the way her mother had let her go.

Tina shuttled between her own flat and her mother's house, trying to stitch together a life. There was chaos all around her, a bombardment of crack, smack, crime and aggravation. Just about everyone she knew was in some kind of trouble. Her best friend had just had both her kids taken away from her by the social workers. She tried to shrug it all off. When a gang of kids from the estate burgled her flat and took everything – the cooker, the fridge, even the hot-water tank – she gave up trying to live alone and handed herself over to her mother as well. She moved in and did her best to take charge of the youngest, *Jason*, and waited for life to get better.

It didn't. Around Christmas time, it got a lot worse. Tina had been seeing a lad called *Donnie* who reckoned he was Jason's father. Tina always told him that he wasn't. She kept telling him that he'd been in prison when she fell pregnant, so it couldn't be him. Donnie wouldn't accept it. He got himself a lawyer to go to court to get custody of Jason and he kept coming round, winding her up, breaking the windows at the front of the house one night when he got angry, dumping a car he'd stolen in the back garden and setting fire to it so the whole house nearly went up in flames. Tina hated him. She told him she hated him. It didn't stop him coming round. But now he started playing little tricks on her, ordering taxis to her address, calling out the fire brigade and an ambulance to go round there, phoning up the police anonymously to tell them there were drugs in the house so that Tina had to deal with two CID men on her doorstep. Then he told the police she had stolen goods in there. Finally, one day, about a month before the custody case was due in court, he turned up outside the house in a taxi and insisted on having Jason for the day. Tina said he wasn't ready to go out. Donnie said there was no time to wait, his taxi was outside, so she handed over the baby and told Donnie to bring him back by three o'clock that afternoon. He didn't. That evening, she called the police. And just after midnight, some police officers turned up at the house.

'Where's my baby?' she said.

'You're not having your baby,' one of them said. 'You haven't been looking after him, you're not getting him back.'

They said Donnie had taken Jason to hospital to be treated for severe nappy rash. She tried to tell them that she was treating it already, with baby cream, and Donnie had taken the baby away before she'd had a chance to change his clothes. But they insisted that she couldn't have the baby. And then they told her that she couldn't have the other four boys either. They had come to take all of them away.

Tina started crying and screaming. The police came into the house. Tina's mother wasn't there to help. There was nothing she could do. At some point, somehow, Tina ended up on the pavement, still screaming and crying and telling them to leave her alone. It was half past one when she saw them carry the four older boys out of the house. She didn't know what to do. There was nothing she could do. She stood on the pavement and cried her eyes out. She could see her children in the back of the car as the police drove them away.

The next day, it was decided that her four oldest boys should be sent to a foster family while social workers decided whether they should be split up or kept together and where they should be placed for the future. Her life had come full circle; her own children had followed her steps into abandonment and isolation. And to add extra pain to her distress, it was decided that Jason should be handed over to Donnie's family.

So now she sits on the battered chair in the bare remains of her home. She is very thin with pinched cheeks and baggy blue Levi's. She is alone. Her mother has moved out permanently. She has no children any more. She does not even have any pictures of her children; she has never had a camera. She has nothing to do. There was a television once, but someone stole it at

Christmas. She wants her children. The other night, she was asleep on a mattress in the front room and she woke herself up because she was crying in her sleep. It was about half past four in the morning and there was no one around and, anyway, she knew by then that no one was interested in what she thought. So she took a biro and she went to the bare plaster wall of the chimney breast in her front room and wrote the names of her five boys. She wrote them again and again. Finally she wrote in square capital letters 'I LOVE MY KIDS' and then again 'I WANT MY KIDS' as if somebody might see it and do something for her.

But how? How can she get them back? There is only one way. She has to persuade the social workers that she is a fit and proper mother, that the chaos of life around her on this end-of-the-world estate will no longer invade her home, that all the damage that was inflicted on her own childhood is repaired now, never to emerge again in a fit of temper or a day of confusion or a bout of forgetful mothering. She has tried. She has dragged her few sticks of furniture and her scraps of tired carpet out into the garden and burned them to blackened ashes, in case anyone says they're too dirty to be near children. She wants to get drunk and cut her arm, but she is controlling herself in case anyone says that the cutting proves she's a bad mother. But the truth screams out of her surroundings, from the two burned-out cars and the charred bed frames in the mess of her back garden; from the two front windows on the ground floor which are still boarded up and broken since Donnie smashed them weeks ago; from the broken glass lying beneath them in the garden with a couple of twisted beer cans and an old towel; from the holes in her hall walls which go clean through the brickwork; from the three leaking pipes which have laid puddles on the bathroom floor; from the mould running up the front wall and the freezing night air in the bedrooms and the bare plaster and the bare boards. She is poor.

Across the other side of Leeds, in the offices of the Department of Social Services, senior officials consider her case. They say her children were neglected and, even though they reacted by removing the children from her, they do not believe that she is truly to blame. One of them says, 'Society reacts in a very odd way to cases of neglect. People prefer not to know about it. Sex abuse is different: they can blame someone. But with neglect they can't, because it is linked to poverty and changes in the benefit system and people do not want to admit that. It opens up too many questions.'

His department have just commissioned an outside agency to review all their cases of child abuse, including neglect. They found they were dealing with sixty allegations a week – children found with no parents and no one at all responsible for them; children abandoned or lost; children homeless or evicted; children beaten or raped or generally made miserable. The city's child protection unit handled 1,057 referrals in 1989. By 1993, they were handling 2,265 – more than twice as many. Some of that could be explained by saying that the city was trying harder to find such cases and to persuade people to report them. But they knew the real answer. Poverty and child abuse, they were like inseparable twins who went everywhere together.

The city's Social Services chairman, Michael Simmons, has watched the problems grow and multiply: 'We have seen a steady increase in poverty and a steady dismantling of the benefit system. The result is deprivation. And I am afraid that deprivation and neglect go hand in hand.

'People in these circumstances become depressed – clinically depressed. Their physical health suffers: they eat bad food and wear inadequate clothing. They all suffer stress – children as well as adults. We have a young boy now who is literally chewing the ends off his fingers, breaking the flesh, drawing blood. Their kids can't go to school because they can't afford school meals or proper clothing, and they don't have the know-how or the money or the energy to drag five children across Leeds to fill in complicated forms to get help. And now the schools have started turning them away. Since schools have been compiling league tables, there are head teachers in this city who are deliberately excluding children like this to avoid damaging their statistics. Some of these children just can't cope with school. There was one family who simply couldn't communicate. The children just cried all the time. Why? They were extremely unhappy. And who can blame them?

'It all flows from this extraordinary idea that we have to give rich people an incentive to work by giving them more money and poor people an incentive to work by taking money away from them. These people are not evil. If they're bad parents, it's not because they don't care about their children. It is because they cannot cope. We see cases like this every day of every week. You are talking about a fairly routine occurrence, but it is an area which most people are quite happy to ignore.'

Tina's life has been mapped out for her for years, almost since birth, when she was surrounded by poverty, certainly since she was seven, when the effect of poverty and stress broke up her own family and propelled her into care. Now her own children have followed her. The social workers call it a cycle of deprivation, each generation dragged down by the suffering of the last.

Tina will fight. The glue-sniffing kids will break into her house once more and accidentally burn it down, but she will get another flat and save £10 a fortnight from her £67 income support to buy wallpaper and make it look decent. Briefly the authorities will return Jason to her. Briefly, they will approve and say she is a mother after all and that she and her new boyfriend are fit to care for her child. And then one day, she will take him to the doctor's for a routine appointment, and someone will notice a red rash on his throat and they will say he must stay in hospital overnight for a check and then they will say that this is the mark of a strangling. Tina will protest and insist and swear that they're wrong. She will throw her boyfriend from the house and promise never to have another man around her, she will beg for her child. But they will shake their heads and say that they are sorry, but she cannot have any of her children – not Jason, not her four older boys, not even a future baby. If they ever hear that she is pregnant, they will move instantly to take the child into care as soon as it is born. Tina will return to her empty flat and take a sharpened blade once more to the inside of her arms.

She looks to the future and sees the past repeating itself. 'With my mam, I don't class her as my mam. I class her as a friend. I can't go up to her and give her a kiss, like some children can. I can't. I don't know. There's a brick wall between us. Because of me being in care and everything. And I can see mine – they are going to come back to me and say, "You didn't love us, you put us away, you must have hated us." I can see it. I think that's what I'm most scared of. That's why I want them home. I don't want them to think that I neglected them.'

19

The idea that poverty mangles the emotions of those who live with it is harder to grasp than the more familiar idea of poverty simply inflicting material hardship. The hardship is often immediately obvious in the clothes and homes of the poor, but, on closer examination, the emotional damage is equally clear. Apart from the fact that it comes screaming out of the stories of these people, it also turns out to be a familiar idea to a small army of academics and other experts.

During the 1980s, numerous studies traced the links between deprivation and emotional damage. Peter Townsend, in *Poverty in the United Kingdom*, found that deprivation caused stress; Ross and Huber, in a study of hardship and depression, found that low socioeconomic status caused 'fatalism', the feeling of powerlessness; Marmot, Shipley and Rose found that economic hardship reduced people's ability to fulfil their roles, whether as breadwinner or homemaker, and so caused depression; Marmot and Wheaton in separate studies found that the poor were less likely to have good friendships, thus stripping them of one of the most effective emotional defences against the effect of stress or depression.

Stress, depression, anxiety, sleeplessness – these are the true colours of the country of the poor, fluttering like flags declaring the rule of this secret tyranny. A school full of children in a state of despair, a full-time thief who is not yet twelve years old, streets full of abuse, a young mother whose children slip through her fingers like water – these are the subjects of this regime.

And the greatest single cause of this emotional damage is unemployment. Bartley, in 1994, found that people who were unemployed had lower levels of psychological wellbeing and were at higher risk of depression, poor self-esteem, neurotic disorders and disturbed sleep. This was partly the result of stigma and embarrassment, because of the attitude to unemployment in society as a whole; and partly the result of their feeling that they had no purpose, no structure to their daily life. They didn't belong anywhere or matter very much.

Debt is not far behind unemployment in the league table of causes of emotional damage. A National Children's Home survey of 347 families, *Deep in Debt*, found that 71 per cent of those who owed more money than they could afford were depressed, 50 per cent were unable to sleep, 40 per cent said they could not cope, 39 per cent were smoking more, 21 per cent felt that their relationship with their partner had suffered.

There is hopelessness here. It has a great deal to do with the feeling of being trapped. In 1993, when there were 3 million men and women officially registered as unemployed, a million of them had been out of work for a year. It was becoming a permanent feature of their life. It was not just that their own problem was a long-term one. When they looked around, many would see their friends and neighbours and relatives stuck in the same position. In July 1995, two researchers from the London School of Economics found that in the UK there were some 2,000 housing estates which had been overwhelmed by poverty. These are estates where up to 60 per cent of the adults have no work, where a third of the families with children are headed by only one adult, where nearly half of the residents are under twenty-four. Six months later, the Joseph Rowntree Foundation similarly identified 2,000 estates that were struggling under 'the statistics of despair'. It is this density of unemployment – as well as its apparent permanence – that does so much to suffocate hope among those who live with it.

There is anger, too. The Joseph Rowntree Foundation looked back at the way that wages had developed over the previous thirty years. They found that between 1966 and 1977 wages of all men in all social classes grew at about the same rate. From 1979, they started to diverge. Between 1979 and 1992, the highest wages grew by 50 per cent; those in the middle grew by 35 per cent. But the wages of the lowest paid hardly increased at all and, by

1992, they were lower in real terms than they had been in 1975. Those who were left at the bottom of the earnings scale, watching everyone else take off into affluence, could be forgiven for feeling that life was unfair, for feeling a deep and resentful anger.

By the mid-1990s, the United Nations discovered that while the average income in Britain was £11,096, the poorest fifth of the population were receiving only £2,548. This meant that they were marginally better off than the poorest fifth of the population in Hungary, emerging from the Soviet Union's ransacking of their economy and the chaos of post-Soviet capitalism. But the Hungarian poor did not have to live in the midst of a carnival of wealth and self-indulgence.

Some of them turn this anger on themselves. In the ten years after 1979, the suicide rate among young men aged between fifteen and nineteen shot up by 45 per cent. Richard Wilkinson, from the University of Sussex, explored the significance of inequality and noticed that suicide rates for young men aged between fifteen and twenty-four started to rise very rapidly from about 1983. He suggested that there were three reasons for this: during this period, young people had found it particularly hard to get jobs; those who had found work had seen their wages fall compared to those of adults; those who were left without work saw their benefits cut back almost every year.

Others turn their anger outwards, on the people and the objects around them. The National Child Development Study, which followed the lives of 17,000 people who were born in 1958, traced a clear link between poverty and 'deviant' behaviour, which they defined as 'disorders of emotion or conduct'. They were talking about deep damage. This went well beyond a loss of sleep or heavy smoking.

The Commission on Children and Violence, which was set up by the Gulbenkian Foundation after the murder of Jamie Bulger in Liverpool, talked about children's personalities being damaged by poverty, and they noted that murder rates were highest in countries with the highest economic inequality.

The damage moves in cycles as one distorted generation struggles and fails to protect the next from another wave of harm. A 1995 study by the Office of Population Censuses and Surveys found signs of disabling behaviour and psychiatric problems among children in the inner city. By the time they were three years old, 7 per cent of them were already said to be displaying moderate or severe behavioural problems. As the children grew older, more of them showed signs of these problems.

A study by Demos, published in September 1995, found that more than a third of young people aged between eighteen and thirty-four were alienated and derived a sense of pride from being outside the system and flouting its rules. They joined gangs, engaged in aimless rioting and stole cars to go joy-riding and, in general, 'have the capacity to ruin pretty much everyone's quality of life'.

There is a mass of evidence like this, diligently collected by expert researchers, all of it reinforcing the message that is implicit in the stories of the people who live in poverty. If adults are tired and angry and lonely and depressed, inevitably they will spill some of those feelings onto their children, in slaps and rebukes, in indifference and curses, and sometimes, it is clear, in outbreaks of real violence and abuse. Equally inevitably, these children will rapidly learn that they should not trust anyone or care for anyone or expect anyone to care for them. They will survive and that is all, and then they will have children of their own, and there is likely to be more damage.

But not all this damage is emotional. There is another kind of damage, equally insidious.

20

A t first, when she walks in to see Dr Dowson, her problem seems quite clear: she has two small boys who are as mad as monkeys. They slide and wrestle around the floor, they yell and scream, they drag anything loose off Dr Dowson's desk and start a tug-of-war with his stethoscope, while she sits with her shoulders slumped and says that she gets headaches and needs some tablets.

She is a big woman, morose and silent, but Tim Dowson has been doing this long enough to know that he has to dig, so he asks her where she lives – and out comes one long string of problems. She has been through five addresses in the last three months, starting with her own home, from which she was expelled by her husband's violence, and two flats on the kind of estate where the fire brigade won't visit without a police guard and where she was hounded out by neighbours. The council then said they couldn't help her, because it was her own fault she was homeless. So she and the boys went first to a women's refuge and then to a single room in a bed-and-breakfast hotel, where they have spent the last ten days with their belongings in bags and all of them on top of each other.

And what about her husband? Out comes another string of problems. He is still in the family home, but he is not the father of the boys. They are two other men, who do nothing to help. And her own family? She has a father, but she doesn't want to see him, because when she was a child, he forced himself on her. And it's not just the headaches. She admits she's been thumping the kids, and she weeps a lot, though she says she can't see why,

177

and the other day she did take a bit of an overdose. All this she confesses through a blizzard of sound from her children.

In theory, Dr Dowson is an 'outreach GP', one of half a dozen in the country whose job is to provide medical help for those who have no fixed address – all those who have been shoved through the holes in the tattered safety nets of the old welfare state. In effect, he is the last hope of the hopeless. A day in his roving surgery soon reveals how the constant emotional stress of living without hope can break out into physical illness.

He works out of all kinds of odd corners. This morning, he is sitting in the foyer of the Kirklees Housing Department in Huddersfield, with his black bags at his feet, while council officers wander by and receptionists tell visitors to take a seat. He sits with his patients in a quiet corner and if he needs to examine them, he can take them into the toilets.

Most of them arrive with a single complaint, but invariably he discovers that they are infested with clusters of problems, some emotional and some physical, all feeding off each other and collectively ruining the lives of their victims. With few exceptions, these are people who are vulnerable because they are poor, who have been pushed over the edge by some additional problem, and who then fall with alarming speed, because there is no longer anything there to stop them.

The first man who ever consulted him here came because he felt depressed. Dr Dowson noticed he was walking rather stiffly, took him to the toilet for an examination, where he discovered a red raw gash around his throat: the man had strung himself up from a tree two days earlier only to have the rope break. It turned out that he had been struggling along in Leeds and started to use a lot of speed. He had fallen out with his girlfriend and then had a bust-up with some dealers, from whom he had fled. He was now completely lost, emotionally and practically, with nowhere else to turn.

With some patients, it is the break-up of a relationship that pitches them downwards. Here is Alan, aged forty-seven, who left his wife seven years ago, lost his home and went to live in a caravan, where he became depressed and eventually subsided into a diet that consisted entirely of beer. By the time he saw Dr Dowson, he had developed problems with his lungs which sounded suspiciously like cancer. But he insists he is 'feeling better, just a bit tired, not sleeping too well'.

With others, a fragile life breaks apart in a sudden burst of tension as some underlying problem explodes. One family have been fire-bombed out of their home in north Kirklees, apparently because neighbours did not like the white mother being married to a black man. Another family have fled a rock-bottom estate, where their adult son has been systematically attacking them as well as hospitalising three other people in the street and taking his thirteen-year-old brother out thieving. They turn up in his surgery with headaches and asthma and chest pains and insomnia.

Almost all of them are on the reject list of the new welfare state. There is a steady trickle of homeless teenagers who are not allowed to claim benefit, who come in with chest complaints and ear infections. There is a 22-year-old man whose stepfather has thrown him out of the house. Sleeping rough, he could not get to work on time, and so he lost his job. He tried to sign on but he was told that he was classified 'voluntary jobless' and so his benefit was cut to £30 a fortnight – just over £2 a day. With no home, no job and next to no money, he started stealing to survive. He says he feels depressed.

There is a young woman with three children, suffering variously from earache, asthma and hyperactivity, who explains that she is homeless because she defaulted on her mortgage. She had gone to court to try and save the house and agreed to make regular weekly payments but every time she put the money aside, she found she had to borrow from it to pay for nappies and children's clothes. She was told that the bailiffs were coming. She offered to make smaller weekly payments, but the building society refused, and so she fled. Now she is waiting to hear whether the council will help her or whether they will rule that she is intentionally homeless. Dr Dowson fears she will fail their test.

There is a steady trickle of women with children fleeing violence or destitution, all of them at risk of being told that they can have no help because they have made themselves homeless. One of them has vicious asthma and, lugging three children and several bags around with her, it takes her a full ten minutes to gather the breath to talk to the doctor. When she does, she tells him a story of the most horrible symbolism – how she saw her sister on

Sunday and had a terrible asthma attack because she started to laugh, for the first time in ages, and she didn't have the breath to do it.

There are some cases where Tim Dowson can see the state's failure actively adding to the suffering of his patients. One of the women who came to him after fleeing a violent husband was stranded by the council with her three children in a tiny temporary flat while they waited to find somewhere more suitable. As the delay stretched on, she agreed to allow her five-year-old daughter to spend a weekend with her father, who then refused to bring her back. The woman went to a solicitor, who arranged an emergency court hearing, at which the judge heard all about the father's drunken aggression and all about his criminal record and nevertheless decided that since the mother was unable to offer stable and suitable accommodation, the little girl should stay with him.

Sometimes, he can manufacture some kind of assistance. For some of those whose social security has been stopped, he can try to write a sick note, so that they are entitled to sickness benefit. Similarly, for some of those who are deemed 'intentionally homeless', he can try to certify that they are particularly vulnerable on physical or mental grounds and smuggle them back on to the council's increasingly brief list of responsibilities. He can lever some patients back into the NHS, as he did with a man in his thirties who had become so depressed about the tattoos on his hands that he had started removing them with sandpaper because he thought they were preventing him finding work. The health service refused him an operation, but Dr Dowson was able to prise him on to a surgeon's list.

Sometimes there is nothing he can do. There was a woman of twenty-three who turned up complaining of inter-menstrual bleeding but who turned out, after gentle questioning, to have heard her mother being murdered in the next room when she was nine, as a result of which she was put into care, from which she emerged at the age of fifteen in a state of complete confusion. She moved in with a boyfriend, a decision which alienated her surviving family. She had two children, but then the boyfriend walked out, so she repeatedly tried to kill herself, as a result of which the boyfriend was given custody of the children. She was now effectively homeless and just before her visit to Dr Dowson, she had swallowed a bottle of paracetamol. He gave her an urgent referral to a psychologist, but she never turned up.

Or there are times when the only cure available is almost intolerable. There was a family who traipsed through his surgery with a familiar cluster of medical problems, whose real difficulty was that the father had gambled away his income, as a result of which they had failed to pay their mortgage and been evicted. The council ruled that they were intentionally homeless and not entitled to housing. The only way in which Dr Dowson and his health visitor could cram them back into the system was for the mother to plead 'nonacquiescence' in her husband's actions. That would qualify her and the children for a roof – but not the man. They could have a home, only if the family broke up.

For many, the doctor can offer nothing more than sympathy and tablets. He cannot cure their problems any more than a bucket can mend a leaky roof. Where once these people lived in a society that offered them national assistance and equality of opportunity, they must now rely on temazepam and fluoxetine and amitriptyline. Welfare by Prozac.

21

D isconnection is a thing of the past. Ask any electricity
company, and they'll tell you that in the new world of
privatised electricity, no one has to live in the dark and
cold any more. If someone has trouble with a bill, they can have
a pre-payment meter. Then they just pop down to the showroom,
buy a token, push it into the meter and there it is – fuel without
fear of debt.

Lucy and Natalie Godfrey were used to living by candlelight.
They had been doing it for more than two years. Lucy was five
and Natalie was only three and Natalie, in particular, was scared
of the dark, so they always slept with a candle in the room. Their
mother, Denise Godfrey, used to buy special safety candles in a
tin-foil holder, the ones that automatically put themselves out
when the wick burns down. It was the candle in the girls' bedroom
that started the fire at their home in Great Chesterford, Essex,
just before dawn one dark August night.

The girls were fast asleep. Denise and her boyfriend Granville
were asleep, too, in the next room. They were all tired. Denise
was seven months pregnant with twins and she had just come out
of hospital where she had been treated for a complication in the
pregnancy, and they had been decorating the third bedroom so
that they were all ready for the birth of the twins. No one knows
how the fire started. Maybe one of the girls turned and knocked
a blanket onto the candle. Maybe it was one of their dolls or a
book that fell off the bed. The fire moved very fast. By the time
Denise heard her children screaming, it had already swallowed
their bedding and filled the doorway with flames. She stood on

the landing, crying for help, rooted by fear to the spot, while Granville ran out to the neighbours.

Dave Bruce was one of those who came running. He lives twenty yards away, in the next street, and by sheer luck, he is a part-time firefighter. He reached the landing, saw the flames billowing out of the girls' room and knew that his only chance was to duck down to the floor, to try and get under the heat. Down on the boards, he could see both the girls lying on the floor, as if they had started to scramble out of their beds before the flames dragged them down. The fire was roaring over them. The one nearest to him was whimpering and moving slightly and he managed to crawl towards her and grab her. He pulled her towards the doorway, but his chest was now so full of smoke that he could no longer breathe and he had to fall back. His fingers were burned. Another neighbour, Pat Henry, was behind him.

Pat knew the family. His house backed onto theirs and he used to like to listen to the girls playing in the garden, fooling about on the swing. He had a little routine with them whenever he walked by their house; they would see him and both start shouting 'Yahoo, yahoo', and Pat would shout back, 'Yahoo to you, too.' He always said they were like two little dolls. Now he swallowed air, crawled into the doorway and dragged out the nearest girl. It was Lucy, the five-year-old. As he took her in his arms and carried her down the stairs, he could see she was ruined by burns.

By now, the fire brigade had arrived with two engines. Dave Curtis, the fire officer in charge, took one look at Lucy and shook his head. He was afraid she didn't have much chance. Then Dave Bruce and Pat Henry told him there was another child still inside and he sent in four men, all wearing breathing gear, working in two pairs, one to shoot an umbrella of water into the flames, one to go in under it and see what they could do. Outside, Dave Curtis and the neighbours waited. There was a series of muffled bangs: the tins of paint which Denise had bought for her new babies' room were exploding in the heat. A few minutes later, the four firefighters stumbled out. One of them was carrying Natalie across his arms. She was dead.

Denise had been taken into a neighbour's house and Dave Curtis had to go and find her to tell her about Natalie and that Lucy was in an ambulance on her way to Addenbrooke's Hospital in Cambridge. He did his best to break the news gently, but she was distraught, apparently unable to believe it was true. He arranged for her to be transferred to a maternity hospital, where she lay all day in a cocoon of sedatives. She awoke to discover that after twelve hours in intensive care, Lucy, too, had succumbed to her burns.

The firemen went back to the smouldering house and studied the ruin. They found the seat of the fire in the girls' room. They found the little tin candles in all the rooms. They found a smoke detector, brand new in its cellophane container, waiting for the decorating to be finished before it was put up. And, most important of all, they discovered that there was no electricity at all in the house. At first, the firefighter thought that the family had been disconnected. But the new world of privatised electricity is cleverer than that.

Officially – for all political and statistical purposes – Denise Godfrey was receiving a regular supply of fuel. In truth, however, her supply ran through one of the new pre-payment token meters and it supplied heat and light to her council house only if she was able to afford to buy tokens to feed it. Since she was separated from her husband and living on income support, it frequently happened that she could not afford them. In the old days, if she had been unable to pay for electricity, the company would have cut her off and would have shouldered whatever moral and political responsibility went with it. With the new system, Denise Godfrey cut herself off. For her family, the result was exactly the same, but for the electricity companies, it made all the difference between a guilty plea and a clean sheet.

Denise Godfrey had been struggling with Eastern Electricity for several years. She had cleared her debt by paying extra for her tokens but even then, Eastern Electricity had insisted that she must keep the meter and so, whenever the lights went out, she travelled four miles to Saffron Walden on the bus to buy new tokens. Three weeks before the fire, she called Eastern Electricity and told them the meter was broken. An engineer visited and said it was just that the token had run out. She says she was then billed £70 for the visit, though Eastern Electricity deny this. She had not bought a token for eight days before the fire.

No one knows how many of these 'hidden disconnections' are

taking place. They don't show up in statistics. But there are clues. When researchers at the University of Wales carried out an independent survey in 1995, they found that just over half (51 per cent) of those using pre-payment meters reported that from time to time they were forced to disconnect their own electricity supply. Many of these were families with young children.

Candles are not the only solution. Some try to find fuel by going to loan sharks. Some buy home-made 'black boxes' which are designed to bypass the meter and which frequently overheat and melt. Most end up in the dark. Many of those who spoke to the University of Wales said that they were compelled to choose between food and fuel. One pensioner said she was left with only £10 a week for food. Some took to their beds to stay warm. One couple reported that when their two children were cold in the early evening, the whole family climbed fully clothed into one bed in an attempt to warm themselves.

The simple problem of living with a meter spawns secondary problems. Some households can't understand the meter, call for help, are charged for it, cannot pay, are summonsed to court and then face court charges and fines as well as their unpaid bill. Those who try to bypass the meter risk starting a fire; some get caught stealing electricity, are prosecuted and are then presented with a new meter. The privatised electric companies have introduced a new policy of passing on to the consumer the cost of their own meter, with the result that even if they have no debts to repay, those who are on meters nevertheless have to pay more for each unit of electricity than those who are able to pay their bills at the end of each quarter. Once a meter has been installed, families find it almost impossible to persuade the electricity companies to return them to standard quarterly bills.

In Birmingham, the fire brigade have reported answering calls where people have lit fires in their flats even though they have no fireplaces. In the East Midlands, an electricity worker found a family who had systematically prised up the floorboards of their home and burned them for heat.

The privatised water companies have followed the same route. In 1995, the National Campaign for Water Justice reported that five thousand homes had been disconnected during the year but that thousands of others had been left without water after being given meters for which families could not afford to buy tokens. They reported that people had been begging water from neighbours and fetching it from public toilets. Some had run hosepipes into their neighbours' kitchens. The British Medical Association called for the disconnection of water supplies to be outlawed in order to prevent the spread of dysentery and hepatitis A. The then Social Security secretary, Peter Lilley, replied that those with no water were wasting money on 'bingo, smoking and doing the lottery'.

Out on the grass behind All Saints' Church in Great Chesterford, there was a mound of flowers, some of them knocked sideways by the wind and rain. In among them lay the souvenirs of two lost lives: two tiny china unicorns, a wooden butterfly painted with gay colours, a couple of toy hedgehogs, a little plastic goose, a bright-red wooden ladybird. At the head of the mound of flowers, there was a wooden cross, no more than twelve inches high, with a mother's locket hanging from its side and a gilt plaque bearing the words 'Lucy and Natalie Godfrey'.

In the year that Lucy and Natalie died, Eastern Electricity declared gross profits of £143 million.

22

Poverty kills. In 1991, three British academics reported that if the poorest half of the population of Britain were as healthy as the more prosperous half, there would be 42,000 fewer deaths each year. The effect of poverty on the health of Britain is the same as a plane crashing and killing 115 passengers every day of every year.

Poverty kills with subtlety and skill. This is not the clumsy tyranny of the Third World dictator, leaving his subjects in twisted pieces by the roadsides. This is clever.

Poverty will use the damaged emotions of its victims as a deadly weapon, driving them to suicide and to violence against each other. Poverty will inject its victims with stress and anxiety and take away their sleep and watch their hearts slowly succumb to the poison. It will feed damp through the walls of their homes, night after night, until eventually their lungs suffocate in their own liquid. The Royal Institution of Chartered Surveyors reported in 1995 that more than 2.5 million homes in Britain suffered from dampness.

Poverty will set up accidents – an easy thing to do in homes with no money to pay for fire guards or stair guards or safety rails or window bars, where the parents cannot afford a nanny or an au pair, where the only playground is the street with its company of cars, or where mothers are compelled to light their children's rooms with candles. In September 1996, the Institute of Child Health disclosed that poor children were five times more likely to die of poisoning than affluent children. The institute also found that they travelled in small cheap cars and so they were much more likely to be badly hurt in accidents; and they lived in substandard houses without smoke detectors and were much more vulnerable to fire. Between 1981 and 1991, death by fire among affluent children dropped by 28 per cent; among poor children, it rose by 39 per cent.

Poverty will go straight for the belly of its victims, leaving them with children who are shorter and lighter than their more affluent peers. The Policy Studies Institute in 1995 found that half the mothers in low-income families regularly went without food in order to provide for their children. Some had been reduced to living on toast and water when the money ran out at the end of the week. Action for Children suggested in 1994 that a woman on income support would not have the money to give her child the equivalent of the diet laid down in Victorian workhouses. Doctors suggested that the children of the poor were up to 13 centimetres shorter than the children of more prosperous families.

A member of a Department of Health team which was investigating the diet of the poor told the *Observer* in 1994, ' "Malnutrition" is an emotive word but, yes, given the levels of vital nutrients, vitamins and minerals that is found routinely in the diet of the poor, that is exactly what it is.'

Poverty has a sense of history in its choice of weapons. In the 1990s, it has seen the overcrowding of families crammed into tiny houses and watched the sleeping bodies stretched out around the pavements of the cities and it has reached back more than a hundred years to revive its most traditional tools – tuberculosis, rickets, scabies, scurvy, diphtheria. By 1993, doctors were seeing a resurgence of them all.

Poverty has seen the cracks in unattended water pipes and watched the families whose water has been cut off altogether and it has sprinkled dysentery among them. In five years, during the early 1990s, two things trebled: the number of households that had no water because they could not pay their bills; and the incidence of dysentery. It has seen the pipes of sewers unreplaced and unrepaired, and brought herds of rats out into the open, spilling their infections wherever they go. The Central Science Laboratories in June 1995 analysed a field study by environmental health officers covering 11,000 homes and found a 39 per cent increase in the number of homes infested by rats.

Poverty sneaks through the maternity wards. From the poor, it takes 700 babies each year – babies who are stillborn but would have survived if they had had the same chance of life as the babies of more prosperous families. If it misses them in the maternity ward, poverty stalks them in the home, taking 1,500 children during their first year of life – again, children who would have survived if they had had the same life expectancy as those in richer homes. Accidents, asthma, bronchitis. A child from an unskilled social class is twice as likely to die before the age of fifteen as a child with a professional father.

Poverty kills the poor whatever their age. Death for death, the British poor die at four times the rate of the affluent. During the 1980s, for the first time in fifty years, the falling rate of death among men all over Britain was reversed – but only in deprived areas. The country that once had been tenth in the Organisation for Economic Cooperation and Development's league table of life expectancy slipped and slipped again, until by 1994 it had fallen to seventeenth place.

In 1995, the Department of Health admitted that those born in social class five (manual workers) could expect to die seven years earlier than those born in social class one (professional workers).

When it was not killing, poverty inflicted illness on its subjects. In his final report as chief medical officer, Sir Donald Acheson wrote in 1990: 'The issue is quite clear in health terms, that there is a link, has been a link and, I suspect, will continue to be a link between deprivation and ill-health.'

In April 1995, the *British Medical Journal* said that if a chemical plant caused illness on the same scale as poverty in Britain, it would be closed down immediately.

Part IV

Dark Heart

We were cut off from the comprehension of our
surroundings. We glided past like phantoms, won-
dering and secretly appalled, as sane men would
be before an enthusiastic outbreak in a madhouse.
We could not understand because we were too far
and could not remember.

Joseph Conrad, *Heart of Darkness*, 1902

23

A lot of people are frightened of the *Jacksons*. Their reputation has spread all around the city. Even people who have nothing to do with crime or drugs or prostitution have heard that the Jacksons are to blame. There are three generations of them, going right back to *Dobber* and *EG Man*, the two brothers who came over from Jamaica in the early 1960s, through their numerous children and then their grandchildren who are now old enough to make an impact of their own. This sprawling clan of nephews and cousins, males and females, is credited by just about everyone who has heard of them with being the premier black crime family in the city. But there is more to their story than fear.

The Jacksons are, by all accounts, certainly not unique. In cities all across Britain, there are families who live with a similar notoriety. Those of them who are black serve to embody the worst fears of a suspicious white society about its black incomers. For some, their reputation is proof of a racial failure by black people to adapt to British society.

And yet, when the Jacksons speak, when they tell their whole story – not just the colourful crime, but the whole history from high hopes to violent death – they reveal a truth that is far more complex and important. The history of this single notorious family carries within it the story of the black ghettos of Britain. It suggests that the idea that young black people have embraced mugging and pimping and drugs as a way of life is not simply a racist cliché. It is also a clue to another layer of damage inflicted on those who live in the undiscovered country of the poor.

★

To understand the story of this community, you have first to understand its roots, which were sunk thirty or forty years earlier when the first Jamaicans made their way from the ports of Southampton and Liverpool to arrive in the Midlands of England with their battered luggage and their shining ambition.

It was during those days, in the mid-1950s, that people like *Benny* arrived. This was four or five years before Dobber Jackson and his brother EG Man made the journey. By the time the Jacksons arrived, the black community in Britain had already started to grow. Benny, however, was one of those who opened up the frontier.

Benny had no doubt about what was going to happen to him in the mother country. He was going to be a doctor. He was going to earn and save and send money home to Jamaica and then go home there himself and try to make his country a better place.

This was not just some hokum dream. Benny meant it. He'd been brought up a Christian and, like everyone else he knew in Jamaica, that meant the Bible on the Lord's Day and the strap on every other day of the week. When he was seven, his father, who was a farmer, had sent him to La Corva School in St Elizabeth and he had learned the meaning of respect. If he didn't respect the teacher, he got the strap. If he didn't respect a woman – like the time he tried to show off to his friends by carrying a Portuguese girl's books – he got the strap. If he was rude, if his khaki uniform trousers didn't have a crease down the middle, if he didn't make it out of bed by five in the morning and feed the cows and cut the firewood and trot along the gravel road to school by the time the bell rang, he got the strap. It was all that any Jamaican child knew.

Benny grew up a respectful and a fearful man: he respected God and the government and his family and the law and women and men and white people and, in particular English white people, and, truth to tell, he was too damn scared of another strapping to question his respect for anything that smacked of power and asked for obedience. England was a disappointment to him.

He could still remember how one day soon after he arrived, he had stood up on a bus to give a lady a seat and some people had laughed at him. He had run into trouble with the language, even though he had taken elocution lessons at Gaynsted High School where his father sent him when he was fifteen. He had trouble finding work – he was told he was overqualified or underqualified or too tall or just that the job had gone. England was supposed to be an industrial giant. He had grown up with this fact as something like the eleventh commandment. Something inside him began to crumble.

Benny soon understood what his real problem was. Pretty soon, he learned to carry a knife with him, in case some of those teddy boys attacked him. Pretty soon, he learned not to be seen in the street near a white woman. For the first couple of years, he was living in Birmingham, in a broken-down patch of the city which was beginning to fill up with Jamaicans. The white people who already lived there were angry with them, and Benny got caught up in a race riot in Walsall, and he broke his arm trying to fend off a flying chair. Pretty soon, he learned that it was going to be a long time before he became a doctor or obtained anything else that he really wanted in this white man's country.

He managed to get himself work at Aston Railway Station, shovelling ash for the old steam engines, but it was no good, he felt like a slave. He felt demeaned because he was an educated man and most of the educated men like himself from Jamaica were migrating to the United States and Canada and now he found himself working alongside the kind of people who would have worked for him if he had stayed at home. They had nothing to say to him, and the white people didn't have anything to say to him either. The work paid badly and it wore him out. He had no time to study and nowhere to learn. He began to feel dispirited and, curiously, he began to feel the lack of his mother's love. His parents had split up when he was small and, although his father had continued to be responsible for him, he had spent a lot of time with his grandmother, and his mother had become a stranger to him. He had found a way to live his life, to discipline himself before someone else did it for him, to find respect, but deep inside, he knew that his childhood had done him some wrong. Now he felt restless and unwanted and he threw in his job at the railway station and headed for another city, where he had heard that there might be a better chance.

He wanted to open a business, but he had no money and no premises and no chance of selling anything very much to white people nor of borrowing from their banks, so he did what he had seen a couple of Jamaican men in Birmingham do. He started a card school, organising endless rounds of poker in his room, laying on a little food and drink, taking 10 per cent of the stake for his trouble. It was illegal – he had no licence to gamble nor to sell alcohol – but that was what the customers were paying him for, to take the risk. He had always liked playing cards and, besides, it was the only way he could see to survive with his self-respect intact.

Benny ran the card school full time, and he did well, though he felt as if he was living in a different world. In the Jamaica that Benny had left, you didn't see people kissing in public or even holding hands. There was no pop music. On Sunday, the shops were shut and the churches were open and that was it. Life here was so different. Life here was wild and it was tough. No one was going to pay you respect here just because you worked hard and went to church on Sunday.

Benny and the others had tried to go down to the pubs and clubs in town, but the teddy boys had beaten them and finally even set fire to some of their own clubs to keep them away. So they had started their own places, unlicensed 'shebeens' where they could drink without being hassled, unlicensed 'blues' parties where they could drink and dance for a day and a night without any kind of trouble, unless the law burst in. They didn't want trouble with the police. In Jamaica, they could drink in licensed bars, the same as anyone else, but here they had no choice but to start their own, with or without the blessing of the law.

After a couple of years, Benny had saved enough money from his card school to open his own little nightclub, the Misfit, and he sincerely enjoyed the knowledge that it had once been the home of the Conservative Club. He did well, made money, gained a kind of respect at least among black people who came to the club. But he wasn't happy. He knew he had forsaken his ambition, though he tried not to think about it, and somehow he couldn't seem to settle down with a woman. Over the years, he kept changing partners, looking for something that wasn't there. Some of the young white girls who came into the club seemed to like him, and he liked them. He liked to fool around with them, maybe take them home.

Instead of becoming a doctor, he had come to enjoy gambling and took to betting his profits in other people's clubs, but he knew himself well enough to know that he wasn't doing it for the money. He was doing it to occupy his mind, to keep the bad feelings away. He knew it was no good: if he lost he had nothing; if he won, he gambled again, until he lost and ended up with nothing all the same. That was how he lived. As far as he could see, that was how more and more black men in this country lived now.

He looked at his brother Jamaicans and he felt sad to see their loss. He saw they had no money and no families and no respect from white people. He saw, too, that they had no respect for each other. He was a Jamaican man himself but he didn't trust Jamaican men any more. They had lost their self-respect and they would steal a couple of pounds off you as if it were a game. The Asians were different: they respected each other, they kept their culture, they worked hard and saved their money and they prospered.

Benny looked around him and he saw Jamaican men drinking too much, gambling, losing their religion, and pimping. That was a new thing. No one he knew ever did this pimping in Jamaica. They had more respect for a woman there, but here he saw them starting to pimp as if it was the only way to live. They had learned how to do it from white men. It was almost as though the British government wanted them to become pimps: they made them live in the poorest, roughest parts of the cities, where crime and prostitution had existed for years; they denied them decent work and then dangled in front of them the prospect of an easy, well-paid life by selling women. Soon enough, Jamaican men started copying the white guys who were already earning a living that way.

Benny could not understand why the white girls let themselves be treated this way. He saw them all coming to the shebeens, looking for black men, almost as if they were some kind of fashion item, and competing with each other to win a big man's favour. Jamaican men weren't used to any of this. At home, the women didn't run around after the men like this, looking after them and running and fetching and doing everything they wanted for them. The wives didn't do it, and the mothers didn't do it; half these men were like Benny, they had never known their mothers. But these little white girls couldn't do enough, and pretty soon the Jamaican men started to take advantage. Then there was no stopping them. The white girls might think they were in love but so far as these men were concerned, they'd got a woman in their hands and they were going to squeeze her like a lime. The men all had their explanations so they could swat away their conscience. They said it was just a way of surviving, like opening a card school. They said these women were all the same, they were all going to go with other men behind your back anyway, so you might as well get paid for it. They said these white girls liked to work, so they could prove they were worth loving. Benny knew that none of that made it right.

He watched it all. It made him feel ashamed and angry, but it made him wonder, too. He always had liked the young white girls. They seemed to like to hang around his club, to hang around him, as if they thought he was cool, cooler than the little white boys. He knew they had heard these stories about the sexual prowess of black men, and sometimes he liked to play the part they gave him. He thought it would be OK to go with them from time to time. And maybe it was true that they did want to work. And surely, if they were going to work, they were better off working in a club than standing on some street corner where every cop and vagrant could hassle them.

It wasn't so long before Benny was arrested and charged with living off immoral earnings and keeping a disorderly house in his club. He protested his innocence, he fought off most of the charges, but in the end it was no good. They found him guilty of running a disorderly house – a whorehouse, in plain language – and they sent him to jail.

So Benny's name was made. He never did become a doctor. He became a gambler and a pimp. He was ashamed. He never went home to Jamaica, never even visited the place, let alone returned there with his learning and his skill to help to improve his people's lives. And he never saw his father again. He couldn't. He couldn't bear to look him in the eyes and see the respect all gone.

★

This was the community in which the Jacksons settled. They came in ones and twos, first Dobber, who travelled alone in 1960; then his wife *Violet* and the oldest girl, *Carol*; then two of the boys, *Raggsie* and *Micky*; and finally the youngest girl, *Elizabeth*, and the sharpest of the boys, *Terence*.

Terence was thirteen when he and Elizabeth arrived in March 1966 to discover the world in which their family was beginning its new life. His head was full of dreams of becoming a lawyer. He reckoned he could make it. He had been doing well at the Barracks School in Spanish Town, sometimes top of the class, always taking pride in himself and his life. He deeply wanted to succeed. He had seen how hard life had been for his father, literally scraping a living out of the earth with his bare hands. Many years later, Terence still remembered how as a small boy he used to trot along behind Dobber in the early morning when he fetched his donkey and led it down to the river. There, he watched his father claw sand out of the tidelines and hump it into baskets on the donkey's back so that he could take it into town to try and sell it for an income. Other days, he watched Dobber earning what he could by mixing iced water with a little syrup and selling it on the pavements of Spanish Town. They had had barely enough to survive and it was even more difficult once Dobber and his mother had gone to England. For four years, Terence and Elizabeth lived with friends of his mother's while they waited for their turn to travel; their family was broken up, not because they failed to care for each other but because they could not afford to live together.

Terence and Elizabeth flew into Manchester Airport, clutching their bags and staring at the strange sights around them. As the car swept them away from the airport, Terence saw through the windows the smoke pouring out of the chimneys and, remembering all he had heard about the industrial might of the mother country, he guessed that all these buildings must be factories, row after row of them, with little gardens in back. It was cold. There was no light in the sky.

Everything in England was strange. There were two adults who were virtual strangers, whom Terence had to adopt as his parents. There was a house, which was nothing like the tenement yard in Spanish Town where he and Elizabeth had been sharing one room with two adults and another child, cooking on the landing outside. This new house had several bedrooms – his parents even had a room of their own. The house had its own toilet out in the back yard and a tub in the front room for bathing.

There was a school. It was huge. Each class was divided into streams. On the first day, the teachers asked Terence to read a passage out of a book. He knew he could read fine – and write and do maths and everything else – but the one thing he knew he couldn't do well was to speak English. It wasn't his language, he didn't have the vocabulary. At home in Spanish Town everybody spoke broken English. At home in England now it was the same. But he didn't like to cause trouble or draw attention to himself, so he did his best to read the passage out loud – and he ended up in Stream C. He knew he was good enough for a higher stream than that, but there it was. It was the same for all the Jamaican kids. They were all marked down as no-hopers.

The whole neighbourhood was completely different from Spanish Town. Most of all, it was the home of white people as well as Jamaicans. These were poor people, who worked in the old factories. Some of them had been born in the area, a lot of them had moved down from Scotland in search of work, and it was the Scots – particularly the Glaswegians – who ran the place. Their kids joined street gangs who went out thieving from houses and then they grew up and carried blades and went out thieving from banks and offices. When you walked to school, you had to be careful of the white kids.

This was not the mother country that Terence had been expecting, a land of power and wealth and beautiful manners and great, fine buildings. This was a place where people told you that you were a jungle bunny and made jokes about eating bananas – things he had never come across in Jamaica. As the months went by, Terence saw that the Jamaicans had made a life here that was very different to the life they had once led in Jamaica, and, after a while, he began to see his own family slip into it, too.

By the time Terence arrived, shebeens had become a regular feature of black communities in every city in England. Jamaicans had had enough of being hounded by teddy boys in the white clubs and pubs ('What time is it?' the white boys used to shout across the street, and then they'd answer their own question,

'Time the monkeys went back to the jungle.'). So they had opened
their own places, and even though it had never been part of the
plan, Dobber now opened one himself. Dobber had planned to
become a carpenter but he had soon discovered that the only jobs
he could get were doing the work that the white man didn't want.
He had become an unskilled labourer but then the work had
damaged his spine and he had been forced to quit. In search of
an income, he and Violet had started selling Jamaican meals from
the dining room of their home, serving up curried goat and
mutton stew and dumplings and rice and yams, and black people
came from all over the neighbourhood to eat at Dobber's Place
and spend a little money in the bookie's across the road. Often,
they stayed up all night, drinking and debating and playing cards,
until the sun came up and Dobber pushed them out on to the
pavement.

Terence watched them and he began to learn how life really
was in the mother country. These men were not like the Jamaicans
he had known at home. They were tired men who were doing
their best to find a laugh. They lived in poor housing in poor
neighbourhoods. Some of them had found work as bus conductors or labourers, but most of them had turned up too often at
factory gates where they had been told yet again that the vacancy
had just been filled, and slowly they had given up trying. They had
signed on for their national assistance and they had just got used
to the idea that this was as good as life got. All the promise of
the mother country had turned out to be a big con. But there
was no point going back to Jamaica: they couldn't afford it and,
anyway, there was nothing for them there. So they waited and, as
they waited, they drifted.

Some of them drifted into crime. It was small stuff – they
robbed electricity meters mostly or took to shoplifting – but the
police fell on them like thunder and made sure they saw the inside
of an English prison. Most of the men that Terence saw wanted
nothing like that, but that didn't stop the law from chasing them.

The pimping that had attracted Benny and some of his friends
had now become a way of life. The Glaswegian gangs who had
once controlled all the prostitutes in the area had lost their grip,
if only because they couldn't control events in the Jamaican
shebeens. Now Terence watched these men sitting in Dobber's

Place playing cards, maybe running out of money for a stake until some young white woman knocked on the door and emptied out her handbag so her man could carry on gambling. Terence saw some of these men with gold rings and flash cars, showing off wealth like a white man, all of them doing well out of their women. They seemed to have this power just because they had these women, as if they had come to own them just by going to bed with them. There were a few who had become notorious, like Brenton Bulford Barton, who was exposed by the *News of the World* and ended up getting nine years in jail; and Fabian Mendes who got busted for beating up some young girl with a poker and ended up dying in a car crash. But mostly, it was peaceful and it became accepted as a way of getting by in England.

A lot of the white girls used to hang around Dobber's Place. Violet seemed to like them. All Jamaican women liked to entertain and they would share their food with their neighbours at the drop of a spoon, but Violet held her home open for anyone. They could come round and, if they were friends, they could sit and eat and sleep all night. If she needed some money to pay the electricity bill or she wanted a little something to take down to the bingo, then she wouldn't be shy to ask her guests. And if these guests were white girls who were spending their time working on the pavement for the men who were eating in Dobber's Place, well, their money was just as good as anyone else's. Terence knew that people were starting to say that his family were pimping, but he didn't think of them as pimps, and they had never been in trouble with the law for pimping. With the Jacksons, it was the ganja that first brought the law into their homes.

Terence had grown up with ganja. It was a part of everyday life in Jamaica. It grew wild like a weed. They smoked it, they drank it, they took it for granted. So it was here. When Jamaicans gathered in their shebeens or at their blues parties, they smoked and it was natural enough that friends and relations would bring a little ganja with them when they came to England. Someone like Dobber, whose home was visited by so many people, was happy to sell a little to his friends.

Down the other end of the street, Dobber's brother was doing the same thing. He had been baptised *Mathew* Jackson, but he hadn't been called that since the day he was born, when the

Governor of Fiji happened to be visiting Jamaica and his father had decided to mark the day by nicknaming his new son Fiji Man. Pretty soon, that got a little bit twisted and Mathew was known for ever as EG Man. A few minutes' walk away from Dobber's place, EG Man ran his own shebeen, selling rice and peas and cans of Double Diamond while his guests danced and talked and smooched the night away, with the help of a little ganja to loosen their minds.

Like all the other shebeens, those that were run by the Jacksons were illegal. Dobber had no restaurant licence. EG Man had no licence to sell alcohol all night. Neither of them paid any tax. Their neighbours complained that their blues parties played music so loud that they could feel it thumping through the ground beneath their feet. And the police followed the smell of ganja like a fox tracking chicken – to Dobber's and EG Man's and to all the other black gathering places. There was plenty of ganja in town. It wasn't very hard to arrest people with it. Yet, time after time people were complaining that they had been planted with the stuff.

By the time the police had finished with Dobber and EG Man and their friends, the black people of the city had been more or less kicked out of the mother country. They might have hung on to the place physically, but for all social purposes, they had ceased to be part of the same community. In the eyes of their hosts, the police proved that these black men were nothing but idle, dishonest offenders. For their part, the Jamaican immigrants were taught to look on the white authorities with fear and resentment.

The trouble had started even before Terence arrived in England. EG Man and a friend had gone to Birmingham for the weekend and ended up being arrested for possession of cannabis. EG Man always claimed he had been planted and slapped around until he signed a statement. No one who counted believed him. Certainly, the court didn't, and he was sent to prison for three months. That was in 1963.

In August 1966, just a few months after Terence's arrival, Dobber too was busted and fined £100 for possession of cannabis. But it was early in 1967 that the real trouble started, the trouble that made big headlines, that meant that things were never quite the same for them again.

It was another one of those cases where there were two sides to the story. The way Terence heard it from EG Man, the police raided EG Man's house and planted some cannabis on him. EG Man didn't have the tiniest scrap of evidence to support his story and since everyone knew that he used ganja like a horse uses hay, it didn't seem to make much difference whether he was telling the truth or not. The court fined him. And that might have been the end of it if several of EG Man's closest friends hadn't come up with a similar story: they were busted and, as they were hauled away, they all complained that someone had set them up, either by tipping off the police that they had ganja in their house or by planting the ganja on them. Dobber found himself being busted along with the rest of them, in March 1968. He swore he had never seen the matchbox containing nine lumps of cannabis which the police said they had found in his front room. He was jailed for three years, though for some reason the police told him to appeal and, when he did, he had his sentence cut in half. Dobber never could understand that, unless the police felt sorry for him, being set up by his own brother.

And that was the truth. It was EG Man. He had been working for the police. Whatever the truth was about how the police had come to bust him in the first place, he admitted now that he had struck a little deal with them – that he would help them to arrest his friends and neighbours if they wouldn't go too hard on him in court. He said that was how come he'd got away with a fine instead of going back to jail for a second time. He hadn't wanted to be a grass, he had tried his best to avoid doing it, he had lied to the cops and run away from them and cheated them but in the end he had done this dirty job, right down to setting up his own brother. He claimed the police had told him that if he couldn't find evidence he should plant it. That was another one of those things which wasn't believed by anyone who counted.

After Dobber's trial, in the summer of 1969, when it all came out how EG Man had been working for the police, EG Man decided he had had enough of all this – of living under the threat of being busted for his ganja, of selling out his friends for the sake of a peaceful life – and since he couldn't go to the police and he didn't know where else to turn, he went off to London to look up some old friends to see if they could find him a handgun.

He made no secret of his plan: he wanted to take that gun back home and shoot the policemen who were giving him a hard time. But the friend he approached in London had a better idea.

He knew a journalist, a guy named Simon Regan, who worked for the *News of the World*. He could help EG Man destroy the policemen without breaking the law. He set up a meeting.

A few days later, Simon Regan travelled up and brought a tape recorder with him. EG Man told him his story – not only of the police who made deals with him but also of the trouble he had had as a black man in a white town. Regan gave EG Man the chance to prove the truth of what he said.

First, Regan set him up with three job interviews and then watched as EG Man approached each employer – a power station, a brick company and a factory that made cigarettes. On each occasion, Regan reported, there were vacancies when the Jamaican went into the building but they were filled by the time he showed his face in the personnel office. Together they worked out that EG Man had been turned away like this on some forty-two occasions.

Then they tackled the police. For three days in late June 1969, EG Man carried Regan's tape recorder with him. At the end of it, they had tapes which they claimed showed that EG Man had been setting up his friends with the active support of maverick police officers.

The tapes appeared to show that EG Man had called a police station and arranged to meet an officer; he had then discussed in some detail how to plant drugs on his friends *Hillie Brown* and *Spencer Chapman*. Then he had gone into a police station where a man had told him, 'Look in my drawer. You'll find two or three pieces.' A few moments later, EG Man had told this man, 'This will do. I can cut it up into dollar draws. Right? . . . I'm not going to make a mistake. I'm going to get up to him and put it 'pon him this evening. I'm going to keep a watch on him and I'm going to phone you. Right?'

According to Regan, EG Man had gone into this police station empty-handed and then emerged with four lumps of cannabis. A final tape appeared to show that EG Man later had telephoned the police station and spoken again to this man and told him he had planted cannabis in his friend Spencer's grocery shop.

That night, Regan and EG Man sat in a car in the street outside Spencer's shop and waited for the police to make their raid, thus providing the final proof that EG Man was telling the truth. But the police never came. EG Man said he could not understand it.

On Sunday 10 August 1969 the *News of the World* splashed their story under the headline 'Police Plot to Plant Drugs'. It caused a national furore. What had previously been a story told only on the grapevine of the black community was now a set of precise and detailed allegations in the biggest selling newspaper in the country. The home secretary appointed an officer from Manchester to investigate the tale. He listened to the tapes and gathered evidence not only from EG Man but also from his friends, who had similar stories to tell, and he reported to the home secretary that he believed that the *News of the World*'s story was true. Three officers were charged with conspiring to pervert the course of justice and, in the autumn of 1970, they went on trial.

Opening the case against them, Cyril Salmon QC told the jury of 'a saga of corruption'. The officers, he said, had 'bullied, coerced and intimidated' coloured immigrants to persuade them to give false evidence against their friends and neighbours. He told the jury that police had made unlawful gifts of cannabis, threatened to arrest and prosecute those who refused to become informants, and rewarded those who succumbed by turning a blind eye to their involvement in prostitution and illegal drinking and by promising to help them in court if they were charged.

The policemen fought back. Their lawyers appealed to the judge not to let the jury hear the tape recordings which Simon Regan and EG Man had made. The prosecution insisted that they must be played. They were the heart of the case against the policemen. They called an expert witness who testified that he could find no sign at all that anyone had tampered with the tapes. But the court had no proof that the tapes were genuine, nor that the voices on the tapes actually belonged to the police officers in the dock. The judge, Mr Justice Kilner Brown, considered the issue and then agreed. The tapes were ruled inadmissible. The jury should not be allowed to hear them.

Then they swore in a jury. The court followed the normal procedure, bringing in a panel of local people from whom twelve men and women would be chosen to sit in the jury box. All of them were white.

The trial began. One after another, EG Man's friends stepped into the witness box to tell their stories. They talked about times that the police had raided their homes and they claimed they had been threatened and planted and ordered to inform. Some claimed they had refused and been punished. Others claimed they had agreed and been given a licence to break the law.

EG Man himself went into the witness box and told the jury that the police had been leaning on him to become an informer ever since they had raided him in February 1967. He went on to describe how two officers had come to him one night, in January 1969, and told him to sign a statement saying that his friend Keith, known as P Sun, had sold him drugs. EG Man told the court that the officers wrote a statement and put it in front of him and then one of them held out a pen in one hand and a lump of cannabis in the other and asked him which one of them he wanted. Afraid that he would be planted, EG Man said, he had agreed to sign the statement. P Sun had been jailed for a year and at the end of the trial, EG Man said, a policeman had come up to him and slipped him a lump of cannabis and told him, 'Go home and have a smoke and forget about everything.' P Sun had written to EG Man from prison, threatening to kill him for the trouble he had caused.

Lawyers for the three policemen undermined the evidence; pushed the witnesses to provide detail, which was often vague and even contradictory; challenged them to admit that they smoked cannabis and showed that some of them were lying. A retired prosecuting solicitor said he had witnessed one of the police raids described in court and the account that had been given was not accurate.

Halfway through this procession of angry black people, the jury interrupted the trial. They sent a message to the judge asking whether they really needed to sit through any more unsupported allegations.

The prosecution were desperate to continue. There were another thirty-eight witnesses who had been listed to give evidence against the three policemen. In particular, there was a prostitute who was willing to swear that she had heard that EG Man was trying to get the police with the *News of the World* and she had tried to earn a favour with the police by going to them to warn them that EG Man and this reporter were waiting for them outside Spencer's grocery shop, waiting for the raid that would provide the final link in EG Man's story.

The judge agreed with the jury. There and then, the trial was abandoned. There was no reliable evidence on which to proceed. The judge praised the jury and told them that they had proved that the coloured community need have no fear of a British jury. The three policemen were freed. EG Man and his friends were discredited. The vice chairman of the police authority told the local newspaper, 'This is excellent. This is wonderful. It is regrettable that the force has been deprived of these officers for so long on the evidence of people who have never done a day's work since they came to this country.'

EG Man and his friends went home to their part of the city, not understanding what had happened, convinced that the only thing that mattered in the court or anywhere else in this mother country was the colour of their skin.

24

As Terence Jackson grew up, he watched his generation totter towards disaster.

They weren't like Dobber's generation, who had dabbled in crime without any great intent or success. The younger people were angrier, less respectful, willing to take more risks and to organise themselves. They had grown up without the solid certainties of life in Jamaica, rejected by the society around them, feeling insulted and disrespected. Now they advertised their hostility. They had had enough of being picked on in the street, so they clustered together in street gangs. They had had enough of waiting at the back of the queue for the work, so they went out and found their own ways to make a living, to earn themselves some respect, to have themselves some power. They weren't afraid to stand out on a street corner to sell their weed, to carry a knife for a pavement robbery, to break into houses and steal sound systems and televisions. It was as if they took it for granted that this country was going to attack them, so they attacked it first.

By the mid-1980s, Terence's older sister, Carol, who was then in her late thirties, had seen her life grow into a tangle of crime and confusion. She had been uprooted from Jamaica, a process which had seen her lose first her father, when he went off to England, and then all of her friends and the rest of her family when her mother took her off to join him. Then she had grown up in this makeshift world that the Jamaicans had patched together in England. Maybe it was because she somehow lost herself among all these changes. Maybe it was because she was pitched into this world of shebeens and pimps when she was only fourteen years old. Whatever the reason, the fact was that she started selling her body on the streets to earn herself some cash. By the time she was fifteen, she was pregnant. By the time she was twenty, she had given birth to five children. All of them had different fathers. All of them had left her. No one was even suprised. By then, everyone knew: that was what Jamaican men did.

For many years, Carol herself had left her children. She had tried to survive with them. She had worked in dead-end jobs, run organised rings of shoplifters, stealing top-of-the-range women's clothes; she had sold herself and robbed her punters. But she had been busted and so, in the early 1970s, when all her five children were small, she had tried to make a break. She had moved to London and got herself a job checking the books in the Lucky Seven Bingo Hall in Camberwell, but she had been earning only £70 a week. It cost her most of that just to hire a baby-sitter. She couldn't handle it. She couldn't cope. Originally, she had wanted to be a nurse. She had even set herself up to become a cadet at the hospital where Violet had started working as an orderly, but that was when she was still at school. Her first pregnancy had put an end to that. She had tried other work, working in the screw factory, minding a conveyor belt. None of it gave her the life she wanted.

And in London, struggling from her overcrowded flat to her underpaid job, her life had become hopeless. One day, she had gone back home, to Dobber and Violet's house, and asked Violet to look after the five kids for her – not just for the day but for ever, or at least for as long as it took Carol to find a life for herself. Her oldest, *Patrick*, was nine then, and the youngest, *Annette*, was only four. By the time she saw them again, eleven years had passed and they were drifting into trouble of their own.

Carol had never meant to break up her family. The truth was she had never meant to start one in the first place, but she had been young and pretty and she had had no idea at all about sex. Back home in Jamaica, people just didn't discuss a subject like that. Violet had never told her anything. When she started her periods, she had gone to Dobber, and he had given her some money each month to buy her necessities. It had been Dobber who had realised she must be pregnant when she stopped asking him for the monthly money. Carol had had no idea. The father was in his thirties, more than twice Carol's age. Dobber told him to bugger off or he'd call the police on him. After that, it just seemed to be one baby after another. The men didn't want her. They seemed to take some pride in leaving, as if they had done enough by taking her to bed, as if that was enough to prove they owned her.

Once she had lost her children, Carol wandered off, following one day into another. She ended up traipsing around Western Europe, dancing in nightclubs in Switzerland and Germany and Denmark, sitting at tables with white businessmen selling her smile. Occasionally she would send a little money home to her children, sometimes a photograph. Often she wondered about them – left without a father, just like she had been, and without a mother, just like her brothers and sisters had been when Violet had been forced to go off to England without them. When she finally came back to England, after eleven years in Europe, she fell in with a man who was trading in stolen cheque cards. The police came, the man fled, Carol ended up serving three years in prison. None of this was what she had planned.

By the mid-1980s, Terence's older brother, Raggsie, had drifted into a similar mess. Like all of his friends, he had left school with no exams. In Jamaica, he had done well and he had lived with discipline (he could remember being whipped just for having dirty fingernails) but here, he had been marked down because he couldn't speak English properly and he'd learned very soon that he wasn't wanted in this country, so he had walked out of school at the first opportunity, with next to nothing to show for it.

None of his friends wanted to work in useless jobs. There had to be something better to do. Raggsie did try. He got himself a job as a welder, but it damaged his eyes, and his mates were always hanging around. There were all these young black guys – 'rude boys' they called themselves – who had white girls working for them.

They had seen the older men do it. They had envied their lifestyle and, since they had just about no one else in their community to look up to, it was natural enough that they had followed in their footsteps. But the young men didn't waste too much time talking about love or worrying about whether this pimping was right or wrong. They competed for trade. All the working girls would go to the blues, all dressed up and vying for attention,

while the men tried to steal each other's women. Some of the
men wanted to be Tobins, the Jamaican equivalent of a white
woman's toy boy, and so they demanded to be pampered and
spoiled by the girls. Others had a kind of anger in them and talked
about how white people had made slaves of them and now it was
pay-back time and the little white bitches were going to do the
slaving. Often there were fights. A man would reckon he owned
some white girl, so when he saw her at a blues talking to another,
he'd come over raving, slapping her or cracking a bottle on her
head, or pulling a knife on the other man. Or one of the women
would do the same, throwing bottles at a treacherous pimp. But
in the end, the men usually won and they set about recruiting
extra girls to work for them, bullying and flirting until they got
their way. 'You won't have to work so hard if there's someone
else to bring in the money,' they'd say.

They started running strings of girls, they had big money, and
they drove flash new cars and splashed out on fine wine and fancy
clothes. Some of them branched out, like Raggsie's friend Jazzman
who not only earned himself a living off the back of his white
girlfriend, May, but also broke into music promotion, putting on
concerts and even television shows starring black musicians like
Curtis Mayfield. He bought a house in Kennington in south
London and was well on his way to a kind of success. As the rude
boys got richer, they used to go down to London to spend their
money. There was a black club near Paddington called the
People's, which was more or less carried by their crowd. And this
was a rich place, with crystal glass and fancy furniture.

Pretty soon, they branched out a little. Some of the women
used to rob their clients. The easiest way was just to slip a hand
into the punter's pocket while they were in the middle of sex.
Half of them were drunk. It was easy. Or else they'd take them
back to their room and let their boyfriend do the robbing, jumping
out with a baseball bat or sneaking downstairs to rob the punter's
car. The women used to take the stolen cheque cards out on
shopping sprees before the numbers were cancelled. They got so
good at it that the rude boys realised they could earn a little more
money by fencing stolen cheque books and credit cards. It became
a regular sideline – punting out the 'bread and cheese', the cheque
books and cards. They started to sell cannabis, too.

Some of the street gangs became big businesses. They called themselves posses and by 1985 just about every black housing estate in the country had one. Some of Terence's friends joined *the Fields Posse* which was run like a corporation. It had a board of four directors, each of whom had his own responsibilities: security and the recruitment of soldiers; procurement of weapons and cars; organising work; and the selling of proceeds. The main work was armed robbery. They planned their jobs carefully – wore plain overalls to cover their own clothes, concealed their faces, wore Afro wigs – and they always travelled in stolen cars for the job so that if they were stopped they could admit they had stolen a car but plead that the overalls and the guns in the boot must have been in there when they stole it. As soon as they had finished a job, they would take any gold or silver or traceable stuff to Birmingham where there were a couple of born-again Christians who would smelt it down for them. If the police tried to bust them at the gold smelter's, they'd just say they were having a religious meeting.

The Fields Posse got so strong that they were more or less licensing robberies around the city. Any rude boy who had some information for an armed robbery would take it to them. Maybe they'd give him a car and a gun and take a slice of his earnings. Maybe they'd tell him to lay off because it cut across something they were planning or just because they wanted it for themselves. A few white lads were allowed to work with them, but not as equals. The main men in the posse used to call them 'tampaxes' because they were white and they kept them on a string.

Raggsie Jackson was soon pulled along by the tide of crime. Within two years of leaving school, he was in borstal. He had chucked in his work as a welder and gone off doing little burglaries with his mates. He wasn't too sure that he wanted to do it and, in the beginning, all he did was to play watch-out and shout the alarm if he saw anyone coming.

When he came out of borstal, he tried again to find work. Briefly, he worked in a café and dreamed of owning his own, but soon he was back running around with his mates and this time Raggsie wasn't any watch-out man. He was as busy as any of them, dressing up like an insurance man to knock on the doors of likely houses, smashing the glass to get in if there was no reply, running through the rooms looking for electrical gear and jewellery. By the time he emerged from his second spell in borstal, he was more or less devoted to crime. So he drifted into pimping along with the others.

It was easy. He met a sixteen-year-old white girl called *Marion*, who was working as a window dresser in Richards. She came from a strict Irish Catholic family. She was fed up with being told to be in church every Sunday and to be home at ten every night, and she was ready to rebel. She also loved Raggsie to the bone. She became pregnant, her parents made it very clear that they didn't like Raggsie – he guessed it was his skin that upset them, but he didn't know – and Marion's father insisted that she get rid of the baby. She did as she was told. Then she left home, moved into a tiny flat, lost her job – it never paid much anyway – and, simply for the money, simply because by this time she was hanging around with Raggsie and his friends and she saw other white girls doing it, she decided to go out on the pavement. Raggsie took the money and started looking for other girls who might like to work for him as well. Pretty soon, he was a big pimp with three or four children scattered behind him.

In the meantime, Terence saw his own life drift into a backwater. Ever since he had been a child in Spanish Town, he had dreamed of becoming a lawyer. All through the 1970s, he had clung like a baby at the breast to this vision, but he could no longer see how it was going to happen.

By the time he was sixteen, he had had enough of school and he had escaped it in the only way he could, by going out to look for work. He had found it first in a series of no-hope jobs, just like Carol and Raggsie. Terence wasn't stupid. He had read his history as well as his Bible, and he knew that two hundred years earlier, his ancestors had been compelled to do the most menial jobs and now, he knew, he was still doing the same thing. He was in the bottom stream again, earning the least, looking forward to the worst. He went in and out of the army, in and out of the Job Centre. But, for some reason, he refused to follow his generation into crime.

He would always remember the riots in 1981, how he had been standing on the street outside his back garden when the first bottle flew through the first window, and he had run straight up a wooden ramp that was resting on his garden wall and hidden down there until it was all over. His whole life was like that – hiding from this crime and craziness going on around him. Maybe he was just scared of getting into trouble. Maybe it was because he still clung to the self-respect that Carol and Raggsie were losing. But he was stuck. He could dream all he liked about becoming a lawyer. The reality was that he was living in a ghetto, where he was far more likely to become a pimp. Then, in the early 1980s, he found the strength to take one step further away from crime, to repair the damage that had been done to him by school. He signed up to go to college to learn law.

Now Terence could see a future for himself. If he could become a lawyer, he could live a decent life himself but, more than that, he would have skills to bring home to his own community, just like Dobber's generation had hoped to take their skills home to Jamaica. This was the time of Rastafarianism, and Terence could see how this faith was bringing a new unity to his divided community. Instead of distrusting each other, people were beginning to greet each other in the street, realising that they had something which gave them a direction, which did not depend on white people. Terence felt this was a turning point, not only for him but for the whole community. He began to feel hope. Maybe Carol and Raggsie and the others who had fallen into trouble would find a new way forward. Maybe this whole community would rediscover its respect for itself. Maybe, after twenty years of being lost in this country, they were about to find themselves.

Terence turned out to be wrong. He had no way of knowing it at the time. He had no idea of what was coming. Back then, he had never heard of crack cocaine.

It's hard to be sure but, almost certainly, Raggsie Jackson was the first black man in the whole city to become addicted to crack.

Raggsie first came across it with a white man, an old hippy type of guy who was known as Cool Dick. This was in the late 1980s, when a few people had heard of 'freebasing' cocaine, but no one called it crack.

Cool Dick used to sit in his place, with coke all over the table, sniffing it like Al Pacino in some Hollywood nightmare, and he showed Raggsie how to take the powder and mix it up with baking soda; how to boil it in a pan until the cocaine sank into this heavy scum at the bottom of the pan; how to let it cool and how to pour off the loose liquid and scrape off the crystalline rocks of hardened cocaine that remained. It was stronger than cocaine powder because all sorts of impurities had been boiled off. And the hit it gave you was instant, because you could smoke it instead of snorting it up your nose. Cool Dick explained that this was not like any other hit Raggsie had ever had before. It was a rush in your brain, a feeling like your brain was flaring for half a minute, it was like an orgasm in your mind, but it only lasted half a minute, then it left you feeling drowsy and drained for half an hour or so and then you went looking for more. That was freebased cocaine. That was crack. Raggsie listened with interest but took none of it. He was happy smoking weed.

One day, Cool Dick asked Raggsie if he could get rid of some of this stuff for him. By now Raggsie was earning a steady living off prostitution. He had half a dozen women working for him and he was also earning well from a sound system called the Comet, which Dobber and Violet had started years ago with two little speakers and a 50-watt amp in Dobber's Place. Now, it was one of the biggest black sound systems in the country and Raggsie could travel around with it from one black club to another, playing beautiful music and smoking weed. He didn't need to earn any extra money running Cool Dick's drugs around for him. But, it looked easy and he was sure he would find something to spend the money on, so he agreed. He drove over to Leeds with a load of rocks, sold them to friends there and pocketed the profit. His friends seemed to like them, so a few weeks later, he did the same thing again. They still seemed to like them, so he wondered what this stuff was like.

They said, 'You wanna try?'

He said, 'Why not?'

That was how he became a crackhead. His life was never the same again.

He started smoking every day and he let his friends in on the adventure – his girlfriend Marion who was still working on the pavement to pay her way, and his mate *Sticks* who had been pimping his white girlfriend *Miss Pet* for years.

The four of them soon fell into a steady routine. Marion and

Miss Pet would go off to work in a sauna; Raggsie and Sticks would lie at home and wait for them to come back; as soon as the two women showed up, they would grab their money and go out and get some coke and 'wash' it into rocks; then they'd all smoke until the rocks ran out, and then Marion and Miss Pet would go back to the sauna to raise the money for some more. Slowly, their lives mashed up.

No matter how hard Marion and Miss Pet might work, they could never find enough cash. Raggsie and Sticks started selling their possessions – the television, a chair here, a bed there. Even the television set that Raggsie had bought for his little daughter ended up in a second-hand shop. Still, they ran out of money. They had such a greed for the little rocks that they couldn't bear to lie at home waiting for the women to come back with the money, so they would set off for the sauna and interrupt the two women to take whatever they had earned and start smoking it as soon as they could convert it in to rocks.

Then Sticks and Miss Pet found a way to solve their problem. They got into selling heroin. Raggsie wanted nothing to do with it. He wouldn't touch that stuff. Pretty soon, Sticks and Miss Pet started selling crack too, and Raggsie became one of their customers. They were still friends, but Sticks and Miss Pet wanted their money – they had their own habit to feed. Raggsie started falling into debt to them. He ended up giving them his stereo system from home to try to pay off what he owed. Still he didn't have enough cash, still he didn't have enough crack.

Now, Sticks and Miss Pet started squeezing Raggsie for money. He and Marion had to start knocking out stolen credit cards for them. Any bits of gold they had, any money at all that Marion earned – it all went straight to their former friends.

Pretty soon, crack started to spread through the ghetto like an infection. Terence Jackson saw it happening. By now, he was further and further down his path out of this place. He had passed his exams, O levels and A levels, and he had found himself his first job, as a legal clerk in a criminal-law firm in the city centre. He was a proud man. His dream was coming true. He walked down the street with a spring in his step, believing that he was beating the ghetto, dreaming of how one day he would use his power and his skill to help this place. But all around him he could see the community was stumbling into disaster, led by the scent of crack cocaine.

Terence thought it was almost as though the British government wanted them to become crack addicts. Just as Rastafarianism was uniting black people, just as they were beginning to rediscover respect for each other and for themselves, this drug appeared. It was brought into this country by white people, it was sold into the black community by white people. It was destroying them. Terence was amazed at the speed with which it spread.

One man became a user; he needed money to fund his habit, so he found two or three more people and turned them on so he could sell to them. Then they did the same. In a community where people worked and had a purpose to their life, it would never have spread so fast, but in this black ghetto, where the unity was still so frail, it was perfect. It was not so much that it filled their brains with pleasure for a minute or two – though that was important – but the really big point about crack cocaine was that it became the most saleable commodity in the neighbour-hood. An entire economy grew up around it, of suppliers and street dealers and consumers, all of it linked to the supply and sale of other drugs, all of it linked to the sale of prostitutes. This economy was a source of income on a scale that income support and dead-end jobs on factory floors could never match. Maybe even more important to a community like this, it was a source of status and power.

All this happened at the same time as the black posses started to fall apart. They had had a good run for four or five years but now the police were beginning to get on top of them. The Fields Posse, for example, which had been the best-defended fortress of black crime and status, started to crumble. One of the white tampaxes put up a job for them, where they broke into a rich woman's house and stole a Gainsborough. They spent nearly a year trying to sell it through a chain of middlemen. What they did not realise was that the tampax had grassed them to the police who were controlling the chain of middlemen with whom they were dealing. What the police did not realise was that the Fields Posse had decided to rip them off.

Both sides agreed finally that they would meet at an airfield outside the city. The Fields men turned up with guns to steal the cash from their buyers; the buyers turned up with a small army of police officers to put them in prison. It was a mess, the police weren't armed, one of the Fields men got away; but in the end, the posse was smashed. At that point, the police discovered that the Gainsborough was a worthless fake. Everybody was cheating.

The four leaders of the Fields Posse were at each other's throats. The selling of the Gainsborough was not the first job that had gone wrong on them. Time after time, the police were finding their guns or their stashes of cash. Once, they had disrupted an armed robbery that the posse had been planning for weeks by following them in a marked car, like a drunkard in the dark, deliberately letting them know that they were onto them. The four posse leaders knew there were informers among them but they couldn't be sure who they were and, pretty soon, they lost all trust in each other. They had known each other since infant school but they had been hollowed out by ghetto life. It was the first rule of the streets now: trust no one. Followed closely by the second rule: like no one. By 1990, two of the four leaders were in jail for armed robbery after jobs that had been grassed to the police. One of them had lost his courage. The other led the Fields Posse over the edge into the crack-cocaine business.

Drugs now were the fuel on which this place was running. Everybody seemed to smoke draw – hash from north Africa, grass from South America, and sensimilla, the best of all, from wherever they could find it. They had amyl nitrite, Amytal, barbiturates, Largactil, Physeptone, methadone, methaqualone, amphetamine, Ritalin, ketamine, Temazepam, Tuinal, Diconal, Dexedrine, diazepam, MDMA, MDEA, LSD, PCP and heroin, lots of heroin. Their language blossomed with drugs. They talked about acid, Adam, Es, Love Doves, eggs, jellies, blobs, blow, bush, weed, dope, junk, gear, brown, skag, horse, H, whizz, speed, gas, glue, dust, coke, charlie, uppers, downers, blues, reds, bombers – but none of it, none of these smokes or shots or pills or powders, compared to the brain-breaking bliss and magical wealth of crack cocaine.

By the early 1990s, in his search for crack money, Raggsie had become a prolific and occasionally violent pimp. His younger brother Micky had followed him, first into pimping and then into crack cocaine. Previously separated by age, the two brothers now became a walking crime wave picking up convictions for burglary, theft, twocking, actual bodily harm, assaulting police officers, possessing offensive weapons, unlawful sexual intercourse, living off immoral earnings, and lots of drugs. The stability that had begun to form in their lives was gone. Both of them were hooked in the heart by crack.

Their youngest brother, Anthony, was smoking, too. He had been born in England and was still only in his late teens, but now he had started dealing as well, ferrying cocaine up the M1 from London using hire cars whose number plates would not interest the motorway police, washing the coke into rocks at Dobber's house before selling it on.

Carol, too, had fallen into the same black hole and, even though she was now a grandmother in her early forties, she ended up travelling down to London in a miniskirt and thigh-high black leather boots to earn her crack money on the pavements outside the posh hotels in Mayfair. If she could raise enough money, she set up deals, using young white prostitutes to carry packages of cocaine from Jamaica and New York through Heathrow airport. She could sell the packages for £10,000 a load.

The police soon realised that the younger Jacksons had taken up drugs in a far bigger way than ever Dobber and EG Man had. They raided Dobber's house, where Carol was living, and found an ounce of grass in the garden and £300 of crack. They arrested Violet, Carol, Anthony, and Carol's two sons Patrick and *Johnnie*, who were in their late twenties. They all denied knowing anything about the grass, but Patrick was convicted for the crack – it was hidden in the pillow on which he was sleeping when the police came in.

All the rude boys were being sucked down the same drain. Some of them took over a couple of rooms in a block of flats near the city centre and called it the Coke House. There they scored and smoked and ran their women. Some of the dealers were coming from London, carrying guns, to supply the place.

The Fields Posse had become a dealing machine. Just like in the old days with their armed robbery, they had organised themselves. At any one time, they operated two or three crack houses on their home turf in the Fields estate. The houses had reinforced doors, where the rude boys would look after the day's supply. From time to time they would change the address in case the police were getting too interested. Out on the streets of the estate, there were younger lads on mountain bikes. If a buyer drove on to the estate, he would be pointed towards a kid on a bike, who would take his money, pedal off to the nearest crack house, push the cash through the letter box of the reinforced front door, get the crack back in wrapped rocks, put them in his mouth and head back for the buyer to hand them over. If the police tried to raid the crack house, the whole stash would go down the toilet before they could get through the doors. If they stopped one of the kids on the mountain bikes, he would swallow the evidence. Every Monday afternoon, from about four o'clock, they met in one of the safe houses on the estate so that they could talk business and review security. They all put money into a cooperative fund to pay for guns and bail money. They all earned a good living. It got so that if you weren't selling and smoking crack, you weren't part of this community.

Jazzman, who had built up such a steady business promoting black music, who had bought himself a shop and a nice house in south London and put money in the bank, was now wasted. He had started using his cash to stake crack deals but instead of sitting back and taking his profit, he had broken the first rule of dealing which everyone on the street had learned from Al Pacino in Scarface, 'Don't get high on your own supply.' Jazzman had become a crackhead and he had lost it all. He had sold his house and sold the shop, blown his cash, ruined his business. In the first few years of the 1990s, Jazzman reckoned he had burned something like a quarter of a million pounds on rocks of crack cocaine.

His friend Marshall, who had seen the trouble this stuff caused, had finally succumbed as well. He had been hanging around with some of the prostitutes, especially *Claire* – who was cousin to Raggsie's girl Marion. Claire ran the first real crack house in the city. Crackheads could go in there and pawn jewellery or television sets or anything else to buy gear, and some time in 1991, Marshall started spending most of his time in there. His white girlfriend Lucy suspected he was cheating on her. Lucy was not much more than five foot tall and she was as thin as a pin, but she was scared of no one and she confronted Claire. It did no good.

The next thing, the police busted the crack house and charged Claire and Marshall with supplying a class-A drug. Lucy realised that Marshall was not only probably cheating with Claire but also using her gear. Still, she loved him – she had had eight children with him – and she went to court to tell lies for him. She said that Claire was a junkie and she had been worried about her, so she had sent Marshall round there to take Claire's drugs off her. That was how come he was found in her house with a pocket full of gear. The jury believed the story and let Marshall go. Claire got three years in jail.

Now Lucy thought maybe she could save Marshall – she had taken him to the Maudsley Hospital in London and they had warned her that he had strong suicidal tendencies – so she decided at all costs to get him out of the city, away from all this crack. She packed him off to Jamaica to stay with his family there. She hadn't realised that, by now, Jamaica too was awash with crack cocaine, that Yardie gangs in Kingston had teamed up with corrupt politicians and policemen to become the world's premier salesmen of crack rocks. They were also extremely violent. By the time Marshall came home from Jamaica, the habit that he had started in Claire's crack house had overwhelmed him. As soon as he arrived back in England, he walked into trouble.

One night shortly before his return, Raggsie, Micky and Jazzman had been so desperate for crack that they had gone round to the home of a friend, *Eric Gloucester*, and searched the place. They had even pulled his baby out of its cot in search of hidden rocks. Eric didn't like that. He thought it was disrespectful and – Jackson or no Jackson – Eric wanted to teach these guys a lesson. Now, he offered Marshall two ounces of coke to deal with it.

Marshall was a big hard nut. He caught Jazzman at the back of the Kentucky Fried Chicken place in the middle of town, used a toy gun to corner him and then beat him up by the rubbish chute. Marshall and Jazzman had known each other all their lives, going right back to Jamaica – but you can't be a crackhead and a friend. He caught up with Micky Jackson in a toilet and did the same to him, hurt him badly. Anyone in Nottingham knew that if you wanted a peaceful life, the last thing you should do was to attack a Jackson. There were too many of them. But you can't be a crackhead and lead a peaceful life. Raggsie Jackson heard what was happening and went and gave himself up to the police to get out of Marshall's way. Then Marshall was arrested for assaulting Jazzman and Micky.

Lucy was furious with everyone who had dragged Marshall down. She blamed Micky Jackson for getting him arrested. By this time, some dealers from Brixton in south London had decided to kill Micky because he had taken ten ounces of coke off them and failed to pay for it. They asked her if they could use her house to blow him apart. She was tempted, but she thought better of it. Marshall's family did some sorting and arranged to pay Micky not to give evidence at the trial. But Jazzman didn't want trouble with the police and he went ahead to court and told everyone what had happened, so Marshall went to jail.

In the ghetto, by the mid-1990s, crack was king. When a group of welfare workers from a drugs charity studied the first wave of crack users in the city, in 1993, they made contact with 185 men and women and coaxed them with guarantees of anonymity to tell how much money they were spending each week on buying the little white rocks. The answers varied between £100 a week and £3,000. Adding the figures together, the welfare workers found that, between them, this small group of users were paying their dealers an average of £144,800 each week, every week – an annual cash flow of just over £7.5 million. This was the size of the 'crack economy' among the few users they managed to trace in two small patches of one medium-sized city in 1993, at a point when the market was still relatively young.

For those who lived in the mainstream of the city, this was £7.5 million which they had exported – willingly or unwillingly – into the undiscovered country. In their study, the welfare workers found that most of the crack users were out of work: they might have had jobs when they started to smoke rocks, but by the time that crack cocaine became the overriding obsession of their lives, they had abandoned their work with the same relentless dedication as they had sold their belongings. The £7.5 million which had been spent by that tiny group of users had been siphoned out of the mainstream economy. A small proportion of it came through Social Security benefits, but most of it came through theft and the sale of prostitutes.

In this way, the undiscovered country had generated income out of the mainstream society. Some of this money would find its way back, as successful dealers bought big houses and new cars, but the rest disappeared into offshore accounts or into building projects in Jamaica. For the economy of the city, this was a haemorrhage of wealth, a balance-of-payments disaster, made even worse if they added in the cost of the police and the health and social workers who went to the aid of those who suffered its results. In effect, the country of the poor was converting the mainstream society into a colony from which it extracted cash.

But for those who lived in the ghetto areas of this city, the scale of the trade meant something quite different.

25

By the summer of 1996, the black community in the city had become frantic with crack. Terence had already seen his father's generation turning inward, cutting themselves off from the broken promise of their mother country. He had seen his own generation drift into hostility and crime. Now, crack cocaine injected a new chaos and a new ferocity into his community. The killing had started.

By now, the Jacksons had seen death batter its way through their door several times. It came first to the family of Carol's second daughter, *Kate*, who had settled in her own home with her husband, *Budge*, and their three young children.

Their story was simple and, by now, familiar. Neither of them had any work. Neither of them was very secure in their emotions. Budge got into crime, robbing and dealing. He was jealous if Kate ever went out of his sight. She was angry with him, and they fought. They split up.

Along with most of his friends, Budge was involved in armed robbery. He did a few good jobs and started to drive around in £10,000 of new car. He got in with a big dealer and started making crack deals with him. He decided to rip off some dealers in Manchester, but since he was inexperienced and not much of a criminal, he simply took their drugs and ran off without paying. They came looking for him. Budge couldn't handle that. He went to the dealer for help, and the dealer sold him a gun. Budge understood how to use it but he couldn't see how he was going to take on a Manchester drug gang all on his own.

Budge wasn't happy. He was smoking rock, which was making him paranoid, and he was deeply jealous that Kate might be seeing someone else. He craved his children and, when Kate decided to go to London for three days, Budge said he would look after them. He took them to his mother's house and he brooded. He spent the first day there writing. He spent the second day there doing the same.

On the third day, he posted a fistful of letters, including one to Kate's uncle Terence. It reached him a couple of days later at the law firm where he was working as a clerk and, as he read it, Terence knew immediately that there was something wrong. He didn't know what. The letter made almost no sense. So he took it round to Carol's house to see what she could make of it. Budge was saying something about taking the children away. What did that mean? Terence guessed maybe it meant he was going to take them to America so he could have them to himself. But Carol guessed something different. And she said they had to get to Budge's house. Right now. Before it was too late.

By the time the taxi had come and taken them up there, the police were already cordoning off the road where Budge was living, and Carol ran out of the cab towards the house where her three grandchildren were and she knew already, long before the policeman caught her in his arms, long before they told her the truth, that all of them were dead.

That afternoon, Budge had taken the gun which the dealer had given him and he had laid his three small children down beside each other on the settee and he had shot them through the head. They were so small and the gun was so powerful that he had killed two of them with one bullet. Then he had sat down at the other end of the settee and turned the gun on himself.

Dobber and EG Man had never dealt in violence, but now their children and their grandchildren seemed to swim in it. On EG Man's side of the family, there were young people throwing themselves into it with a force like madness.

He had three young daughters, *Wanda*, *Leila* and *Coretta*. EG Man had fathered seventeen children and these three girls were the same age as some of his grandchildren. They were in their early twenties, they were devoted thieves and they were happy to use a little violence. One of their favourite moves was to assault women and threaten to set their hair on fire if they did not turn over their valuables. Coretta, who used to wear a big black straw

hat wherever she went, with the result that she was always identified, tried this in broad daylight on a woman who was doing her
shopping one afternoon at Tesco's in the city centre. Coretta
knocked her around a bit, produced her lighter, made her usual
threat and stripped the woman of all her jewellery. The sisters
used to go out on shoplifting sprees together, filling their bags as
they went. Leila often took a baby so she could hide the stolen
gear in the pushchair. She still got caught a lot. In fact, she had
been busted for stealing from meters, stealing from shops, assault
and actual bodily harm. The oldest daughter, Wanda, specialised
in robbing people who wouldn't cause her too much trouble –
old-age pensioners, a sixteen-year-old schoolgirl in a phone box,
an absent neighbour whose house she burgled. By the time she
was twenty, she had spent eighteen months behind bars for
robbery and two years for actual bodily harm as well as being
convicted of twocking, possessing an offensive weapon, burglary
and theft.

Their brothers were playing the same kind of games. *Wayne*
joined the Playboy Posse and started a war with the Fields Posse.
They arranged to stage a fist-fight with them, but some of the
Fields people brought knives and Wayne ended up being badly
slashed. He needed sixty-seven stitches. He told the police he
had no idea who had done it, but a month later he and fifteen
others set on five of the Fields lads as they came out of a black
club. They piled into them with broken bottles and knives, Wayne
wielding an iron bar at a lad named *Tommy Whitedge* who survived
with his skull broken in two places. Day by day, Wayne earned
his living by mugging in the streets near his home, particularly
by targeting day nurseries where he could snatch the handbags
of women who were delivering their children. Every so often, his
violence would overflow: he beat up a schoolboy who, he suspected, was planning to burgle his mate's house; he kicked a
traffic bollard in front of a white guy's car, threw a brick through
the windscreen and then tore a four-foot wooden slat off a nearby
fence so that he could beat the driver as he fled on foot.

He spent a lot of time with his brothers *Floyd* and *George*. They
were involved in a rape when a fourteen-year-old girl said that
four lads had pulled her into a garden shed where they had taken
it in turns to have sex with her. Like Wayne, Floyd and George

both had a history of sudden violence. Floyd had carried a knife into the battle with the rival crew. George had carried a broken bottle. For some reason, the fourteen-year-old withdrew the complaint of rape against them.

In the end, the Fields Posse got the better of them or, at least, they got the better of Floyd. They killed him. They were having some row about nothing – a stolen bike – and they piled into him. One of them swung a baseball bat which hit the back of his head like a mallet on a melon. He died right there on the street. Another dead Jackson.

There was no pretence any more that anyone had any time for anything other than their own survival. The pimping, for example, had almost nothing in common with Benny's guilt-ridden games. In the old days, the men had persuaded the girls to work with the illusion of love. Only ten years earlier, Raggsie and his friends still looked upon their women as their girlfriends, even though they took it for granted that they could sell them. Now, with crack running through the streets, pimping had become a vicious business: the bitch works, hands over the money to the man, the man gives her a rock, she smokes it and gets back on that pavement; the man takes the money, scores some more rock, smokes some himself, and waits for the bitch to come back with more cash. That was pimping. That was an economy: £20 for a rock – four or five smokes at, say, £4 a hit; £100 for a sixteenth of an ounce – 'a teenth' – which would be seven or eight rocks at, say, £3 a hit. That was the deal. Never mind love.

In the old days, you would see the successful pimps a mile off, with their two-tone mohair suits and their Tetley teabag hats, cruising the streets in their Ford Granadas, while their women stood at the bus stop and persuaded themselves that they were proud to have paid for their man's comfort. Now, they were all at the bus stop together: the pimps and the girls, all more or less bankrupted by crack.

Raggsie Jackson was running his girlfriend Marion, and also Marva and Norma and Barbara and Pamela and Diane, whose house was full of whips. Micky Jackson was pimping several women too, using Angela Simpson to lure punters to a house where they could be beaten and robbed, using a fourte-year-old girl for punters and for shoplifting too. Micky was bad with his women. He attacked the fourteen-year-old with a hammer (and was battered himself the next day by two guys who wanted her to work for them). And he kept getting his women pregnant. By this time, he had fathered seven children with five different women.

The men were not content only to take the money that the girls earned on the pavement. They were also taking their straight earnings, their social security cheques, walking out with the television or the kids' toys to pay for more rocks. There was one guy whose woman tried to support him by working as a cleaner in a big office block. One night, she saw a pile of blank cheques and decided to steal them. Over the next few days, she managed to collect £25,000 in cash, but when the police went to her flat, they found she had got only £5,000. She had spent a little on herself and given more than £15,000 of it to her man. Who had smoked it.

Sticks was now carrying a cane to beat his girls. He got angry with one of them, Angela, when they were working in Leicester one night, and forced her to walk naked down the street.

All that mattered was the crack. There were some people who couldn't even spare the time to cook it up in a pan; they used a Ronson blow torch or a microwave to do the job instantly.

In a crack house in a red-brick terrace, *Antonia* spent her days lying like a skeleton on a black imitation leather couch with a sheet draped over it, waiting for the Crack Man to come, while her little boy played with an old newspaper on the floor. There was a torn picture of Caspar the ghost stuck to a mirror, and up on the mantelpiece a calendar that the boy had made at school with a drawing of something on the front of it. She had a book called *Simply Delicious Recipes*, a broken fridge which was pulled out from the wall where someone had once tried to mend it, and that was all. That was Antonia.

A young prostitute called Lindsey discovered that if you were strung out on crack, a shot of heroin helped to make you mellow. She liked it so much that she made a mess of injecting her arms, which became riddled with thromboses. The doctors said that all these blood clots could kill her, and they told her that they could save her life only by operating, to slice both of her arms from her shoulders.

Jazzman, who had once earned such a good living promoting music, was now running around doing the bidding of a young white dealer called Pitches, who had lost his driving licence and needed Jazzman to act as his chauffeur in exchange for crumbs of crack. Jazzman got caught up in a bust in a crack house. The front door was pushed in and everyone was charged with possession: the next day, everyone was back in the same crack house, smoking just the same as usual, but now there was a long, thick plank jammed between the end of the radiator in the hall and the inside of the front door.

One night, Jazzman met a woman in a wine lodge and went home with her to give her a smoke and to see if she'd give him some sex. To his surprise, he found that her three sons were up waiting for her. They were aged about eleven, twelve and thirteen, and they wanted a smoke – a smoke of crack. Jazzman was a bit worried about this.

'I can't have your lads smoking crack,' he told her.

'You can't stop them,' she said.

So they all sat down and smoked together and when they had finished, the woman sent the two older boys out to do some robbing so they could get some more.

Nothing else mattered. People didn't matter, family didn't matter, friends didn't matter. You couldn't trust anyone. Because no one would repay your trust. Everywhere, there was cheating.

Old Stewart, who ran the café where the young lads liked to hang out, had always done a little grassing to keep his name in with the police. That way he had managed to hang out a big sign that said 'NO DRUGS' and still let his customers smoke them – just as long as they bought them from him. Now he went further. One of the rude boys tried to sell him some stolen cigarettes and booze, so Stewart took them and simply refused to pay him the price that they had agreed. The rude boy lost his cool and started threatening him, so Stewart went and grassed him to the police. Stewart was safe – until the rude boy went further too, got out of custody and set fire to the café. Stewart went to America till things cooled down.

There were so many firearms around that the most popular black club installed a metal detector inside the main door. It made no difference to the guys with guns: they just walked straight past it and strode into the club, where they liked to salute the music by firing live bullets into the ceiling. There was a riot on one of the black estates where a pub had become a kind of crack-cocaine Tesco's. Different groups of dealers started fighting about who should sell what in the pub and they started shooting at each other. Eventually, the landlord allowed the police to install a hidden camera in the pub and the police moved in and busted the place.

Marshall emerged from prison into this blizzard. Within hours, he was smoking rock. He fell out with Lucy, who suddenly realised one day that she had spent twenty years selling her body for this man and that she had nothing. She hacked off her hair, smashed up her room and told him he could earn his own money. Marshall raged at her. He told her he loved her. Lucy believed him, but she told him it was too late. She could see he was getting depressed and paranoid. No one seemed to respect him any more. She tried to protect him by going up to the crack house, where he was smoking with a sixteen-year-old girl called Nadine. Lucy yelled at him to give it up, and asked him how he would feel if some crackhead was sitting around getting Marshall's sixteen-year-old daughter to smoke pipes. She knocked the pipe out of Nadine's hand. Seeing him sit there, hangdog, she knew she had struck his pride. Now he had lost everything. Lucy hoped against hope that he would see he had to stop the crack. But he could not.

Marshall went off alone, up to the top of the block of flats where he was living with Lucy and their eight kids, and he launched himself into the empty air. He hit the ground and died.

In the midst of all this, there were Yardie gangsters who had learned to kill at the drop of an insult on the crime-drenched streets of Kingston, Jamaica. In the early 1990s, they had moved into London to sell crack – a trade in which they exceeded the strength even of the Colombian cocaine cartels – and now they were moving into the provincial cities in search of new buyers.

The Yardies set a new standard in the black estates. They carried more cash, wore more gold jewellery and packed more firepower than any local black man. Where once the old pimps had been a role model, now the Yardies showed the young rude boys how to make their way in the world. Everyone had heard stories of the Yardies' violent ways – the woman courier they had tortured with a red-hot iron, the US embassy worker in London who had been killed because she had discovered their racket in phoney visas, the dealer in New York who had crossed them and who had ended up decapitated, with his head wrapped in cellophane and being used in a celebratory game of football. No one wanted to cross a Yardie.

One of them was mixing with the Jacksons and selling crack as though he owned the place. Another, a guy named Pepsi from the Rapid Posse in Kingston, was trying to settle down permanently in the city.

Terence Jackson watched as the story of the ghetto became a diary of disaster. Lives crumpled and died like paper in a fire. By the late 1990s, the black community of the city, which had once been the home of ideals about respect and discipline, had become a slaughter bench.

Terence had seen his niece's children murdered, his cousin Floyd murdered. He had seen his older brother Raggsie sent to jail for six years for stealing handbags to fund his crack habit. (Just like his uncle EG Man, Raggsie had been hassled by the police to become an informer and he had tried to cheat them.) Terence had seen his younger brother Micky put on trial for attempted murder after a shoot-out in a black club where some of the local rude boys piled in with knives and swords and firearms to punish two Birmingham dealers who had stolen some crack off one of Carol's dealers. He could see Anthony was travelling the same road, smoking crack and dealing. And now, as this second generation collapsed in disarray, he could see the third generation throwing themselves into the chaos.

Carol's teenage daughter *Louise* became an obsessive crack addict and a prolific street prostitute. Another daughter, *Annette*, took up with a Yardie who was swaggering around crack houses and shebeens in London with a sub-machine-gun in his hand. Carol's eldest son, Patrick, was locked up for a string of offences, came out of jail and within weeks was back inside again after he saw a man at a blues party wearing a fancy gold Rolex watch studded with diamonds. Patrick broke his skull and one of his ankles, stole the watch (which turned out to be worth £50,000) and £2,000 in cash. When he was released from his sentence for that, he and his younger brother Johnnie were beaten up by a crew from Birmingham, who were trying to make their mark in the city's coke trade. That little wave of trouble reached Terence. Somebody torched his car one night when it was parked outside a club and all the Jacksons reckoned it must have been the Birmingham crew trying to hassle them.

Terence tried to shrug it off and concentrate on his work at the law firm, but there was more trouble around. His friend Eric Gloucester got busted with a kilo of coke in London. The police tried to make out that Terence had introduced him to a woman who had acted as Eric's courier, smuggling the coke from Jamaica into Heathrow Airport in two shampoo bottles. Terence put his faith in the system and told the police the truth: that he had sat in his car outside this woman's house while Eric went in to talk to her. Within days, he was on the receiving end of some very threatening phone calls from people with Jamaican accents, telling him he was a dead man if he went into the witness box. When the case came to trial, the judge said Terence need not give evidence, but he had barely talked his way out of that situation when trouble grabbed for him again. And this time it caught him.

He was arrested and accused of a conspiracy to cause actual bodily harm. The police thought that Tererence's two sisters Carol and Elizabeth had hired some Yardies from London to batter the Birmingham dealers out of the city and to get revenge for their beating up Carol's sons Patrick and Johnnie. They said Terence had got involved because he wanted revenge for his car being burned out. Terence hated to be suddenly locked up in police cells and sat in a dock like a criminal, and he was sure this was just the police trying to get at the notorious Jacksons, but all he could do was to put his faith in the system again and hope for the best.

For a brief moment, it looked as though all would be well. When his case came to the magistrates' court, it was thrown out. There was not enough evidence for it to go before a jury. Terence was just about to believe that the system had done its job again when the police did something highly unusual. They went to the Director of Public Prosecutions and asked for a bill of indictment to send Terence and his two sisters straight for trial, even though the magistrates had said there was no case to answer. The DPP agreed. Terence was trapped. Worse than that, his law firm said that they couldn't tolerate this any longer. Terence would have to go. He lost his precious job. He lost everything he had worked for.

When the case finally came to trial, it was a fiasco. A few weeks into the trial, the prosecution were forced to admit that one of the Yardies in the case was a highly paid Scotland Yard informer and that the London police had misled everyone in the case – the police, the prosecutors, even the judge. The trial was abandoned and started again. This time, the Yardie informer gave evidence and told the jury that Terence and his two sisters had hired them to beat up this Birmingham crew. The jury didn't believe the Yardie and acquitted Terence, Carol and Elizabeth. A month later, the Yardie admitted that he had lied throughout the trial. But by then, it was too late for Terence. He was unemployed and penniless. He couldn't even pay his phone bill. He had put his faith in the system, and now he had nothing.

It wasn't just that his own life had plunged into an abyss, nor even that so many of his friends had fallen into the same place. More than that, so far as he could see, the whole black community had collapsed.

Sure, there were some black people who were making it – but not many. Out of his whole class at school, there were maybe two or three who had got decent jobs and managed to make a life for themselves. But mostly, when Terence looked around him he saw young black men who were pimps and dealers and users; he saw young black women trying to settle down and finding no young black men who were capable of living stable lives; he saw black youths who thought nothing of serving a 'life' sentence because they'd still be only thirty when they came out and, more important, they would have respect; he saw the Yardies and the rude boys with money and power, he saw the dealers and the gangsters; and he saw no hope at all. He knew it was a hard thing to say about his own people and he knew there were white racists who would ignore all the reasons why it had happened and simply take his words and twist them into weapons, but he believed the truth had to be told: most of them had lost their way. Terence had tried and he had failed. In the ghetto, it was better to be bad.

26

The true scale of poverty may be hidden from the rest of Britain by the simple fact of the prosperity of the majority. The true damage inflicted by poverty is hidden by something more deliberate.

There are leading figures in black communities who know very well that numerous young black people – particularly the grandchildren of the original Jamaican migrants from the 1950s – have succumbed to a life that is infested with drugs and pimping and crime, that there is some kind of social holocaust raging in these communities. But these leaders are most reluctant to admit it, for fear of bringing down racism on their people.

In the same way, there are social workers and doctors and local politicians who know very well that among some of the very poor white communities, there is something like an epidemic of child abuse – physical, emotional and sexual. But, with a few brave exceptions, they are most reluctant to admit it, for fear of giving the poor a bad image.

It is the same story with the truth about levels of crime committed by poor people, or about levels of alcohol addiction or domestic violence or the neglect of children. Well-meaning defenders of the poor mask the truth about what is happening to them, insist on being positive about their achievements and construct images of their courage in the face of austerity.

In the United States, a society whose poor have drifted some ten or fifteen years further down the path to destruction, this kind of well-meaning collusion has ended. A black leader like Jesse Jackson will address a gathering of black people and ask them, 'Put your hands up, everyone here who's ever been shot or shot at.' And all across his audience, the hands will rise. Then he will ask them, 'Now put your hands up, everyone here who's ever been shot at by white folk.' Just about no hands. He isn't denigrating them by exposing the violence that they inflict on each other, he is advertising their misery, appealing for help, demanding help by demonstrating the damage they have suffered.

The damage is complicated. The experience of the Jackson family suggests that it goes beyond the emotional and the physical. There is also a deep social damage.

At its extreme, this involves the mushrooming of what academics like to call subcultures. The world of the Jacksons is like this, a community that has drifted away into its own way of life, so that any child growing up within it is going to find it almost impossible to escape its grip. The world of the Hyde Park kids is another, or that of the children around the Forest, or of groups within the two thousand estates where boy-thieves like Joey grow up. They are little colonies, looking inwards at their own values and rituals, their own ways of surviving. Little ghettos, fuelled more than anything by crime and drugs – the two clearest and most lethal forms of social damage. But in other, less extreme forms, this social damage bubbles up through the everyday life of the poor in a hundred different ways.

In his studies of the effect of inequality, Richard Wilkinson, from the University of Sussex, has tried to explain the myriad different shapes which this damage might assume:

> The relationship between increasing income differentials and the various social problems it creates is not necessarily a simple one. A large number of different pathways are involved in the links with crime, child abuse, reading standards, school expulsions, drug taking, child prostitution and health problems of different kinds in different age groups. Because the relationships are not always clear and simple, they are denied as an excuse for inaction, and the social and financial costs continue to increase. However, there can be no doubt that relative deprivation is a component in all these outcomes.

There is a complicated maze of pathways which lead away

from the safety of a life with health and hope, into the tangled undergrowth. Sometimes these paths intersect or curl back on themselves, so that cause and effect become hopelessly embroiled.

Some of them run through emotional problems and become social. For example, adults who are stumbling under the weight of unemployment and debt will find themselves becoming anxious and sleepless and angry. Soon they will argue. One study found that half of the couples who had suffered unemployment reported that they were having more arguments, and a third of them said that one partner had either left or, at least, had contemplated leaving to escape the stress. So families collapse and the emotional damage takes on a social shape. In some cases, those broken families then wander even further into the darkness, finding new pathways into damage: the remaining adult may take to alcohol or drug abuse; or become so depressed that social workers start to hover, spotting neglect of the children; the children, too, may wander into truancy and petty crime.

The mid-1980s saw a surge in 'runaways and throwaways' – children who either fled from their homes or were ejected onto the street. These were social incidents which made sense only if they were seen as emotional breakdowns. The children speak of stepfathers who bullied them and sometimes ordered them out of the house; of fathers or occasionally mothers who used them as sex objects; of homes where slaps and belts took over as the common currency of everyday exchange. They ran away from the 'state of despair' in which they lived. As the poverty rose, the number of runaways and throwaways rose. In 1995, on the best available estimate, some 98,000 children took refuge on the streets.

There is one particular pathway to social damage which attracts poor adolescent girls. They fall pregnant at something like six times the rate of girls of similar age in affluent areas. There are politicians and journalists who have never met any of these girls, who paint a colourful picture of manipulative young scroungers totting up their rights under the rules and regulations of Social Services and then trotting out to gather some semen to boost their income and to jump the housing queue. The reality is simpler and sadder. They do it because their sisters did it, because there is nothing else to do, because there is no reason not to do it. And, following the same pointless path, they deliver the babies and bring them up even when they do not want them, because they have no plan, no control. A Dundee doctor who analysed every unwanted pregnancy in his area between 1980 and 1990, found that women from deprived areas aborted only a quarter of their unwanted pregnancies, while those from affluent areas aborted two thirds of them. The affluent women knew what they wanted in life and went out and got it; the poorer women, by contrast, and in contradiction to the easy assumptions of hostile politicians, had no idea what they wanted and were often incapable of controlling their lives in any way.

There is a relatively simple, straight path between poverty and physical isolation. If you have no money, you cannot afford to go out. Alternatively, if you have no money and you live in an area that has spawned a culture of crime, you do not dare to go out and leave your house empty. Single mothers without money find their own path to isolation. They cannot afford to pay anyone to look after their children and so they cannot go out to work or to drink in a pub or to sit in a cinema or to do almost any of the things that parents with money in their pockets can do with ease. It is the simplest of chains. Across the rest of Europe, governments have fought to cut these chains. In Denmark, the government provides day care of some kind for 44 per cent of the country's toddlers aged under two. In Britain, the government does so for only 2 per cent of its toddlers. By the mid-1990s, Britain was almost the worst in all of Europe: only Portugal provided fewer publicly funded places for children under four years old. So the single mothers remain with their isolation.

The early 1990s saw surges in the statistics of social damage around children in deprived areas as this younger generation also found its own pathways to destruction.

The number of children whose names were logged on Child Protection Registers almost quadrupled during the 1980s. The number of children taken into care rose almost as quickly. Some of this may have happened because there was more pressure on social workers to intervene in cases of suspected child abuse. Nevertheless, the trend was clear. When these children were logged onto the Child Protection Registers, there were three reasons that were given more often than any other to explain the background problems of their families: marital problems, debt and unemployment. The *British Journal of Social Work* reported that a child from an affluent background had a one in 7,000 chance of ending up in the care of the local authority; children from deprived homes had a one in ten chance.

With their emotional problems and their behavioural disorders, these children are being excluded from schools on a grand scale, the numbers accelerating each year between 1990 and 1993, from 2,000 to 11,000. The schools complain that they have no option. The new system of league tables means that if they allow these troubled children to stay, they will perform badly in their SAT tests, so that the schools will sink further down the published league tables, attract fewer able children, and hit a downward spiral, losing funding as they fall. The problem goes deeper. Long before they are thrown out by the schools, these children are playing truant – 800,000 of them a year, according to the best estimate, of whom 80,000 are playing truant so frequently that they have effectively abandoned school altogether.

Many of these same children are caught up in the booming figures for heroin abuse which were reported in the early 1990s by community workers from around the country, not just from the bowels of the old Victorian cities, but from the devastated pit villages of south Wales and from the rural disarray of counties like Gloucestershire and Surrey. The number of children who died from sniffing glue and gas raced upwards by 400 per cent between 1980 and 1990.

One of the subcultures that developed during this time involved those who had lost their homes. This means not only the 2,000 or 3,000 who sleep rough on the streets of London, nor even the 5,000 others who join them on most nights on the pavements of Exeter, Oxford, Brighton, Leicester and almost any other provincial city. This means also the 50,000 mostly young people who are living in squats; the 11,000 in bed-and-breakfast rooms; the 10,000 in hostels for the homeless; the hundreds of thousands cramped on sitting-room sofas and on the floors of friends. In total, according to the housing charity Shelter, there are some 1.7 million people in Britain who do not have their own bed to sleep in.

This mass of homeless suffer their own particular kinds of

damage. They are far more likely to become physically and mentally ill, far more likely to see their families split up, far more likely simply to be unhappy and tired and ill-tempered with their children and their partners. Those who sleep rough are truly vulnerable. Shelter reckon that some 600 of them die on the streets each year and that the average life expectancy of a homeless person on the streets of this wealthy country is only forty-seven, somewhat shorter than in most of the very poorest countries in the world.

In the same way, the subcultures that have developed around drugs carry with them their own particular kinds of damage. There are grim infections from sharing dirty needles. At one extreme, by 1997, doctors at the London School of Hygiene believed there were some 5,000 women who were HIV positive who were giving birth to babies who would be born with the infection in their blood. By then, nearly a thousand babies had lost their mothers to AIDS. Others who wander into this subculture sink into debt, turn to crime, reach for prostitution, end up in prison. It is a vortex of destruction.

As poverty rose, crime rose. Between 1979 and 1993, unemployment more than doubled, and so did episodes of recorded crime. In 1994, the chief constables of England and Wales trawled through their own crime reports and discovered that 70 per cent of their offenders were unemployed. The government worked hard to deny that there was any link at all between unemployment and crime. But the facts trapped them. When the Home Office conducted its own internal review, collating information from a huge pool of 397 studies of young offenders in Britain, they concluded that the biggest obstacle to keeping young people away from crime was 'an inability to offer them any realistic prospects of . . . the means of achieving material success'. The Home Office suppressed these research conclusions, which became public only after months of concealment.

Some of this crime is linked clearly and immediately to shortage of money. For example, in 1994, there were 103,000 women who were fined after being caught without a television licence. An offence of poverty. Thousands of them could not afford to pay the fines any more than they could afford to pay the television licence in the first place. By 1994, on an average day in England

and Wales, sixty different men and women were sent to prison for failing to pay fines – more than 22,000 in the year. This is another of the figures that has soared upwards with the rise in poverty, increasing by 37 per cent over the previous four years.

Other crime is generated by the deeper forces of poverty, by the frustration and boredom of the Hyde Park gang or the deep irrationality of the children of the Forest.

It is as if poverty has taken the top off some volcanic reservoir of damage which now flows through Britain, deforming those who stand in its way and, more than that, distorting whole communities into the shape of ghettos where trust and care and self-respect are suffocated, where a man like Terence Jackson is condemned for living by his conscience.

27

I t was dark on the Forest. Several years had passed now since that autumn evening when the fairground workers had been swarming over the recreation ground in the twilight while the two small boys stood in the yellow light of their doorway. The faces had changed. There was no sign now of Jamie and Luke or any of the other children who had opened the door into this forbidding country. Instead, there were others, standing in the same way in the same places.

These children seemed familiar now, and so were their origins in the ocean of old housing estates around the country from which they had been washed up, broken and battered by their haphazard journeys. Now, for the first time, those around them who were part of their hidden world were also recognisable.

This fat young white man, for example, driving in his businessman's car, apparently with nothing more than his trip home on his mind. He is a dealer. His real name is Paul but everyone on the Forest knows him as Coach. He cruises around the Forest in his car with a bag of crack beside him, selling rocks to the working girls on the pavement like an ice-cream vendor selling wafers. He tells them he isn't worried about being busted. If the police stop him, he'll just say that he's found this bag of crack somewhere and he is on his way to the police station to hand it in.

These young black lads who are standing on the pavement outside the Black and White Café on Radford Road. They are selling rocks to passers-by: Smiley and AJ and Courteney and the others. From time to time, they get busted, but they are back out there again the next day.

Just like every other city around the country, Nottingham now has its drug culture. One summer day in 1996, the police in Nottingham had a tip-off that there was a sizeable stash of speed – 50 kilos of the stuff – in a house just down the road in Mansfield. When the police went to the house, they found the drugs in a package in a wheelbarrow at the bottom of the garden, but there were only 18 kilos left. They were told that it had arrived in Mansfield within the previous seven days, and they were left to ponder on the scale of a market which could see more than 30 kilos of speed consumed in less than a week in a small provincial town.

That same summer, in Nottingham, the police came across a factory worker who was enjoying the lifestyle of the chairman of a privatised utility. He had several brand-new cars and a villa on the Mediterranean, and he had recently played host to the chief of police of a Third World city which was notorious for its trade in illegal drugs and for the corruption of its police officers.

This realm of drugs has its own hierarchy, an aristocracy of dealers. Some of them are white, like Wayne Hardy who supplies bouncers to half the pubs and clubs in Nottingham and uses his power on the doors to control the supply of drugs inside. His empire was expanding fast until he was exposed by a television programme in 1996. Others are black and among these barons, one man is king.

Dave Francis makes no secret of his power – which means that he makes no secret of his money. It is not just that he lives very comfortably in a three-bedroom detached house among the white business executives in Compton Acres, nor that he keeps a flat near the Forest in Francis Street, nor even that he keeps a wardrobe full of designer clothes (he is particularly fond of Armani and Versace). Dave positively breathes money. He wears diamonds in his teeth. They have been drilled into the enamel by a specialist dentist – half a dozen sparkling advertisements for his success in life. When Dave smiles, the rest of the world sees his wealth winking back at them. In his ear, he has another diamond, on his wrist he wears a heavy gold Rolex with diamond studs which he says cost him thirty grand. There is gold around his neck, more gold around his wrists. He has a ring full of jewels which he says cost him £10,000. He drives cars that cost a fortune. His latest is

£49,500 of open-top Mercedes with leather seats, although he boasts that by the time he paid for the stereo and other extras, the bottom line was nearer £63,000. There is no great secret about where Dave Francis has found his wealth. He worked his way up through the biggest black gang in Nottingham, the Meadows Posse, where he set up armed robberies, and then he struck out on his own, handling stolen goods and selling drugs. He has now become the biggest dealer in the black community in Nottingham, and he has used the perfect cover.

He is well known to the police. He has a long criminal record with some thirty different convictions for firearms, violence, possession of drugs and unlawful sexual intercourse. He buys from some of the biggest suppliers in England, bringing bulk cocaine into Nottingham from Leicester and Manchester, from Birmingham and Newcastle, washing it into rocks and selling it through runners around the city. But for four years, while he expanded his business, he was also being paid £21,000 a year of public money to run an agency called the Crack Awareness Team whose job was to help people who were addicted to crack cocaine. He could go into any crack house, mix with any crack user and it was all just part of his job.

Dave will deal in anything – crack, Es, grass, jewellery, gold. And women. His runners have the rocks that the working girls want, so he has power over them. Sometimes, he sends them down to London where he has friends who run brothels. Sometimes, he keeps them for himself.

There was a little blonde prostitute called *Fiona*, who came to him when she was only fourteen. By that time she had been abused and used by one man after another, she had run away from a children's home in Nottingham and she was living near the Forest with a pimp and crack dealer called Stumpy Cooper who had turned her into a cottage industry. Stumpy was pimping her to the men in cars on the Forest, selling her rocks and grass, using his video camera to film her in porn movies and having sex with her himself. Eventually, the Nottingham police busted Stumpy and put him away. Fiona went to the Crack Awareness Team for help with her crack smoking. Dave took her under his wing, asked her to come round to the flat he owns near the

Forest. He smoked grass with her, helped her to score crack, let her sit on his car and smoke rocks and he screwed her.

It is not only the drug dealers who share these pavements with the children. There are older prostitutes, too. Joy, who works on TV corner, has been out here since she was eighteen, earning enough to support her heroin habit, and to look after her boyfriend Dicky. She's thirty-six now, she's had both her children taken into care, including one who was born addicted, and she's still out on the pavement every evening with her thigh-high boots and her stiff blond wig. Old Mary works up the hill from her in Southey Street. She must be in her sixties but she still has her regulars who pick her up in the shadows. There's Ann, who looks so thin and ill (everyone says she has AIDS, but no one knows for sure), and Rachel, who was beaten up so badly by her pimp that she finally plucked up the courage to get him jailed, though he'll be out again soon. And then there is Miss Popular, who is a kind of legend.

Her real name is Karen. She is a beautiful blond woman in her early forties who used to live a life of comfort and stability, ferrying her two daughters to ballet classes and going out with her husband to Nottingham's nicer restaurants, until September 1991 when her marriage fell apart and she started to snort cocaine. Within months, she started smoking crack as well and, in order to find a supply, she set off alone one night for a club called the Tally Ho, which was popular then with the Nottingham pimps and their working girls. By the end of the night, she had found herself being escorted home by Spotty Caine. He was a prolific pimp who lived with a white woman named Kath Swanwick, known to all as Miss Kath, who was the biggest heroin dealer in Nottingham. Spotty took one look at the tall poplars in Karen's garden and baptised her Miss Popular. He offered her crack in exchange for sex. She accepted and, even though Miss Kath came to her door and told her she'd kill Karen if she saw Spotty again, she continued to make the same trade with him and with numerous Nottingham rude boys who soon took over her home.

For several months Spotty spoiled her and pampered her until one warm summer's day he came round to her house and told her firmly that she owed him for all the crack he had given her. That afternoon, he drove her down to the Forest with a girl called

Rita, who was working for him at the time, and put her on the game. She never escaped and now, with her waves of blond hair and her elegant style, she is a familiar figure on the streets of vice areas not only in Nottingham but also in London.

On the pavements of the Forest, Jamie and Luke and the children who had taken their places strolled through this world and belonged to it. They were a walking embodiment of the damage that had been inflicted in the country of the poor – emotionally scrambled, physically at risk from a gauntlet of dangers, moulded into the shape of this mutant culture. But there was something else, something that was not yet familiar.

Kit Austin lived with her mother, *Judy*, and her three younger brothers in a small house in a long straight terrace in a dreary street in the western suburbs of Nottingham; and there was something about her that her mother could not understand.

In some ways, she seemed to be a happy child. Each morning, she went off to catch the school bus in her neat black-and-grey uniform and her clean white shirt, and she did quite well in class and talked about becoming an air hostess or an interior designer. In the evenings, after school, she watched television and, occasionally, worked in a part-time job. She was healthy, she was bright, she had a bubbly, likeable sort of personality and, even though she was only fourteen, Judy knew that the boys were already making moves for her.

Judy wasn't saying that Kit's life was perfect. They were only ordinary working people, they had precious little money, there were the three boys to look after and Judy had to lean on Kit for support. This area of Nottingham was drab and tired and there was a fair bit of crime and violence around. Judy's family had grown up around here and over the years they had had their own problems with the law and with some of the neighbours, and they had got a bit of a reputation for using their fists and getting themselves into trouble. Judy's whole family had been knocked off centre by her father's drinking and she and her sisters had grown up with trouble. As a teenager, Judy had started living with Kit's dad but he had left when Kit was only a little baby. He had walked out and gone off to work in Scotland. He had kept in touch, but not very often. After a few years, Judy had got married to a man who turned out to be so jealous that she hardly dared to breathe without his permission. They had had two little boys and then Judy had got so fed up with him that she had thrown him out. Since then, she had taken up with a third man and had another baby boy.

Judy didn't think that Kit missed her dad or her brothers' dad. She supposed it might have upset her to have lost two fathers but, if anything, the two men going like that seemed to have brought Judy and Kit closer. Judy felt she would lay down her life for that girl and there had been times, it was true, when Judy had taken her fists to people who had threatened her daughter. There was a furious affection between the two of them. And yet, Judy knew, there was something wrong.

Sometimes in the evening, Kit would finish her homework and yell ta-ra to Judy and tell her she was just going out with one of her friends, but somehow it didn't ring true. Sometimes she'd tell Judy that she was staying overnight with friends, and Judy would often call to check that the parents were expecting her but, although they always said that they were, Judy was never quite sure. Kit had started to behave badly. Judy would give her a fiver and she'd turn her nose up at it.

'What good's this to me?' she'd say. 'Everyone else gets a tenner.'

Judy found out more or less by accident that Kit had been skiving off school and when she asked Kit why she'd been doing that and where she'd been going, she'd got answers for everything. But none of them really satisfied Judy.

This had been going on for about a year; Kit had passed her fifteenth birthday and started seeing a lot of a boy called *Sam*; and Judy was trying to persuade herself that perhaps the only problem had been in her imagination, when one Friday afternoon in November 1994, she took a phone call from the school nurse, who said she was sorry to have to tell her that Kit had just confessed to her that she was using methadone. Judy had never heard of methadone.

'It's a substitute for heroin.'

'Don't be stupid,' said Judy. 'Heroin? That went out with the ark. Didn't it?'

There was a ghastly excitement about the following months as

Kit went in and out of clinics and hostels and Judy struggled to find out what had been happening to her daughter and how it had started and where it would end, but nothing she did and nothing she thought of seemed to make any difference. Just over four months later, in March 1995, Kit Austin went to London. Judy didn't know quite how it had happened. All she knew was that from that moment, Kit went into another world, a world of immense darkness.

The basement flat at 32 Gloucester Terrace was warm and dimly lit. Outside, the cars went pouring by from Hyde Park towards Paddington Station in a blur of noise. Nobody noticed.

The Victorian terrace had been grand once, the home of lawyers and doctors and entrepreneurs, but now it had fallen on harder times, like some of the people who lived there. The cream paint on the façade of the terrace had started to blister beneath its veneer of grime. The black gloss paint on the iron balustrade outside number 32 was chipped and smudged with dirt. At the entrance to the basement, there were sodden flaps of rubbish clinging to the gateway, and the stone steps that led down to the iron security gate below were cold and hard.

But beyond the iron gate, on the other side of the plain front door, the flat was warm, and the middle-aged woman who came to the door always smiled an easy smile as she welcomed her visitors and ushered them a few steps along the darkened corridor and into a room full of shadows. She was small and slim with ash-blond hair and a thick Slavonic accent. Her name was Suzie Chezie, but everyone knew her as Hungarian Suzie or, occasionally, Suzie Floozie.

She would invite her visitors to take a seat on the extra-soft mattress of the grand double bed which almost entirely filled the floor and then she would disappear for a moment. As the darkness dissolved, the visitor took in the rest of the room: the dark-blue feather boa neatly arranged across the headboard of the bed; the two dim lamps on the little tables on each side of the bed, one with a red bulb and the other with a yellow bulb; the television and video on a trolley at the foot of the bed; the shelves in the nearest corner with the rows of high-heeled shoes and straw boaters; a lacrosse stick perched against the wall; the shop-window torso on the far side of the bed, with a tight black corset clamped to its midriff; the six-foot X-shaped wooden frame that stood behind the door with leather belts for wrist and ankle at the end of each limb; the two leather bullwhips and the thin bamboo cane on the table beside the frame. Then Suzie would return to tell her visitor that the young lady would be with him in a moment.

For Kit Austin, now a few weeks past her sixteenth birthday, the flat in Gloucester Terrace had seemed to offer a kind of salvation. Here, she had been told, she could earn money, she would be looked after, she could survive and feed her gaping appetite for heroin. And the work would not be so bad. So it was that she had found her way down the narrow stone steps and presented herself at Hungarian Suzie's door.

At that moment, back in the spring of 1995, she had had no idea of the step she was really taking. She was only 130 miles away from her home in Nottingham, but already she was deep inside the undiscovered country. She knew no more about this place than her mother did. Like anyone else who walked the streets of London, she could see in every telephone box in the West End the clusters of curious cards offering women for sale but, like almost anyone else who saw these signs, she had no idea of what really lay behind them. Through her eyes, she saw a refuge of sorts. In fact, she was entering into a place that represented all that was most intensely unfair – and all that was most insidiously dangerous – about the undiscovered country and its tormented relationship with the rest of Britain. This was a place of the purest exploitation.

Hungarian Suzie was a small player in this game. Years ago, she had been a working girl herself, but although she was still slim and still moved with a natural elegance, she had become a casualty of her age and she had been forced to become a maid. It was easy enough work. She ran the flat for the working girl, answered the phone, ushered in the customers, tidied up the mess, occasionally cooked a meal for the girl, and took her percentage off the top of the money.

There were other maids like her, behind the doors of other basements, behind the claims of other cards in the telephone boxes: Big Sue, the two Ruthless Ritas in Maida Vale, Jan the

Man, Chris Cave, who had been a woman until the surgeons got to work on her body, Jackie McGwire, Chrissie Flynn. Lucy Cope, who had spent years selling her body in Nottingham and London, was now running her own flat in Warren Street. Her sister Jean was running a flat near Baker Street; and her third sister, May, was out of the business only because the police had decided to drive her away. But, like Hungarian Suzie, these were all small players, maids who ran only one flat with only one girl. They all knew who the big players were, but they knew enough to stay well clear of them and certainly not to talk about them.

Those who simply saw the cards in the phone boxes might imagine, if they took the time to ask the question, that those who ran this hidden industry in the heart of London would be men, probably young, muscular men with chunks of gold jewellery on their hands and wrists. They would be wrong. The most powerful figure in the world of London vice in the 1980s and 1990s was a small woman who was old enough to have claimed a pension for years.

People often said that Mary Daly reminded them of Madge, the downtrodden little shrew who sometimes sits at the feet of the comedian Dame Edna Everage, quivering nervously, serving no great purpose other than to be the butt of the Dame's cruellest barbs. Just like Madge, Mary Daly was small and old and thin, she wore carpet slippers and baggy cardigans, and she liked to sit with her ankles crossed and her elbows gathered in her lap. The smoke from her Silk Cut would drift slowly up across her cheek, adding yet another thin layer to the yellow-brown streak which its predecessors had already painted over the years across the loose grey fringe of her hair. But Mary Daly was not downtrodden, and no one made jokes at her expense.

In the rest of the world, this old woman had succeeded in remaining invisible. Her name was not known. Her business was not recognised. But, in the undiscovered country of the poor, she was respected and renowned. More than any other individual, she was the power behind the cards which now littered the city's phone boxes, advertising young women for sale – for beating, for buggery, for golden showers and hard sports and A levels and O levels and all of the other euphemisms of exploitation. Quite simply, Mary Daly was the biggest whoremonger in London.

Few people knew much about her past. She was a Londoner, who had grown up in Islington during the 1920s and 30s with a family who were hooked into the old gang network of north London, villains who hung around Portobello Road and earned a living by blowing safes and staging armed robberies. Those who claimed to know her past said she had worked as a barmaid, sometimes in illegal drinking clubs; some said she once worked behind the bar of the Blind Beggar pub in Whitechapel where Ronnie Kray shot dead George Cornell because he was running with the Richardson gang. They said she married a senior Islington gangster known as Jimmy Essex and had a couple of sons, one of whom had grown up to become a successful businessman while the other, Mick, started working for her as a card boy. For as long as anyone could remember, she had worked in the West End flats. Her friends said her interest was simple: 'Her God is the £1 note.'

Mary's life ran along the rails of a steady routine. She worked five days on, five days off. On her working days, she would leave her neat suburban home, a few minutes' walk from North Wembley underground station, and travel into the West End, to the basement flat of number 169 Gloucester Place, Marylebone (half a mile away from Hungarian Suzie's basement in Gloucester Terrace, Bayswater). There, she would smoke her Silk Cut and watch the television and answer the never-ending phone calls in her gravelly old voice: 'Yes, sir. And where are you, sir? . . . Today, I have a lovely young girl. She's a genuine seventeen-year-old, with shoulder-length blond hair, she has a full 36-22-34 figure, a warm personality and she offers the full range of services . . . Yes, sir. That is a £60 service . . . That would be an £80 service, sir . . . Thank you, sir. Would you like the address?'

Mary Daly was no simple maid. For one thing, she had made a lot of money. Over the years, she had owned scores of working flats in the West End. At any one time, she had half a dozen, each of them occupied by a maid and a girl; each of the girls paying her up to £175 a day in rent – more than £1,000 a day from the group of flats, more than £7,000 a week in cash for the Old Maid. And most of that was profit. In each of the flats, there was a maid to pay; but the working girl had to cover that out of her earnings. For each of the flats, there was a card boy, who wanted £100 a day for distributing a thousand cards through the phone boxes of the West End; the working girl paid him, too. Mary Daly took bundles of cash each week and invested it wisely, in more property and in gold. But, more than wealth, Mary Daly had power.

For years, she had worked with partners who, between them, had made sure that she remained the biggest player in this dark game.

One was Carolyn Dunk, who was more than twenty years younger than Mary and had spent most of her life as a working girl, in Leeds, Manchester, Brighton and, in particular, in Nottingham, where she had been at the heart of a group of young white women who had fallen in love with charismatic young black men and lived in a circus of drugs and prostitution. She still had links with the Forest and, in particular, with Dave Francis, supplier of drugs and, occasionally, of girls.

By the time she had reached Nottingham, Carolyn had left behind her two small children with a lover in Leeds. In Nottingham, she had fallen for Ray Davis, known on the streets as Jack the Ripper because women fell down at his feet, and, as he had progressed from football to armed robbery, she, too, had progressed from a lowly working girl on the pavements around the Forest, to a force in her own right. So it was that she had been able to bribe her way through prison security to get Ray what he wanted when he was locked up for robbery. She used to meet him some afternoons when he was allowed out to help disabled children learn how to play football. The screw would turn a blind eye and let them have a bit of sex but then Ray – who had a streak of unreliability in him – stole an officer's car and sped off to London, where the police found him holding forth over a pint of beer in a pub in Bayswater. Carolyn realised that one of the officers must have grassed Ray to the police, so she grassed them in return.

While Ray was back in prison, Carolyn returned briefly to Leeds and retrieved her daughter, Nicky, then she settled in London, working in the flats, where she began to rake in some serious money. By the time that Ray was released, Carolyn could afford not only to marry him, in April 1989, but to throw an extravagant party at the Royal Lancaster Hotel, after which he and Carolyn settled down to a life of self-indulgence, picnicking on brandy and Temazepam at their comfortable home in Wyndham Street, London W1.

Carolyn was now one of the most prolific working girls in London, a specialist dominatrix, who took her whip to some of the wealthiest backsides in the city. She caused a furore among some of the other girls by allowing her daughter Nicky to hang around in the flat while she dealt with her clients. The girl grew up to the sound of corporal punishment and commercial orgasms.

Inevitably, Carolyn had met Mary Daly. Carolyn had worked for the Old Maid, as a prostitute and as a maid, and because she was sharper than the other girls, because she could charm money out of the punters like knocking blossom off a tree, and because steadfastly she refused to get herself a drug habit like so many of the others, Carolyn was enlisted by Mary as her partner. She moved into a new house in the same quiet suburban street in North Wembley where Mary lived. The two of them became a force to be reckoned with. They owned more flats, they sold more girls, they earned more money than anyone else in London. But it was Mary's other partners who were the real source of her power.

Within the confines of this private world, just about everyone was afraid of Mary Daly and just about everyone gave the same explanation. It was not simply the many years that Mary had been working that made her the boss (and she went back decades, right back to the 1950s when the Messinas and their Maltese cronies had run vice in London); nor was it simply that for the last forty years she had been on nodding terms with some of the most formidable crime firms in the city; nor even that she was herself a strong and occasionally ruthless character. All these things made Mary powerful, but the real source of Mary Daly's power over the years lay in the friends she had made in the Metropolitan Police.

There were some who said she had made these friends by working as an informer, that she had spent years whispering in the ears of friendly policemen in order to get rid of anyone who trespassed on her patch or who tried to poach one of her girls or who did anything at all to upset her. They said she had grown up using the police as though they were her business partners and that Carolyn had done the same, that she had grassed her way through Nottingham and Leeds, settling scores and getting her way, and that in London she had put away a string of pimps who had crossed her. In their world, Mary and Carolyn together were renowned as the busiest pair of informers in London. They were feared for it.

There were many who believed that the two of them had gone a little further than that with some of their friendships. Everyone in the West End knew that for years during the 1960s and 1970s there had been bent officers in the old porn squad. Before they had finally been exposed by the press, they had had their fingers in the tills of all the porn shops and strip clubs and walk-up flats in Soho. There were plenty of police in the West End who were not bent, but there were very few working flats in those days who didn't keep a few bent officers on the books to give them a licence to operate. That was when Mary had learned the game. If she had to hand over a little of her cash, it was a fair investment, no more than a kind of tax she was paying. Everyone knew that Carolyn had learned the same tricks. She liked to boast about how she had bribed some of the prison officers when Ray was inside. She still boasted about how police officers had fallen in love with her and would do anything for her.

Some of those who were closest to the two women said they had no doubt at all that they still paid for a few friends in high places – a single detective in one of the West End stations would be able to keep his finger on the pulse, tell them if there was going to be a crack-down, slip them a little information from the police computer, keep them informed if one of their girls got arrested on the street. It didn't have to be an officer who dealt with them direct. Any bent policeman would do.

There were working girls who swore they knew that it was not only money that Mary would give to her bent friends – that she had set up sexual favours as well. One girl who had spent years in the flats used to tell how one afternoon Mary had told her she wanted her to do a freebie. 'There's a cozzer coming and we want to keep him sweet.' The girl argued and refused to do it, but Mary insisted. She told her she had to dress up as a schoolgirl and do as he told her. He was a spanker, Mary said. And the girl's job was to let him have what he wanted.

Mary and Carolyn didn't seem to mind if people did think they had a few policemen pimping for them, even if it was now mostly a thing of the past. If a young girl coming into the flats for the first time heard about the two of them and decided that they were too powerful to compete with, too dangerous to cross – well, that was doing them no harm. If, from time to time, Carolyn and Mary were seen with a policeman drinking in a pub off the Edgware Road or sharing an Italian meal in Bayswater, it did no harm at all if people guessed that that must prove they still had coppers on the payroll.

For years, Mary and Carolyn had been the biggest entrepreneurs in the world of London vice. Both of them had criminal records. Carolyn, in particular, had ended up in jail, but mostly they survived and prospered without punishment by living in the grey area where the law did not quite touch them. It was not against the law to work as a prostitute. It was a crime to run a brothel, but the law said that a flat with only one maid and one working girl did not amount to a brothel. It was an ancient English crime to run a disorderly house and during the 1980s a few of the flats who were selling torture had been charged in this way, but now just about all of them sold violence as well as sex and the prosecutors said there was no suitable law to stop them. It was a crime to procure women for prostitution, to solicit for prostitution, to live off immoral earnings, but Mary and Carolyn and many of the other smaller operators survived without provoking a charge. It was almost too big for the police to control.

In the late 1970s, there had been around 50 walk-up flats in Soho and a thin scattering of flats in other parts of the West End who used coy avertisements in contact magazines and tourist guides to bring in the clients. By the late 1980s in the West End of London there were more than 200 'call flats' using cards in the phone boxes and newsagents' windows.

Mary Daly rose with the tide. While others had only one flat, she and Carolyn were running their business in and around Baker Street, Edgware Road, Harewood Avenue, Cabell Street, Maida Vale, Sussex Gardens and Seymour Place. They even opened a penthouse among some of the most prestigious flats in the City of London, in the Barbican, where in Seddon House, Lauderdale Place, next door to captains of industry and senior civil servants, they managed to run a four-bedroom brothel complete with dungeon, torture room, two other working rooms and a video fantasy room. But most of all, they worked in Gloucester Place, north of the Marylebone Road, where a cluster of basement flats were the nearest thing that London had to a concentrated red-light district. Tourists might look in Soho, but genuine punters went to Gloucester Place and looked for a high-heeled shoe in the window of a basement flat. Over the years, in this single block of Gloucester Place, there had been flats in the basements of 138, 142, 144, 152, 158, 164 and 169. While Mary used 169 as her headquarters, Carolyn was based opposite at 152. This was the heart of their empire.

When Kit Austin, a few weeks past her sixteenth birthday, walked down the steps half a mile away at number 32 Gloucester Terrace, it was this world that she was entering. The route which had taken her there was alarming, but terribly simple.

In Nottingham, that winter of 1994–95, Kit's mother had reacted to the news from the school nurse by struggling for months to keep her daughter safe. Judy had heard about people being addicted to drugs, and she had always thought that it meant that they really liked them. She never knew it meant that they just couldn't stop. She knew all about people being addicted to alcohol. Her father had been an alcoholic for years and she had seen how he had dragged down everyone around him, how her mother and her brothers and sisters had all become victims of his madness and his violence. She could still remember him hauling her through the streets, chattering, poncing fivers off people as he went, always brilliant, always dangerous. She wasn't going to go through something like that again, with Kit. So she tried everything she could think of to help her.

As soon as the school nurse told her that Kit was on methadone, she called the police and asked them to find the dealer, because she imagined that Kit was buying from only one person and if she could just get him arrested, then that would be the end of the problem. The police did come to interview Kit, but they never arrested anyone. That same day, she called her doctor and took Kit to see him. He got Kit to admit that she had been smoking heroin as well as swallowing tots of methadone, but all he could do was to refer her to an agency called Open Doors, which tried to help young people who were in trouble with drugs. Judy managed to get Kit admitted to Thorneywood Hospital, where the doctors assessed her and attempted to wean her off her habit. Judy thought maybe that had done some good, but, a week after Kit was discharged, apparently free of heroin, Judy noticed her behaving oddly.

She had spent the day at Open Doors and she had come home giggling and laughing about nothing. Judy, who was now alert to every oddity, watched Kit closely when she said ta-ra that evening and walked off up the street, and so she saw her stop in the winter darkness and very deliberately place something in a rubbish bin in the street. When Kit walked off, Judy scuttled out into the street, reached into the bin and retrieved a small silver bag containing a black tube, several syringes and some needles. Kit was still using.

Judy exploded in rage at Open Doors. A woman from the agency came round to her house and tried to explain that they had given Kit this little silver bag, because if she was determined to use drugs, it was best that she used clean equipment. Judy saw red, threw herself at the drugs worker and tried to batter her, then she turned on Kit and said she couldn't have her in the house if she was going to be using drugs, not with her boys around. That night, Kit left home and went to a hostel. Alexandra Court stood next to a hospice full of dying people opposite a street corner where prostitutes who could not find a beat on the Forest came to sell themselves. Halfway between death and sex. Judy thought she would be safe. She had no idea that on her first night in the hostel, Kit would be approached by a volunteer worker from Open Doors, an amiable young man named Pete, who first would sit down in her room and smoke grass with her and then would ask her if she could help him to buy some more.

A few days later, Kit was transferred to the Nottingham Clinic, a specialist unit which ran a strict regime in which no drug abuse was permitted and which was supported by counselling and advice. In there, behind closed doors, Judy thought that at last Kit might find the help she needed. But Judy did not know that Kit was now sharing a room with Miss Popular.

In the years since Spotty Caine put her on the streets, Miss

Popular had lived like a pinball in a flipper machine, bouncing in and out of the kind of places that used to exist only in the inner cities of the United States – drug houses with gunmen on the door, illegal gambling clubs among the high-street shops, squats full of crackheads and prostitutes. Spotty had shunted her down to London and put her to work on the pavements around the Seven Sisters Road, but she had managed to get away from him. He and his friends were too busy running packages of crack cocaine up the M1 to Nottingham to watch her all the time. But she had run straight into the arms of another crackhead. Over the months that followed, she had been passed from man to man. One protected her. Another anally raped her. One pumped her full of crack and beat her when she disobeyed him. Another saved her life when she filled herself with sleeping pills. All that mattered, all that gave her purpose, was to find another pipe of crack. She hired herself out to men in cars and flats and hotel rooms and in the windswept corners of the Homebase car park in Seven Sisters. It was a world of chaos.

One crazy weekend, she found herself sitting in a seedy hotel called The Carlisle which was run by an old African man named Moses, just across the road from Kings Cross Station. The prostitutes were bringing in the cash; the rude boys were handing out the crack. She was no longer surprised by any of it. She just wanted to smoke. Sitting in the hotel was a wealthy pimp with big gold rings on his fingers, who had made a lot of money out of making pornographic films. He was disgusting, but he had money and a bag of rocks. He took a shine to Miss Popular – 'I like this bit of beef' as he put it – so she agreed to go off with him to his big, plush house. There, they smoked a lot more pipes and she let him have his sex, and since he still had a lot more rocks left, she agreed to stay overnight with him and to make a pornographic film for him the next day. Then he made a mistake. He fell asleep, with his gold rings and his watch on the bedside table. One of the rings had a stone the size of a prune in it.

Ten minutes later, Miss Popular was dressed, she had a pocketful of his jewellery and she was scrambling out over the high wall around his house. She hailed a taxi, drove halfway across London looking for a jeweller's that was open on a Sunday morning, sold her stash for £900, headed for Mayfair and spent several hours drinking champagne with her taxi driver. Then she wanted crack. She headed the taxi driver to Stoke Newington to buy rocks, found a dealer she knew called Bigga who took £150 off her and was just about to hand over a couple of rocks when two other dealers raced up in their car and beat him to the ground, yelling that he was selling 'stingers' – phoney crack. She looked down at Bigga, who seemed to be having convulsions; she grabbed back her money and left him twitching on the ground and found another dealer further up the street, and then she smoked and smoked until all of the £900 was gone.

Eventually she had fled back to Nottingham, hiding in the toilet of the train in case the pimp who currently claimed to own her tried to recapture her. By then, she had picked up a criminal record and lost the custody of her two daughters. She had lost her self-respect and all her ambition, and she had cried until the mascara trailed down to her chin. And now she was in the Nottingham Clinic, desperate to prove that she was good enough to be taken back by her former husband, desperate to be with her kids again, to be normal again.

She liked Kit Austin, she thought she was a laugh and she felt sorry for her, a kid of that age with a heroin habit. The two of them got on well. Miss Popular was more than twenty years older than Kit and she felt protective towards her. She lent her clothes and told her about life on the streets and tried to help her to sort out her future. But Miss Popular had long since lost contact with ordinary life. For all that she longed to return to her former self, to her children, to a day without violence and dread; for all that she was here in this clinic, trying to clean out her body and sort out her mind, she was lost now, deeply devoted to crack cocaine. Barely a day went by when she did not long for it. Worse than that, she had come to enjoy the excitement and the madness of her life in the undiscovered country. So, when Kit told her that sometimes she didn't really want to stop using heroin, and that she wanted to go to London to earn some money, Miss Popular decided to do her a favour.

Miss Popular had worked long enough in London to know who was who and, although she had spent most of her time working on the pavements, she had dabbled with work in the flats. Briefly, she had taken a flat with a maid who knew exactly what she was doing, who had taken one look at this middle-class woman with her big breasts and her tumbling blond hair and seen a valuable investment. The maid had taken her straight off to Harrods to buy her make-up and clothes and she had boasted about how well connected she was with all the right people and how much money they would make together. This maid was Carolyn Dunk.

Miss Popular knew that if anyone could find work for little Kit Austin, it was Carolyn. But she wasn't going to call her herself. She thought she might not be too welcome: after Carolyn had spent good money kitting her out and set her up in a flat near Gloucester Place, Miss Popular worked for only two days before she got fed up with the routine and took the cash she had earned and went out looking for the Crack Man. But she knew someone else who could act as a go-between. His real name was Arthur Williams, but everyone knew him as Moonie.

Moonie came from Leeds but he had spent plenty of time in Nottingham and he had played the same games as all his friends. He had run women in Leeds and Nottingham and then he had started selling them in London. He always liked to deal with Carolyn, because her money was the best. He did well, although one of his girls, who was called Maria, caused a lot of fuss and was almost suicidal when she discovered that this smooth man with whom she had fallen in love was, in fact, farming her like a young heifer.

Moonie had known Carolyn for years. She had made it her business – quite literally her business – to stay in touch with the Nottingham pimps. There was always a demand in the flats for clean, young girls – the blonder the better and the younger the better, as long as they were at least sixteen. Carolyn often took Nottingham girls. It was primarily because of her connections with Nottingham and her influence in the West End flats that the single city of Nottingham provided something like half the working girls in London. She took them from Lucky Golding and his brother Romeo, from Ivan Pinnock, from Esmond, from Spotty Caine, who was living with her old friend Miss Kath. She had a more or less independent business with the Shand boys. One after another, the Shands picked up young white girls in Nottingham and brought them down to Carolyn to earn money. There was one family of white girls where there were three daughters and each one of them was brought down to London one after the other and sold into the flats by the Shand boys. Even the Shand sisters joined in. One of them was involved in setting up Frank Bough, the television commentator, when the story of his love of cocaine and working girls was sold to Fleet Street.

Carolyn also took girls from her oldest friend in Nottingham, Dave Francis, who had become her lover while Ray 'Ripper' Davis was in jail. He was well placed to find them, with crack-crazy adolescent girls trailing through the CAT office, looking for help. Dave had already introduced little Fiona to Carolyn, who told her she would love to use her once she was sixteen.

When Miss Popular called Moonie from the Nottingham Clinic and told him that there was a sixteen-year-old blond girl who wanted to work in the flats with Carolyn, Moonie hit the motorway. That afternoon, he rolled his car into the tarmac square in front of the clinic on Ransome Road, just northeast of the centre of Nottingham, and asked to speak to Miss Popular. The clinic told him to go away. No visitors. Not allowed.

Moonie slunk back to his car. And from one of the ground-floor windows at the front of the clinic, Miss Popular saw him. Kit was standing beside her. Miss Popular rapped on the glass with her knuckles and signalled to Moonie, pointing her finger at Kit, nodding wildly and giving him a thumbs-up. Moonie understood.

Miss Popular was never quite sure how he did it. All she knew was that a day or so later, she did a runner from the clinic and went down to London and, after a few days of madness, she was walking through St Pancras Station and she saw Kit with a worker from the clinic, evidently waiting to go back to Nottingham. She didn't know what they were doing, but she knew what Kit was carrying – Miss Popular's own handbag, one that she had left some weeks ago at Moonie's place in Ealing. Kit must have been inside Moonie's flat. Somehow he had got her out of the clinic and taken her to London.

On that day, Kit went back up to Nottingham, to the clinic, but soon she was released from there and then she disappeared into undiscovered London, like Alice going underground. Most of the time, she stayed with Moonie and his sidekick Freddie in Ealing. When she wanted to go home for a few days, Freddie drove her to St Pancras. When she wanted to return to London, he was there to ferry her back to work. Moonie made good use of her.

This wasn't exactly about sex. Very few of the flats sold simple sex. Mostly, they sold violence, violence that the punters wanted inflicted on themselves, or violence that they wanted to inflict on the women, and sheer craziness.

Some of the clients were almost legendary. In flats in Earls Court and the City and Gloucester Place and Mayfair, the same characters were regulars.

There was one man who turned up in Carolyn Dunk's penthouse flat in the Barbican and, in a single evening, he blew something like £20,000 in cash. He sat there with four working girls, smoking pipe after pipe of crack cocaine, occasionally announcing that he wanted to bugger one of the girls or to tie her up and beat her senseless with a riding crop. He became a regular. In one flat after another in central London, the same well-spoken man in the elegant suit would turn up at night with a bundle of cash and, in a single evening, he would blow it all on girls and on rock after rock of crack cocaine. He would pull money out of his briefcase, out of his pockets – once he scooped it up in handfuls from the boot of his car – and he would literally throw it around. He had money. He had power. He had a whip in his hand.

He had virtually no sex. He smoked so much crack that he was almost impotent. But he would sit for hours, smoking pipes of crack cocaine with the girls, talking about his Swiss bank accounts and his clever stockbroking deals and his mighty bonus payments, telling the girls exactly what he wanted to do to them – which was usually something sadistic – and handing out bundles of cash until the money had gone. Then he would drive off into the night in his Porsche, which he changed at least twice a year, or his other car, a new Ferrari. A night or two later, he would be back in the same flat or else in another. Three or four times a week, this man was turning up in the flats and blowing a small fortune. His supply of money seemed endless. He had bought himself a large town house in St John's Wood and a country house in Hertfordshire, he was sending his son to Harrow and, when he turned up in the flats, his money bestowed on him an absolute power. What he wanted, he could buy: crack; a young girl to whip; another young girl to poke around. He was rich. They were poor. He had desires. They had needs. They did as they were told.

It was the same in all the flats. Rich, old men did whatever they liked with poor, young women, most of them crackheads. They used chains and cuffs and crops and canes, they played with whipping stools and flogging frames, they ordered up the women as nurses and schoolgirls and nuns and teachers, they tied them and poked them and hurt them and smeared them. They didn't apologise for their tastes. They just paid and did as they liked.

There was a man who used to make the girls dress up in school uniforms so that he could cane them; he turned out to be a real headmaster. There was another who liked to pretend to be a magistrate. He'd set up a court in the bedroom, charge the girl with driving without due care and attention or drunken driving and then try her, convict her, and, inevitably, punish her with a stick. The oddest thing about him was that he used to turn up with what appeared to be genuine court papers to help him in his fantasy. How had he got hold of them? The girls could only guess that somewhere in some real court, he truly was a magistrate.

Some of the men dredged up desires that beggared the imagination. The Hangman liked to have a rope tied around his neck so that a girl could haul him upwards on a pulley, throttling him to orgasm. Another man was desperate for clingfilm. The girl had to strip him, wrap him in clingfilm from his ankles to the top of his head and then stand back as the plastic wrapping gripped his body and, in particular, his face, cutting off his air so that he slowly started to suffocate. His aim was to have an orgasm before he ran out of air. The job for the girl was to watch his feet: when he wagged them, he was dying and needed to be unwrapped. Some of the girls placed bets about how long he would survive before he died in one of their flats. If he did die, they'd have to drag him out and prop him against a lamppost somewhere. You couldn't have corpses in the working flats. But the man just kept on turning up, carrying his four-foot roll of industrial clingfilm in his arms.

There were a handful of politicians who liked to turn their

backs on national power to exert a power of a more personal type. One was a Member of Parliament – a likeable left-of-centre young man – who was a compulsive visitor to the flats where he spent a small fortune indulging some terrible obsessions. He would not put a foot through the door unless he was assured that there was no one in the flat apart from the maid and her girl. He wore a pair of black-framed spectacles which the girls were almost sure were false. He always wore the same beige mac, apparently hoping to conceal his real clothing. But the girls knew him. He gave them his real first name; once or twice he even paid by cheque. More than that, they had seen him on television, perched politely on the green benches of the House of Commons, waving his order paper. Once, when he was busy, one of the maids had peeked in his briefcase and found it full of official paperwork.

His routine was always the same: the girl was to wear white knickers; she was to go into the bathroom, while he waited for her in the bedroom; she was to shit into her knickers, come and knock on the bedroom door, and then let him peel the knickers off her while he excited himself to orgasm. Then he put the soiled knickers in his briefcase and went away. The girls used to see him on television with the same briefcase by his side, and shake their heads in wonder at what must be in there. Sometimes, on his most crazy days, he would add one terrifying extra scene to his routine. Before he left, he would produce hospital suture needles, strip from the waist down and lie on his back on the bed and order the girl to squeeze his testicles until they were as hard as rocks – and then drive the needles into them.

He never hurt the girls. He was not one to whip them, like several of his Parliamentary colleagues, but he took them into this nightmare of his own making. He needed someone – some pretty young girl – to join him inside it, and so he used his power to buy her.

The working girls didn't like him. After a while, they ceased to like any men. All they saw was sickness imposed on them. There were some men who never even touched them. One beautifully dressed stockbroker in his early forties wanted nothing more than to swallow the contents of used condoms in the wastebin while his mobile phone trilled in the background. Nightmares. This was the world that was waiting for Kit Austin.

28

It was months before Judy Austin found out what had really happened to her daughter.

Kit's friends reluctantly unfurled the story of how Kit had found her way from the life of a schoolgirl to that of a heroin addict. Their main point was that it was easy.

Judy heard that Kit had been eleven years old – in her first year at secondary school – when she had started to smoke grass. She had done it because everybody else at school was doing it – well, almost everyone. It turned out that in the mornings, when she had gone skipping off down the street in her black-and-grey uniform and her neat white shirt, she had often stopped and smoked a spliff on the way to the bus stop. She was usually stoned in her lessons, they said, and, in the lunch hour, she and her mates would wander down to the little shop in the high street, where they bought cobs and chips, and they'd sit on the bench outside or on the low wall and have another spliff or two before they went back to class.

In the evenings, it was the same. She and her mates would go to this crappy little bit of public grass which they called Crazy Park, where they'd sit and shiver in the winter or sunbathe in the summer, and they'd smoke more spliffs. Almost everybody did it. It wasn't just kids from Kit's school. There were other kids from other schools who lived round her part of Nottingham, and older kids as well who had nothing better to do than hang around with them. They called themselves the Crazy Crew.

Pretty soon, Kit tried speed. It was her auntie's boyfriend who got her into it first. He lived up in Broxtowe and he was a well-known dodgy character. He sold second-hand cars and he always knew how to get rid of video recorders and televisions that the kids brought round to him, and he gave his little niece some speed when she was twelve or thirteen. Some of her friends said Kit was sleeping with him for it, but they weren't sure. She said she was, but maybe she was just saying it. There was another place they used to get speed, much nearer to Kit's home. Just around the corner, there was this elderly man, who looked like a really respectable gentleman but who used to have all this drug-taking in his house. He was into all sorts of weird things, palm-reading and star signs. As far as her friends knew, it was the summer of 1994, when Kit was fifteen, that she first got into heroin.

There was this lad called Wayne, a scruffy, runtish little guy who was a junkie. He used to hang around the old gentleman's house – they'd seen him in the toilet there one day, with the door open, injecting himself. Kit started going round to this Wayne's house, and he offered her little tots of methadone, which he'd been prescribed by the doctor as a substitute for heroin. He told Kit she could have a tot, and it would really get her out of her head, as long as she gave him some sex. And she agreed. Her friends said that was the thing about Kit: she'd always been fearless, she'd always been more mature than most of them, even down to carrying a little handbag and talking in a very grown-up way. One evening, her mate *Tessa* had been with her down in town and this carload of lads had gone by whistling and Kit had waved at them. The lads had driven round again and stopped next to them, and the next thing Tessa knew, Kit had got in the car with them and gone off.

Pretty soon, her friends said, Kit started turning up at school with these little tubs of methadone, sharing them with Tessa and some of the others during the lunch break. Then she found another dealer who started giving her loads of heroin – 'brown' she called it now. By coincidence, he was called Wayne as well. He was a big, swish idiot, who used to go off to Thailand all the time. When he was in Nottingham, he'd hang around young people's pubs with his sidekick, who looked like a monkey. He'd made the same deal with Kit as Little Wayne: he gave her brown, she let him use her body. In the lunch hour now, Kit and her mates would sit on the wall outside the shop and smoke heroin.

Tessa got so sick on it one day that she thought she was going to die in her French lesson, but Kit just thought it was hysterical.

After a while, the two Waynes started to get heavy with Kit. In the beginning, they'd been OK, all they wanted was a blow job, but after a while they started saying she had to give them money for her brown, so Kit had started doing a lot of shoplifting. Well, the truth was, the friends said, that she'd always nicked things. She used to get her Christmas presents that way, but now she got so good at it that she'd nick to order and get everyone else's Christmas presents for them, too, and sell them to them at half-price. She started taking things from home – Judy knew herself that a lot of jewellery had gone missing – and the friends said there was no doubt about it, Kit had taken it and sold it. She'd got to the point where she didn't mind what she did.

She'd broken up with Sam, who smoked a lot of weed but didn't like her using heroin, and she'd tried to make out that she was pregnant and needed an abortion. She said Sam had to pay her £200 for it, but Sam knew it was bullshit. The next thing he knew, Big Wayne and his monkey friend turned up at the place where Sam was working and told him that if he didn't pay Kit £200, they'd break his legs. Kit must have known they were doing it – they were saying he had to pay the money to her, not to them – and Sam felt pretty bad that his girlfriend would try and do that to him. He told his mum, who knew some people who sorted Wayne out. Kit found other ways to make her money – out on the pavement around the Forest.

Judy didn't really want to hear that. She knew there were kids selling themselves there. There was a girl in Kit's school who was doing it – Judy's sister had seen her – but it was hard to think of her own daughter doing it. And, at the time, she had known nothing. In the spring of 1995, all she knew was that Kit had come out of the Nottingham Clinic towards the end of March and gone down to London. Once or twice, during April, she had been back, and she had seemed OK, but there was no knowing what she was doing down there. Judy hoped she was with friends.

Kit had come into London on the train from Nottingham and walked out of St Pancras Station into the world of Kings Cross – cheaper and rougher and tougher than anything she had had to deal with in Nottingham. Kings Cross was like a great drain, a plughole for the city of London, into which the weakest and the poorest were sucked without hope of resistance.

There was a woman called Marilyn Lowe who was almost a walking biography of Kings Cross. She had worked here for fifteen years, usually at the top of Belgrove Street, taking the punters around the corner up against the post-office wall or into the cramped hotels in Argyle Square – £20 for the service, £20 for the room and a towel. Her life was full of trouble. She had a huge drug habit, she was a police informer, she always had fines to pay, she often had angry punters chasing her because she had robbed them ('clipping them', she called it). And there was something else, something deeply sad inside her. Most of the time, she said nothing about it, just carried on hustling, but occasionally, when she was out of her head in the small hours of the morning, she would talk about how her little boy had died in his cot back in Sheffield.

Marilyn used to spend a lot of time in the old Carlisle Hotel, before the police busted it. There were dealers in there serving up crack, working girls smoking, punters smoking, while old Ivan who owned the place and Moses, his manager, calmly watched over it all. All the Kings Cross people used to go in there: the chubby Irish girl who gave birth and was back on the street within forty-eight hours; Joanne who had just been in prison where they had discovered she was six months pregnant; Addie, the half-caste Ghanaian, with his £10 bags of brown; the blond girl whose face had been bashed by a punter because she had tried to stop him buggering her; Ron the meat man, who survived on a diet of 100 per cent meat and sold porn videos to pay for it; Twiggy who sold herself along with her adolescent daughters. Marilyn was always in the Carlisle.

When Marilyn died, aged only forty-one, they all talked about what had happened to her. They said she had been beaten so badly in a porn movie that her heart had given out, that she had been killed by someone she had grassed on, that she had overdosed on heroin or crack, that she had been killed by dealers who said she owed them money, that the police had done it because she had threatened to tell what she knew about the drugs they were selling. She could have died so many ways.

They buried her and then they carried on.

Kit Austin walked through this world like a day-tripper in Disneyland, surrounded by some kind of fantasy version of real life. There were the girls hovering around the post office door, occasionally breaking off to buy a Kit-Kat, chucking the chocolate on the pavement so they could use the silver foil to cook up a smoke. There were the black lads with hoods over their heads shuffling their feet outside the amusement arcade on Kings Cross Road and by the cinema on the Pentonville Road. They kept the rocks of crack wrapped in clingfilm, stuffed up inside their upper lip, where they could tongue them out and swallow them if the police came and hassled them. They could hold twenty rocks a time like that. There were girl dealers in there, too, like Pauline Read, who became one of the biggest dealers in Kings Cross before she was even twenty years old. The girls used to keep the rocks up inside their vaginas – 'in the fridge'. There was one dirty white dealer called Fox who used to keep his wraps up his backside. Then, if he had a buyer, he'd wriggle around in the back of his pants and finger it out and, sometimes, if he was selling to a woman, he'd put it in his mouth and kiss it into hers. The girls usually had no idea where the rock had been. He liked that. 'A Kings Cross kiss,' he called it. He was proud of it, until one of the papers published pictures of him doing it.

There were no heroes here. There was a girl who coughed so loud that it sounded like laughter. She was trying to have a fight with a dealer, standing with her arms stiff with anger, telling him she'd paid him, she'd fucking paid him, and coughing till she cackled, while the dealer shook his head and walked away. There was Avril with her tin of Tennants, battered and bruised, one of the walking wounded from her family's battle with its demons. There was Maureen with the stained red hair, and someone else who seemed to be her sister but who turned out to be a man. And there was Vinnie, as close as you got to a hero in Kings Cross.

Vinnie had a kind of strength. Once, he had been a successful pimp in the West End and he had owned his own house near Argyle Square. Now, he was a serious crackhead who lived off the Liverpool Road in Islington in a small, dark flat that looked like a stage set for a play about a junkie – bare boards, an old sheet nailed up across the window, no sound system, no television, no books, no nothing that could have been sold. He lived with two women, not because they were having sex, but because they kept each other alive. Vinnie cooked lamb stew and scored crack. The women earned money. Each afternoon, as the rest of the world headed home, they started to stir. Heather would pull on her Sunday-best clothes, comb her hair, pick up a knitted brown bag with wooden hoop handles and go off to work as a shoplifter. Beverley would haul her skeletal frame out of Vinnie's bed, briefly flashing her ribs like a collection of coat hangers beneath her pale white skin, she would bath, find a bottle of unusually strong wine, and start searching the place for make-up. If she couldn't find any, she'd grab the tub of margarine which usually lay among the pipes and cigarette ends on the little table by the bed and she would dab it into the shadows under her eyes. Finally, when she was ready, when she had had another couple of mouthfuls of wine, she would head for Kings Cross and the streets of the city, hoping to avoid the policeman who threatens her with arrest unless she gives him blow jobs without a condom, hoping to find a punter she could clip before the night was too old.

Vinnie knew everyone. He had known Marilyn for years – he was one of the few men she told about her dead son. He had lived with Miss Popular when she first came to London and ran away from Spotty Caine, and, despite his many years of experience on the streets, he had broken a rule and fallen in love with her. He had found himself hanging around with a hammer waiting to bash any punter who abused her. But he was fading now, physically weaker from his crack habit, broke, about to be kicked out of his crummy flat for failing to pay the rent, a step or two away from sleeping on the pavements of Kings Cross.

Kit Austin stepped through Kings Cross and headed for the West End, where the working flats were. She passed along the Strand, where every evening saw the homeless pull themselves into shop doorways for the night. Like Kings Cross, this, too, was a little world on its own.

There were men and women who had lived here for years – like Bob Easton who had first made his home in the shop doorways here more than ten years earlier. Bob knew how to stay clean by ducking into the showers at the Oasis sports centre; how to get a free drink by mingling with the audience at the first nights in the theatres and galleries on the South Bank; how to get a free cake from the lady at Sheraton's by Waterloo Bridge; how to stash his bags during the day on the fire escape of the Vaudeville Theatre, which was like an unofficial left-luggage department for the homeless.

But there were children who drifted into a place like the Strand with almost no idea of how to survive. Bob Easton met a girl like this tripping along the street one night, looking small and scared and lost. She was fifteen years old, she was called Sharon and she had no idea of how to look after herself. In fact she looked so helpless that even though Bob had always told himself that you could trust no one on the street, that your only job was to look after yourself, he invited her into his doorway and set out to look after her himself.

By that time, Bob could see there was a whole new generation of young people pouring onto the streets, and they were nothing like the old-timers like himself. Most of the old homeless were on the street because they were misfits of one kind or another – alcoholic, epileptic, schizophrenic, simply sad – anyone at all who was marked out by some frailty and then punished for it by the crowd. Some of them kept their true lives secret, tucked away behind matted beards and rheumy eyes: the university physicist whose life had been ruined by schizophrenia; the senior social worker who'd studied classics at Durham and been destroyed by drink. But there were others whose pain was beyond disguise. Like Sylvie, who had been sleeping rough round Lambeth ever since the war. She'd been in some kind of concentration camp as an adolescent – she still had the blue number tattooed on her skin – and there were times when she was still crazy with it and she'd stand on her bedding and yell, 'Yes, commandant! No, commandant!' Or she'd go out on the pavement by North Lambeth Day Centre and take off her shirt and flap her naked breasts at the buses going by. There was old Peggy, who shuffled round Waterloo Station, picking up titbits from the cafés there, her whole life bent out of shape by some faraway torment. And Sean, who had become so depressed that he had staggered onto the wall of Waterloo Bridge and leaped into the Thames. The tide was out and he had broken both ankles.

The streets were a kind of oblivion where people went to forget and hoped to be forgotten. Only rarely did they come to terms with the pasts they had left behind.

There was one strange fellow who was known as Little Michael, who had spent years living round St Martin-in-the-Fields church. He was in his sixties, he always had a fresh carnation in his buttonhole, which he got from Janet the flower lady on the Strand, and he was almost always drunk. He was a happy fellow. He'd sit for hours with his bottle of cider, being cheeky to the people passing by, inviting them all to give him a kiss, particularly the good-looking young men. One day, he was found dead in a doorway and, although everyone had always thought he spent all his money on drink, it turned out he had been steadily saving a little bit of cash each week for years so that he could have a big funeral service in St Martin's. He'd quietly told Janet the flower lady about his relations. And suddenly, this lonesome alcoholic man had filled the whole church with friends and family from the life he had left behind him decades before.

But when Bob Easton looked at young people like Sharon, he saw something different. They weren't escaping on to the streets. There was no escape for them because the source of their pain was the whole of their lives – useless, pointless, hopeless lives. They had grown up to believe there was nothing for them in life – no real interest, no good work, no genuine help, no future worth fighting for. So they had walked out on their run-down schools and their broken families and left behind the world they had been offered. They hadn't been pushed out like most of the older homeless, they had walked out on the world and now they were sitting with their backs to it, daring it to come after them. They weren't burying their misery. It was more like they were advertising it.

You could see them at seven in the morning, already at the Special Brew and the tins of Tennants, and then it was wacky baccy, speed, smack, crack – anything at all that might mess them up. All day, every day. They just seemed to stumble from one pointless moment to the next. They'd steal your blankets to go begging and then, when they'd finished, they'd just chuck them in the river. If they didn't like you, they'd set on you with knives and scaffold poles. While the old ones struggled to survive, the young ones seemed to be addicted to disaster. They didn't care about anything. It wasn't even as if they were trying to destroy themselves. They didn't care either way. A useless, pointless, hopeless world.

When the young people had first started pouring out on the streets – when the government took away their benefits in the late 1980s – Bob had watched them trying to make little communities for themselves, where they could look out for each other. They used to chase away troublemakers and drug dealers. They even set up little letter boxes in cardboard boxes for messages. A few of the older generation had become leaders down there, especially old Cowboy, who would sit outside his cardboard bash, sharing his thoughts about the world. He was well respected, but then he had got sick and ended up in some home in Oxford.

These communities had never been very stable and when the police came in and broke them up a few times, they had all fallen apart. Now almost all the young ones were into the drink and some of them were into the drugs as well. And it all brought trouble down on their heads. To get the drink and the drugs, they had to get money, so some of them stole and some of them became prostitutes and the rest of them begged, so then there was trouble with the law and, worse than that, they'd got these 'taxers', some of the bigger, tougher homeless kids who ran around taking their earnings with the threat of a kicking. Bandit, Mad Geordie, Paul Harrington – bad people. There wasn't even that much money to be made out of begging. The police reckoned that when they arrested them, they usually found about three pounds in their pockets. They were so vulnerable. Someone had had their cardboard 'bash' firebombed down in the Bull Ring subway near Waterloo. And there was a young girl down there who had been raped and horribly mutilated. No one had helped her.

More than anything, Bob Easton wanted to protect young Sharon from all this. He showed her how to live on the streets, taught her his tricks, got her selling the *Big Issue* so she had some cash, tried to stop her drifting. But all the same she did.

She would vanish for days at a time, usually when some young lad came by offering her tablets and things. Bob would wait anxiously, and sooner or later she would come back. Then, one day, she went off with some bloke he'd never seen before, and days passed without any sign of her returning. Bob started tramping the streets in search of her, all the way up to Kings Cross, in and out of back streets, in the arches near Waterloo Station. No sign. A couple of weeks passed and one day, Bob was sitting in his doorway on the Strand when he saw a young lad who had often hung around Sharon. The lad noticed Bob sitting there and said, 'You hear what happened to Sharon?'

Bob shook his head.

'She's dead,' said the lad. 'They found her in a gents' toilet in New Cross.'

Bob Easton sat alone in his doorway.

'Some kind of overdose,' the lad said.

All along the Strand, the shoppers and the tourists came and went, homeless people panhandling the flow, taxis lining up outside the Savoy, winos crumpled in doorways, all these people. He didn't know any of them.

Kit had slipped into this city like a light going out in the dark. Moonie had let her stay at his flat in Ealing and screwed her until he was content and then he'd made himself a little cash by selling her to Carolyn Dunk. Carolyn earned a little money from her by putting her to work in one of the flats.

So this was London. Everybody in the world knew London. It was where the Queen lived, where they had black taxis and red buses and streets full of theatres and restaurants. The London that enveloped Kit was a different place. It was not just the working flats or the street people. There were the crack houses, too, and the shebeens and the gambling houses and the illegal clubs. A world within a world.

Most of it was new. The first crack house in London had been set up on the North Peckham Estate in 1988. It was well fortified with iron bars on the windows and an iron grille at the door. No one came in. The buyers made their deals through a little flap in the door. Pretty soon, there were crack houses everywhere, a lot of them run by Yardies from Jamaica.

There was crack in Camberwell, where Pepsi, who had led the Rapid Posse in Kingston, set things up before he moved on to the Midlands. He was running things out of a barber's shop in

Camberwell Church Street, selling into reinforced houses on all the local estates. There was crack in Peckham, where Squiddley from the Black Rose Crew in Kingston was moving a lot of gear – through a different barber's shop – until he died in a police station in south London. His death didn't make any difference to anyone. The crack kept coming. Stripes and Parrot and Teacher and Big Lee just took over where Squiddley had left off, setting up houses and keeping them supplied.

There was crack in Brixton, where Wayne and Paul sold from the steps of a church. There was crack in Harlesden, where Dooley and Clint Eastwood sold through houses on the Stonebridge Estate and set up a trade which spread all across the borough. There was crack in Clapham, where Redman and Elvis from the Georges Lane Crew in Kingston were washing crack in a house in Bedford Road, selling it to Lisa and Lover and Binie, who was a gunman from Concrete Jungle in Kingston. Redman had a pump-action Remington shotgun, two pistols and a collection of new 9-mm Brownings which he had stashed at a house in Felmersham Close in Clapham. He ended up getting shot, though he survived and refused to give evidence against the woman who had shot him. He wanted her to be free so he could kill her himself.

There were crack houses all over Notting Hill, in All Saints Road and Lancaster Road and up and down Ladbroke Grove, where Marcia Beckford and her mate Marva had run the scene for years. Marcia had a crazy life. She had been living with a Yardie musician known as Tapper Zoochie who had pictures of her with a mouthful of his cock and a gun at her head. Marcia had scars all over her body which she said were the marks of Tapper Zoochie's belts and guns. She said that Tapper Zoochie had raped her daugher Nereeka when she was only a child. Nereeka lived in fear of him – particularly after her friend Genevieve went back to Jamaica and got raped and tortured to death with her eyes gouged out. Nereeka was sure it was friends of Tapper Zoochie who had punished Genevieve as a message not to talk about his affairs.

After that, Nereeka took refuge with a Yardie in London called Ratty. He usually carried an Uzi sub-machine-gun with him because he had killed some guy whose friends wanted his blood.

He looked after Nereeka and kept her safe, until he got shot on All Saints Road in July 1993. The doctors patched him up and he survived long enough to get himself to New York, where he found himself a fight and finally got shot dead. Ratty was lucky in a way. He'd nearly ended up in jail for life. A Yardie called Eaton Green, who was grassing for Scotland Yard, had decided to put him away, so he'd told Ratty he'd pay him to kill a musician who owed him some money for a crack deal. Ratty went to do it; the musician went down on his knees and begged; Ratty wasn't too moved by that, in fact it made it nice and easy to shoot him through the eye, but Nereeka was in the room and she said she didn't want him to do it and after a while, Ratty put his gun away, so Eaton Green never got to grass him for murder.

The police were after Marcia for a long time. They busted her sister Joanne, thinking it was her, and her brother, Thin Hand Barry, too. He had been brought up by Bob Marley in Jamaica and got caught up in the political violence and now the police in London were after him, because he was supposed to have shot a guy called Ritchie in a bar in Hackney. Marcia got busted in the end in her house with a transvestite guy called Tina and a local black lad called Hitchcock, who had been grassing to the police. She got seven years. In the crack houses down Ladbroke Grove, Marva and the others carried on just the same.

By the time that Kit Austin started wandering through the streets of this unseen London, there were guns everywhere in the crack houses and the shebeens. There had been a time when a gun was a rare thing in the London ghettos. Even in the Jamaican ghettos, in the early 1980s kids used to saw off the crossbars of bicycles to make their own shooters. In London in the late 1980s, there had been a big scare when a guy called Cutter Dread arranged to import a load of 9-mm Glocks from New York so that he could do some shooting at the Notting Hill Carnival. He was bringing them over in packets of soap powder, with the barrels in tubes of lipstick. But the guns never got through. One of his women, Sweet Pants, told the police they were coming; some bent officers got to hear of her information and tipped off Cutter Dread, so he made a deal with them and grabbed his passport and ran before the guns arrived.

Now, it was different. In Jamaica, all the big Yardies and all the little rude boys had handguns and semi-automatics, they had Uzi sub-machine-guns and M-16s. And in London, everybody in the crack houses and the shebeens carried a gun. They'd go to Maxim's in Kingsland High Road or the Pyramid Club or Steppers in Brixton or Trends in Stoke Newington, and when they liked the music well enough, they'd salute the sounds by firing live bullets into the ceiling. They'd also shoot each other at the drop of a word.

In August 1988, a guy called Rohan Bailey, known as Yardie Ron, got shot to pieces in a row about crack in Harlesden. Seven different people took shots at him, they hit him with twelve bullets. He was the first crack killing in London. Now, they were killing each other on all sides.

Rankin Dread, who at one time was the most powerful Yardie in London, had been on the wrong end of a shooting in the Four Aces in Stoke Newington. He had been shot at by Patrick Roach, whose brother ended up shooting himself dead in the reception area of Stoke Newington police station. Rankin Dread had ducked the bullets in the Four Aces and one of them had ended up in Donald Brown's eye.

Miss Popular told Kit how she had been in a crack house in Stoke Newington with two young black guys and without a rock in sight or smell. They were getting desperate and the two guys, who were brothers, decided to scrape out an old pipe and try and smoke the scrapings. One of them was using a kitchen knife and a screwdriver to clean out the pipe, while Miss Popular and the other guy sat and watched. Finally, the pipe was clean and the guy who had cleaned it went to light it up. His brother started to protest, claiming that he ought to have the first toke. An argument developed, and the guy with the pipe grabbed the screwdriver and stabbed his brother through the chest.

There was always violence; people setting up deals and ripping each other off, people pulling guns because they liked the look of someone else's gold medallion. There was a guy who walked into a shebeen on the Harrow Road wearing a fancy pair of hand-tooled leather shoes. The guy next to him at the bar reckoned these shoes had been stolen from his house a week earlier, so he shot the guy dead. There were no friends in these places, only people who were stronger than you, whom you treated with respect; and people who were weaker than you, whom you ripped off, no matter how long you'd known them. There was always danger.

Miss Popular had been to score crack from a big dealer in Stoke Newington, a Greek guy who was known as George Michael, who made the mistake of going out of the room and leaving Miss Popular alone with his stash. She walked away with the lot. About eight months later, some guy she had met took her up to the top floor of a block of flats in Islington. Because she was good-looking and blond, she got in through the security gate, past the two guys with guns on the door, past the racks of televisions and sound systems that people had brought there to trade for rocks, and she came face to face with the dealer, who turned out to be one and the same George Michael. He recognised her, thought seriously for a while and informed her that he was going to have some fun with her. He took her into a quiet room, set up a video camera on a tripod, gave her a huge hit of crack cocaine and prepared to screw her for the camera. He had barely started when a competing posse decided to raid the flat. They were outside on the landing. George's minders were going crazy threatening to shoot everyone. George grabbed a gun and a mobile phone and started calling in back-up from the streets where his people were dealing. As they arrived, waving their guns, the other posse ran and then George's only interest was to clean things up in case the police arrived, so he kicked Miss Popular out.

There were so many feuds that it was hard to keep up. Blue came over from the Top Road Crew in Dunkirk, a suburb of Kingston, and teamed up with Patrick, a big crack dealer in Brixton who was having a war with Burro. Blue's job was to kill anyone who threatened Patrick. But he wasn't so good at his job, and he got shot dead himself.

Mikey Sprang was trying to kill Brigga C and Tonto and Vivien. In Brixton one time, he opened up on them with a machine gun, but they got away. Some friends of his got Brigga C all the same and shot him to pieces.

Squiddley from Peckham stole a load of drugs from Little Andy, but Little Andy's crew beat the blood out of him to teach him a lesson. Chunkie had shot and killed Ozzie in Kingsland High Road, and he was having a war with Binie, who was supposed to have shot a lad in Ladbroke Grove. Now Chunkie also shot Munchie in the crack house in Bedford Road. (Munchie never had been lucky. She had once found $2 million in cash from a Colombian cocaine cartel in a motel room and made the mistake of telling her brother Willy, who was in the Black Rose Crew. They stole the lot off her.)

Tuffy was getting ready for a big war in London, importing hand grenades and Uzis. Back in Kingston, he killed people on behalf of the Jamaican Labour Party who controlled his home patch in Tivoli Gardens, and he could see a bunch of opposition killers from the People's National Party putting themselves together in London. They were all from the Spanglers, whose American arm had been busted in Florida for multiple murders and millions of dollars of crack. There was Zeekes, Chin, Blacker John, Spanner and Juggaland, who was the nearest thing there was in London to a leader of the PNP. They were selling huge amounts of crack in Hackney and Stoke Newington. They'd even set up a street-cleaning company which got itself hired by a council in south London so they could go into the estates and sell all the crack they liked. Tuffy did an armed robbery at a gambling house in Dalston and found Juggaland in there. Tuffy sauntered over to him, stuck a gun in his belly and told him to get down on his knees, and then made him suck the barrel of his gun while everyone stood around and jeered. It looked as if a war was going to begin. Then Tuffy got himself shot dead in a flat in south London, Juggaland decided to concentrate on selling crack, and a kind of peace broke out.

A little blond schoolgirl like Kit Austin was welcome in the crack houses and the shebeens. She was a good customer, she was good to screw, and, if money was short, she was good to sell out on the pavements.

By the middle of April, Kit was using just about anything she could lay her hands on – heroin, cocaine, crack cocaine, pills, lots of weed – and she was working hard. She had decided to pick up some extra cash in a massage parlour in Maida Vale run by a woman called Maggie. It was a rub-and-tug place where there were girls who did real massage and then, if the customer wanted it, Maggie would send in Kit to give him a hand job. When she went back up to Nottingham and saw Tessa, she seemed happy and she did her best to persuade Tessa to come and join her in London – lots of brown, she said, lots of money, lots of friends. The truth, however, was that Kit's life was becoming a torment.

It was Good Friday, 14 April, when Kit first worked in Gloucester Terrace, where Hungarian Suzie needed someone to stand in for her usual girl who had gone away for the Easter holiday. Suzie was nervous about the girl, not least because another maid kept calling and warning her that she was underage. Kit told her the truth, which was that she had passed her sixteenth birthday in January. The police always said that a girl had to be eighteen to work in the flats, but Suzie decided that she was just legal and the two of them got to work on the punters.

By the time a week had passed, Kit had had enough. She had had enough of the warm, dark basement flat and the punters with their creepy habits, and she had had enough of London, this unreal city, and so, on that Friday evening, 21 April, after a week's work, she left the flat in Gloucester Terrace with a little more than £1,000 in her handbag and went along to the Caravan drug project near Paddington Station and called an Open Doors worker in Nottingham and told her she wanted to come home. She wanted someone to drive down from Nottingham to pick her up. The Open Doors worker told her to get on a train; they would pay for her ticket. But Kit didn't.

Instead, she wandered off towards Sussex Gardens, looking for somewhere to score. Some time later on that night, she met David Gilligan, a young heroin addict from Cumbernauld in Scotland who financed his habit by working as card boy for a local prostitute. Gilligan was staying with a friend of his around the corner in the kind of hotel where your feet stick to the carpet. It was called the Metro and it was well known to the working girls on Sussex Gardens who used to take their punters there, while Sid the manager looked the other way. Kit had been up to Gilligan's room a couple of times during the week, smoking heroin, and he had told her that he knew how to inject. He didn't exactly have to tell her that: there was a hospital sharps bin in the corner of the room in the Metro Hotel which was overflowing with needles.

Now, Gilligan saw that Kit had money and he said he knew somewhere they could score. Kit wanted somewhere to sleep and she liked the idea of injecting, if it would give her a better hit. So, soon after midnight, they walked up the sticky staircase at the Metro Hotel on Craven Street, past the call bell with the broken button, up to the top floor and into room nine, where Gilligan's roommate, a middle-aged Yorkshireman named Martin Cowap, was crashed out on one of the two beds, stewing in the Valium and heroin he had taken earlier that evening.

Gilligan found a dessert spoon, dropped heroin into its bowl, squirted it with lemon juice until it was sodden, mixed it with a little water, and then heated it with his cigarette lighter until the heroin dissolved in bubbles. He took a clean syringe, drew it half full, gripped Kit tightly by the right arm, watched the vein swell in the pit of her elbow, pierced it with the syringe and shot her full of brown. He took another needle and did the same for himself.

An hour or so passed. Martin Cowap woke up and declared an interest in screwing Kit. Kit said she'd massage both of them if they liked – she'd learned how to do it at Maggie's – and if they'd fix her another bit of brown, she'd use talcum powder and give them both a good rub. They agreed. She massaged their backs. David Gilligan cooked up some more brown, and some time in the small hours of the Saturday morning, 22 April, the three of them crashed out.

More than twelve hours passed. There was a lot of banging at the door. Martin Cowap managed to stagger out of his bed to open it and on the landing outside, he found a black guy called Christian Allen, looking sick and demanding a fix. What time was it? Something like six in the evening. Where was Gilligan? He'd gone.

Cowap waved his visitor into the room, beckoned him to sit down on the spare bed and turned to sort out a little brown. Kit was still lying quietly in Cowap's bed, where she had spent the night. And it was Christian Allen who leaned across and looked up at Cowap and told him he reckoned she was dead. Cowap took a look. She wasn't breathing. Her lips were purple blue. He touched her skin. Yeah. She was dead.

Cowap sat down on the bed and cooked up the heroin and wondered if they should do something. Christian Allen rolled up his sleeve and the two of them had a good fix. They lay down for a while. An hour or so later, they came round and it was about then that Cowap realised that not only was David Gilligan gone but so was Kit's roll of cash, about £1,000 of it. Allen said he needed a drink, he was going to the pub. Cowap wondered out loud if they should do something about this dead girl. Allen said he'd call the police, so Cowap lay down next to Kit's still body and Allen went to the pub. After he'd had a drink, he called the police, and they came and took the body away. Cowap still had nearly a gram of heroin left.

Kit's death is a clue to the final truth. Partly, this is because of the particular part of the undiscovered country where she died. The brothels of London are a point of connection, where the affluent meet the poor. There are other points like this. Although most of the country of the poor is invisible, nevertheless, there is still the moment when the shopper steps over the sleeping body on the pavement, or when the couple come out of the opera and dodge the beggar at their feet, or when the rest of Britain finds out about two bored inner-city ten-year-olds who abduct a toddler and batter him to death.

But the brothels are special. At that particular point of connection, the affluent not only see the poor, they not only feel frightened or disgusted or sorry or sad, they directly and physically exploit them and, furthermore, they do so entirely for their own pleasure. This has absolutely nothing to do with the needs or wants or cares of the working girl. She is merely a stimulant.

These flats are a perfect symbol of exploitation. The flat in Gloucester Terrace where Kit Austin lost her way, or the one in Gloucester Place where the Old Maid, Mary Daly, runs her empire encapsulate the truth about the relationship between rich and poor. The maids in the flats reported one statistic that has escaped the most diligent of the academics who have investigated the poor. In the last decade or so, the price of thrashing a young girl in London has fallen dramatically. Where once the men who visited the flats had to pay £100 for each stroke of the cane they inflicted on a young woman's back, they can now indulge themselves for only £10 a stroke. Supply and demand. There is a market surplus of desperate young women.

But more than that, Kit Austin's death points straight into the heart of the darkness. There is something about the people she was mixing with that goes beyond mere physical or emotional or social damage, something that lingers in the background to the stories of almost everyone in the country of the poor.

It was there in a conversation between Jazzman and Terence Jackson, when Jazzman had been trying to explain that although he had lost a quarter of a million pounds and everything he owned as a result of his addiction to crack cocaine, he had not lost his sense of right and wrong. For example, he told Terence, he had been in a crack house a few weeks earlier and there had been this young girl there, she was a working girl and unlike most of them she was a black girl. 'In fact, you know her well,' he added.

Terence didn't need to have it spelled out for him that this was his niece, Louise, his sister Carol's young daughter. Jazzman went on to explain with some pride how he had helped Louise. He described how she had been begging for crack, she had run out of money and so she had been giving her body to anyone who wanted it, trading it time after time for another pipe, on her back, on her knees, up against a wall, and Jazzman recalled with some force how he had watched this happening to Terence's little niece and how he had felt very sorry for her. He had decided to help her out.

And so he had taken a little rock of his own crack and called over a white working girl who was hanging around the crack house looking for a pipe and he had offered her a deal. She could have this £20 rock all to herself, if she would do one little thing: just sit Louise down in that chair and get down on her knees in front of her and give her some oral sex. And, of course, the little white girl had agreed.

Jazzman told this story and looked at Terence for approval for this good thing he had done for his niece.

This man has travelled a very long way and what he has lost along the road is far, far more than he has ever counted. He has lost much more than money, more than self-respect or even the sense of right and wrong to which he believes he is still attached. This man has lost touch entirely with his humanity. He can look at himself – half-starved, manic, inclined to paranoia, devious, ruthless, desperate – and believe he is still basically sound inside himself. He can look at Louise Jackson, he can faintly discern in the darkness a glimmer of wrongness about what is happening to her, but he can no longer see what it is that is wrong – and certainly he cannot see what is right. He can sit and tell this story to Terence Jackson and genuinely expect Terence to thank him for being so kind to his niece.

People have become objects.

Looking back, this was there all the time. There was that pimp who bought Miss Popular for the night. ('I like this piece of beef'); Miss Popular stealing from him – he was just a lump of income in a bed – and going off to buy crack from a man who was then beaten to the ground, where he lay twitching and fitting, while Miss P. stepped around him and walked off to find someone else to score off. 'That was his problem' she said.

Look at the lads in Hyde Park who tormented their neighbours and drove Jean Ashford out of her own home; or the guys who run the Fields Posse who have known each other all their lives but who have learned not to trust or even to like each other anymore; or the women in the Forest – Fat Natalie and Wanda – who trapped children into prostitution. The country of the poor is littered with people like this – people who have had their humanity squeezed out of them. Like the two Waynes in Nottingham who used heroin to tie down a schoolgirl so they could enjoy her body; or the women in London who sold her for profit; or the two junkies who sat and got themselves stoned while she lay dead beside them.

It is not that poor people are bad – that is simply the self-serving story of those who are responsible. The truth profoundly is that poverty is bad for people. It brutalises them. It has produced a mutant society in which, after all the physical and emotional and social damage which has been inflicted on the poor, it becomes clear that there is also a deeper damage – something that strikes them in the core, robbing them of their humanity. For want of a better way of describing it, they have also suffered a spiritual damage.

29

WHen Judy Austin first heard that her daughter was dead, she wanted to know who to blame.

Judy came from a rough family who had never been slow to use their fists to make a point, and one of her sisters had already been round to Wayne's home. This was the scruffy, runtish Wayne who had first traded Kit a tot of methadone for some sex, and he had put up almost no resistance as Judy's sister laid into him with her fists and gave him a good pasting. In a way, she had been right enough. It was Wayne's fault that Kit had got into heroin. He had done that to her. But, of course, in another way, it wasn't his fault at all.

Why was Wayne an addict? Why was Wayne the sort of person who really thought it was OK to slip addictive drugs to a fifteen-year-old schoolgirl in exchange for a little sexual cooperation? What had happened to him? What had happened to the other Wayne or Moonie or Carolyn Dunk or Hungarian Suzie or any of the others who were part of the chain that linked Kit, the bright-eyed schoolgirl, to the half-naked body in the Metro Hotel? Beyond that, what had happened to the kids in Hyde Park, or to Jean Ashworth, or to Natalie Pearman lying dead in a lay-by, or the boy-thief Joey, or Tina Sampson with her five boys all in care, or any of the other subjects of the undiscovered country? Who had damaged them? Whose fault was that?

There is an answer to these questions. It is not as if this is all some kind of accident. Looking back into the history of the country of the poor, it turns out that it was created quite deliber-ately, rather like the great penal colony of Australia was planned and created by politicians in London two centuries earlier. This poverty was produced for a purpose.

Almost any human settlement grows around a source of food and water. The country of the poor first began to expand when a current of ideas which had flowed underground for several decades bubbled up into the open in the late 1970s. Two ideas, in particular, started to flow freely.

The first was the idea that there was nothing socially useful or morally desirable about equality. This was a maverick idea which contradicted the values that had defined British politics since the war. For years it had been embraced by only a handful of thinkers who worked on the extremes of political debate.

In the United States, Milton Friedman had been arguing for the virtues of inequality since the 1960s. His thinking was reflected in more philosophical form in the works of F.A. Hayek, who was merciless in his attack on ideas of social justice.

In his review of socialism, *The Fatal Conceit*, Hayek hammered his point home:

> The phrase 'social justice' is . . . simply a semantic fraud . . . It is probably true that men would be happier about their economic conditions if they felt that the relative positions of individuals were just. Yet the whole idea behind distributive justice – that each individual ought to receive what he morally deserves – is meaningless . . . The demand that only changes with just effects should occur is ridiculous . . .

For years, these were lonely voices, lost somewhere on the political fringes, accepted by no one of any weight in the main-stream of politics – until 1975, when a senior British Member of Parliament made a speech in New York in which this kind of thinking broke through into the currency of British political exchange. The key thought in the speech was expressed at its clearest in a single sentence: 'The pursuit of equality is a mirage.'

Four years later, in April 1979, the MP who made that speech became the prime minister, and as she moved into Downing Street she opened the door to ideas which had once lived only on the margins but were now allowed to take their place in the most powerful office in the country. No more equality.

The second idea that stimulated the growth of the country of the poor was equally explicit. The welfare state was to be dismantled.

In a 1971 pamphlet entitled *Down with the Poor*, the right-wing Conservative MP Dr Rhodes Boyson attacked the very idea that the government should care for its vulnerable citizens:

> The moral fibre of our people has been weakened. A state which does for its citizens what they can do for themselves is an evil state . . . In such an irresponsible society no one cares, no one saves, no one bothers – why should they when the state spends all its energies taking money from the energetic, successful and thrifty to give to the idlers, the failures and the feckless?

Hayek had been arguing this same point for more than twenty years. In 1960, for example, in *The Constitution of Liberty*, he had suggested that government welfare spending should be limited to providing no more than 'security against severe physical deprivation'. No more welfare from cradle to grave, no more automatic protection for those in need, no more guarantee of education and health and housing for all.

In April 1979, this idea too found its way across the doorstep of Downing Street, where its implications were clearly understood. In his history of the welfare state, Nicholas Timmins recounts how the new prime minister spoke to her first secretary of state for Social Services, Patrick Jenkin.

'I think we will have to go back to soup kitchens,' she told him and paused. Then, noting his reaction, she continued, 'Take that silly smile off your face. I mean it.'

Soon these ideas flowed out of Downing Street and started to flood the intellectual terrain of the whole country. Although large groups of mavericks continued to huddle together under the shelter of left-wing magazines or community groups or rebellious local authorities, the mainstream of opinion was soon flowing fast with these new ideas. The centre ground was swallowed. Although many millions of people continued to object, the central debate was no longer about whether or not there should be equality but about how best to reward enterprise; no longer about how to sustain the welfare state but about where first to cut it.

Once these two ideas started to flow freely, they nourished the seeds of a whole crop of new proposals.

The banishing of equality allowed conservative thinkers to speak up for the interests of the rich, to promote the idea that enterprise and initiative were being stifled by taxation. The affluent must receive more. Over the next eight years, they would have their top rate of tax cut from 83 per cent to only 40 per cent. They would have their basic rate of tax cut from 33 per cent to 23 per cent.

At the other end of the social scale, however, the same thinkers insisted that the trade unions and their members were 'pricing themselves out of their jobs'. The workers must accept less. They must accept lower pay. So the wages councils were abolished, first for workers under twenty-one, and then for all employees; the trade unions, whose central purpose had been to lift the living standards of their members, were weakened by new laws; the employment rights which had protected the wages and conditions of workers would now be granted only to those who had kept the same job for more than two years. The number of 'working poor' rocketed by 300 per cent between 1979 and the early 1990s.

The workers must also accept unemployment. After decades when governments had ensured that unemployment never rose above 3 per cent of the workforce and was often below 2 per cent, the Downing Street that was no longer afraid of inequality allowed unemployment to soar. Some of this unemployment was generated by forces beyond the government's control – by the introduction of new technology, for example – but much of it was engineered as part of a conscious economic policy. In order to 'make British industry more competitive'; in order to increase the productivity of manufacturing industries; as part of the 'globalisation of the economy' in which British labour must compete with low-paid workers in the Third World; in order to 'choke inflation out of the economy' with high interest rates: jobs must be cut. Twelve years later, in spite of the thirty changes of measuring stick, the official register of the unemployed broke through the 3 million mark, and Norman Lamont, who was then the Conservative Chancellor of the Exchequer, still described it as 'a price well worth paying' for lower inflation.

The dismantling of the welfare state meant that just as low pay was becoming lower, just as jobs were becoming rarer, the government started to strip away the safety nets which for decades had ensured that the poor could not fall too far.

During her first government, between 1979 and 1983, Mrs Thatcher cut the benefits of the unemployed, pensioners, strikers, pregnant women, the victims of industrial accidents and the disabled. These were the first real cuts in social-security benefits since the 1930s. Most of these groups suffered real drops in their income. By 1983, for example, allowing for inflation, every state pensioner in the country was worse off each week by £1.45, unless they lived in a couple, in which case they were worse off by £2.25.

In 1984, the new secretary of state for Social Security, Norman Fowler, embarked on the what he called 'the most substantial examination of the social security system since the Beveridge Report forty years ago'. He set up review teams of Conservative politicians and business executives, who considered the life of the poor and suggested that the government should cut, among other things, death grants, maternity grants, pensions, housing benefits, all benefits to those under eighteen, some benefits to those under twenty-five, crisis grants for the very poor, and free school meals. They also suggested that more of the poor should have to pay local taxes and water rates, and they said that they wanted to scrap supplementary benefit in order to introduce a new bottom-line benefit called income support with new rules about who could receive it.

As these plans took root, they were swept by a hurricane of protest from those who had resisted the shift in thinking and from others who began to see the grim consequences of this approach. The Confederation of British Industry, the Church of England, the welfare lobby, the pensions industry, the *Financial Times*, the trade unions and parts of the Conservative Party all warned of the terrible results of such cuts. The Select Committee on Social Services told the government that if they carried them out, they would inflict financial losses on almost every vulnerable group in the country. The young, the single and the unemployed would lose the most. The committee's chairman, Frank Field, aware of the cuts that had already been imposed on the poor in the previous five years, said, 'I see signs in my constituency that I have not seen in London since I was a boy. I see pinched faces, shuffling feet and ill-fitting shoes, which are all signs of poverty. It is from these people that we are taking money away.'

The government lost a few of its ideas but it was able to shelter most of them from the protest. On 11 April 1988, Norman Fowler's changes passed into law. The Benefits Research Unit at Nottingham University calculated that as a direct result of the biggest single change – from supplementary benefit to income support – just over 2 million poor people were materially poorer. Researchers at Oxford University later suggested that it was probably nearer 2.5 million.

It was at this time that young people aged under eighteen lost their general right to receive any benefit at all; those under twenty-four had their benefit cut back to only £36.15 a week; and the Social Fund was introduced, attacking the poor at the bottom of the scale. For years, those who were in greatest need had been able to get extra help if they ran into a crisis. If they were burgled, if their cooker broke down, if their furniture was ruined by flood or fire, they had been able to get a small grant to help them through. Now, the grants stopped. Instead, there would be loans from the Social Fund. And these would be 'discretionary': they would be given only if Social Security officers authorised them; and they could authorise them only if they had the money in their budgets. By 1992, the budget for these payments had fallen from £504 million to only £91 million.

Those who were lent money from the Social Fund struggled to repay it. Eventually, the system reached gridlock when 116,095 claimants were refused crisis loans to buy cookers or beds or clothing – on the grounds that they were too poor to pay back the money. So the very poor lost their final safety net because they could not afford to pay for it themselves.

It was during this period of intense attack on the welfare state that the government realised that many of the poor were reacting to this new regime by simply failing to pay their bills, and so they introduced new powers for the Department of Social Security to deduct money from benefit before it was handed over. By 1993, there were about a million claimants who were receiving even less than the breadline benefit to which they were still entitled. Money was deducted for crisis loans, for rent, water, electricity, fines and old poll-tax debts. When the DSS commissioned a group of independent academics to look at the results of this change, they found that by 1992 almost 70 per cent said that their repayments left them without enough money to live on; more than a third said they had to cut back on food, clothing or on paying bills; and a fifth borrowed money from other sources to cope with their reduced incomes. By 1994, officials had chopped £435 million out of the income support which was paid to the poor. On average, claimants were losing a total of £19.68 a week from benefits which had been calculated to do no more than cover the essentials and which, in the view of independent researchers, were already too low.

As the years went by, every limb of the welfare state was affected. Free school meals and children's milk were restricted. In some areas, all school meals were stopped. Child benefit was frozen for three years. Rules were rewritten to shave a few more pence from the purses of the poor: child allowances were to be upgraded in September, instead of on the child's birthday, thus taking away from many several months' benefit; family credit would be cut as soon as a child left school instead of waiting for the end of a six-month period, thus taking away several months more. Poor families were told that if one of them died, they could no longer have any help towards the cost of the funeral if there was a single relative who was still in work.

Nine years after scrapping supplementary benefit and introducing income support, the government rewrote the rules again, throwing out income support and introducing in its place the job seekers allowance. The result was similar. Benefits were cut to the unemployed if they were aged between eighteen and twenty-four; if they had a partner who was working; if they had managed to save more than £3,000; or if they were disabled without being incapacitated.

While all of these benefits were being cut, the government had launched a separate attack on public housing. Previously, this had been the greatest 'benefit in kind' paid to the poor.

The government stopped the construction of council houses, cut the payment of improvement grants for homes in need of repair, cut the housing-maintenance budgets of local authorities, and oversaw the transfer of tens of thousands of council homes from the care of the local authority to the possession of professional landlords.

During her first government, Mrs Thatcher raised the rents for those in council houses and cut spending on housing by 70 per cent. Within six months of winning the 1983 election, her government cut the housing benefit paid to those who were struggling with their rent: half a million people lost all their housing benefit; 4 million others were affected, losing an average of £1.57 a week, although some of them lost as much as £12 each week. Then she cut housing benefit again in 1984 and in 1985 and 1986 and 1987. By December 1987, a million people had lost all their housing benefit; a further 5.5 million had seen their housing benefit cut.

And there was more. In 1995, the government cut the 'exceptional hardship' payments which had allowed extra housing benefit to be paid to the elderly, the sick, the disabled and the very poor. Local authorities were told that each of them would now receive only £6,000 a year to cover all of these payments. In 1996, the government introduced new rules which meant that even those who had kept their benefit could no longer expect it to cover all their rent. Housing charities estimated that this would leave a further 1.5 million tenants out of pocket.

In the background, the government had stopped the construction of all council houses. They had provoked local authorities into selling £47 million worth of council houses and although some of this was diverted into housing associations, the government soon cut back on its grants to them, leaving the associations to borrow the outstanding cash, paying market rates of interest which could be covered only by pushing up rents.

The government attacked not only the money that was paid directly to the poor in their benefits, but also the money that was paid to them indirectly through services.

They cut the rate support grant to local authorities, forcing them to cut all their provision – money for books and teachers in schools, for libraries, buses, repairs to houses, the collection of rubbish and the control of rodents. Although all of these services were available for the whole community, most of them were of special importance for the poor, who were more likely, for example, to rely on public transport or public housing or public libraries. All were cut. Many became more expensive.

They reduced housing subsidies, forcing councils to raise the rents in public housing. Between 1979 and 1995, council-house rents rose by 100 per cent. This pushed more people onto the housing benefit which was being cut so dramatically.

The combined effect of these changes was to create poverty on a scale that had appeared to have been buried in the past, and of a kind that had never been seen before. Some of the damage was directly linked to specific actions by the government.

By the end of the 1980s, with its assault on housing, there were 1.5 million homes that were unfit for human habitation, 2.5 million homes that were damp – and an epidemic of bronchial illness.

By the end of the 1980s, with its attack on the budgets of the poor, there were fifty per cent fewer children taking school dinners, a general drop in the nutritional standard of school food – and experts talking of 'malnutrition' among the poor.

When the Government took away the benefits of young people who were under eighteen, they built a bridge between their homes and the streets. It was in the wake of these changes that young people began to drift onto the streets of the big cities and, from there, into the red-light areas. It was then only a matter of time before their younger brothers and sisters crossed over the bridge to join them.

When the government cut into the weekly income of the poorest, when they ensured that there was nothing there for them to fall back on in the event of a crisis, they guaranteed not only the stress and physical illness which afflicted many of the poor, but also the creation of an alternative economy, based on crime and drugs and prostitution.

The final financial result of all this activity was stunning. By 1987, Mrs Thatcher's cuts in the welfare state had yielded a total saving of £12 billion. Some of this was used to pay off public debt which had built up under previous governments. Some was used to fund huge increases in military spending.

But most of it – £8 billion – was used to pay for cuts in taxes for the affluent. For example, within four weeks of Norman Fowler's changes passing into law, with all of their devastating effects for the poor, the Chancellor Nigel Lawson gave away more than £2 billion in tax cuts. The richer they were, the more of the poor's money they were given. The richest 5.5 million gained an average of £6,000 a year and within that elite, the richest 550,000 gained an average of £33,300 a year.

In the new world without equality, the new wealth of the rich was paid for entirely by the new poverty of the poor.

Spiritual damage. It runs deep and into unexpected places.

With those who are absorbed by drugs, it is intense. Soon after Kit Austen died there was a revealing sequence of events which involved some of those who had led her to her death and which saw everyone treating everyone they came across as though they were mere objects.

It began when Miss Kath and Spotty Caine got busted with a big stash of heroin in their home in Nottingham. The police missed three kilos of heroin, which had been hidden inside one of the doors in Miss Kath's house. From prison, she managed to get a message to Carolyn Dunk, who hurtled up to Nottingham with Ray the Ripper, who was out of prison for once, went to Miss Kath's house, tore this door apart, found the heroin and stashed it in a safe house back in London. However, Carolyn's daughter, Nicky, found it, stole some of it, stashed it up her vagina and headed back to Nottingham, where she checked into the Royal Moat House Hotel and embarked on a binge which ended up with her being arrested for trying to get out of the hotel without paying her bill. In custody, she grassed her friends, as she often did.

In the meantime, Carolyn had moved the rest of the stash to Mary Daly's house – apparently without telling her what she was doing. But somebody grassed Carolyn and the police took out a search warrant. Somebody then grassed the police to Carolyn who managed to get to Mary's house and move the stash ten minutes before the police arrived, leaving the Old Maid to have her home searched and to submit to an internal examination. No one looked out for anyone. No one cared. No one cared even about themselves, as soon became clear when Carolyn Dunk tumbled into disaster.

For years, Carolyn had chewed temazepam like smarties and

smoked weed like air, but she had never been addicted to anything. She had seen the trouble it caused.

She had seen Nicky hurtle into oblivion, driven on by a crack
habit that consumed her life. Nicky cheated everyone around her.
She had a fist fight with Miss Popular who ended up with a grape-
sized blister from a cigarette burn on her breast. She attacked a
child prostitute because she discovered the girl was carrying
money from a drug dealer to Carolyn. She had abandoned her
own two sons. She beat up anyone who got in her way and then
tried to grass her way out of custody. When she got out, she liked
to boast of how she had grassed to the police and told them
nothing but lies. Carolyn had seen her husband, Ray, go the same
way. Soon after they had played hunt-the-heroin with Miss Kath's
stash, Ray was arrested yet again, for taking a screwdriver to a
man in the street, trying to steal something to fund his habit.

Carolyn had seen the decline of the City crackhead – the well-
spoken man in the elegant suit who blew thousands of pounds a
night on crack and girls. She had watched as he lost his Ferrari
and his great big house in St John's Wood. His wife had left
him and taken the children with her. He was forced to sell his
house in Hertfordshire to pay off debts. He lost his job and now
he was being investigated for corruption. Along the way, she
knew, he had been arrested in a crack house in Notting Hill by
police who tried to persuade him to become an informer, he had
been picked up by the police on the Mozart Estate – also known
as Crack City – and around Kings Cross, when he had been
scoring off the street dealers there. In the old days, the police had
busted him because they guessed that anyone who drove a Ferrari
in places like that must be a dealer. More recently, they busted
him because they knew he was a screwed-up crackhead.

Carolyn had played her part in his downfall, letting him throw
his money around, giving him credit if he ran out, making it quite
clear that his health would suffer if he didn't pay up. There was
one time when he had failed to pay up, and Nicky had heard
about it and taken it upon herself to call his wife and tell her
everything. That had caused him some deep trouble. But he still
came back to Carolyn's flats for more. It was amazing how far he
had fallen.

It had all started with some working girl ten years earlier.

Although he was married, he had taken to using the girls for sex from time to time and, one day, one of them had offered him a pipe.

'Try this,' she had said.

So he had. He had liked it, and the next day he had gone back to the girl for more.

'That girl ruined my life,' he used to say.

Carolyn knew he'd tried to get shot of his habit, but he couldn't. He'd been on expensive detox courses three times but he had always reverted. Now he looked like a tramp. He lived in a poky little flat where he darted in and out in fear of crack dealers and working girls to whom he owed money. He was caught up in one of the biggest investigations that the Department of Trade and Industry had ever run. Still, Carolyn used to say, that was his problem.

But even though she had seen all of this, Carolyn now made the biggest mistake of her life. She started smoking crack – as if her own life now meant as little to her as those of the people around her. She developed a habit of monstrous proportions. She was smoking £1,000 of crack a day, staying up for forty-eight hours at a time. In the first six months of 1997, she reckoned she had blown £100,000 on crack. She took her pipe everywhere, she couldn't walk down Oxford Street without ducking into a ladies' toilet for another rock. She blew out her credit cards and suffered the indignity of being arrested by store detectives. She couldn't pay the bill on her mobile phone, so she lost that, too. And, for the first time in a long career, as she became more and more ruthless, she started to lose her grip on the working girls.

At this time, she was working in a flat in Seymour Place, a few minutes' walk from Mary Daly's flat in Gloucester Place, and she started to let crack dealers base themselves in the flat so they would sell to the girls and perhaps to the punters, and to herself. In the middle of all this she lost her regular girl, so she phoned up a sixteen-year-old blond girl called *Lola* whom she had noticed in Nottingham. Lola was no working girl, she had never had anything to do with prostitution, but Carolyn knew she was pretty and petite, she was young and looked fresh, and she was out of work.

Carolyn dangled the prospect of a fortune in front of her. Lola was nervous. She wouldn't mind some money but she didn't like the sound of it. Carolyn promised her she wouldn't have to do anything hard core. She didn't even have to have sex with the punters – just dress up in the uniforms, spank them and give them hand jobs. She could earn £1,000 a day if she did well, Carolyn told her. She'd pay for her train fare and have a taxi at St Pancras Station to pick her up. All she had to do was say yes. So Lola did.

The young girl arrived that evening from Nottingham, slept the night in Seymour Place and then started working the next morning. She got £150 from her first punter. She hated it. She hated the punters and their horrible ideas. She hated the flat and the men sitting in there with their pipes of crack. Pretty soon, she started to hate Carolyn, who had sounded so nice and sympathetic. Carolyn was just smoking and smoking.

By the end of the first day, Lola had been through so many punters, she could hardly stand up. She had made at least £1,000. Carolyn hadn't lied about that. But she had lied about everything else. She had promised her it would all be a secret – there'd be no one else in the flat. But there were working girls coming from all over to smoke crack, there were these men dealing, there were several women dealing, too. And Carolyn started making her do things with the punters that she didn't want to do.

'This is London, darling,' she kept saying. 'You can't say no.'

By ten at night, Lola had had enough. She told Carolyn she wasn't working anymore, she wanted to sleep, but the phone kept ringing and Carolyn kept telling the punters to come round, and she'd wake up Lola and tell her to work.

'You have to do more, darling. You have to do more.'

And she'd take the money and keep on smoking and smoking.

In the morning, Lola woke up and said she wanted to go home. Carolyn said she couldn't go. She was still smoking. She told Lola she had to stay and get on with the work like she was told. Lola protested. Carolyn insisted. The punters started calling and Lola headed into another working day, wrestling all the time about what she would do and wouldn't do. By evening time, she was ready to drop.

Nicky turned up. She was five months pregnant with her third child, she was out of her head on something and desperate for more. She begged Lola to let her do some of the punters so she could buy some crack off her mum. Lola had had enough of punters, so she let Nicky do a few. Nicky scored and smoked and vanished into the night. The punters kept coming, Carolyn kept smoking and hassling Lola to earn them more money, and when Lola said she had had enough, Carolyn had an idea.

'Have a little smoke, darling,' she said.

Lola knew she shouldn't. She had been smoking weed, but there was no way she wanted to smoke crack. Carolyn said it would pick her up and make her feel better and then she could do some more work. She should just try it, she said, just have a little blast. So Lola did.

The punters kept coming. Carolyn kept smoking and smoking. Lola started talking about leaving. Carolyn said she'd lock her in the flat. A big black guy came and wanted to screw Lola. She didn't want him, so she said no. Carolyn went mad, started shouting at her, telling her she had to have him, he was a regular, they needed the money. She was still smoking and smoking. But Lola had had enough. She said no, she was going home, she didn't care what Carolyn said, she wanted her money. More than £2,000, she had earned, and she wanted it now.

Carolyn said it wasn't quite like that, darling – there was the rent to pay, and the card boys, and then there was her own pay for maiding. Lola could have £800. And that was all. Lola knew when she had been ripped off, but she had had enough. She called a taxi and paid the driver to take her all the way home to Nottingham. And the next morning, she called Mary Daly.

Lola had heard from the others in the flat all about the Old Maid and now the young girl poured out her complaint to her. Mary Daly listened as Lola told her about the crack dealers in the flat, even though Mary had a strict rule barring dealers from her flats; about Nicky coming in and doing punters, even though Mary had banned her from the flats for fighting and stealing; about Carolyn smoking and smoking, even though Mary had trusted her for all these years not to get a habit.

Mary had also been getting calls from friends in the police who had heard that there were dealers crawling all over the flat in Seymour Place. If Carolyn didn't cool it, there would be no way out of it: somebody was bound to raid the place.

That afternoon, Mary sacked Carolyn. The partnership was over. Never mind the years of partnership. Never mind that they were supposed to be friends. Carolyn was out. No friendship. No trust. No care. Not for anyone and not for themselves.

There is one thing more here, behind this merry dance of death and trade. This spiritual damage was not confined to the country of the poor.

How is it that the mainstream society of Britain has allowed this dark heart to grow up within it? The answer is that many of the affluent, too, have come to look upon the poor as mere objects. If the poor have been encouraged by circumstance to treat each other as objects, it is a lesson they have learned from mainstream society.

It is the lesson of the privatised electricity company squeezing its customers regardless of the danger to their children; or of the absentee landlords buying up old council houses and raking in the rent while the houses and their tenants slowly rot. It is the fairground full of happy people with two rent boys in its midst. It is the taxi drivers at Victoria bus station in Nottingham watching Slim being beaten up by the black lads and doing nothing to help him. It is the endless stream of ordinary men sniffing around the pavements of the inner cities where the damaged children sell themselves. It is the government which set out to squeeze the poor and which pursued policies that were, in the words of Sir Ian Gilmour, one of its original members, 'unrelentingly divisive and discriminatory against the poor, whose human dignity was relentlessly ignored'. It is the replacement of human values by economic ones, the commercialisation of human relations.

The economic reality is that there are several million British workers whose labour power is no longer needed. Their role as labour has been stolen away by new technology, by the availability of much cheaper labour in Asia and South America, by the drive for higher productivity. They are in the deepest sense redundant. Looking at them from a strictly economic point of view, these former workers and their families are worthless. More than that, they are an expensive burden – at least, they will be if they are to be properly housed and clothed and fed, if they are to be given decent schools and hospitals. So, why bother?

From a human point of view, of course, there is no doubt at all that they have value, just as much as any human, and that they have a moral right to live secure and happy lives. But this is an inherent human value – nothing that the market can put a price on. From an economic point of view, they are worth nothing, they will be given the bare minimum. For these redundant humans, the creation of poverty is the final solution.

And this is a two-way relationship. A mainstream society that is losing its humanity is willing to create a poor country in its own image, but the destruction which sweeps through this undiscovered country then causes a new cycle of damage to the affluent.

The poverty of these neighbours is a constant warning of what can happen to those who fail to conform to expectations and generally to those who fail. Since the core of this failure will be financial, the closeness of this poverty is an incitement to focus still more blindly on commercialism. It is a constant invitation to the affluent to jettison their humanity. How can they step over the body in the street, ignore the beggar outside the opera, drive straight past the endless devastated housing estates unless they take their feelings of humanity and junk them? So they have done, and one government after another has endorsed them. Every time a government minister from any party stands up and declares war on the welfare state, every time some respected thinker jeers at the idea of equality, or contrives a case for stripping the poor of yet more benefits, they give a cloak of credibility to this hardness.

So the mainstream society succumbs to a coarseness of values, to a trivialisation of caring. It is as if they had hired some Pied Piper to cleanse their society of pests – of socialists, and trade unionists and civil libertarians – and he played this merry, merry tune of commercialism and junk culture and, sure enough, he purged their homes of the old infestations. Then the piper, who had seemed so colourful and attractive, turned on them and stole their children and handed them over to greed and selfishness and a ruthless self-indulgence – to the values at the dark heart of Britain.

The Labour government which was elected in May 1997 saw the damage which had been created by the new current of conservative thinking, and their leaders announced their intention to dam it at its source. They declared that they would rehabilitate the idea of equality; and they would call off the attack on the welfare estate and restore the public services which had been dismantled.

In a newspaper interview ten months before he became Prime Minister, Tony Blair risked his reputation to underline the point. 'I believe in greater equality,' he said. 'If the next Labour government has not raised the living standards of the poorest by the end of its time in office, it will have failed.'

But when he walked into Downing Street and ordered the tide to retreat, he found he had thrown away the weapons that might have given him the power he needed.

If he is to attack the economic origins of the new poverty, Tony Blair has to do two things; he has to restore the millions of jobs whose removal has drained the life out of communities across the country; and he has to repair the welfare nets which have been shredded by cuts. However, by the time he took power he was committed to economic policies which prevented him doing either of these things. In the two years before the 1997 election, both he and his chancellor, Gordon Brown, embraced the macroeconomic policies of the Conservative government – low public spending, low taxation, low inflation. There was no secret about this. It was an explicit and well-advertised part of their strategy to secure the support of the City and to reassure middle-class voters that they would be safer under a Labour government.

However, this policy means that they cannot secure anything like full employment; to do so would mean injecting into the economy the kind of extra cash which is bound to send inflation upwards. Or, as they put it, in the jargon of the day, the economy will 'overheat'. Given the choice between low unemployment and low inflation, the Labour chancellor has followed his Conservative predecessors in deciding that high unemployment is a price worth paying for lower prices. So, far from reviving employment, Gordon Brown, in his first Financial Statement as chancellor, assumed that over the next three years there would be no fall at all in the number of jobless. 'If it happens,' his spokesman said, 'it is a bonus, but we are not forecasting it.'

In the same way, this economic strategy makes it impossible for the new Labour government to repair the welfare state. They have undertaken not to borrow more money. They have also undertaken not to raise more money through new taxes. If they honour those undertakings, they cannot afford to restore the scores of benefits which have been removed from the poor or to revive the ailing public services on which they once relied.

This does not mean that they are doing nothing. But the few steps which they are taking betray a deeper loss of direction, an ignorance of what life is really like for the poor.

The Labour government suggested quickly that they would try to revive the family by cutting benefits to single parents, assuming that if mothers were unmarried, it was their own fault – or even that it was their own design in a deliberate attempt to secure extra benefits. They have never met Tina Sampson or Terence Jackson's sister, Carol, both of them deserted by one man after another, each of them finally left with five young children they loved and had no hope of caring for. They have never met the single mothers in Hyde Park, drifting into pregnancy because there is nothing else to drift into, too depressed to plan anything, organising nothing in their lives, not a meal for that evening, not even a condom, and certainly not a strategy for exploiting loop-holes in benefit regulations. Most of all, they have never considered the very clear possibility that when they cut the benefit to women like these, they push them not into happy families but onto the dark pavements of places like the Forest or the working flats of people like Mary Daly.

In the same way, the Labour government announced that they would skim the excess profits of public utilities and use the money to pay companies to hire 250,000 young people. Their critics warned them immediately that this would count for nothing as long as there were not enough real long-term jobs in the economy: these companies would hire these young people only for as long as they were paid to do so by the government and then they would drop them. More than that, the government threatened to cut the benefits of any young person who refused to take up the job that he or she was offered. If the Labour leaders had spent any time with any of the young people who run with the Fields Posse or if they had sat on the pavement with the Hyde Park Gang, they would see that they have misunderstood the choice which is confronting the young people they are trying to help.

This choice is not whether to get a job or to rely on benefit. It is whether to try to live within the law, surviving on breadline benefit or on wages no higher than £250 a week; or to turn instead to the booming and lucrative economy which provides the only regular employment on their estates – the distribution of drugs, where even at the lowest level they can easily earn £1,000 a week tax-free. To cut the benefits of young people on these estates is like running a recruitment campaign for the nation's drug networks.

Labour thinking seems to take no account of the damage which has been inflicted on the poor in the past twenty years. It assumes that even though these communities have been riddled with drugs and drink and depression and stress; that even though tens of thousands of young people have abandoned their schools without any thought for the future; even though hundreds of thousands are now unskilled and alienated while millions have been drained of hope and motivation; that nevertheless by flicking the switches of the benefits machine, these people can be manipulated into families or into work or out of crime as though they were carefully calculating their rational self-interest, as though their lives and sometimes their personalities had not been scrambled by the experience of the last twenty years.

Worse, it is clear that Labour thinking has been polluted by another new stream of thought which has bubbled up out of the hinterland of right-wing thinkers and into the mainstream of debate. It is the product of the same conservative thinkers who were so keen to kill off equality and dismantle the welfare state and who have watched with some anxiety as crime and social disintegration have spread relentlessly across the country. Neatly, they have sidestepped responsibility, suggesting that the blame for all this should be placed not on their own ideas but firmly on the shoulders of the poor themselves.

A right-wing columnist, Bruce Anderson, who was a Downing Street confidant to Margaret Thatcher and John Major, articulated this view with particular clarity in an essay in the *Spectator* in August 1996, in which he suggested that the parents of juvenile criminals should be punished for their crimes, or, as he put it, they should be 'treated as toads under the harrow'.

He continued: 'We are in the grip of the post-modern vaga-bond. We have expensively constructed slums full of layabouts and sluts whose progeny are two-legged beasts. We cannot cure this by family religion and self-help. So we will have to rely on repression.'

Although this kind of aggressive celebration of the results of the new thinking is rare, academics and journalists who claim to be open-minded have begun to give credibility to the general idea that the poor are to blame for their poverty. They have taken up the theory of 'welfare dependency' which confuses cause with effect and suggests that it is the availability of state help for the poor which is producing the symptoms of poverty. If men and women are out of work, it is not because factories have closed but because these feckless work-shy families choose to rely on the generosity of benefits. If unmarried women become pregnant, it is not because they are too alienated and aimless to take any control of their lives but because they calculate that the child will help them to jump the housing queue. If young men sit for hours on pavements, it is not because they are jobless, hopeless and bored to the bone but because the welfare state has killed off their incentive to work.

Rather like the ideas of Hayek and others in the 1970s, this theory comes originally from the United States, from the fringes of intellectual thought, where it was popularised by an academic named Charles Murray. The theory is self-serving, in that it allows the affluent to justify more cuts to the welfare state which in turn will pay for more cuts in their own taxes. It was produced by academics and propagated by politicians, none of whom spend any time on estates like Hyde Park or in places like the Forest. Even at the most superficial glance, it looks suspiciously like claiming that if only there were fewer hospitals, there would be fewer sick people. And yet, despite its obvious flaws, the theory has been adopted by liberal journalists and Labour politicians, by academics and commentators and think-tanks, and now flows over the centre ground just as the ideas of Hayek did nearly twenty years earlier.

So it is that the economic strategy which first created the new poverty in Britain is allowed to remain in place. In a country where values have been commercialised, morals are less than chaff in a breeze. A taint of imbecile rapacity blows through the land, like a whiff from some corpse.

There is no crusade against poverty in Britain. No leading politician demands full employment for the country's workforce. No prominent public figure insists that the wealth which was taken from the poor and given to the rich during the Conservative years should now be returned. There is only the immense jabber of the powerful who are surrounded by the victims of their affluence and who yet continue to know nothing of the undiscovered country of the poor.

'If, after full and exhaustive consideration, we come to the deliberate conclusion that nothing can be done, and that it is the inevitable and inexorable destiny of thousands of Englishmen to be brutalised into worse than beasts by the condition of their environment, so be it. But if, on the contrary, we are unable to believe that this "awful slough" which engulfs the manhood and womanhood of generation after generation, is incapable of removal; and if the heart and intellect of mankind alike revolt against the fatalism of despair, then, indeed, it is time, and high time, that the question were faced in no mere dilettante spirit, but with a resolute determination to make an end to the crying scandal of our age ... "Darker England" is but a fractional part of "Greater England". There is wealth enough abundantly to minister to its social regeneration so far as wealth can, if there be but heart enough to set about the work in earnest.'

William Booth, *In Darkest England*, 1890

'My earnest hope is that the book may serve to give the rich a more intimate knowledge of the sufferings, and the frequent heroism under those sufferings, of the poor – that it may teach those who are beyond temptation to look with charity on the frailties of their less fortunate brethren – and cause those who are in "high places", and those of whom much is expected, to bestir themselves to improve the condition of a class of people whose misery, ignorance and vice, amidst all the immense wealth and great knowledge of "the first city in the world" is, to say the very least, a national disgrace to us.'

Henry Mayhew, *London Labour and the London Poor*, 1851